PRAISE FOR LEONARD GOLDBERG'S FICTION

"Imaginative, murderous ... captures the top shelf in the mystery world."—*Kansas City Star*

"Rushes along at a brisk clip."—*Chicago Tribune*

"A medical thriller ... with uniquely ghastly murders."—*Los Angeles Times Book Review*

"A page-turner with medical realism and characters who command our sympathies."—*Charleston Post and Courier*

"Fascinating ... devilish."—*People Magazine*

"Outstanding specimens of suspense."—*Knoxville News-Sentinel*

"Diabolical."—*The Virginian-Pilot*

"Bone-chilling and provocative."—*Tulsa World*

"The stuff of nightmares."—*Library Journal*

"Cool cuttings by a sure hand ... scalpel-edged."—*Kirkus Reviews*

"Compelling and suspenseful."—Associated Press

"Fascinating and fast-moving."—*Booklist*

PLAGUE
SHIP

LEONARD GOLDBERG

PLAGUE SHIP

MIDNIGHT INK
WOODBURY, MINNESOTA

MIDNIGHT
INK

FIRST EDITION
First Printing, 2013

Book design and format by Donna Burch
Cover art: iStockphoto.com/3708074/Shaun Lowe, 149147/4x6, 5495905/James
    Steidl
Cover design by Ellen Lawson

Midnight Ink, an imprint of Llewellyn Worldwide Ltd.

This is a work of fiction. Names, characters, places, and incidents are either the product of the author's imagination or are used fictitiously, and any resemblance to actual persons, living or dead, business establishments, events, or locales is entirely coincidental.

Library of Congress Cataloging-in-Publication Data
Goldberg, Leonard S.
  Plague ship / Leonard Goldberg. — First Edition.
     pages   cm. — (A Ballineau/Ross Medical Thriller ; #2)
  ISBN 978-0-7387-3837-6
1. Plague—Fiction. 2. Terrorism—Fiction. I. Title.
  PS3557.O35775P53 2013
  813'.54—dc23
                                        2013018073

Midnight Ink
Llewellyn Worldwide Ltd.
2143 Wooddale Drive
Woodbury, MN 55125-2989
www.midnightinkbooks.com

Printed in the United States of America

*For Sheran, who took the biggest hit
and came out just fine*

Historically, plague ships carried either the dead or people dying with infectious diseases, in an attempt to prevent them from infecting others.

PROLOGUE

THE LAST BIRD IN the formation was having difficulty keeping up with the others. It flapped its wings frantically, but to no avail. The long-necked bird fell farther and farther behind, its muscles and lungs weakened by a rapidly replicating avian influenza virus. Below was the gray Atlantic Ocean, and the infected bird knew instinctively that if it landed in the rough seas it was dead. Its wet wings would prevent it from ever taking flight again.

Now the flock was turning to a more southerly course and, as the wind stiffened, the sick bird found itself losing altitude. Desperately it searched for a landing site in the murky waters, but all it saw was a gray mist. Lower and lower it dropped until it was less than a thousand feet over the ocean. It flapped its wings vainly in a final attempt to survive, but all of its energy stores were depleted. The bird dropped even farther and, sensing the spray of the rough swells below, gave up the fight.

Then suddenly it spotted a shadow on the water's surface. It was a giant, moving shadow that seemed to rise above the swells. With a last-ditch burst, the bird beat its wings and dove for the moving haven. A moment later it crashed onto the deck of the luxury liner the *Grand Atlantic*.

ONE

THE STORM THAT BATTERED the *Grand Atlantic* and caused so many of its passengers to become seasick was finally subsiding. But occasional, large swells were still slamming into its steel hull with enough force to make glassware and the other unfixed objects vibrate and move about. These sounds and motions made all but the most experienced travelers ill at ease, despite the repeated reassurances by the ship's captain, whose gravelly voice was now coming over the public address system.

"We are currently passing through the outer edge of the storm and will shortly reach calm waters. The remainder of our voyage should be smooth and uneventful."

In a posh portside cabin, Carolyn Ross growled her annoyance as a small bottle of Joy perfume rattled noisily on the dressing table before her. Quickly she grabbed the expensive vial to prevent it from slipping away.

"Damn it, David!" she grumbled aloud. "How long will it be until things really calm down?"

"Not long," he answered. "The swells are coming farther and farther apart."

"You said that ten minutes ago."

"It was true then too." He grinned and came up behind her to rub her neck. "I thought you nurses were supposed to be so patient."

Carolyn smiled at David Ballineau's reflection in the mirror and wondered why he had been so unaffected by the rough seas. He hadn't taken any medicines or used any skin patches to prevent seasickness. It just didn't seem to bother him, like it did most of the other passengers. "Maybe the poor ship's doctor will be able to get some rest now."

"He wasn't that overworked," David remarked. "All he had to do was pass out Antivert and Dramamine pills."

"He was overworked enough to beg you to come back and help him."

"It wasn't a big deal," David said with a shrug.

"More than a hundred sick patients would say otherwise," Carolyn argued mildly, as she reached back to fasten the latch on her pearl necklace. "It was really unfortunate that the other ship's doctor wasn't available."

"He and his nurse-wife were down with a double dose of seasickness," David said. "Make that a triple dose."

"That bad, eh?"

"So bad they had to crawl to the bathroom just to throw up," David went on. "They both plan to get off the ship in Bermuda and fly home."

Carolyn gave David a long look. "Are you telling me they'll leave the *Grand Atlantic* with only one doctor and one nurse?"

"Only temporarily," David told her. "The ship will arrange to pick up replacements in Montego Bay."

"And until then, suppose another hundred passengers show up with seasickness?"

"If they ask me, I'll lend a hand again," David said with another shrug, thinking that another hundred straightforward cases of seasickness would be a relatively simple matter to treat. Pass out pills, tell patients to lie down with a damp washcloth over their forehead, and sip liquids sparingly. And all would soon be well. Easy enough, David thought to himself. Far easier than dealing with a handful of critically injured patients at University Hospital in Los Angeles where he was director of the emergency room. That was life and death. Seasickness was a transient inconvenience.

"Would you help me with my necklace?" Carolyn asked, fumbling with its latch.

"Sure."

They were standing in the dressing area of their opulent suite near the bow of the luxury liner. All of the suites aboard the *Grand Atlantic* were oversized, with rich fixtures and furniture, plush carpeting, and hanging tapestries on the wall. In addition to the dressing area next to the bedroom, there was a separate parlor and a marble tiled bathroom that was large enough to have a bathtub and walk-in shower. The ship was considered the most elegant passenger liner in the world, built to accommodate the tastes of the wealthy, particularly those who enjoyed old-world splendor. But it was special in other ways too. To ensure the comfort of the passengers and to minimize the intrusive and disturbing instruments of modern-day life, the use of cell phones was prohibited in public gathering places, particularly in the dining areas, theaters, and libraries.

To encourage passengers to follow these regulations, all calls made from the individual suites went through a central phone bank and were free of charge, regardless of destination or length of conversation. At a cost of $8,000 to $12,000 per passenger, depending on the location of their suite, everyone expected and was given the best of all worlds on a ten-day cruise that went from New York to Bermuda to Montego Bay to San Juan and back.

"There," David said as he secured the latch on Carolyn's string of Mikimoto pearls. "Now you're perfect."

She nestled the back of her head against his chest and smiled. "I feel like we're in another world."

"We are," David agreed. "It's as if someone turned the clock back a hundred years."

"I heard one of the passengers comment that the suites on this ship were modeled after those on the *Titanic*."

David nodded and kissed the nape of her neck. "Not only the suites, but a lot of other things too. According to some naval historians, this liner is remarkably similar to the *Titanic*. It has the same structure, style, and dress codes. Even the ship's officers are all British, just like on the *Titanic*."

"So they copied everything but the name."

David nodded again. "They'd be way beyond stupid to ever use that name again."

"The *Titanic*," Carolyn said in a soft voice. "Everyone on the *Grand Atlantic* was probably thinking about the awful fate of that ship when we were going through the worst part of the storm."

"We were never in any real danger," David commented.

"I knew that," Carolyn said. "I suspect all the passengers knew that. But the memory of the lifeboat drill we went through just before leaving port still made everybody nervous. Jesus! They just gathered us all together, then had us put on life jackets and stand beneath those huge, hanging lifeboats, while they informed us what to do if the ship began to sink. The memory of that rehearsal was in everybody's mind as the ship bounced around in those rough seas."

"The ship's crew was only following regulations," David told her. "The drill had nothing to do with the impending weather."

"I wonder if the passengers on the *Titanic* went through a lifeboat drill."

"One had been scheduled," David said, his mind going back to a book about the ship's sinking. "But they canceled it at the last minute for unknown reasons."

Carolyn's eyes widened briefly. "And our final lifeboat drill was also canceled at the last moment."

"Supposedly because of the bad weather."

Carolyn shook her head. "It wasn't that bad."

"But the passengers kept bitching and moaning about it until the captain finally gave in."

"And I'll bet the passengers on the *Titanic* bitched and moaned their way out of their lifeboat drill too."

"You're probably right," David agreed. "The rich and pampered don't like to be inconvenienced."

"Well, let's hope the similarities end there," Carolyn said, then turned to David and smiled. "There aren't any icebergs in the Caribbean, are there?"

"None have been spotted recently," David jested.

"That's comforting to know," Carolyn said dryly, then reached up to center his black bow tie. "There! Now you're perfect too."

They briefly studied their reflections in a large wall mirror. He was wearing a white dinner jacket with a cummerbund, she an Audrey Hepburn–type cocktail dress with thin shoulder straps. That was another requirement aboard the *Grand Atlantic*. Everyone had to be formally attired at dinner.

"You look very distinguished with your graying hair," Carolyn observed.

"You think so, eh?"

"I know so."

David gazed at himself in the full-length mirror. In his mid-forties, he was tall and lean, with an angular face, pale blue eyes, and close-cropped salt-and-pepper hair that turned gray at the temples. His clean-cut good looks were marred by a jagged scar across his chin. According to Carolyn, most women thought the scar made David appear dangerous. He shrugged indifferently at the notion. The only effect the scar had on him was to bring back memories of a time and place he wanted to forget.

"Well?" Carolyn asked. "What's your opinion?"

"You're right," David said as he turned away from his reflection. "I do look distinguished."

"Jesus!" Carolyn chuckled and poked his chest playfully.

"How about a drink before—"

The phone rang loudly. David picked it up on the second ring and spoke briefly. His face grew more serious as he pressed the receiver to his ear and asked for additional details. "What type of jerky motion?" … "Is the patient conscious?" … "Can she talk?" … "I'll be right down."

David replaced the receiver and glanced over to Carolyn. "That was the ship's doctor. It sounds like someone is having a seizure."

"Oh Christ!" Carolyn groaned.

"I'll run down to the sick bay and get things squared away."

"Do you want some help?" Carolyn asked. "I was pretty good with seizures when I was a MedEvac nurse."

"Nah," David said. "I can handle it."

"You sure?"

"Positive," David told her. "Tell you what. If the seas calm down as expected, let's meet on deck near the bar for a drink in thirty minutes or so."

"See you then."

David dashed out of the suite and down a narrow passageway, rushing by strolling passengers. He hurried through an exit door and took the stairs down, two at a time, all the while going over the differential diagnosis of sudden onset seizures in a middle-aged woman. A brain tumor was at the top of the list, followed by other space-occupying lesions, such as a subdural hematoma or arterio-venous malformation. *But a brain tumor would be the most likely diagnosis*, he thought miserably. *Shit!* David moved to the side of the staircase and made room for a pair of joggers who were running the stairs for exercise. The lead jogger, a handsome, well-built man in his early thirties, huffed aloud, "Make way!" and rudely brushed by David. Behind the man was a very pretty young woman with streaked blond hair held in a ponytail. She offered no apology as her elbow caught David in his lower ribs.

"Careful!" David called out.

The man stopped abruptly and gave David a hard stare. "What did you say to her?"

"I said be careful."

"Ah-huh," the man snarled, with an expression of disbelief. "It sounded like you said something else."

David ignored the man's challenging stare and continued down the stairs. His mind switched back to the patient waiting for him in the sick bay. The first order of business would be to get her seizures under control. He wondered how extensive the ship's pharmacy would be. Surely they would have injectable Dilantin and Ativan on board. *Jesus H. Christ! I hope so.* From his brief stint helping the ship's doctor with the seasick passengers, David recalled that the sick bay consisted of a small reception area, two examining tables separated by a curtain, and a radiology room capable of taking only the simplest x-rays. It was like a first-aid station when compared to the ER at University Hospital, where the most sophisticated equipment and resources were immediately at hand.

"Well, just make do," he muttered to himself as he left the staircase at the G level.

David rushed by the ship's spa and entered the sick bay. A plump, heavily bosomed nurse, with dyed black hair, frantically waved him into a nearby room. The middle-aged patient was lying on an examining table, obviously agitated. Her head was tilted to the side and twitching with rapid, jerky motions. But the most disturbing features were bulging eyes that were staring up and back in a fixed position. The woman was making unintelligible sounds because her tongue was protruding far out of her mouth.

"It's the strangest seizure I have ever seen," the small, bespectacled, ship's doctor said. Arthur Maggio ran a hand nervously through his thinning gray hair. "Only her head and neck seem to be involved."

"What medicines has she received?" David asked at once.

"None," Maggio replied. "I wasn't sure of the diagnosis."

"No, no," David clarified his question. "I meant, was she given any drugs prior to all this happening?"

"Only a shot for her terrible nausea," Maggio answered. "It was given fifteen minutes before the seizure began."

Maggio coughed without turning his head away. David immediately detected the smell of alcohol on the elder doctor's breath and hoped it only represented the ingestion of a single cocktail before dinner. "A shot of what?" David asked hurriedly.

"Compazine."

David nodded to himself. "This isn't a seizure we're seeing. It's a dystonic reaction to Compazine." He quickly turned to the nurse and said, "Draw up five ccs of Benadryl in a syringe for me. Put a 23-gauge needle on the syringe."

The nurse looked over to the ship's doctor, who gestured his approval. She dashed over to a medicine cabinet and busied herself following David's instructions.

"I've never seen this type of dystonic reaction," Maggio said honestly.

"It's called an oculogyric crisis," David elucidated. "It's a very rare reaction to Compazine-like drugs."

"And it only involves the head and neck?"

"Only the head and neck," David said. "Typically the muscles around the eyes and face go into spasm. And the tongue is frequently involved, which explains why it was protruding from the patient's mouth."

The nurse came over and handed David a syringe fitted with a 23-gauge needle and filled with a clear liquid. "Each cc has 25 milligrams of Benadryl."

"Good."

David used an alcohol swab to clean the patient's antecubital fossa before inserting the needle into a vein. He began to very slowly inject the Benadryl solution. Almost instantly the woman stopped twitching and jerking. Then her eyes returned to their normal gaze, and her tongue withdrew itself back into her mouth. A moment later the patient sat up on the examining table and asked, "What in the world happened to me?"

Maggio shook his head in wonderment. "I've never seen anything like that before."

"The response is always impressive," David said and turned to the patient. "You had a severe reaction to the drug you received for your nausea. It's called Compazine. You should never take it again."

"You needn't worry about that!" Edith Teller had an attractive face now that the spastic contortions had left it. She had prominent cheekbones and dark eyes from her one-quarter Cherokee heritage. "I won't go anywhere near Compazine."

"If any of your symptoms return, let us know at once," David advised. "Another shot of Benadryl will stop them in their tracks."

"Will they return?" she asked anxiously.

"Probably not."

"With my luck they will," the woman said sadly. Then tears welled up and began to roll down her cheeks. "This cruise is turning into a disaster for me. Only two and a half days out, and I've experienced rough seas, nausea, dizziness, and a bad reaction to a drug." She looked away and sniffed her tears back. "You save up for the trip of a lifetime and you end up in a sick bay, certain you're about to die."

David nodded sympathetically while the woman spoke on and on about being a librarian from Ohio and dreaming of taking an ocean voyage on a great luxury liner and meeting interesting people and visiting exotic places. David appeared to be listening, but he wasn't. He didn't want to hear her sad story, and he didn't want to know about her wishes and hopes and dreams. That's why he was an emergency-room physician. There he didn't have to listen to people complain about life's disappointments and heartaches. His ER mantra was *See 'em, fix 'em,* and *send 'em* on their way. All interchange was strictly medical, and that's how he liked it.

The woman was still talking when David patted her on the shoulder and gently interrupted, "Well, you're fine now. Let's hope all your bad luck is behind you now."

With a wave to the ship's doctor, David left the sick bay and walked over to the elevator. He wished again that he hadn't taken the cruise aboard the *Grand Atlantic*, because it wasn't turning out to be a vacation at all. He was trapped on a giant ocean liner that had 750 passengers, with a retired military doctor and a seasick general practitioner as the only healthcare providers. And the ship's doctor now knew that David was an experienced ER specialist. So, in case of any real emergencies or mass illnesses, David would be called in. He grumbled to himself as he thought about the sun-drenched beaches of Hawaii. That was where he wanted to go. But his twelve-year-old daughter, Kit, and his girlfriend, Carolyn, ganged up on him and insisted they all take a cruise on a fantastic luxury liner. David was good at a lot of things in life, but negotiating with women wasn't one of them.

The elevator door opened, and David stepped into a crowded car. The air within was filled with the aroma of heavily perfumed women who seemed to all be speaking at the same time. Their bored husbands looked on, mute as stone statues. Once more David thought about the white-sand beaches at Waikiki. The elevator stopped, and most of the splendidly dressed passengers got off at the C level, where the huge dining room was located. With a jerk, the empty elevator continued upward. David was still thinking about white sand beaches and wondering if he could talk the girls into disembarking at San Juan and enjoying the sun before flying back to Los Angeles. Or maybe they could get off at Montego Bay, which was closer, with even better beaches.

The elevator door opened, and David walked out into a cool breeze. Beyond the lounge chairs he spotted Carolyn standing by a small bar and looking absolutely gorgeous. She was tall and slender, with soft, patrician features and long brown hair that curled slightly as it reached her shoulders. But it was her perfectly contoured lips that fascinated him, particularly the way she could use them to change her expression. One moment she could seem frank and serious, the next amusing and playful, the next sympathetic and engaging. All by just moving her lips a bit one way or the other. But her eyes were always the same—deep, dark, and sensuous. David had once told her that a man could get lost in those brown eyes and never find his way out. And he meant it.

David waved and strolled over to the bar. "You're beautiful," he said, pecking her lips.

"You say that to all the girls," Carolyn grinned.

"Only the pretty ones," David said and kissed her again.

"You're going to mess up my makeup."

"Do you mind?"

"No," Carolyn murmured softly and kissed him back.

"You're my type of girl, you know."

"And you're my type of guy." Carolyn took his arm and guided him away from the other couples at the bar. Quietly she asked, "What happened to the woman with seizures?"

"It wasn't seizures," David said and told her the details of the patient with an oculogyric crisis caused by Compazine. "She had a textbook picture of the disorder."

"I haven't seen a case of that in years," Carolyn thought back.

"Same with me," David said. "But it was totally foreign to Maggio."

Carolyn slowly shook her head. "Most doctors would have made that diagnosis in a split second."

"Not if they had spent most of their professional career as a military physician doing mainly administrative work."

"Well, I guess the cruise line owners figured they didn't need a specialist from the Mayo Clinic to be one of their ship's doctors."

"I guess."

The wind stiffened, coming in from the northeast, and the temperature seemed to drop abruptly.

Carolyn shivered in the sudden coolness. "Let's have that drink in the dining room."

"Sounds good," David said and reached for her hand.

They strolled past the lounge chairs on their way to the elevator. In the fading light, neither noticed the large bird, with a quivering wing, curled up beneath the end chair.

TWO

A YOUNG MAN IN a white waiter's jacket bowed and opened the ornate glass door for David and Carolyn. Before them was a wide mahogany staircase that descended into a large anteroom. Like many of the other passengers, they were struck by how closely the opulent anteroom resembled the one seen in the movie *Titanic*. Everything was polished wood except for the immense ceiling that was dome-shaped and made of frosted glass. Even the walls were impressive, with their exquisitely carved, gold-rimmed inlays. David gazed around the magnificent setting, then down at the elegantly dressed couples as they mingled and chatted with one another prior to dinner.

"It looks like an Easter parade in slow motion," David said.

Carolyn chuckled under her breath. "The women just want to find out what the others are wearing."

"It's the jewelry they're interested in."

"That's part of what they're wearing."

They walked down the stairs and through the crowded ante-room, nodding to those they recognized. Most of the couples were middle-aged, but some seemed old and frail, with bent postures and shuffling gaits. There was a scattering of aluminum walkers and wheelchairs for the infirm. David sighed to himself as he viewed the elderly as prospective patients. One misstep by a senior citizen could result in a broken hip or fractured skull or worse. David wondered how long it would take for a MedEvac helicopter to reach them.

Carolyn broke into his thoughts, asking, "Why do you think we were invited to sit at the captain's table tonight?"

"I don't have the slightest idea," David said.

"I don't think it was just a random choice."

"Me neither."

Carolyn grinned at him. "Your daughter believes we were picked to be window dressing."

David smiled back as a picture of his twelve-year-old daughter flashed into his mind. Kit was bright and beautiful, with a flawless, cream-colored complexion and raven-black hair—all lovely features she had inherited from her mother. Now another picture came to David's mind, and his smile vanished. It was Marianne, his former wife, with her soft voice and gentle touch, who had made his life perfect. It was a storybook marriage that most people could only dream about. Then, out of the blue, she became ill with acute myeloblastic leukemia and was dead in six months. And David's perfect world came crashing down. That was almost nine years ago, he thought sadly. And eight of those years were filled with loneliness and emptiness. Then Carolyn came along. She made life good again. Not perfect, but damn good. And she and Kit were best buddies, and that made it even better.

David put his arm around Carolyn's waist and gave her a tight squeeze.

"What was that for?" Carolyn asked softly.

"Everything."

"That covers a lot of territory."

"It was meant to."

They entered the resplendent dining room, with its gleaming chandeliers and large, round tables that were set with enough sterling silverware to serve four courses. The wine glasses were Waterford, the dishes Royal Doulton. There was an individual waiter for each table. A string quartet far off to the side was playing Mozart.

David guided Carolyn over to the captain's table, which unlike the others was rectangular and had four chairs aside. The ship's captain, William Rutherford, was a large, heavyset man, with a neatly trimmed gray moustache and beard. He was dressed in a naval outfit and seated at the head of the table. Quickly he rose to greet the new arrivals.

"Dr. Ballineau, let me thank you and Miss Ross for joining us tonight."

"It's our pleasure," David said as he pulled out a chair and waited for Carolyn to be seated.

"And I wish to thank you for helping out the ship's doctor with the passengers who became ill," Rutherford went on, his voice deep and distinctly British.

"It was no trouble at all."

"Nevertheless, I thank you." Rutherford waived his hand expansively to the two other couples at the table. "Also joining us tonight are Mr. and Mrs. Sol Wyman and Mr. Richard Scott and his companion, Miss Deedee Anderson."

Everyone nodded to one another and began chatting about the rough spell the ship had gone through. Of particular interest was a loud bang that had occurred at the height of the storm and caused the *Grand Atlantic* to vibrate momentarily. Most of the passengers had attributed it to a large wave slamming into the ship.

"No, it wasn't a wave," Rutherford told the group. "The strong wind dislodged a panel from the rear of the bridge and it landed well aft on the deck. There was no significant damage to the ship, and we continue to steam along in the somewhat choppy Atlantic at a steady 28 knots per hour."

Rutherford's statement was half true. The *Grand Atlantic* was moving along at 28 knots per hour. But the damage caused by the falling panel was not insignificant. The half-ton panel had crushed the heliport and created a huge, deep crack in its surface. The entire area was now covered with canvas and roped off, with a NO ADMITTANCE sign prominently displayed. A crew member was posted to guard the area to ensure no passengers wandered around the damaged, unstable heliport. Repairs were scheduled to be made when the ship docked at the next port of call.

The conversation shifted to the calm waters of the Caribbean and white sand beaches of Jamaica. The captain had lived in Montego Bay as a boy and knew the island's history in detail. His storytelling held everyone's interest, except for Deedee Anderson, who kept glancing down to make certain she was showing the right amount of cleavage.

A waiter appeared out of nowhere and began filling the wine glasses with Chateau Lafite Rothschild '95, to go with the first course of Beluga caviar.

"How do you take your caviar, sir?" the waiter asked David.

"Unadorned," David replied.

Nibbling on the delicacy, David studied the man sitting directly across from him. Sol Wyman was stout and middle aged, with a round face and thinning hair. He looked uncomfortable in his Armani dinner jacket that seemed a size too small.

"Me and Marilyn got married a couple of years ago," Sol Wyman was saying. "First for me, second for her."

"My first husband passed away," Marilyn Wyman added softly. She was a slender woman with an aristocratic face and carefully coiffured, auburn hair. "We'd been married nearly twenty years."

That was eleven more than I got, David thought unhappily. *And seventeen more than poor little Kit. Shit!* He shook his head at the sad remembrance. *Get your mind out of the past. It's long gone and never coming back. Just be thankful you've got someone as wonderful as Carolyn at your side now.* David brought his attention back to the table. Sol Wyman was now talking at length about the wholesale jewelry company he owned, giving one detail after another, with particular emphasis on platinum settings. David quickly took the measure of the talkative man. The jeweler's loquaciousness was a reflection of his nervousness in the extravagant surroundings. Sol Wyman was a steak-and-potatoes guy, who was worth a lot of money but was unaccustomed to a posh lifestyle. His wife seemed to be the opposite. She appeared reserved and refined, and an unlikely match for Sol Wyman.

"What about you, Mr. Scott?" Sol turned to the man seated next to him. "What line are you in?"

"I'm an investment banker," Richard Scott answered importantly.

"Ho-ho-ho," Sol said, and rubbed his hands together. "We could all use some of your advice during these tough economic times."

"I'm afraid that would present a problem," Scott said in a condescending tone. "My client list is rather restricted and exclusive, you see."

Sol's face colored and his head dropped, like a schoolboy who had just been put in his place.

David glared at the insolent investment banker and his snobbish behavior. Richard Scott now had a satisfied look, obviously pleased with causing Sol Wyman's public embarrassment. It took David a moment to recognize Scott as the jogger who had rudely brushed by him on the stairs down to the sick bay. The banker was a handsome man, in his late thirties, with sharp features and sandy hair that was swept back and gelled into place. His eyes were steel gray and cold as ice. The woman next to him, Deedee Anderson, was close to beautiful in her tightly fitted white cocktail dress. She had nicely contoured lips, doe-like brown eyes, and blond hair that came straight down to her shoulders without even a hint of curl. Her silicone-filled breasts seemed too large for the rest of her body.

"Ah-hmm," the ship's captain cleared his throat, breaking the silence. "As you can see, we have two empty chairs. I asked Dr. Maggio and his wife to join us, but perhaps they were held up with more sick patients."

"Or maybe he's just worn out," Carolyn suggested. "David told me he had over a hundred patients to care for."

"And he did really well," David exaggerated. "He's a fine old doctor."

"With an emphasis on the word *old*," Scott scoffed. "God help us if he's confronted with anything more than a common cold."

"Oh, I'm certain he'll do well," David said easily. "After all, his clientele is rather exclusive and restricted, you see."

Everyone at the table smiled politely, except for Richard Scott, whose eyes seemed even colder now. David saw a flash of anger cross Scott's face, but it quickly vanished. The banker was mean as a snake, but under control. He could be a very dangerous man, David concluded.

"Tell me, Dr. Ballineau," Marilyn Wyman inquired. "What type of doctor are you?"

"I'm director of the emergency room at University Hospital in Los Angeles," David replied.

"I've heard that University Hospital is the Harvard of the West," Marilyn said.

"We like to think of Harvard as the University Hospital of the East," David jested.

Marilyn smiled at the quick retort and softly clapped her hands. "Well said, Dr. Ballineau."

"David, please."

"David, then. And please call me Marilyn."

"Good," David said, liking the woman instantly. "Now, Marilyn, I have to ask your husband for some advice about diamonds. Would you mind?"

"Not at all," Marilyn said. "As a matter of fact, diamonds are his specialty."

"Excellent." David turned to Sol Wyman, who was struggling to keep his caviar on his biscuit. "Sol, I need to know how to choose the best diamond. Tell me the features I should look for."

Sol straightened up in his seat, a man now in his element. "What do you know about diamonds?"

"Very little."

"Then let's start with the basics," Sol began, like a man well rehearsed. "When it comes to diamonds, you have to know the four Cs—carat, color, cut, and clarity. Those are the features that determine a diamond's value."

"Well, I know about carats," David told him. "They measure the weight of a diamond."

"Right," Sol said at once. "But what the hell does that tell you? It's like saying a car weighs five thousand pounds. Isn't it a beauty?"

David laughed at the analogy. "But carats do count some."

"Oh yeah," Sol agreed. "But keep in mind, a diamond is most valued by its brilliance. A big diamond only glistens when it's clear, colorless, and perfectly cut."

David nodded slowly. "So it's really a combination of all four Cs that tells you the quality of a diamond."

"Right again, although it's the cut that is most important when it comes to brilliance," Sol went on. "But the majority of people don't know much about cut or color, and they know even less about clarity."

"What determines clarity?" David asked.

"The number of inner flaws," Sol answered. "The fewer, the clearer. But you've got to see inside the diamond to determine that."

"So you're really at the jeweler's mercy."

"Absolutely," Sol said. "And there are more than a few thieves in the business. But I've got a friend in L.A. who is straight as an arrow. I'll give you his name, if you like."

"I'd appreciate that."

"By the way, who is the diamond for?"

"Someone very special," David said and touched Carolyn's knee under the table.

Sol smiled broadly at Carolyn's radiant face. "I'll bet she's elegant."

"Doubly so."

"Then you'll want an Asscher-cut diamond," Sol advised. "It's an emerald cut, with cropped corners. It goes best with elegance."

A messenger rushed up to the table and handed the captain a folded note. Rutherford put on his reading glasses and quickly read the message. He turned to David and said, "Dr. Ballineau, I'm afraid you're needed in the sick bay urgently. Someone has an airway obstruction."

David jumped up and grabbed Carolyn's hand. "Come on! I'll need your help on this one!"

They hurried between the round tables and past startled diners, then darted into the anteroom and up the mahogany staircase. A uniformed crewman led them to a waiting elevator and pushed the G-level button.

"What do you think is causing the airway obstruction?" Carolyn asked as the elevator descended.

"Probably aspirated food," David replied. "But with the number of elderly people aboard, it could also be a dental fixture or bridge somebody sucked down into their airway. Either way, they'll need a tracheotomy if we can't get the damn thing out."

"Do they have a trach setup tray in the sick bay?"

"I'd guess not. You'd better plan on improvising."

Carolyn quickly listed in her mind the instruments that would be needed for a tracheotomy. Scalpel. Hemostats. Some type of tube. Packing gauze. "If he doesn't have a pulse, what do you want to do?"

"It depends on how long he's been pulseless."

The elevator jerked to a stop and the door opened. David and Carolyn ran at full speed down the corridor and past the ship's beauty spa. David was still thinking about the possibility of encountering a pulseless patient. And whether or not he should perform CPR. Even if he could bring the patient back, there was little chance of survival with the lack of an ICU aboard the *Grand Atlantic*. And if the patient did survive, they could end up with a brain-dead vegetable on their hands. Again David thought about the white sand beaches of Hawaii, where he wanted to vacation in the first place.

He led the way into the sick bay and saw his daughter Kit standing by the reception desk. She looked badly frightened and had tears welling up in her eyes.

David quickly knelt in front of the young girl and asked, "What's wrong, sweetheart?"

"My—my friend Will," Kit stammered. "He's got a gumball stuck way down in his throat and it won't come out. You've got to help him, Dad!"

"I will," David promised and hurried into the treatment room. A young boy, no more than twelve, with tousled auburn hair and freckled cheeks, was seated on the edge of the examining table. His labored breathing caused an audible wheeze, but his skin color was good.

"Hi, Will," David said calmly. "I'm Kit's dad and I'm a doctor, and I've seen plenty of cases like yours."

Will nodded rapidly and pointed to his lower throat. He sucked deeply for air and that made him wheeze even louder.

"I want you to talk," David requested. "Tell me your full name."

The boy swallowed and squeaked, "Will Harrison."

"Good," David said. "The fact that you can talk means air is passing through your larynx and that means you're not blocked off all the way. And that means we can take our time getting that gumball out. Okay?"

Will nodded nervously.

David turned to the ship's doctor. "Did you try a Heimlich maneuver?"

"Three times," Maggio answered. "And the obstruction didn't budge."

"Let me give it a go."

"Be my guest."

David moved behind Will and, using clasped hands, forcefully compressed the boy's upper abdomen. The gumball stayed stuck in place. He tried once again, with the same result. "I'll need a laryngoscope," David said to Maggio. "I trust you've got one."

"We do," Maggio replied. "But the boy kept fighting me and turning away, so I couldn't insert it."

"Did you anesthetize his throat before trying it?"

"We don't have any topical anesthetic sprays."

Carolyn stepped forward. "Do you have Xylocaine?"

"Yes," Maggio said. "But it's only for injection."

"It'll do," Carolyn told him. "We'll need a couple of ccs drawn up in a syringe."

Maggio looked at her oddly. "But you can't inject—"

"Stop wasting time and get the Xylocaine," Carolyn cut him off, then turned to the nurse. "And bring me some long cotton swabs."

The nurse hesitated and glanced over to Maggio for his approval.

"Now!" Carolyn barked.

The nurse hurried away.

David patted the boy's shoulder and said, "Will, we're going to get that gumball out, but you have to do exactly what we say. Got it?"

Will nodded, his eyes dancing around the room anxiously.

"For a moment you'll feel like you're choking, but then it'll be over and you'll be breathing fine." *And if he puts up a fight*, David told himself, *I'll sedate him with IV Valium, assuming this ship has IV Valium.* "Okay?"

Will's eyes bulged with fright. "Ch-choking?" he managed to say.

"Just for a second."

The nurse returned with a syringe of Xylocaine and a handful of cotton swabs. She handed them to Carolyn, who promptly squirted the Xylocaine onto the cotton ends of the swabs until they were soaked.

"Now, Will," Carolyn said soothingly, "I want you to open our mouth real wide, so I can touch the back of your throat with these cotton swabs. It'll taste bitter, but it will numb your throat and that will let us get that old gumball out."

Will followed Carolyn's instructions and, despite repeated gagging, allowed her to paint his posterior pharynx with Xylocaine.

Meanwhile, David was examining the sick bay's only laryngoscope. It was adult-size.

"Have you got anything smaller?" David asked Maggio.

"I'm afraid not."

"Terrific," David muttered sarcastically, thinking he was aboard a luxury liner that cost a billion dollars to build, but had a second-rate sick bay. "We'll have to make do."

Carolyn called out, "He's numbed up!"

"All right," David said and turned to Will. "I want you to lie down, open your mouth, and close your eyes. It'll be over before you know it."

"Will it hurt?" the boy asked meekly.

"Not if you do what I tell you."

With Will on his back, Carolyn moved to the front of the examining table. She held the youngster's head tightly in her hands and immobilized it, then hyperextended his neck.

David quickly inserted the laryngoscope and squeezed it past the hard palate and into the boy's hypopharynx. Will gagged forcefully, but David was still able to see a small gumball that was lodged aside the laryngeal opening. It was partially dissolved and beginning to come apart. David knew he had to be doubly careful because the gumball could easily fragment into pieces, which could be sucked down into the boy's lungs. He grasped the gumball gently with long forceps and felt its firmness give, but the ball stayed intact. Slowly he extracted the mushy sphere, then held it up to the light for inspection. There was no evidence of fragmentation.

"Okay, Will," David informed him. "We're done."

The boy sat up quickly and took several long, deep breaths to make certain his airway was now wide open. Relieved and reassured, he smiled at David and Carolyn and said, "Thanks."

"Any time," David said. "But I think you should stay away from gumballs. They can be dangerous."

"This never happened before," Will retorted, obviously not liking the prospect of no more gumballs.

"Well, I think we should make certain it never happens again."

Will thought for a moment, then said, "Maybe I'll just stick with chewing gum."

"Good idea," David approved. "Now scoot. There's someone waiting for you outside."

Will climbed off the examining table and, after taking a few more deep breaths, dashed out to the reception area. He smiled at Kit, saying, "Your dad is really cool!"

"I know," Kit said proudly.

David watched the pair run out into the passageway, laughing and talking at the same time, as if nothing untoward had happened.

"God!" Carolyn marveled. "They're so resilient."

"If they weren't, they'd never reach adulthood," David said.

Leaving the sick bay, David put his arm around Carolyn's waist and gave her an affectionate squeeze. "You were great! Without that Xylocaine, I could never have passed that laryngoscope."

Carolyn shrugged off the compliment. "That old doctor and his nurse aren't much good in emergencies, are they?"

"They're mainly for show," David said. "You know, to treat colds and seasickness."

"And that's all the sick bay is designed for too."

David nodded. "It's little more than a dispensary."

"Why would they cut corners on something as important as a sick bay?"

David considered the question before answering. "I suspect the people who designed the ship weren't interested in a high-tech sick bay. From a business standpoint, it doesn't make sense to spend a lot of money on something you don't anticipate using."

"Suppose a really serious medical problem arises," Carolyn thought out loud. "Like one involving a lot of people on this ship."

"Then the sick would be in real trouble," David said grimly. "And unless we could reach shore quickly, they'd be in deadly trouble."

THREE

"WE'RE WELL AWAY FROM the storm's path now," David said as he gazed out at the gray-blue Atlantic Ocean. The water was calm except for a few choppy swells here and there. "I think we've seen the last of it."

"Good riddance," Carolyn said. "Let's hope it takes all the emergency cases along with it."

They strolled by the swimming pool area that was crowded with people in lounge chairs basking in the sun. Children were jumping into the pool and causing big splashes under the watchful eyes of their parents, while waiters were bringing over drinks from a nearby bar. A voice from the PA system told passengers that lunch would soon be served.

David groaned good-naturedly. "They never stop serving food aboard this ship, do they?"

"Most of which sounds better than it tastes," Carolyn opined.

"Do you really mean that?" David asked.

"I sure do. As a matter of fact, I'm almost glad we missed the rest of dinner at the captain's table last night."

"Why?"

"Because I'm not very big on pheasant, and it gave us an excuse to go to that nice little restaurant and have those delicious hamburgers."

David shrugged indifferently as they walked by a group of joggers coming from the stern of the *Grand Atlantic*.

"Didn't you love those juicy hamburgers?" Carolyn asked.

David shrugged again. "I'm a chili dog man, myself."

Carolyn poked him gently with an elbow. "Eaten standing up, of course."

"Of course," David agreed. "Otherwise you'll drip all over yourself."

Out of nowhere there was a sudden, loud burst of rifle fire.

Reflexively, David dropped down to one knee and raised his left arm to protect his head. With his right hand, he reached for his weapon. But he couldn't find it! Frantically he searched the deck for the semiautomatic M16.

"David! David"! He heard a voice calling him as he came out of the flashback. Slowly he got to his feet and collected himself, then waited for his heart to stop racing.

"Are you all right?" Carolyn asked, concerned.

"I'm fine."

But in his mind he could still see himself in Somalia over twenty years ago. He, along with seven others in the Special Forces unit, were surrounded by a mob of jihadists, all screaming at the top of their lungs, "Death to Americans!"

The only thing that saved him was a heavily armed helicopter sent to pick them up and ferry them back to a destroyer stationed offshore.

"I thought those damn flashbacks were finally fading away," Carolyn said, keeping her voice low.

"I did too."

Richard Scott came racing over. He was holding a shotgun, with its breech open, by his side. "I was only doing a bit of skeet shooting. I had no idea it would frighten you the way it did."

"It didn't," David told him.

"Well, the way you hit the deck," Scott went on, "I would say otherwise."

"Just drop the subject," David said, now aware of the small crowd gathered around them.

"Is that an order?"

"It's a request."

"I'll think it over." Scott turned to the bikini-clad Deedee Anderson, who had come up beside him. "I'm afraid we scared the doctor with our skeet shooting."

Deedee thought for a moment before saying, "Then he should stay away from guns."

"Or learn about them," Scott said and nodded at his own suggestion. "Yes. Perhaps I should instruct him in the proper use of guns. What do you say, doctor?"

"No, thanks," David refused the offer.

"It's quite easy." Scott checked the open breech on his shotgun and blew away and imaginary speck of dust. "I'll show you everything you need to know."

"Maybe another time."

"You don't have to be afraid of guns," Scott persisted. "If you know how to handle them, they can't hurt you."

"Oh yes, they can," David said, then added darkly, "There are graves everywhere filled with brave men who knew all about guns."

Before Scott could reply, David took Carolyn's arm and walked away. Behind him he heard Richard Scott telling his girlfriend, "Skeet shooting is a man's sport. Not everyone is cut out for it."

David slowed momentarily and wondered how macho Scott would be with a hundred bloodthirsty terrorists charging him, all intent on slitting his throat so they could drag his body through the streets of Mogadishu. Once more his mind went back to Somalia and the piles of corpses and the overwhelming stench of death. All for nothing. Not a damn thing had changed over there.

"He's got a big mouth," Carolyn broke the silence.

David nodded as they strolled on. "He's insecure and trying to prove he's not."

"To us?"

"To himself."

Carolyn moved in closer to him and asked, "Do those flashbacks ever go away altogether?"

"I don't think so."

"Does everyone who ever fought in a war have those damn things?"

"Not everyone," David said somberly. "Just those who came back alive."

Up ahead they saw Marilyn Wyman, who waved and walked over to them. She was wearing a yellow sundress that was cut low enough to expose the upper part of her breasts. David noticed a small horizontal scar at the top of her left breast. It was a biopsy site.

He hoped the lesion had turned out benign. She already had enough grief for one lifetime.

"Thank you so much, David," Marilyn gushed. She reached out and gave his hand a grateful squeeze. "Thank you for saving my son, Will."

David was taken aback. "I didn't know that Will was your son. He told me his last name was Harrison."

"It is," Marilyn explained. "Harrison was my former husband's name."

"I see," David said, nodding. "Well, he's certainly a brave little fellow."

"Would you believe he didn't tell me anything about the choking episode?" Marilyn asked. "I learned everything from Dr. Maggio this morning. He told me you saved Will's life."

"He wasn't in any real danger," David downplayed it. "The gumball was off to one side of his throat."

"But he still could have sucked it down in this lungs. Right?"

"It could have happened," David agreed mildly.

"Then you saved him from *possible* suffocation," Marilyn insisted. "And we owe you a debt we can never repay."

"No payment is necessary."

"Just the same. I want you and Carolyn to join us in the lounge before dinner for a nice bottle of Dom Pérignon."

"We'll look forward to it."

The skeet shooting resumed, with one shot after another in rapid fire. Marilyn waited for the noise to quiet before continuing. "I wonder if I could impose on your medical knowledge a little further," she said hesitantly. "I hope you don't mind."

"Not at all," David said and again thought about the sandy beaches of Hawaii where he and Carolyn and Kit should be now. His eyes drifted to the well-healed scar on Marilyn's breast. "Are you ill?"

"Not me," Marilyn answered. "Sol."

Carolyn grumbled to herself, but kept her face expressionless. Poor David, she thought, had suddenly become the ship's go-to doctor. He would never be able to relax and enjoy himself on the *Grand Atlantic*. She felt like hanging a DO NOT DISTURB sign around his neck.

"What's wrong with Sol?" David was asking.

"He has coronary artery disease," Marilyn confided. "He's undergone bypass surgery, but still has to take a variety of medicines to prevent his angina from recurring. We were assured there would be excellent medical care aboard the ship in case of any problem. But now I'm not so sure. The little doctor downstairs is a very nice man, but I'm not certain he's up to date."

Try twenty years behind time, Carolyn wanted to say but held her tongue.

"If any problem arises," Marilyn went on, "could we turn to you for help?"

"Of course."

"You're very kind," Marilyn said and reached into her purse for an envelope, which she handed to David. "And here is the name, address, and phone number of Sol's friend in Los Angeles. He's the one who knows so much about diamonds."

"Thanks," David said and winked at Carolyn.

"I wonder who the diamond is for?" Carolyn asked with a grin.

"I can't tell you," David grinned back. "It's a surprise."

Carolyn chuckled softly, delighted that her life was once again smooth and wonderful. The depression that followed her mother's death from Alzheimer's disease had finally lifted, and the memories of several failed relationships, which should have led to marriage but didn't, had faded away. Now she had the ideal man and everything in her world was perfect. "Big secret, eh?"

"For now."

The threesome strolled on as a warm breeze from the south freshened. The women chatted about the ship's beauty spa and salon, and about shopping in the luxury stores located on the arcade level. Names such as Gucci, Bottega, and Bulgari were discussed at length. David blanked out the conversation, but his mind was still on Marilyn Wyman. A pleasant, attractive woman, well-to-do and refined, who seemingly had everything in the world. But that was on the surface. Scratch a little deeper and one found a world of sadness. A first marriage that ended in the premature death of her husband. A second marriage to a man with heart disease, who she constantly worried about. And then there was the biopsy on her breast that may or may not have revealed a malignancy. But chances were she palpated her breasts daily, looking for another lump to appear. The woman had bad karma and was waiting for the next terrible event to occur.

"Hi, Dad!" Kit's voice brought him out of his reverie. She ran over to give him a tight hug.

"Hi, kiddo!" David hugged her back, loving her more than anybody or anything on the face of the earth. "How are you doing?"

"I'm fine," Kit told him, "but Juanita is still not feeling good."

"Is she still seasick?"

"I guess," Kit said with uncertainty. "She just says she feels bad."

"Well, I'd better stop down to see her." David kissed his daughter's cheek and tried to think why the nanny would continue to be seasick. The sea was now calm and the few swells that did occur shouldn't noticeably affect the stability of the *Grand Atlantic*. But David knew that even a few swells could cause the ship to gently bob, and that might be enough to exacerbate the symptoms in those suffering from severe seasickness. Like the second doctor and nurse aboard the luxury liner, who were still dizzy and nauseated. David kissed his daughter's cheek again and said, "We have to take good care of her, don't we?"

"I love Juanita," Kit cooed.

"I know."

Juanita Cruz was a naturalized American citizen who had left her native Costa Rica to get away from an abusive husband. She began working for the Ballineaus when Marianne was six months pregnant with Kit. After Marianne's death, Juanita moved into their guest house and helped David raise Kit, like a surrogate mother. Juanita became an integral part of the family and loved Kit almost as much as her own daughter, who was currently a registered nurse at Grady Hospital in Atlanta.

"You'll make her well, huh, Dad?" Kit said.

"I'll get her fixed up," David promised.

As Kit reached up to hug David again, a small notepad slipped out of the back pocket of her jeans and fell to the deck. She quickly retrieved it and smiled up at David. "I love you, Dad."

"I love you too."

Securing the notepad in her back pocket, Kit blew him another kiss and ran back to a small restaurant that was just beyond the pool. She picked up her half-eaten hot dog, added more mustard, and bit into it, all the while talking with her new best friend, Will, who seemed to have most of his chili dog on his face.

"She's adorable," Marilyn commented.

"And bright as can be," David noted with pride.

"Will thinks so too," Marilyn said. "But tell me, why does she carry around that notepad?"

"She wants to be a writer," David said. "So when she sees or hears something interesting, she immediately writes it down, then rewrites it in her diary for possible use in the future."

Marilyn shook her head in wonderment. "Has she written anything thus far?"

"A play for her class in school based on a Harry Potter novel," David replied. "It was surprisingly good."

"It's amazing how soon some children realize exactly what they want to do with their lives."

"Yes, amazing," David agreed, stealing another glance at Kit and thinking about how fast she was growing up right before his eyes. "What about Will? Has he decided what he wants to do later in life?"

Marilyn nodded. "He'd like to be a veterinarian. The boy just loves animals and taking care of them." She laughed briefly to herself. "He wouldn't come on the cruise unless I allowed him to take along his pet goldfish and turtle. And of course he also had to bring his book on what to do if pets get sick."

"He sounds great," David said and meant it.

"He is," Marilyn beamed. "My only problem is coming up with ways to feed his interest in animal care. I've already bought him a dozen books on the subject."

"What about more pets?" David proposed.

Marilyn rolled her eyes to the sky. "In addition to the goldfish and turtle, we have two dogs, a cat, and a parakeet. I don't think more animals is the answer."

"May I make a suggestion for Will?" Carolyn offered.

"Please do," Marilyn said promptly.

"Well, when I was growing up, the boy next door was a real animal lover," Carolyn told her. "Like Will, he really enjoyed looking after his pets. So his father arranged for him to work on the weekends, without pay, for the local vet. That boy is now the town's veterinarian. You could talk with your vet and see if he can arrange a similar position for Will."

"What a wonderful idea!" Marilyn exclaimed. "Thank you so much for that."

"You're very welcome," Carolyn replied.

"Both of you are becoming so special to me," Marilyn said warmly. "We'll have two bottles of Dom Pérignon around seven tonight. Is that convenient for you?"

"Perfect," Carolyn and David responded almost simultaneously.

"And thank you for agreeing to look after Sol if the need arises," Marilyn said to David.

"No problem," David said.

"See you two at seven then."

David watched Marilyn walk away, her husband's illness still on his mind. Sol Wyman required medications to control his angina, despite having undergone coronary bypass surgery. And that meant he continued to have coronary artery insufficiency and was an ideal candidate for a full-blown myocardial infarction.

"What's causing that faraway look on your face?" Carolyn broke into his thoughts.

"I was thinking what would happen if Sol blocked off his bypass and had an acute myocardial infarction," David answered quietly.

Carolyn shuddered to herself. "We'd never be able to handle it. The sick bay hasn't got any monitoring equipment and no anticoagulants or antiarrhythmic drugs."

"And if he went into shock, he'd be dead," David added.

"A nightmare," Carolyn thought aloud.

"We'd better hope it doesn't happen."

Carolyn took his arm and hugged it. "This ship is turning into another ER for you, isn't it?"

David nodded. "It seems like it so far."

"This was supposed to be a vacation away from all that stress," Carolyn said wistfully. "A nice, relaxing time. But then again, doctors are never really off duty, are they?"

David shrugged. "It comes with the territory."

———

Munching on a giant bag of potato chips, Kit and Will carefully studied the list of movies available on the *Grand Atlantic*. The luxury liner had two large theaters as well as a library filled with DVDs of the most recent hit shows.

"Look!" Kit called out. "They've got the newest *Spider-Man*!"

"I saw it," Will told her.

"Is it any good?"

"Real good."

"Want to see it again?"

"Sure," Will said enthusiastically. "We can get a big box of popcorn and some sodas on the way in."

Kit checked the listings, then her watch. "Shoot! It doesn't start for over an hour."

"I know something we can do to pass the time," Will said, and looked over to the pool area to make sure no one was within earshot. "It'll be really cool."

"Like what?"

Will hesitated as he glanced around once more. "Can you keep a secret?"

"Of course."

"Even from your dad?"

"Yeah," Kit said with uncertainty. "I guess."

"You've got to promise," Will insisted.

"Okay," Kit said and crossed her heart. "I promise."

"Let's go!"

They hurried past the pool and lounge chairs, and through a door that opened into a narrow passageway. The area was hot and humid, with a staircase that went down at a sharp angle. Carefully, they descended the stairs, watching their every step. Will led the way while he held Kit's hand.

"We've got to go real slow," Will cautioned. "Everything is covered with moisture and really slippery."

"Okay," Kit said in a low voice. She was excited to be on a new adventure with Will, but not at all nervous. Although she'd known Will for only a few days, she trusted him. And she knew why. They shared something important that they could talk to each other about. Both had lost a parent—Kit, her mom and Will, his dad—and that left both of them emotionally scarred. It made them different from the other kids. A lot different. They always felt a sadness and emptiness when trying to remember things about their dead parent. Other people didn't understand it. One had to have lost a parent early in life to know the feeling. "Where are we going?" Kit whispered.

"You'll see," Will whispered back.

They went down another flight of stairs and came to a metal door that had a sign on it:

DANGER
HIGH VOLTAGE

"Will!" Kit cautioned. "I don't think we should go in there."

"We'll be fine," Will said confidently. "Just follow me."

They entered a large room that was hot and sticky despite several ventilation ducts that circulated the air. Behind one wall were giant, screened-off generators. The opposite wall was lined with bundles of wire and big metal pipes.

"Will, if you get us electrocuted, I'll never forgive you," Kit warned.

"That's not going to happen," Will assured her. "Now watch."

He reached down beneath a large pipe and pulled out a crumpled-up blanket. Atop the makeshift nest was a big, gray bird. It lay motionless except for a brief fluttering of one wing. There was a thick discharge drooling from its beak.

"It's a goose," Will explained. "I found it up on deck under a lounge chair yesterday. I think it landed accidentally on the ship and hurt itself."

"Is it dying?" Kit asked, concerned.

"I don't know," Will replied. "I gave him some food and water, but he barely touched it. That's not a good sign in animals."

"Maybe you should tell the captain."

"No! No!" Will refused adamantly. "They'd probably destroy it or throw it overboard. With some rest, he might be able to fly again." He considered the matter at length. "Maybe the food I left for him is something he doesn't like."

"Or maybe he's got a broken bone," Kit suggested.

"Maybe. But yesterday he was still moving his wings, and that means nothing important is broken."

Will bent down farther and was now face to face with the bird. The large goose quivered as spittle drooled off its beak. Then it had a cough-like spasm, and more spittle sprayed out.

"Watch it, Will!" Kit admonished. "That stuff will get all over you."

"Don't worry," Will said. "I'll wash my hands when we leave."

He carefully fluffed up the small blanket to construct a better nest and keep the bird more comfortable. Then he pushed the small bowls of food and water closer to the bird's beak.

The large bird coughed again and sprayed the air with droplets that were heavily laden with the avian flu virus.

Some of the deadly droplets floated toward the children. Others drifted up into the ship's ventilation system.

———

David peeled off his T-shirt and began some stretching exercises to relieve the stiffness in his scarred upper back. "I think I'll shower before dinner."

"Want some company?" Carolyn asked playfully.

"Oh, yeah."

As Carolyn slipped out of her jeans, she shivered noticeably. "Jesus! It's cold in here. Should I turn down the air conditioning?"

"Leave it on high," David said while starting a series of shoulder rolls that caused the large joints beneath his deltoids to crack pleasantly. "I like it cold."

Carolyn nodded thoughtfully, remembering that heat bothered David, particularly at night when he always slept under a single sheet, with the air conditioner on full blast. If he began to perspire in his sleep, he would suddenly throw off the sheet and start yelling, "Get out! Get out! Get out!" At first David refused to talk about it, saying it was just a bad dream. But Carolyn persisted and prodded him and, after two episodes happened in the same evening, he finally told her why oppressive heat triggered his subconscious outburst. They were nightmarish flashbacks to a firefight that occurred in Somalia during the hottest part of the summer. David was a member of an elite Special Forces unit sent in to destroy a militant group that was terrorizing the shipping lanes in the eastern Indian Ocean. After completing their mission, the unit was on their way back to an airstrip when they were ambushed by an overwhelming force of Islamic terrorists. Somehow, in the intolerable heat, they fought their way back to a waiting helicopter, but paid a heavy price. Two members of the unit were killed and three others badly wounded, including David, who had a shattered jaw and severe shrapnel wounds in his upper body. It took two months and multiple surgeries at Walter Reed Hospital to put David Ballineau together again.

Carolyn brought her mind back to the present and studied David's face in profile, focusing in on the contour of his chin that had been restored with a plastic implant. A faded, jagged scar was the only remaining evidence of that terrible wound. But the emotional wounds of war, the ones you couldn't see—those lasted a lifetime.

Carolyn moved in closer to David and watched him rub at a deep scar on his shoulder. The scar still had flecks of black buried in it. According to David, the surgeons weren't able to remove all the debris from the wound before they sutured it. The embedded metallic particles caused the scar tissue to itch and burn when the muscle beneath it was stretched too far.

"Is that scar bothering you again?" Carolyn asked.

"Nope."

"Your expression says it is."

"Maybe a little," David said absently. But it wasn't the twenty-year-old wound that now had his attention. It was an intuitive sixth sense that was suddenly telling him that something was wrong. *Something was amiss!* On more than a few occasions the sixth sense had alerted him and saved his life as well as the lives of the others in his Special Forces unit. *But what the hell could be amiss here, on a giant luxury liner in the middle of the ocean?*

Carolyn tried to read his face. "Your mind is a million miles away, isn't it?"

"It's right here in the cabin," David said, improvising quickly. "I was just thinking how lucky I am to have a beautiful girl like you."

Carolyn smiled at him. "You don't lie very well."

David smiled back. "But I think I'm getting better at it."

"Not really."

David rubbed more vigorously at the scar, digging into it before admitting, "That goddamn itch is back."

Carolyn reached up and scratched the area with her long fingernails. "Better?"

"A little."

"Well, let's try this." Carolyn stood on her tiptoes and kissed the scars on his shoulders and back. Then she ran her tongue and lips back and forth over them. A flick here. A gentle nibble there. "How's that?" she breathed.

David felt himself stir as her tongue came up his neck and into his ear. "You're asking for trouble," he shuddered.

"Among other things."

David spun her around and kissed her lips hard, then threw her down on the bed. They both quickly wriggled out of their clothes, their tongues and mouths going everywhere. Clinging to each other, they made wild, passionate love. The air now filled with sighs and moans and the sound of their headboard hammering against the wall. Yet there was no hurry. They went long and slow, long and slow, then deep and easy. Then deep and easy gave way to faster and harder, and faster and harder, until they both groaned simultaneously—a long, sustained groan—as their climaxes met, with Carolyn's seeming to go on and on.

Finally, Carolyn went limp and caught her breath. "Jesus! That was the best ever," she whispered.

"Nah," David whispered back and gave her a tender kiss. "Just the best so far."

"Do you know you're the perfect lover?"

"Only when I'm with the perfect partner."

Carolyn smiled and kissed his chin, then cuddled up close to David. "I love you, David Ballineau," she said softly and drifted into a deep sleep.

David closed his eyes and he too dozed off, despite the return of his sixth sense that kept telling him that something was wrong. Had he stayed awake a little longer he might have remembered the last time he ignored the warning from his sixth sense. It cost him a shattered jaw and nearly ended his life.

FOUR

Richard Scott resumed skeet shooting at midmorning the next day. A small crowd of admirers gathered near the stern of the ship and watched as he blasted one clay pigeon after another out of the sky. With each successful shot, they applauded lightly, urged on by Deedee Anderson.

"Pull!" Scott bellowed. He kept his eye on the flying disc, then squeezed the trigger of the shotgun. There was a loud bang before the disc exploded out over the ocean.

Scott increased the difficulty by calling for the discs to be released more rapidly. His marksmanship remained excellent, with nine out of ten perfect hits.

Off to the side, Carolyn watched Scott's last shot before turning to David. "He's pretty good, eh?"

"He's better than good," David said.

"Particularly in front of a crowd."

David nodded. "He needs the crowd. Men like Scott need to be the center of attention. It's their lifeblood."

Carolyn spotted Scott making his way through the crowd and coming directly toward them. She gestured with her head and said unhappily, "Look who wants to join us."

"Let's find something else to do," David said hurriedly. "Make believe you don't see him."

"Too late," Carolyn muttered as Scott waved to them. He was dressed in a shooting vest that had a padded shoulder for the butt of the shotgun to rest upon. "I'm surprised he's not wearing a bandoleer."

David smiled at Carolyn's quick wit and thought she had the man pegged just right.

"Well, well," Scott called to them, "I see you're getting over your fear of guns. The way to eliminate fear is to face it, you know."

"So I've been told," David said and kept his expression even despite his intense dislike for the man.

"I take it you've come for a lesson or two." Scott spoke in a voice loud enough for the small group behind him to hear. "We'll start with the basics."

"I'd rather not," David refused politely. "But thanks anyway."

"Oh, come on," Scott insisted. "The rifle won't bite you. I can assure you it has no teeth."

Deedee laughed weakly at the remark, as did a few others in the crowd. "Even I can shoot it," she challenged. "And I'm just a sweet little girl."

The only thing little about you is your brain, David thought, but held his tongue. "Perhaps another time."

"Don't be such a pussy," someone at the rear of the group yelled. The small crowd laughed harder at the crude comment.

David's jaw tightened when he saw Kit standing off to the side by the railing. The dejected look on her face told David she had heard every disparaging word. He felt his heart breaking.

Scott bit down gently on his lip to stifle a grin. He seemed to be enjoying David's obvious discomfort. "It's really quite easy, doctor. You simply place the weapon firmly against your shoulder, aim, and squeeze the trigger. Here, I'll show you."

David glanced over at Kit again. She was staring down at the deck, averting her gaze from his public humiliation.

"Push your fear away, for Chrissakes!" Scott blurted out.

David's anger was rising, and his eyes, now cold as ice, were flashing a DON'T FUCK WITH ME sign. But Scott didn't see it. He was too busy putting on a show for the crowd.

Scott reloaded the shotgun and handed it to David. "Let's begin with the correct stance. First, you must—"

"Just aim it and squeeze the trigger, eh?" David interrupted abruptly.

"Yes. But first—"

"Stand back," David ordered and used his forearm to shove Scott aside. He took a moment to expertly examine the shotgun, then released its safety and shouldered the weapon. Firming up his stance, he called out, "Pull!"

A clay pigeon flew skyward.

David fired and the clay disc exploded over the ocean.

"Pull!" Another disc went out and David fired again, and again the target exploded. In rapid succession, David called for eight more discs to be released, one after another. His aim was on the mark every time. After the last shot, David handed the weapon back to Scott and said, "You were right. It's really quite easy."

The crowd buzzed with stunned admiration. "Jesus! Did you see that?"… "That guy is a pro!"… "Ten out of ten. That's amazing!"

David took Carolyn's arm and strolled away, unhappy with the display he'd just put on. Now people would ask him about his marksmanship and want details. And that would bring up the past, which he was continually trying to forget. In a low voice, he said, "Richard Scott is going to be miserable for a while."

"Because you outshot him?" Carolyn asked.

David shook his head. "Because he lost center stage."

"That was some exhibition you put on," Carolyn praised. "It looked as if you'd been doing that all of your life."

"Only for a few years."

"Did you learn to shoot like that when you were in Special Forces?"

"Yeah."

"I'm not going to ask you how many men you killed."

"Good, because I never counted."

The wind suddenly picked up, gusting in from the northeast. It stiffened enough that they had to bend forward to walk against it. Then the air became heavy with moisture. It all seemed to happen in a matter of seconds.

Carolyn huddled up next to David and said, "Jesus! I wonder what caused the weather to change so fast."

"That." David pointed out to an approaching band of thick, black clouds. "That's a squall line. We're about to hit rough seas again."

Carolyn grumbled under her breath. "Accompanied by a lot of wind and rain, no doubt."

"It won't last long," David told her. "Squalls usually come and go in under an hour."

"That's enough time for everybody to become seasick again."

"And for Dr. Maggio to be overwhelmed with more patients than he can deal with."

"And of course he'll plead with you to help."

"Of course," David said and thought about the other doctor and nurse aboard the ship, who were still so nauseated, they could barely hold down liquids. If their symptoms persisted, he'd have to start them on IV fluids. "We'll handle it just like before."

"They should be paying you to be on this damn cruise," Carolyn complained.

The wind gusted across the deck and blew lounge chairs around. David and Carolyn turned away as paper cups and debris flew by them. The sky darkened more, then big raindrops began to fall. David glanced about hurriedly and searched for Kit. For an anxious moment, he didn't see her. Then she appeared. She was holding up a plastic plate to protect her hair from the rain.

"Kit!" David yelled to her. "We're over here."

Discarding the plastic plate, Kit ran to them and grabbed David's hand to steady herself against the strong wind. "Shouldn't we go below, Dad?"

"I think that's a good idea," David said and gazed around the rapidly emptying deck. "Where's your friend Will?"

"He doesn't feel so good," Kit answered. "So he's staying in bed."

"Is he seasick?" David inquired.

"I think he's got a cold," Kit said as a sudden blast of wind pushed against them. She grasped David's hand tighter as they approached the elevator. "Dad, how did you learn to shoot so well?"

"I used to practice a lot."

"Did mom practice too?"

David shook his head. "She hated guns."

"I hate them too."

"Good," David approved.

"I really hate them a lot."

"That's because you're smart."

They stepped into the crowded elevator and heard the wind howl behind them. Everybody in the elevator was complaining about the weather and how it was ruining the trip. A few were considering asking for a refund once they reached the Caribbean. The elevator moved sideways for a brief moment, and all the voices quieted abruptly. At the rear of the elevator, a woman made a retching sound. Everyone held their breath and hoped the woman wasn't about to throw up. The elevator came to a stop and most of the passengers hurried out at the arcade level, relieved to be away from the confines of the swaying car.

The elevator continued down, empty now except for David, Carolyn, and Kit. It seemed to wobble and vibrate as the strong wind outside continued to pound the luxury liner. David estimated it would take gusts of at least 35 knots per hour to make the *Grand Atlantic* rock noticeably in the water.

"Why didn't the captain see the squall coming?" Carolyn asked nervously.

"They can come up very quickly," David explained. "And there's really no way to get around them."

"But for a ship this size, squalls aren't dangerous, are they?"

"Not in the least," David assured her.

Kit inquired, "Dad, how do you know so much about boats?"

"I spent a lot of time on ships when I was in the military," David said and thought about the destroyer he had been ferried to after being wounded in Somalia. Involuntarily he raised his hand and felt the scar on his chin where his jaw had been shattered. The destroyer carrying him to a naval hospital had hit rough seas, too. But he barely noticed it. The terrible pain in his jaw had all of his attention.

The elevator jerked to a stop, and the three of them quickly exited. Kit led the way down the passageway, unaffected by the swaying of the liner. David watched his daughter prance along the corridor, skipping from side to side so she could touch each closed door. He remembered the old Navy adage—you're born with sea legs; either you have them or you don't. Kit had them.

"Dad?" Kit asked as she looked back. "Are you going to check on Juanita?"

"I think I'd better," David said.

"And I think I'd better go lie down for a while," Carolyn told them.

David studied her briefly. "Are you getting seasick?"

"I'm a little unsteady," Carolyn admitted.

"Take an Antivert tablet before you become nauseous."

"That's my plan," Carolyn said and headed for the door to their cabin.

David and Kit continued down the narrow passageway. They went by an open door and heard people within retching and throwing up. The ship began to sway more in a side-to-side motion. Both David and Kit kept a hand on the wall to maintain their balance as they came to the cabin where Kit and Juanita were staying. A DO NOT DISTURB sign hung on the door.

"Listen to me, kiddo," David said seriously. "Don't start eating candy or potato chips while we're around Juanita. That could make her even sicker."

"I gotcha, Dad."

"And don't even mention food or drink."

"Right."

David rapped on the door and entered the cabin. Kit was a step behind him. Juanita Cruz was lying on the sofa in the sitting room, with her eyes closed. She was dressed in a thick bathrobe and had a wet washcloth draped over her forehead. The air in the room had a faint but definite aroma of vomit.

"Juanita," David said softly. "Are you feeling any better?"

"Not much," Juanita murmured, opening her eyes.

"That's because she won't take her pills," Kit interjected.

"Why won't you take the medicine, Juanita?" David asked.

"Because as soon as I swallow the pills, I throw them back up."

"Then we'll try something new," David offered. "It's a medicine patch you put on the skin behind your ear."

Juanita moaned loudly. "Just let me die."

"Death will come later," David said, "when you are an old woman."

"I'm old now."

"Not old enough," David argued and reached for a skin patch containing scopolamine. He placed it firmly behind her ear. "The medicine will be absorbed through your skin, and you'll feel better soon."

"If I die, send my body back to Costa Rica," Juanita requested.

"Don't talk like that!" Kit said, clearly upset by her nanny's death wish. "You do what my dad says and get well."

"Okay, Little One." Juanita managed a weak smile as she called Kit by the pet name she'd given the child years ago. The nanny closed her eyes and drifted off.

"She'll be okay, won't she, Dad?" Kit asked quietly.

"She'll be fine."

"You promise?"

"I promise," David said, then stroked his daughter's raven-black hair. "Now, what do you say we go and catch a movie?"

"Which one?"

"Maybe the one about soccer," he suggested, aware of Kit's love for the game.

"You mean *Bend It Like Beckham*?"

"Nah. That's old. There's a new one from England about a girl's soccer team that has to overcome a lot of problems."

"Great! When does it start?"

"We'll check and—"

There was a loud knock on the door.

Carolyn rushed into the cabin and urgently waved David over. "Marilyn just called from the sick bay. Her son Will is really ill! It sounds double bad."

"What are his symptoms?" David asked quickly.

"His face has turned purple, and he's coughing up bright red blood."

"Oh Lord!" David said and ran for the door.

FIVE

MARILYN WYMAN WAS TERRIFIED by her son's appearance. Will's face had a grotesque, bluish-purple hue, and he was struggling for every breath.

"Wh-what's causing his complexion to have that awful color?" Marilyn asked frantically.

"Lack of oxygen to his tissues," David answered and reached for a stethoscope.

"Why can't he get oxygen to his tissues?"

"Let me listen to his lungs, then we'll talk more." David placed his stethoscope on the boy's chest and heard a cacophony of wheezes and crackles. But the breath sounds were clearly diminished. It was an ominous sign. He looked up at Marilyn and said, "Will has widespread pneumonia."

"Oh, my God!" Marilyn moaned.

"Which explains why his oxygen level is low," David said, as he touched Will's forehead. The boy felt like he was burning up, yet he seemed to be shivering. No gross chills, just shivers. David glanced over to Carolyn. "Get a temperature for us."

"It was 102.8° a few minutes ago," the sick-bay nurse volunteered.

Carolyn nodded, but still applied a digital thermometer to the skin over the boy's temporal artery. With her free hand, she adjusted the plastic mask on Will's face that was delivering oxygen at a rate of three liters per minute. The supplemental oxygen didn't seem to be helping. Will's lips were as blue as ever.

David quickly looked to the sick-bay nurse. "Do we have a chest film on him?"

The nurse nodded. "Dr. Maggio is reviewing it now."

"What about a complete blood count?"

The nurse shook her head.

David turned back to Carolyn. "Draw some blood and do a stat CBC."

"What about blood gases?" Carolyn asked.

"You're dreaming." David was almost certain that tests to determine the blood levels of oxygen and carbon dioxide weren't available in the ship's small laboratory, but to be sure he asked the sick-bay nurse, "Can you do blood gases down here?"

The nurse shrugged, apparently not understanding what the term meant.

Carolyn gazed at the digital thermometer and reported, "His temperature is 103.6°."

"Give him two Tylenol tablets," David directed.

"He won't take anything by mouth," the sick-bay nurse said. "He just shakes his head and babbles incoherently."

"What about Tylenol suppositories?" Carolyn suggested, as she drew blood from Will's arm.

"We don't have any of those," the nurse replied.

Christ! David growled to himself, thinking again that the sick bay was like a mediocre dispensary. He knitted his brow and concentrated on other ways to lower the boy's temperature. "You wouldn't happen to have a cooling blanket down here?"

The nurse shook her head.

"Then wrap his extremities in towels that have been drenched in ice water," David ordered. "And continue doing it until his temperature is down to 102."

He hurried into the radiology area and saw Arthur Maggio peering up at a viewbox that held Will's chest film. Even from a distance, David could see the abnormal findings. The x-rays showed dense, nodular infiltrates, which were concentrated in the hilar region of both lungs. But the peripheral areas were spared. Instantly he knew the diagnosis and it was even grimmer than he originally thought.

"Pneumonia," Maggio pronounced. "The x-ray fits with his earlier symptoms of fever and chills and cough."

"Yes," David agreed. "And it's bilateral, too."

"Which antibiotics will work best here?"

"I doubt that any of them will work, because I don't think he's got bacterial pneumonia."

Maggio studied the x-ray again, looking for any telltale clues. "You believe it's viral, eh?"

"Most likely."

Maggio nodded slowly. "That would explain the boy's terrible headache and myalgias and, in particular, the pain behind his eyes, which his mother told me about."

David nodded back, now thinking he may have underestimated the old physician's diagnostic abilities. "You sound like you've come up against viral pneumonia before."

"A long, long time ago," Maggio said wistfully. "I was a young Air Force doctor stationed in Japan when we had a sudden outbreak of influenza. It spread like wildfire among the enlisted men who lived in crowded barracks. Some of them ended up with influenza pneumonia, and all of those died terrible deaths." He paused and sighed deeply to himself. "And we couldn't do a damn thing for them."

"We still can't," David told him. "We have no effective treatment, so most of the people with this disease die from it."

"Do we have anything at all to offer the boy?"

David shrugged. "We can try him on antibiotics, just in case he has a bacterial super infection."

"Of course, there's still a slight chance the boy's pneumonia is in fact bacterial," Maggio mused.

"That's not going to happen," David said bluntly.

"Well, I like to leave room for a glimmer of hope."

Carolyn came to the entrance of the area and stuck her head in. "Will's CBC is fine. His white blood cell is 6,200, with a normal differential."

"Your glimmer of hope just walked out the door," David said to Maggio, and shook his head at the bad news. If Will had bacterial pneumonia, which could be cured with antibiotics, the white cell count would have seen greater than 10,000, with a very high percentage of polymorphonuclear leukocytes. But that wasn't to be. The boy's fate was sealed. "How is his cyanosis doing?"

"Worse," Carolyn reported. "His face is turning deep purple, despite the oxygen."

David turned to Maggio and asked, "Do you have a positive pressure ventilator down here?"

"We don't have a ventilator of any type."

David came back to Carolyn. "Hook up another tank of oxygen and see if you can somehow get it to flow into the mask."

"That can't be done," Carolyn said promptly. "But maybe I can increase the delivery of oxygen using nasal prongs."

"Give it a try."

Maggio watched Carolyn dash away, then repeated her description of Will's complexion. "That deep purple face," he said quietly, his mind going back forty years. "I knew I had seen it before, yet I couldn't place it. But now I can. That was the face I saw on the boys in Japan who died of influenza pneumonia." He sighed sadly at the memory. "That awful purple color, so gruesome you thought it was painted on."

"Severe cyanosis does that to the skin," David said. "Virtually no oxygen is getting to the boy's tissues."

"But why so severe?" Maggio queried. "You never see this degree of oxygen deprivation in bacterial pneumonia."

"Did you notice that Will was coughing up blood?"

"Yes, and plenty of it."

"Well, that's just the tip of the iceberg," David went on. "The virus is causing Will to hemorrhage into his lungs. And that blood is filling up every bronchi, bronchiole, and alveoli, to the point no oxygen can get through."

"It's as if he's drowning in his own blood," Maggio said, after reflecting briefly.

"Exactly."

"What can we do for him?"

"Nothing aboard the *Grand Atlantic*," David said candidly. "We have to transport him to a critical care unit ASAP."

"How can we accomplish that?"

"With Captain Rutherford's assistance, I hope."

David raced back into the examining room. Marilyn was holding Will's hand and crying, as she tried to understand his high-pitched babbling. The boy's face remained deep purple, despite the increased oxygen he was now receiving through nasal prongs. Will coughed, and up came bright red sputum that oozed around the edge of his oxygen mask. It began to bubble, trapping even more oxygen. David watched the soundless bubbling increase within the mask. It was a graphic depiction of what was happening inside the boy's lungs, he thought darkly. Soon no oxygen at all would be getting through.

David took a deep breath and walked over to deliver the bad news. "Marilyn, it looks like Will has severe viral pneumonia."

"Can he be treated?" Marilyn asked in a rush.

"It can," David said, deciding to withhold the grim prognosis for now. "But it requires that Will be looked after in a critical care unit."

Marilyn quickly glimpsed around the sick bay before asking, "But we don't have one here, do we?"

"No," David replied. "He'll have to be transported back to the mainland. I'll have Captain Rutherford make the necessary arrangements."

"I'll want to go with him," Marilyn said at once. "I will insist on that."

"Of course," David agreed. "And Sol too, if you wish."

Marilyn nodded her answer. "He'll need care as well. Sol has the same symptoms as Will."

"Is his face turning purple?" David asked immediately.

"No. but he has fever and is coughing up a little bit of blood."

"Is he short of breath?"

"No."

"Good," David said with an optimistic tone, but he knew that dyspnea would start soon. And so would the change in face color. "I have to go see Rutherford now and make the arrangements for Will to be transported."

"Thank you, David," Marilyn said gratefully.

David dashed out and down the passageway, digesting and assimilating all the medical facts he'd just encountered. The diagnosis was certain. All the signs and symptoms fit. But there were several things out of place that bothered him. First, he had never seen more than a few cases of influenza pneumonia, but they always occurred during a major influenza outbreak. And that wasn't happening now. The only other case was Sol Wyman, who had gotten it from close contact with his stepson. So there was no outbreak, yet there were already two cases of influenza pneumonia. The second bothersome point was that neither Will nor Sol were elderly, had compromised immune systems, or had preexisting pulmonary or rheumatic heart disease. Those were the conditions that predisposed individuals to influenza pneumonia. Yet none of those factors were present in Will and Sol. Peculiar business, David thought to himself, very peculiar.

He went to the staircase and darted up the stairs, still thinking about the out-of-place facts. David had learned from past experience never to discard facts that didn't fit the diagnosis. They were invariably trying to tell him something. Something important.

SIX

William Rutherford's face paled as he listened to the nightmare about to unfold on the *Grand Atlantic*. David was speaking to the ship's captain in a very low voice so the other officers on the bridge couldn't overhear him.

"How far is it to the nearest U.S. port?" David asked.

"Eight hundred miles," Rutherford replied.

"How long would it take for us to reach the mainland?"

"At full speed, just over a day."

David grumbled under his breath. "The boy will be dead by then."

Rutherford gazed down at the expansive deck of the luxury liner. Passengers were strolling along the railing or dozing in lounge chairs, all taking in the bright sun and unaware of the disaster about to occur. "Perhaps the boy and his father will be isolated cases."

"Don't bet on it," David said forthrightly. "Chances are this virus will spread, particularly among the elderly, and we'll end up with a lot of very sick people on our hands. And those with pneumonia, like Will, will die."

"Is there any possibility the boy will survive?"

"Only if we can transport him to a critical care unit. And even then, his outlook is poor."

Rutherford sighed heavily, unsure of what to do next. "Dr. Ballineau, as an ER physician, you must have dealt with similar situations. I'm referring to patients with terrible diseases caught in remote places. How did you handle those predicaments?"

"Usually with a helicopter," David said. "But most of them have a range of only 400 miles, so you'll have to contact the Navy and see if they have any ships with helicopters nearby. And if so, maybe they can pick up Will, then hop and skip their way back to the mainland."

"There's a problem with that solution," Rutherford said unhappily.

"What?"

"Our heliport was badly damaged during the storm," Rutherford confided. "That large panel that fell from the bridge onto the deck split the heliport wide open. It's so unstable that no one is allowed to walk on it, much less land a helicopter."

"Shit," David growled.

"Indeed," Rutherford agreed. "Do you have any other ideas?"

"None at the moment."

David hurried from the bridge and took the stairs down as he tried to come up with an answer to the dilemma. Without a heliport, there was no way a helicopter could land safely on the *Grand Atlantic*. And even if a naval ship with a helicopter came to their aid, how could they transport Will to it? In a lifeboat or a dinghy? Christ! He'd never survive that. The trip alone would kill him.

David continued down the steps, concentrating his mind on other solutions to the problem. The Navy SEALs, as good as they were, would be of no help here. Nor would the speedier Coast Guard cutters, which would still require transferring Will over rough seas. And it was impossible for a seaplane to land and take off in the choppy swells of the ocean. So for now, David concluded, there was no way out. They were all prisoners aboard the *Grand Atlantic*. And to make matters even worse, without a heliport, they couldn't bring in life-saving equipment, like ventilators and additional supplies of oxygen.

At the G level, David left the staircase and dashed down the passageway. He went by a spa that was crowded with people waiting for a body massage or facial or some other beauty treatment. All were sitting close to one another, all breathing the same air in and out. It was a perfect setup to spread the virus quickly. David could only hope that his diagnosis was wrong. Maybe, just maybe, Will would turn out to have some strange type of bacterial pneumonia that would respond to antibiotics. But David knew he was hoping against hope. There was a nasty influenza virus on this ship, and it would search for any available host to live and replicate in.

He entered the sick bay and walked through an empty reception area. It was a good sign, David told himself. At least ill patients were not piling in to be seen. At least not yet. In the examining room he saw Marilyn sobbing, with her head resting on Will's chest. The boy was still cyanotic, his extremities still wrapped in ice cold towels.

Carolyn glanced over and silently mouthed out Will's temperature: 103°.

David nodded at the improvement. That was some better, but not much. The goal was to keep the temperature below 104°, because above that point it could begin to fry the boy's brain.

Marilyn looked up, her eyes puffy and red from constant crying. "Did you make arrangements with Captain Rutherford to have Will transported to land?"

"We're trying to get things set up," David lied.

Marilyn studied David's face, as if aware of his half-truth. "Will isn't going to make it, is he?"

"If we can get him to a critical care unit, he stands a chance," David said and gently squeezed the woman's shoulder. "Don't give up hope yet."

Marilyn put her head back on Will's chest and began sobbing again.

David resisted the urge to comfort the woman further. At this point it wouldn't help. She knew instinctively that her son was barely clinging to life, and all the kind words in the world weren't going to change that. Mothers had inborn antennas for those sorts of things.

David gazed down a makeshift chart of Will's vital signs that Carolyn had constructed. The boy's blood pressure had dropped to 95/60, and his pulse was now racing at 120/minute. But most disturbing was a respiratory rate of 40/minute, which was three times normal. Will was trying to suck air into lungs that were rapidly filling up with blood. It was a hopeless endeavor.

David was about to reach for a stethoscope, but decided not to. He already knew what he would hear. There would be widespread wheezes and crackles and decreased breath sounds bilaterally. The only thing missing would be a death rattle. That would come soon enough.

In his peripheral vision he saw Maggio waving him over to the radiology room. David softly squeezed Marilyn's shoulder once more, then walked away and joined the old physician in a far corner of the sick bay. The expression Maggio's face told him that something had gone wrong. Terribly wrong.

"What?" David asked.

"I've gotten emergency calls from two other passengers. They're complaining of high fever and cough. Both have awful headaches." Maggio hesitated and lowered his voice to a whisper. "And one of them is coughing up blood."

"Oh Christ!" David groaned.

"It's spreading," Maggio said and tried to swallow back his fear. "And it's spreading fast."

SEVEN

DAVID PUT ON TWO surgical masks, one on top of the other, and hoped the double layer would afford him added protection against the virus. Then he placed a stethoscope around his neck to give him the appearance of a physician, and knocked on the cabin door. He heard movement inside, followed by silence, and sensed he was being looked at through the peephole.

"I'm Dr. Ballineau," David called out. "Dr. Maggio asked me to pay you a visit."

The door opened immediately. A colorfully dressed, middle-aged man, wearing a brown smoking jacket and yellow ascot, ushered David into the overheated sitting room.

The man introduced himself as Thomas Berns and said, "I should begin by telling you I'm HIV positive, and so is my partner." He gestured to a younger man lying on the sofa and bundled up in a white terrycloth robe. "Ralphie has become quite ill, as you can see."

David glanced over and studied the dark, handsome man on the sofa. He had his eyes closed and he was breathing normally except that he coughed with every third breath. From a distance his skin color appeared healthy. But there was a Kleenex in his hand that was heavily stained with blotches of blood.

"We're both on a triple drug cocktail for HIV," Berns informed. "I assume we should continue taking it."

"You should," David said. "Now tell me, when did your symptoms begin?"

"Late last night," Berns replied. "We both felt feverish, and chilly. Ralphie's temperature was higher than mine. A hundred and one, I think."

David quickly estimated the incubation period for the virus. Will had been ill for two days at the most. So assuming he was the source of the contagion, the incubation period was in the range of forty-eight hours, which was very short. The usual incubation period for the influenza virus was four days. A virulent virus with a brief incubation period, David thought grimly. It was a perfect combination for a major outbreak. At length David asked, "Do either of you have shortness of breath?"

"Not really," Berns said and tried to suppress a wet cough.

"Are you coughing up any blood?" David inquired.

"A little," Berns said. "But not nearly as much as Ralphie."

David walked over to the sofa and placed a stethoscope on the chest of Ralph Oliveri, which was the name embroidered on his white robe. The man opened his eyes to peer at David, then closed them without saying a word. Ralph Oliveri's lungs were filled with crackles and wheezes, and his breath sounds were distant. Bad, David told himself, knowing the worst was yet to come. He studied the man's face again and now saw a blue tinge to his lips. Another ominous sign.

The phone in the cabin rang. Berns quickly answered it, then held the receiver out to David. "It's Dr. Maggio, for you."

David put away his stethoscope and reached for the phone. "Yes?"

"More bad news," Maggio reported. "Two of the deckhands now have symptoms of the flu. Both are coughing their heads off."

"Do they have hemoptysis?" David queried.

"Not yet," Maggio said. "But my biggest concern at the moment is the crowded quarters they're occupying. The beds for the crew are pushed together, almost side by side. They're going to infect everybody down there, if they haven't already."

"Somehow you've got to isolate them," David urged.

"That can't be done. All the cabins are taken."

David knitted his brow and concentrated on the problem. Somehow the infected crew had to be separated from the others. But how? There was no good way to do it, so they'd have to settle for a not-so-good way. "Put surgical masks on the sick deckhands, then push their beds into the corner, as far away from the others as possible. Finally, see if you can arrange to have some curtains put up around their beds."

"I don't think that'll be of much help."

"It'll have to do for now," David said. "I'll meet with you in the sick bay shortly so we can make further plans."

David hung up the phone and came back to Berns. "The virus you have is beginning to show up in other parts of the ship. It's obviously very contagious, so here is what I'd like you to do. First, don't leave the cabin unless you absolutely have to. And don't allow any visitors in. If you do leave, wear surgical masks that I will have sent down to you. Second, avoid all places where crowds assemble, such as the dining room and movie theater."

"What shall we do for food?" Berns asked.

"We'll provide room service," David said and headed for the door.

"Nasty virus, eh?" Berns called after him.

"Very."

David hurried down the passageway with a worried look on his face. The virus was spreading so rapidly to all parts of the ship. The cases would really begin to pile up now, particularly among those with impaired immune systems. Like the couple he'd just seen. *Christ!* He wondered how many more HIV-positive people were aboard the *Grand Atlantic*. They would go first, along with those on chemotherapy, then the elderly and infirm, then those with cardio-pulmonary problems. But there was still one big question in David's mind. *How did Will contract the virus and develop influenza pneumonia? How?* He was a healthy kid, yet he caught it and passed it on to Sol, with whom he had close contact. And Marilyn would be next because she too had such close contact with ...

David stopped in his tracks. Close contact! The people who had close contact with Will were most likely to become infected with the virus, and nobody had closer contact than Kit! They played and ate and went to movies together every day. And who knows? They may have even kissed! Oh Jesus! Oh Jesus!

David broke into a run and dashed to the staircase, then up the stairs at full speed. He sprinted by startled passengers as he went through a door and down a long passageway, still thinking about how close Kit and Will had been. They had been closer than Will and Sol—that was for damn sure. David grumbled to himself, remembering how cute he thought it was for Kit to have found a little boyfriend. Then it all seemed so innocent. Now it could turn out to be all so deadly.

He came to Kit's cabin and, after a quick rap on the door, entered. Juanita was sitting on the sofa, reading a Spanish magazine. The sliding glass doors were opened to an empty balcony. Kit was nowhere to be seen.

"Where's Kit?" David asked anxiously.

"She's taking her afternoon nap," Juanita replied. "Why? Is something wrong?"

"No, no," David said, gathering himself. "Is she feeling all right?"

"She is fine," Juanita told him. "It was I who insisted she take a nap. Children need their rest too, you know."

David breathed a sigh of relief. "Has she had any symptoms of a cold? Like fever or chills or cough?"

"No," Juanita said and eyed him carefully. "Why do you ask this?"

"Because there is a virus going around."

"The Little One is fine," she reassured him. "See for yourself."

David tiptoed into the bedroom and saw Kit sound asleep, hugging her favorite teddy bear. He watched her breathe, without even a hint of a cough or wheeze. Again he was struck by the child's beauty. The flawless skin. The raven-black hair. The rosy pink lips that always seemed to have a half-smile on them. She had inherited so much from her mother, David thought for the thousandth time. Those wonderful genes that made her doubly special. He moved silently to the bed and kissed the top of her head, careful not to wake her. As he turned to leave, he saw Kit's diary on the nightstand. It was open. Reaching over to close it, he noticed there was a paragraph about

Will at the top of the page. He had always considered Kit's diary to be her private business, and none of his. But now things were different. Will was sick and dying from a vicious virus, and Kit was still very much at risk.

David sat quietly in a chair and began to read the diary.

Wednesday

Will showed me his big secret. We went through a door by the pool and down some real slippery steps to a place where there was a lot of pipes and electric things. Then Will showed me his secret. It was a sick bird he had found under a deck chair. He had it on a dirty old blanket and was giving it food and water. But the big bird—Will says it's a goose—wouldn't drink or eat. Maybe because it was so sick. The bird kept coughing up stuff and it got all over Will's face and hands, but he promised to wash it off later. Then Will put the bird back under the pipes and we left.

David stared at the page of the open diary, stunned, with his mouth agape.

Oh, my God!

EIGHT

David took William Rutherford's arm and guided him to the outer deck of the bridge. He glanced over his shoulder to make certain no one was within earshot of their conversation.

"We've got a full-blown disaster underway on this ship," David said gravely. "And it's going to explode right in our face."

"Are you referring to the viral pneumonia?" Rutherford asked at once.

David shook his head. "I'm referring to avian influenza. We have an outbreak of bird flu aboard the *Grand Atlantic* and it's spreading fast."

Rutherford was shocked speechless. He stared at David for a full ten seconds before asking in a whisper, "Are you sure?"

"Ninety-nine percent," David replied and recited the details of the sick bird in Kit's diary, then told him about the newly ill passengers. "So we've already got six who are sick, and that's just the beginning of this nightmare."

Rutherford clasped his hands together tightly, a man now clearly out of his depth. "Wh-what should we do?"

"A number of things," David said and immediately prioritized the list. "First, we have to find the damn bird and place it in something airtight. My daughter told me it's located down some slippery steps that lead to a large room with screened-off generators on one side and pipes and wires on the other. Do you know where that is?"

Rutherford nodded promptly. "It's a restricted area just beyond the pool."

"Does it have ventilation ducts?"

"Of course," Rutherford answered. He didn't see the significance of the question at first, but then it came to him. "Do you think the virus is traveling to all parts of the ship via the ventilation system?"

"Yes," David said. "That's exactly what I think."

"So, if we can remove the sick bird, we can stop the virus in its tracks," Rutherford said and brightened at the prospect.

"Maybe, maybe not," David said carefully. "Usually the H5N1 bird flu virus is not easily transmitted between humans. Most of the cases have occurred in poultry workers who were exposed to large doses of the virus from the sick birds. But for some reason, the bird virus aboard this ship is spreading rapidly from person to person. In essence, we have a transmissible killer on the *Grand Atlantic*."

Rutherford's face turned ashen. "Can—can a virus change itself into such a virulent form?"

David nodded gravely. "It happened in the great flu epidemic of 1918. And I suspect it's happened here. In all likelihood, a fair number of people have already been infected. When they develop symptoms and start coughing, they'll become carriers of the virus and be able to transmit it to other passengers. Nevertheless, the sick bird remains a major source of the virus."

"So it's still important to remove the bird," Rutherford thought aloud.

"Oh yeah," David said at once. "The only question is who's going to go down there and stick his nose next to a sick bird whose body is teeming with a deadly virus."

Rutherford hesitated a moment, then said bravely, "As captain of the ship, I should do it."

"Don't be stupid," David said. "You have to stay in command of the *Grand Atlantic*. You're one of the people we've got to keep healthy."

"Who then?"

"Me."

Rutherford squinted one eye. "Do you know how to do it with any degree of safety?"

"No, but I think I know somebody who does," David said, then refocused his mind on the list of tasks for Rutherford to do. "Now, while I'm busy learning how to bag that bird, there are a number of things you must do pronto. First, I'll give you the names of the infected passengers. We have to keep them isolated from the others at all times. They are to stay in their cabins and have all their meals delivered."

"Done."

"Secondly, two of your deckhands are down with the illness," David went on. "You have to find a room to put them in, so they don't infect the entire crew."

"Done."

"Next, go through your passenger list and cull out those who wrote down the present or prior professions as doctors or nurses. Call each of them and have them gather in one of your conference rooms."

"I could do that faster on the PA system."

David shook his head. "That could cause people to panic, and that's the last thing we need."

"Right, you are."

"And one final thing," David concluded. "Did you contact the Navy regarding our problem?"

"Not yet," Rutherford replied. "I decided to put in a call to the ship owners first, and I'm waiting to hear back from them. I thought it best to go through the owners, and see if they could come up with a way to transport the boy back to the mainland."

"Cancel the request," David said hurriedly. "Tell them Will has suddenly improved."

"Why?"

"Because for now we have to keep the virus limited to the *Grand Atlantic*," David explained. "Will is now a huge reservoir of the avian flu virus, which we already know is highly contagious. If Will is taken ashore, he would spread the virus to everyone he came in contact with. And I mean everyone. The helicopter crew, the Navy personnel on the ship, the medical staff on land, and on and on. He would be ground zero for an avian influenza pandemic."

Rutherford swallowed hard. "Are you saying the entire ship should be placed under quarantine?"

David nodded. "Until we get instructions from the Centers for Disease Control on when and where to make port."

"I should discuss this matter with the ship owners," Rutherford said, more to himself than to David.

"I wouldn't," David advised. "They might panic and do something foolish. Let's wait for instructions from the CDC."

"When will—"

"Captain!" the first officer called out from the door to the bridge. "We have a problem!"

"What?" Rutherford called back irritably.

"There's another storm brewing in the Bahamas," the first officer reported. "And we're headed straight for it."

"What are the winds?"

"They're Category 1, at seventy miles per hour."

Rutherford turned to David. "We'll have to change course to avoid the storm."

"And?" David asked, noticing the added worry on the captain's face.

"And that will take us even farther away from port."

"By how much?"

"That depends on the size of the storm and how rapidly it moves."

David walked away, grumbling and thinking that everything was going against them. Now the virus had even more time to spread and infect everyone aboard the *Grand Atlantic*.

NINE

PEOPLE AROUND THE POOL area stared at David as he stepped out
of the elevator. He was wearing a hospital gown and latex gloves
that were taped down onto his sleeves. Atop his head was a shower
cap, and over his nose and mouth were three surgical masks lay-
ered one upon another. His eyes were covered with snorkel goggles.

"Everyone step back, please," Rutherford ordered from David's
side. "Please step back and make way."

The crowd slowly moved apart and gave David an open path to
the staircase leading down to the sick bird. He walked awkwardly,
with his feet apart, because his shoes were wrapped in thick towels.
The passengers' eyes were glued on David's outrageous outfit, so no
one noticed the partially hidden long forceps in his left hand or the
folded-up plastic bag in his right.

"What's going on?" someone in the crowd cried out.

"Please be patient for now," Rutherford urged.

"What the hell is that strange getup?" another voice yelled.

Rutherford ignored the question and reached for the door to the staircase. Under his breath, he told David, "Good luck."

"I'll need it," David said. "Now remember, when you hear me knock, open the door and step away—far away."

"Right."

David gathered himself and rehearsed in his mind a final time how to grab the sick bird and bring it up without contaminating himself. And how to make certain he didn't carry any of the avian flu virus back on deck with him. *Son of a bitch!* he growled silently. *I should be on a white sand beach in Hawaii now. I should—"*

"What's this all about?" Richard Scott broke into the silence of the crowd. The banker pushed people aside as he made his way from the volleyball court over to David and Rutherford. He carefully eyed David's bizarre outfit and remarked snidely, "Is it Halloween already?"

"Please, Mr. Scott," Rutherford implored. "We're doing something of the utmost importance."

"Like what?" Scott demanded. He was wearing only tennis shorts on his well-muscled body that was covered with beads of perspiration.

"Please," Rutherford urged. "Now is not the time to—"

"I don't move until you give me some straight answers," Scott interrupted.

"Yeah," another volleyball player joined in. He was in his mid-thirties, with a tattoo of a red rose on his deltoid area. "Nobody does a damn thing until we get to the bottom of this."

Scott shoved Rutherford to the side and confronted David face to face. "Well, Dr. Sharpshooter, it seems the captain has suddenly gone mute. So it's up to you to give us some answers."

"Your best move would be to back off," David said stonily.

"Maybe you'd like to make me," Scott challenged.

The man with the tattoo moved in closer. "Maybe you'd like to make me go away too."

The move was so quick nobody could swear they actually saw it. In a fraction of a second, David dropped the folded plastic bag and brought his hand up to Scott's throat, grasping the banker's Adam's apple and squeezing it. Scott's face when from tan to red as he sucked for air.

"If I squeeze a little harder, you'll be breathing through a tube for the rest of your life," David said without inflection. "You'll be a banker with a tracheostomy."

Scott was now wide-eyed, his face deep red from lack of oxygen.

"When I let go, you walk away," David went on. "And you take your tattooed friend with you. Got it?" He waited for a response and when none was forthcoming, David added, "You'd better nod before you lose your larynx."

Scott nodded hurriedly.

David released his grip and watched Scott crumple to his knees. He turned and gave the man with a tattoo a hard look, and that was all it took for the man to back off and retreat into the crowd.

David reached down for the folded plastic bag and glanced over at Rutherford. "All right, let's do it. And remember, when you hear my knock on the door, open it and step way away."

"What if those two idiots gather their courage and come down after you?"

"They'll wish to God they hadn't," David said simply. "Now open the door."

David stepped in and heard the door close behind him. The air was humid and hot, and David could feel his temperature rising beneath the layers of clothing he was wearing. He waited for his eyes to acclimate to the dimness before starting down the stairway. Like Kit had written in her diary, the stairs were covered with moisture and slippery, so he moved very slowly, not touching the walls or railing. His mind went back to the instructions he had received from Lawrence Lindberg, the director of Global Migration and Quarantine at the Centers for Disease Control in Atlanta.

"Don't touch anything unless you absolutely have to," Lindberg had cautioned in their phone conversation. "Just about everything in that passageway could be swarming with that virus."

"Well, I'm going to have to have contact with the damn bird," David had told him.

"Not if you do exactly as I tell you."

Lindberg then instructed him how to put together a makeshift outfit that would protect David from the deadly virus. But there were still a dozen ways the virus could contaminate David, and both men knew it.

"Place the bag containing the sick bird in a secure container," Lindberg had continued on, "then attach the container to a very long rope."

"How long should the rope be?"

"At least two hundred feet," Lindberg had replied. "That should be enough to reach the ocean from the deck."

David knew from past experience that Lawrence Lindberg was a very careful man who always did his homework. Two years earlier, David had seen a Pakistani in the ER at University Hospital who was suspected of having smallpox. The patient came from a remote village in one of the tribal areas, had never been vaccinated, and had a rash that closely resembled that of smallpox. Lindberg had flown to Los Angeles and expertly guided the quarantine medical team until the disease was proven not to be smallpox, but rather a rare, relatively benign disorder that was seen only in South Asia. *Maybe the virus aboard the* Grand Atlantic *will turn out not to be the avian flu variety,* David thought hopefully.

Maybe it will be some other, less lethal microorganism. But deep down he knew that was only wishful thinking.

David's foot suddenly slipped on a wet step, and he had to grab the railing to steady himself. *Goddamn it! Concentrate or you'll end up rolling around in the virus, and then start coughing your guts out, like little Will.* Carefully David continued down the stairs, trying to watch his feet in the dimness. The towels wrapped around his shoes were already soaked with water and made a slushing sound with each step. He moved on, now uncomfortably hot and sweating beneath the multiple layers of clothing. The light became brighter and he saw the bottom of the staircase, with screened off generators to his right.

David walked slowly, staying in the center of the passageway, until he came to the rows of pipes and wires. Bending at the waist, he spotted the outer edge of the blanket-nest Will had built. He pulled the nest out and saw the motionless goose, with one of its wings drooped awkwardly off to one side. The sick bird looked dead. David unfolded the large plastic bag, then, using long forceps, grabbed the bird by its neck and lifted it up. The bird made a weak, squawk-like sound, but offered no resistance. David quickly deposited the dying bird into the large plastic bag, and spun the bag shut before clamping it tightly with a thin wire. Then he started up the stairs, holding the bird well off to the side. The bird began to move, and David wondered if it was strong enough to peck its way through the plastic. *I should have killed the damn thing,* he thought miserably. *It still would have served its intended purpose.*

At the top of the stairs, David pounded on the steel door. Rutherford promptly opened it and handed in a large suitcase. Hurriedly David opened it and stuffed the bird in, then closed and locked it.

"Rope!" David yelled.

Rutherford tossed in the end of a long rope that David tied securely to the handle of the suitcase. He tested the knot to make certain it was firm.

"Is the deck clear?" David called out.

"All clear!" Rutherford called back.

David kicked off the soaked towels on his feet, wiggled out of his hospital gown, and ripped away his masks, cap, goggles, and finally his gloves. Then he dashed out onto the deck, holding the rope attached to the suitcase well away from his body. The door slammed behind him.

He sprinted across the deck to the railing and hoisted the suitcase over the side. Slowly he lowered it, giving out the rope a few yards at a time. Only now did he become aware of the large crowd that had gathered less than a hundred feet away. They watched in dead silence, all sensing that something terrible was happening or about to happen.

David let the rope out a final five yards before tying it tightly to the railing. Then he trained his eyes on the horizon and waited.

"Please, captain!" A voice pleaded from the crowd. "Tell us what's going on."

Rutherford paid no attention to the request, and like David, kept looking out at the open sea.

"Did a terrorist put a bomb aboard?" another voice in the crowd asked.

"No, it's not a bomb," someone answered. "They would have just thrown it into the ocean if it was a bomb."

"Then what?"

That question was met with silence.

David glanced down at his wet tennis shoes and wondered if the virus had penetrated through the soaked towels. *Shit!* He groused and kicked the shoes overboard. Better safe than sorry, he reminded himself, thinking he'd do the same with the rest of his clothes as soon as he got the chance.

David checked his watch. The Navy was late and twilight was setting in. If it became too dark, the Navy would have to abort the mission. And that would put them ten more hours behind, which could mean the difference between life and death to a lot of people.

In the distance, David heard the sound of an approaching helicopter. He focused his hearing and picked up the distinctive putt-putt noise of a Seahawk. The Navy was sending in one of its rescue teams! A speck on the horizon grew larger and larger as the noise intensified. Then the helicopter appeared and swooped down a hundred yards starboard of the *Grand Atlantic*. It hovered over the ocean while a rescue team dropped into the sea, followed by an inflatable Zodiac. Moments later, the team was speeding toward the luxury liner.

The crowd began to applaud, as if the Navy was coming to solve whatever problem existed.

The rescue team came alongside the hull and signaled up to begin lowering the suitcase. David untied the knot from the railing and slowly began to let out the rope. The Navy team opened a large metal container and guided it into a position that allowed the suitcase to drop directly into it. Then the container was closed and hermetically sealed. Another Zodiac came up, carrying a stack of big cardboard boxes. One by one, over the course of ten minutes, the boxes were attached to dangling ropes and hauled up onto the deck of the *Grand Atlantic*. When the last carton was aboard, David gave the Navy team a thumbs-up signal and watched them speed away to their waiting helicopter.

Rutherford moved in next to David and said quietly, "We've got to tell the passengers something. They won't stand for our silence much longer."

"I know," David agreed. "Let me do it."

David approached the crowd of onlookers. He stared at them for a moment, carefully choosing his words and deciding to be as direct as possible. The crowd stared back, all expecting the worst.

"Listen up!" David said in a commanding voice. "I'm Dr. Ballineau, and I've got good news and bad news. The bad news is that we believe there's been an outbreak of bird flu aboard the *Grand Atlantic*. It's already sickened six people, and it's likely to infect a lot more."

A string of loud murmurs went through the crowd.

"Oh, Jesus!"

"We're all going to die!"

"I want off this damn ship!"

David held up his hands and quieted the crowd before continuing. "The good news is that the Navy has delivered us a good supply of specialized masks, which we'll all wear and which will prevent us from catching or transmitting the virus."

"The hell with that!" a voice bellowed. "I want off this goddamn boat now!"

A chorus of onlookers joined in, all demanding to be let off the luxury liner.

David ignored the outburst and went on, "In addition, the Navy dropped off a large supply of Tamiflu, which of course protects the individual against the influenza family of viruses. It's a pill, easy to take, and has no side effects."

The crowd murmured its approval. Some applauded.

"All right!"

"Now you're talking!"

"I took it before. It worked like a charm on my flu."

The mood lightened even further. More and more people in the crowd applauded, delighted with the good news.

But David didn't join in. Lawrence Lindberg had told him that a sizable proportion of patients with avian influenza didn't respond to Tamiflu or any other antiviral agent. They just got sicker and sicker and, despite all measures, they died.

TEN

THE TURNOUT OF DOCTORS from the passenger list was disappointingly small. Carolyn glanced at the two physicians sitting at the conference table and again decided that neither would be of much help. One was an elderly, retired surgeon who'd had a stroke and required a walker to get around, the other a middle-aged radiologist who never saw patients, only their x-rays. *And no nurses*, Carolyn grumbled to herself. If the virus continued to spread, patients would stack up, and there'd be far too few personnel to start IVs and check vital signs and adjust oxygen flow rates and perform a dozen other critical functions. *God! Let the Tamiflu work!*

"What's the delay?" the old surgeon demanded. "You don't need specialists to pass out some pills."

"I know," Carolyn said soothingly. "But Dr. Ballineau thought it best to gather as many experienced hands as possible." Then she added in a more somber tone, "Just in case there's a need."

"And who is this Dr. Ballineau?"

"He's director of the emergency room at University Hospital."

The surgeon straightened up in his chair. "University Hospital in Los Angeles?"

"Yes."

The surgeon and the radiologist exchanged firm nods, a silent message passing between them.

Oh yes! Carolyn thought without expression. University Hospital in Los Angeles were magic words to any medical professional. Like the Mayo Clinic and Johns Hopkins, University Hospital was among the very elite of medicine, and everybody knew it. But so what? Carolyn thought on. In the situation they were in, reputation didn't matter a damn, particularly to a killer virus.

There was a brief knock on the door.

"Ah! A third," Carolyn murmured to herself, hoping for an internist with experience in critical care.

The door opened, and a strikingly attractive woman entered the conference room. She was in her late thirties, with deep blue eyes and ash-blond hair that was held back in a ponytail. Her tight-fitting tennis outfit revealed graceful legs and a curvaceous figure.

Carolyn was stunned speechless. It took her a moment to collect herself. "Hi, Karen."

"Hey, Carolyn!" Karen Kellerman flashed a smile that showed pearly white, perfectly even teeth. "I didn't expect to find you aboard the *Grand Atlantic*."

"Nor I you."

"Is—ah—David with you?"

"He sure is," Carolyn said and wished that David had bought her a diamond ring at Bulgari on the shopping level of the ship rather than waiting for them to return to Los Angeles. God! She'd love to show it now and watch Karen Kellerman's reaction. "But he's tied up with some very sick people."

"How many?" Karen asked at once.

"Six, but only one with full-blown avian flu," Carolyn replied. "But there'll be a lot more if the virus spreads like David thinks it will."

"But we've got Tamiflu now," the old surgeon interrupted.

"Right, you are," Carolyn said, annoyed that she'd been so loose-tongued. "I was only doing a worst-case scenario."

"Well, let's wait for Dr. Ballineau to give us facts instead of your off-the-cuff scenario," the surgeon huffed. "We need an expert here, not a nurse."

Carolyn's face colored. *Fucking surgeons! They always have to be in control, even when they're not in control.* And the old doctor was probably ignorant as could be about avian flu and how it could spread and how ineffective most treatments were. Carolyn took a deep breath and let her anger pass, remembering that the elderly surgeon came from another generation in which nurses wore caps and white, starched uniforms, and followed physician's orders with obedient nods, and never voiced an opinion unless asked. That wasn't another generation. That was another world.

Her gaze drifted over to the oval conference table in the center of the room. The two male physicians were introducing themselves to Karen Kellerman and drooling over her. Karen did that to men, all men, including David. The two had once been lovers until David discovered that Karen was a liar and a thief. The co-director of anesthesiology at University Hospital was so pretty and, according to David, so dishonest. And so stupid, Carolyn added on, to lose David over an invention Karen could easily have shared with him.

Carolyn thought back to the distasteful episode that she'd first heard about in hospital gossip. David had filled in the details later. He had come up with an idea for a portable cooling blanket that would be particularly useful in MedEvac helicopters transporting patients with sky-high fevers. Unbeknownst to David, Karen took the idea, redesigned the blanket with a few modifications, and sold the patent to a large corporation that manufactured medical equipment. David was furious at her dishonesty, and from that point on he rarely spoke to her and only when he absolutely had to. He vowed never to forgive her, and never had.

The door to the conference room suddenly opened and David hurried in. He was carrying a carton of N-95 high-filtration masks and a handful of Tamiflu packets. He quickly counted the backs of the heads at the conference table and dashed over to Carolyn.

"Is that all we've got?" David asked in a whisper.

Carolyn nodded and whispered back, "And two of them aren't going to be of much help. One is an old, retired surgeon who has had a stroke, the second is a radiologist."

"Shit," David muttered. "And the third?"

"Surprise of all surprises. It's Karen Kellerman."

David jerked his head around and stared at the anesthesiologist for a few seconds before waiting. "Hello, Karen," he said neutrally.

"Hello, David," she said back and gave him her best smile. "It's nice to see you again."

David nodded indifferently, disliking her as much as ever, but still struck by her beauty. "Are you traveling alone?"

"Yes, as a matter of fact, I am," she said, with a mischievous lilt.

"That's unfortunate," David said. "It would help us if you were traveling with another doctor from University Hospital."

"I'll keep that in mind next time I board a luxury liner," Karen retorted. "Just in case there's an outbreak."

She was still very quick, David thought. Too bad some of her other qualities were so unappealing.

Karen crossed her legs and her tennis skirt slipped farther on her thighs. David was careful to keep his eyes trained on her face. But despite his effort, his gaze dropped and he felt himself stir. Quickly David turned to the other physicians.

"We'll save the introductions for later," he began. "For now, I'll pass out packets of Tamiflu, which you should take as directed. I also have N-95 masks, which should filter out viruses. Please wear them at all times until further notice."

"Are the masks really necessary?" the old surgeon asked, fumbling with the duck-billed mask because of his palsied hand. "The Tamiflu should protect us since we're all still asymptomatic."

"Maybe it will, maybe it won't," David said, recalling Lawrence Lindberg's words of caution. "The CDC still doesn't know where the bird got infected or why this virus suddenly acquired the ability to infect humans so readily."

"What the hell does the origin of the virus have to do with anything?" the old surgeon groused.

"Well," David said slowly, "let me give you the nightmare picture. There is currently an ordinary influenza A virus in Scandinavia that has become resistant to Tamiflu. Maybe a pig picked up this human virus in Scandinavia, then combined it with the avian flu virus that was already in its body. Now you've got a mutant virus that's half human flu virus and half bird flu virus, and it's resistant to Tamiflu. The end result is a mutant that infects like the human flu virus and kills like the bird flu virus. And maybe the pig that has this mutant virus transmitted it to the infected bird that landed on the *Grand Atlantic*. That being the case, we could well be facing a highly contagious, deadly virus for which there is no treatment."

A chilled silence went through the room.

"Are you saying this virus may be resistant to Tamiflu?" asked Thomas Steiner. The radiologist was a portly, balding man, with gray-brown hair and wire-rimmed glasses. He cleared his throat and asked again, "Is that what you're saying?"

"Yes," David said straightforwardly. "That's exactly what I'm saying."

"But that's all hypothetical," Steiner persisted. "Right?"

"Right," David answered. "But let me tell you what's not hypothetical. We've got a deadly virus aboard this ship, and it can be transmitted person to person."

"Whoa!" Karen interrupted. "The only person who has the full-blown disease is the boy who had direct contact with the bird. All the others probably caught it through the ventilation system. And that problem has been solved since the infected bird is gone and no longer transmitting the virus via the ventilation ducts. Thus, there's no evidence for person to person transmission."

"There you go!" Steiner agreed strongly. "The source of the virus is no longer on the ship, so transmission to passengers won't be a problem."

"Damn masks won't work anyway," the old surgeon chimed in.

"You'd better hope they do," David warned. "Because there's still a source of that virus that could reach the ventilation system."

"Which is?" Karen asked.

"Anyone who is infected and coughing," David replied. "If you can catch if from the ventilation system, that means the virus is airborne. And that means anybody coughing up virus-laden droplets can infect the person standing next to him. Which means person to person transmission any way you cut it."

"Which means we could all get infected with a Tamiflu-resistant virus," Karen said, her face now horror-struck.

"Yeah," David said bluntly. "And that's more than hypothetical, according to the CDC."

"When will we know if this virus is resistant to Tamiflu?" Steiner asked nervously.

Karen replied, "When the CDC finishes its tests on the bird, however long that takes."

"Or maybe sooner," David told the group. "If passengers taking Tamiflu start coming down with bird flu pneumonia, we'll know the virus is resistant."

"And we'll all know we're aboard a plague ship," Steiner added darkly.

"This is not in any way the plague," Karen corrected.

"I was using the term plague ship in a generic form," Steiner said. "In the Middle Ages, a plague ship carried either the dead or people dying with an infectious disease so as not to infect other members of society."

"But...but," the old surgeon stammered, "when we make port, surely they'll let us disembark so the sick can be attended to."

David shook his head slowly. "They'll never let us in, not with the prospect of starting a pandemic caused by a Tamiflu-resistant, bird flu virus."

All eyes stayed fixed on David, but he had nothing more to say. Instead, he put on a high-filtration mask and secured it in place.

The others quickly followed suit.

ELEVEN

"Dad, can I go see Will?" Kit asked.

"It's best you don't, sweetheart," David replied. "He's really sick with the flu and you sure don't want to catch it."

Kit thought for a moment. "But I can visit him after he gets better, huh?"

"Absolutely," David lied, straight-faced.

"Maybe I'll just send him some candy for now."

David smiled at his daughter, thinking the child was so much like her mother, Marianne. She was kind and generous and always concerned about the other person. It must run in the genes, David decided. "I'll let you know when he's up to it."

"Good."

"But for now," David went on, "you've got to protect yourself and Juanita against the nasty virus. So you must take your pills as directed and wear your special mask at all times. And remember, don't touch the duct tape that's covering the ventilation duct. If a piece comes off, tell me and I'll replace it."

"It's going to get really hot in here, Dad," Kit complained mildly.

"That's why you should keep the sliding door to the balcony wide open. It'll let fresh air in from the sea." David's gaze drifted out to the balcony of the cabin and to the ocean beyond. The water was becoming choppy again, the sky grayer, as the outer forces of the storm began to reach the *Grand Atlantic*. The storm was monster-sized, measuring 200 miles in diameter, with winds clocked at over eighty miles an hour. The luxury liner was currently moving away from the other edge of the tempest, heading on a southeasterly course. This maneuver would delay the ship from making landfall by an additional seven hours. "And don't forget," David said at length, "you and Juanita must stay away from crowds. All meals will be served buffet style, so take your food on deck and eat away from all the other passengers."

"What should we do with our plates?" Kit asked.

"There'll be giant bags to put them in," David answered, then quickly warned, "but don't touch those bags."

"I won't," Kit said and coughed briefly.

David stiffened in his chair. "Do you have a cough?"

"No, Dad," Kit told him. "I was gargling with some mouthwash and a little of it went down the wrong tube."

David hurriedly glanced over to Juanita, who nodded, verifying the incident. "So," David came back to his daughter, "no cough at all."

"None," Kit replied.

"And no fever or chills either, eh?"

"None," Kit said, unconcerned. "I feel good, Dad."

"Great!" David gave Kit a tight hug and watched her run out to the balcony, where she spread her arms out wide against the wind, like a bird about to take flight. In her diary, which David now read secretly, Kit had written she wished she and Dad and Juanita and Carolyn were all birds that could take wing and fly away from the sick ship. That's what Kit called the luxury liner—a sick ship. And for some, David thought on, it was going to turn into a death ship. He got to his feet and walked over to Juanita. In a low voice he told her, "Make certain Kit follows my instructions. Watch her closely."

"She will not leave my eyesight," Juanita promised.

David left the cabin and decided to take the stairs down to the sick bay. Even with his mask on, there was no way he was getting on an unventilated elevator that was crowded with passengers. It would be the perfect contagion zone. Others must have had the same idea, because the staircase was now filled with people. As David started down the steps, his mind returned to Kit. *How in the world did she avoid catching the virus?* he wondered for the hundredth time. *How?* Like Will, she had been so close to the infected bird that was spewing the avian flu virus into the air. Maybe she had some type of immunity to the virus or maybe it was only pure luck. But there was another possibility that made David shudder. Perhaps Kit had gotten a relatively small dose of the virus from the bird or from Will, and it was only a matter of time before she too came down with the illness. *God! Don't let that happen! Please don't let that happen!* Just the thought of a deathly ill Kit unnerved him. Taking a deep breath, he collected himself and exited the staircase on the G level.

The beauty spa and salon was closed, its doors locked shut. Masked crewmen were wiping down the walls in the passageway with a disinfectant, while others sprayed the air with something that smelled nauseatingly sweet. All those precautions were mainly for show, David told himself. A group of people coughing continuously would fill the air with a billion times more virus than the disinfectant could kill.

In the reception area of the sick bay, Arthur Maggio was slumped in a chair, totally exhausted, with dark circles under his eyes. He looked like he hadn't slept in a week.

"Any new cases?" David asked.

Maggio shook his head. "Not so far, but the boy is deteriorating rapidly. And his mother is now coughing as well."

"With bloody sputum?" David asked quickly.

"Not that I've seen. But her cough is coarse and raspy."

"Shit," David muttered under his breath. He had hoped that Marilyn would somehow avoid catching the virus, despite her close contact with Will. But deep down he knew it was inevitable. "What about the boy's stepfather?"

"Mr. Wyman's fever has apparently spiked up," Maggio said. "Your nurse has gone to his cabin to see if she could be of some assistance."

"And the other two sick passengers?"

Maggio shrugged weakly. "I haven't heard from them, so I assume there's been no change."

"Don't assume," David told him. "They could be so sick they can't even pick up the phone. Or they may be dead. You might want to call them and see how they're doing."

Maggio wearily pushed himself up from his chair and reached for the phone.

David entered the examining room that had two tables side by side. On the table nearest him, Will Harrison was gasping for air. His face had a purplish-red color, with bloody sputum caked around his oxygen mask. David didn't bother to listen to the boy's chest with a stethoscope because he could clearly hear the sounds coming from Will's lungs at a distance. There were loud wheezes and rhonchi—noises made by air trying to flow through bronchial tubes obstructed with blood. The only good sign was that the boy had lost consciousness and would die peacefully.

On the examining table across from Will was his mother, Marilyn Wyman. She appeared pale and worried, and was coughing intermittently.

"You might be more comfortable in your cabin," David suggested softly. "I could look after Will for you."

"I have to be here, just in case he needs me," Marilyn said in a quiet voice.

David nodded, aware that all the forces in heaven and hell couldn't pull the mother away from her dying son. "I know."

Marilyn wetted her parched lips with her tongue and coughed up phlegm that rattled in her throat. "Is there any drug that will help him?"

"I'm afraid not," David said honestly. "But we'll support his breathing with everything we've got and hope he makes it through."

"You've been very kind to us, David."

"Well, you're one of my favorite people."

Marilyn managed a shadow of a smile, but it faded quickly. "I took the Tamiflu capsules, like you directed."

"Good."

"Will it help?"

"Time will tell."

Marilyn coughed again and swallowed it back. "My immune system won't be able to put up much of a fight against the virus, you know."

"Why not?"

"Because I finished a course of chemotherapy for breast cancer last month," Marilyn informed him. "My oncologist told me my immune system would be suppressed for a while."

"That may not matter since Tamiflu's action doesn't depend on one's immune system."

"Well then," Marilyn said as the faint smile returned to her face, "score one for the home team."

David patted her shoulder, admiring the woman's pluck and courage in the face of a deadly virus. She was the perfect example of Ernest Hemingway's definition of courage, which was grace under pressure.

Out of the corner of his eye David saw Thomas Steiner, the radiologist, waving him over to the x-ray room. He patted Marilyn's shoulder once more, telling her, "I'll be back in a minute."

David strolled over to the radiology area and closed the door behind him. Steiner was standing in front of a row of viewboxes that held a series of x-rays.

"The boy is as good as dead," Steiner said in a clinical voice. "His chest film shows a complete white-out."

David studied the x-ray briefly. Will's lungs were now totally opacified, with no evidence at all of any aeration. Instead of air, the boy's lungs were filled with blood and mucus. "Nobody survives this," David said grimly.

"Nobody," Steiner agreed.

"Have you got a chest film on the boy's mother?"

Steiner shook his head. "Does she need one?"

"Not yet," David said. "But she will soon, I'm afraid."

"Then she too will die," Steiner said somberly. "But not before watching her only child pass away. Can you imagine anything sadder?"

"No," David said, with a deep sigh. "I can't."

There was a loud rap on the door.

"Come in!" Steiner called out.

Carolyn rushed into the room and over to David. "Rutherford needs you on deck pronto," she said urgently. "He's got a revolt on his hands."

TWELVE

Dozens of masked passengers crowded around William Rutherford and shouted obscenities and yelled invectives at him. Leading the uproar was Richard Scott, who towered over Rutherford and was making threatening gestures.

"You'll turn our goddamn phones back on or there will be hell to pay," Scott raged.

"But it's not under my control," Rutherford tried to explain. "I can't—"

"Bullshit!" someone in the crowd interrupted.

"Truly," Rutherford pleaded. "All phone service, including your cell phones, was cut off by order of the Centers for Disease Control."

"Then order them to turn it back on," Scott demanded.

"I can't," Rutherford told him. "It's an agency of the federal government, and they have jurisdiction over all—"

"We want our phones!" a voice bellowed out, and others joined in, repeating the line in a loud chorus.

"We want our phones!"

"We want our phones!"

"We want our phones!"

David pushed through the crowd that had now grown to over a hundred, with even more passengers on their way. The gathering was becoming increasingly surly, and it showed in the group's manner and appearance. The men were unshaven and poorly groomed, the women with little makeup and unconcerned with their attire. David nodded to himself, remembering that when survival was at stake, outward appearance was the first thing to go. Staying alive took precedence over how one looked.

Finally David reached Rutherford's side. The captain's face showed no obvious evidence of him being riled by the menacing crowd, but the underarms of the man's shirt were soaked with perspiration.

"I hear you've got some trouble," David said calmly.

"More than a little," Rutherford replied under his breath. He muffled a cough and cleared his throat. "I can't seem to get through to them about the phone service."

"Let me try."

"Be my guest."

David turned and raised his arms, palms out, to the crowd. "May I have your attention?"

The hostile throng booed loudly.

David tried again. "May I—"

The crowd booed even louder, then a voice cried out, "Give us back our phones!"

"Yeah! Yeah!" a dozen others joined in.

"Quiet!" David roared above the voices. "Quiet, damn it!"

"Who the hell are you?" a man in the second row yelled.

"Somebody you'd better listen to," David yelled back. "Particularly if you want to know how the bird flu is going to affect this ship."

The crowd went silent, but they still shifted around uneasily.

Richard Scott stepped forward and came face to face with David. Again he was wearing only tennis shoes and a swimming suit. He was the same height as David, but his well-muscled body and broad shoulders made him seem a lot bigger. "Screw you and your lecture!" he snarled. "We want our phone service back!"

David gave the investment banker an icy stare. "Now would be a good time for you to zip it up."

"And what if I don't?" Scott challenged him.

David controlled his temper, now wondering if Scott was going to make a stupid move or was just showing off in front of a crowd again. "You're a slow learner, aren't you?"

"Not according to my friends," Scott said with a smirk.

Scott's friends moved in behind him. There were three of them, and all had the look of well-conditioned athletes. The one closest to Scott was the man with a rose tattoo on his arm. His face was impassive, but he had his fists clenched tightly. The crowd was now dead quiet as they watched and waited to see which side would give in.

David quickly sized up Richard Scott and the men with him. Scott and the tattooed man were the most dangerous. The other athletic types were less aggressive and would hesitate before jumping into a fight. That would give David all the time he needed. David moved slightly to his left to give himself a better angle at Scott's neck. Scott moved with him, keeping his eyes locked into David's.

The tension between the two grew so heavy, it seemed to hang in the air.

Rutherford leapt in and separated the two men. "We'll have no fights!" he ordered. "We have enough trouble aboard this ship as is."

David continued to stare at Scott, waiting for the banker to make any movement at all. *Watch the head*, he told himself. The head always moved before the hands.

"Please!" Rutherford begged. "Listen to what Dr. Ballineau has to say. He can answer your questions far better than I."

The crowd remained silent and turned their attention to David. Rutherford used his bulk to put even more distance between the two men.

David stepped away, but kept Scott in his peripheral vision. He didn't trust the banker one iota and knew the man was capable of attacking from the front or rear, whichever gave him the clearest advantage. And Scott's three muscular friends would soon join in. That would make it four against one. David decided he'd still win, but there was a real chance he'd get hurt.

"Please, Dr. Ballineau," Rutherford urged.

David stood on a lounge chair so he could see more of the crowd. "We couldn't turn our phones back on even if we wanted to."

"Why not?" Scott pressed.

"Because the United States government has an Air Force plane circling above us and jamming all incoming and outgoing calls," David answered. "The plane is called an EA-18 Growler and it can block any and all electronic transmissions. Currently it is blocking all cellular and landline phone service to and from shore. The only communications allowed are radio calls involving the federal authorities, and landline phone-to-phone calls aboard the *Grand Atlantic*."

"Well, it can't stay up there forever," Scott challenged. "And when it goes to refuel, our cell phone lines will be open again."

There was a chorus of "Yeah! Yeah!" from the crowd.

"That won't happen," David explained calmly. "When that plane leaves to refuel, it'll be replaced by another Growler. There's a squadron of those planes on an aircraft carrier that's following every move we make."

A few grumbles arose from the crowd, then they went silent. Several of the passengers walked away slowly, dispirited, but most stayed, their eyes glued on David.

Finally Scott spoke again, "How do you know so much about these planes?"

"The federal authorities gave us all the details," David said, with a nod to Rutherford. "And they also told us they intend to keep your phone lines jammed for the immediate future."

"Why would they do that?" a female voice in the middle of the gathering asked.

"To prevent you from doing exactly what you're doing now," David told him.

"And what's that?"

"Panicking and acting like a bunch of fools," David said bluntly.

"How should we react?" the man with the red-rose tattoo spoke out. "For Chrissakes! We're trapped aboard this ship with a goddamn virus that will kill all of us!"

"That may not be true," David said in an even tone. "As you know, we've had an outbreak of bird flu aboard the *Grand Atlantic*. Only a few have been affected, and the rest of you are now wearing protective masks and taking Tamiflu. So there's every reason to believe that this outbreak will be limited and future cases will be mild, so mild that—"

"Well, if that's the case," Scott cut in, "why take away our phone service?"

"Because there's a second possibility," David went on, "which is a nightmare scenario. It's possible that many of us have already been exposed to this virus and will soon become sick. And it may turn out that this virus is resistant to Tamiflu. In that event, we'll end up with a ship filled with terribly sick people who are very contagious."

"But that still doesn't tell us why we've been shut off from the world," Scott pressed on. "We won't spread the virus by making a phone call."

"But you will spread the word and demand to be rescued, for which you'll pay any price."

"Damn right," Scott said at once. "I'll write a check for a hundred grand right now to be airlifted back to New York."

"So would I!" a voice from the rear of the crowd vowed.

"And so would a lot of others," David continued. "And suddenly ships and boats and helicopters would arrive in droves to rescue you and take you ashore, where you'll transmit this killer virus to God-only-knows how many people. And a fair number of those will end up like the little boy down in the sick bay whose life we're trying to save. In essence, then, you'd be starting a worldwide, bird flu pandemic."

The crowd went silent as it digested the distinct possibility of being ground zero for a pandemic affecting every country on the face of the earth. The men stood stone-faced and tried to hide their fear. Some of the women began to quietly weep.

"This is all bullshit!" Deedee Anderson screeched. "If we're going to get sick, why not go ashore and right to the hospital?"

"Because there's no city in the world that has enough hospital beds or isolation wards to look after hundreds and hundreds of very sick, highly contagious patients," David answered. "So you'll have to disperse to other cities by car, plane, or train, with family members or with strangers, and you'll spread the virus. It'll suddenly show up in ten different places, then twenty, then fifty. Then it will come in waves until it engulfs the entire world."

"You're a big expert on this, eh?" Scott growled and moved closer to the lounge chair.

"I'm not, but the CDC is," David said. "I'm only repeating what they told me."

"How do we know you're not embellishing their words?" Scott moved in closer, now just over an arm's length away.

David watched him carefully and tensed his muscles, readying himself to lunge. "One more step, and it'll be the last one you take for a long time."

Scott stared up at David for a moment, then retreated, but only a half-step.

David turned back to the crowd, still keeping Scott in his peripheral vision. "Then there's the chance that terrorists will learn of the ship and try to take it over. Maybe some Muslim jihadists will decide it's time to end the world."

"Where the hell would they go?" the tattooed man asked.

"That's a good question," David said, recalling that it was the same one he'd asked Lawrence Lindberg at the CDC. "They could sail to Somalia or Yemen, which are controlled by radicals who would happily start a pandemic."

"You're making this up as you go along, aren't you?" Scott said derisively.

"I'm telling you what could happen," David snapped. "And only a fool wouldn't be frightened by it. This isn't make-believe. This is reality, whether you want to accept it or not."

"Screw you and your scare tactics!" Scott blurted out. "We're going to take over this ship and somehow get our phones reconnected."

God! He's foolhardy on top of being dangerous. "Really?" David asked tonelessly. "And who will sail the ship? Who will navigate?"

"The crew," Scott answered promptly. "They'll do exactly what we tell them to do, if they want to stay healthy."

Deedee joined in support. "Yeah! They'll do whatever we tell them to do."

The crowd murmured their backing of the plan.

Someone at the rear of the large gathering yelled out, "And we'll head straight back to New York."

Another voice piped in, "Yeah! The greater New York area has plenty of hospital beds."

"Let's do it!" two others shouted.

Scott turned back to David and parted his lips in a hollow smile. "It seems like you're outnumbered." He waited for a response and when none was forthcoming, he added, "And if you try to stop us, you'll get hurt. I promise you that."

"Kick his ass!" Deedee encouraged.

David eyed Scott's Adam's apple. One quick blow, and the larynx would be fractured. A little harder blow, and the larynx would cave in and shut off Scott's airway altogether. Then a karate chop would shatter the tattooed man's clavicle. It would be over in seconds, and the crowd would scatter. David flattened out the palms of his hands and prepared to spring at his targets.

Suddenly Rutherford began to shake. The chills grew worse as his fever shot up. Then he coughed up sputum through his N-95 mask. It was streaked with blood.

"Oh, no! God, no!" Rutherford cried, his voice thick with fear.

"Oh, Christ!" a passenger in the first row shrieked. "He's got the disease! The captain's got bird flu!"

Rutherford's knees gave way, and he started to stagger. David rushed over to support him, but it was too late. The captain slowly sank to the deck, his entire body now shaking. The crowd backed away horror-struck, most of them realizing how close they were to the highly contagious virus. The passengers in the rear began to run from the scene. All the others, including Richard Scott, were right behind them.

David grabbed a cushion from a lounge chair and placed it under Rutherford's head. The captain's face was flushed with fever, his forehead burning hot.

"The Tamiflu doesn't work," Rutherford sputtered between coughing spasms. "It's the nightmare scenario."

THIRTEEN

FROM THE FOOT OF the bed in the captain's quarters, David watched Rutherford transfer command of his ship to the first officer, Jonathan Locke. It was being done in an orderly, prescribed manner, despite the dire consequences. Rutherford was a sea captain to the very end, David thought, the man obviously more concerned about the ship and its crew and passengers than himself.

"So follow these instructions and you will get the *Grand Atlantic* home safe," Rutherford was saying. He paused to raise his head off the pillow and cough before continuing on. "You are to depend on Dr. Ballineau for all medical matters. His word, which comes directly from the CDC, will be law. Understood?"

"Aye, sir," Locke said obediently.

"And be particularly wary of Mr. Scott," Rutherford warned. "He's rebellious and rambunctious and, if there is to be a mutiny, he will lead it."

"I'll watch him and hopefully be able to reason with him."

"Good luck," David murmured to himself, thinking that Scott would intimidate Locke and push him aside in the blink of an eye. The first officer was a thin, quiet man, middle-aged, who wore horn-rimmed glasses and looked more like a college professor than a sea captain. His appearance would not engender confidence among the passengers.

"And always stick to your seafaring instincts," Rutherford instructed. "No matter what, stick to those instincts. They will serve you well."

"Aye, sir."

"Finally," Rutherford concluded as he lay back on his pillow, now totally exhausted, "you will bury me at sea."

"But, sir," Locke argued mildly, "you may pull through."

"Not very likely," Rutherford said, accepting his fate. "Remember, at sea, wrapped in a simple cloth."

David and Locke left the captain's quarters and headed down a long passageway that led to the bridge. The corridor was clear except for two masked crewmen washing down the walls and doors with disinfectant. A third deckhand was on a ladder mopping the ceiling and ventilation ducts.

"Is it as hopeless as the captain says?" Locke inquired.

"I'm afraid so," David said honestly.

"And what about burying the captain at sea?" Locke asked. "If his body is loaded with the virus, won't it infect the ocean's food chain?"

It was a good question, one that David hadn't thought of. "I'll pass it by the CDC."

And what about Will Harrison and the others who are sure to die? David asked himself. *If they can't be buried at sea, where could the bodies be stored to prevent them from contaminating the entire ship? Perhaps in the food freezers. No! No! Then the food would become—*

"I'm concerned about Richard Scott," Locke broke into David's thoughts. "How should I deal with him?"

"You don't have to for now," David said. "He'll wait to see if the infection spreads to the whole ship or is limited to just a few."

"What if is spreads?"

"Then you'll have your hands full," David replied. "And, in all likelihood, Scott will encourage the others to take over the ship."

"We do have firearms, you know," Locke said, lowering his voice.

"And how many do you think you'll have to shoot to put down a mutiny?" David asked. "One? Five? Maybe ten?"

Locke sighed to himself and slowly nodded. "I see your point."

The men walked through a door and entered the bridge. The three officers at their duty stations straightened their postures, all aware that Locke was now in commend of the ship. But their expressions and eyes told David that, to a man, every one of them wished that Rutherford was still at the helm. Not that it really mattered, David thought darkly. Because, regardless of who was captain, the luxury liner would stay at sea, isolated and quarantined, until the virus problem was solved or everyone aboard was dead.

Locke called out to the officer piloting the *Grand Atlantic*, "Have we passed the outer reaches of the storm?"

"We'll be clear within the hour, sir," came the reply.

"Steady as you go, then."

Locke led the way out to the narrow deck at the front of the bridge. The air was still so heavy with moisture that the plants around them were dripping wet. David gazed out at the gray, gloomy sky, then down to the expansive deck beneath them. It was deserted and eerily quiet. There were no strollers or joggers or anyone relaxing in lounge chairs. The passengers were frightened, all staying in their cabins away from others who might infect them.

"I feel like I'm captain of a ghost ship," Locke remarked.

More like a plague ship, David started to say, but held his tongue.

"How long will they remain in their cabins?" Locke wondered aloud.

"Until they know for sure whether the virus is spreading."

"And then?"

"And then, those who are sick will stay in their cabins because they have no choice, and those who aren't will take over the *Grand Atlantic* and try to jump ship."

Locke looked at David oddly. "But we're surrounded by a thousand miles of open sea."

David pointed to the lifeboats that hung along the sides of the ship. "They'll use those."

"But they'll never make shore."

"Desperate men do desperate things."

The door to the bridge opened, and an officer stuck his head out. "Excuse me, sir, but Dr. Ballineau is needed urgently in the sick bay."

David hurried through the bridge and down the passageway to a waiting elevator. The door was open, the elevator deserted except for a deckhand mopping the interior with disinfectant. David motioned the man out and stepped in, then pushed the button for the G level. He was convinced that the washed-down elevator would be less contaminated with the virus than the staircase, which was being used by virtually all passengers because they feared being crowded into a small space with infected people. And their fear was justified, David thought miserably. The high-filtration N-95 masks and Tamiflu were supposed to protect them, but it was now clear that those measures had limited effect at best.

The elevator jerked to a stop and David quickly exited. The passageway was empty except for two people sitting in chairs outside the sick bay. They were an elderly couple dressed in Ohio State warmup outfits. Both looked sick and were coughing up bloody sputum. Neither was wearing a mask.

"Where are your masks?" David asked brusquely.

"We couldn't keep them on," the man answered in a hoarse voice. "They were filling up with phlegm and we couldn't breathe through them."

"We'll get you new masks," David said and wondered how many other people the maskless couple had infected.

The inside of the sick bay looked like an emergency room with mass casualties. A dozen or more people were slumped down in chairs or sprawled out on the floor, all coughing harshly through their blood-stained masks. Two were having shaking chills and had wrapped themselves in woolen blankets. David stepped over a portly man who was lying on his side and gasping for air. It was Sol Wyman. A woman near the wall called out and pleaded for help.

David held up a hand in a gesture of *I'll be with you in a minute*, and entered the examining room. Off to his left he saw a scene of overwhelming grief, and it tore at his heart. Marilyn Wyman was sobbing uncontrollably as she rested her head on the chest of her dead son. Will's face was now pale, and one could see his freckled cheeks, which, along with his tousled hair, made him look like a sleeping little boy. David choked for a moment, then swallowed back his sadness. Out of the corner of his eye, he spotted Carolyn, who was finishing a phone call, and walked over.

"When did Will die?" he asked.

"About ten minutes ago," Carolyn whispered, then lowered her voice even more. "Marilyn won't allow us to cover the boy."

"Let him stay the way he is," David said and thought about the terrible grief a parent must feel when they lose a child. It had to be beyond unbearable. "We'll move the body to her cabin later."

Carolyn nodded. "And it won't matter to her or Sol because they've both got the disease."

David nodded back and tried to come up with the logistics of moving the dead boy. It would have to be done on a gurney late at night when everyone was asleep. They'd use an elevator programmed to only stop at the level where Marilyn's cabin was located. And they'd leave the boy's head uncovered, for Marilyn's sake.

The phone rang.

Carolyn answered it and quickly put the caller on hold. "This is spreading like wildfire, David. I've already spoken to at least a dozen passengers with the disease, and the calls keep coming."

The phone rang again and Carolyn ignored it. "How should we handle it?"

David thought for a moment before giving specific instructions. One thing was certain. The sick bay could not accommodate those who were already sick or those who were about to become sick. "Have everybody return to their rooms, even if you have to use wheelchairs and gurneys. For those who call in, get their room numbers and tell them to stay put. Somebody from the medical staff will come by to see them."

"What about medications?"

"Tylenol or Motrin for fever."

"And their coughs?"

"There's nothing we can do for that."

Carolyn glanced over her shoulder at the coughing patients. Half had their masks up or off, so they could breathe. "They're taking their masks off because the damn things are filling up with bloody sputum."

"Then give them new masks."

"Our supply is running low."

"I'll get more," David said and quickly looked around the sick bay. "Where's Maggio?"

"Still asleep, I guess."

"Wake him up," David directed, then asked, "What about Karen?"

"I tried her room, but there was no answer."

"And Steiner?"

"He's with his wife," Carolyn replied. "She has asthma and is coughing her guts out. He's not sure if it's asthma or the avian flu."

"Shit!"

"Yeah."

David snapped his fingers suddenly as a thought came to mind. "What about the other ship's doctor and his nurse-wife? You know, the ones who were so seasick."

"Now they're both sick as hell with the bird flu," Carolyn reported. "His wife is already turning cyanotic."

"Shit!" David said again, even louder. "This is turning into a full-blown nightmare."

"And it's going to get worse," Carolyn added.

"Hold the fort," David said, turning for the door. "I'll be back."

Before leaving, David stopped by the examining table that held Will Harrison's body. He gently patted Marilyn's shoulder and waited for her to look up, then said, "You stay with Will. I'll return in a little while to be with you."

Marilyn nodded, and placed her head back on Will's chest and began sobbing again.

David hurried out of the sick bay and down the passageway, zooming by more people on their way to the medical facility. Quickly he estimated how many passengers had come down with avian influenza. At least three dozen, he decided, which meant the virus now had an ever-increasing reservoir to thrive and multiply in. The air would soon become so thick with the killer virus that there'd be no escaping it.

As he reached the bank of elevators, the door suddenly opened and Karen Kellerman stepped out.

"David! Thank goodness!" She reached out and grabbed his arm. "I've been looking for you everywhere!"

"For what?" David asked quickly.

"Your daughter," Karen said and, winded, paused to swallow and catch her breath.

"What about her?" David cried out, instantly alarmed. He grasped Karen's shoulders and shook her. "What about Kit?"

"She's really frightened," Karen went on. "She thinks Juanita has the bird flu."

"Oh Christ!" David groaned.

"Kit ran into me in the passageway and begged me to look at Juanita," Karen told him. "Apparently she couldn't find you, and all the phone lines to the sick bay were busy."

David waited for his heart to stop racing. He was still rattled by just the thought that Kit might be ill with the deadly disease. *Thank Goodness Karen was there when she was needed*, he told himself. And Kit knew she could turn to Karen for medical help. They had become friends when he and Karen were lovers. Good friends. Kit was so disappointed when the two broke up. Despite repeated questions from Kit, David never told his daughter the real reason why the couple had split apart. He saw no need to. Finally David asked, "Did you examine Juanita?"

Karen nodded. "She's sick, but I'm not certain it's the bird flu. There are conflicting signs. She has a cough, but fever is low-grade and she's had no chills."

"It sounds viral, though."

"But that doesn't make it bird flu."

"Chances are it is," David said glumly, recalling that he had given the nanny Motrin for her recurring headaches. And that drug, like all the anti-inflammatory agents, could suppress the early symptoms of flu. Even bird flu. *Shit!* His mind turned quickly to Kit, who had been in almost constant close contact with Juanita. "Where is Kit now?" he asked in a rush.

"I thought it best to put her in my room."

"Good."

"You should examine Juanita to see if she really has bird flu," Karen suggested.

"I will shortly," David said. "But there is something very important I must do first."

"What?"

"Find out if there's any way to treat her," David said and hurried into the elevator.

FOURTEEN

THERE WAS A PROLONGED silence on the phone line connecting the *Grand Atlantic* with the Centers for Disease Control in Atlanta. David and Karen stared at the speakerphone and waited for a response.

"They're in a real quandary," Karen whispered in David's ear. "They've never encountered anything like this."

"Nor has anyone else," David whispered back.

They were sitting in a small communications room that was adjacent to the bridge. Except for an oval, teak table and chairs, the windowless room was unadorned, with no ornaments or special electronics other than a flashing green light atop the phone that indicated the line was secure. The room was designed to be private and used only for extraordinary circumstances.

Suddenly a burst of static came over the speakerphone. In the background, they could hear isolated words, which sounded like *isolation* and *quarantine*. This was followed by a chorus of muttered, unintelligible phrases.

Karen asked quietly, "Do you think they're trying to come up with ways to get us ashore?"

David shook his head. "More likely they're devising plans to keep us out in the middle of the ocean."

"Can you imagine the public outcry if they learned the CDC was doing that to us?" Karen paused to swallow back her growing fear. "It would be like an execution order for everyone aboard this ship."

David shrugged. "The public won't be that upset. It would be a choice of their survival or ours. Which do you think they'd choose?"

Karen rested her head on David's shoulder and said, "I'm getting scared out of my wits."

"Welcome to the club."

"You're really not frightened, are you?" She glanced up at his face and studied it briefly. "How come you never show fear?"

"It's a genetic defect."

A faint smile came to Karen's face, then faded. "Did they teach you how to do that in Special Forces?"

"I guess," David answered, but he knew the trick wasn't to mask fear, but rather to push it into a side compartment of your brain and ignore it and not let it interfere with the task at hand. You can shake and scream later. Or have flashbacks. He felt Karen nestling her head against him, her warm breath brushing by his ear. For a moment, it caused him to shiver pleasantly. He peered over to Karen, with her gorgeous face and slim body, and again realized there would always be a part of him that was attracted to her. There was no getting around that. But, like fear, he would push the feeling into a side compartment of his brain and ignore it.

Lawrence Lindberg's voice came over the speakerphone. "Dr. Ballineau, I'm sorry about the delay, but we're trying to develop a plan that will save as many passengers on the ship as possible yet keep the virus from spreading to the mainland. I think you can appreciate the difficulties we're facing."

"Concern yourself with saving the lives of the passengers," David said bluntly. "The virus can't reach land as long as we're at sea."

"Your point is well taken," Lindberg said. "And of course our primary focus will be on the passengers aboard the *Grand Atlantic*."

Bullshit! David thought, but remained silent.

"First, there are a number of questions we still have," Lindberg went on. "And we need specific answers. If you don't know, say so."

"Get on with it," David growled impatiently.

"Are you certain the sick passengers took their Tamiflu capsules?"

"I'm certain the captain of the ship did," David replied. "I asked him specifically, and, to be sure, I checked his blister pack of Tamiflu. The correct number of capsules were missing. And the little boy who died was started on the drug within twenty-four hours of his initial symptoms."

"What about the others?"

"I'll have to ask them," David said. "But I'll bet they did because they're really frightened. They're facing death and they know it."

"Please check for us."

"I will."

"And keep in mind that Tamiflu is not a cure," Lindberg continued on. "In most patients it will only make their illness somewhat shorter and less severe. Now that may not seem like much, but it could make the difference between life and death."

"What about other antiviral agents if the virus proves to be resistant to Tamiflu?" David asked, glancing down at a list of questions he had for the experts at the CDC.

"The virus is being tested against a variety of such agents, including Relenza, Ribavirin, and M2 ion channel blockers," Lindberg said. "Hopefully, the virus won't show resistance to these as well."

"And if it does?"

"Then our problem becomes magnified a hundredfold."

David and Karen exchanged knowing glances. The prospects for their survival were looking dimmer and dimmer.

"But even in that case, it is still possible to avoid the disease," Lindberg went on. "The N-95 masks can be very protective. They're not perfect, but they will be your best chance to keep the virus at bay."

David leaned toward the speakerphone, bothered by Lindberg's phrase *They're not perfect*. "When we talked initially, I was told the N-95 masks offered excellent protection. Has something happened to change that?"

"Not really. The masks are quite good, but not perfect."

"Define 'quite good,'" David pressed.

"In the best-controlled study from China, the masks protected 75 percent of the individuals exposed to the influenza virus."

"Were they exposed to the high concentration of virus that the passengers aboard the *Grand Atlantic* will encounter?"

There was a long pause before Lindberg answered, "Probably not."

David groaned inwardly. The N-95 masks weren't working nearly as well as he had hoped. With a sky-high concentration of avian flu virus in the air, the infection rate on the ship could easily surpass 50 percent. That would amount to over four hundred very sick patients. *Shit!*

"Ballineau? Are you still there?"

"Still here," David said, coming out of his reverie. "Are you finished with your questions?"

"Yes."

"Good, because I've got a lot of things to discuss with you." David again glanced down at the list he'd prepared earlier. "First, we need more N-95 masks. The passengers are taking them off because the filters become clogged and they can't breathe through them."

"Oh, no!" Lindberg raised his voice. "They must keep them on at all times!"

"Have you ever tried to breathe through a mask that's filled with bloody sputum?"

"I'll see that you're supplied ASAP."

"Next, we've already had one death, and there are surely more to follow. We should keep them isolated so they don't serve as a reservoir that continually contaminates the ship. Unfortunately, we don't have a satisfactory storage area, and burial at sea doesn't sound like a good idea."

"No burials at sea!" Lindberg demanded sharply.

"That's what I figured," David said. "Do you think it could infect the ocean's food chain?"

"Perhaps," Lindberg told him. "But an equally terrifying prospect is that migratory birds might see the floating bodies and decide to feed on them. Then we'd have infected birds flying to all the continents."

David shuddered at the thought of infected birds traveling up and down the great flyways of North and South America. The birds would represent the perfect way to start and perpetuate a worldwide pandemic. And, as long as there were birds, the disease would persist. A nightmare! A nightmare come true!

David refocused his mind on solving the body problem. "The safest way to deal with the dead is to place them in body bags, which you'll have to supply us with."

"Done."

David's eyes went to the last item on his list. "And finally, I've set up a quasi-isolation plan for the ship, which consists of the following. All infected passengers will stay in their rooms and have food and medicines delivered to them. The others will be told to avoid any gatherings or crowds and wear their N-95 masks at all times."

"How will you keep an accurate record of those who are sick and should be confined to their rooms?"

"Let me think about that for a moment."

"Take your time," Lindberg said. "But also come up with a mechanism to alert everyone that a particular room has a sick person in it and will be heavily contaminated with the virus."

David concentrated his mind for several seconds, then nodded to himself. "I'll have the doors of the sick marked with a splash of red paint."

"Kind of like Passover," Lindberg remarked without humor.

David nodded again as he recalled the Jewish holiday of Passover, in which God punished Pharaoh by instructing the Angel of Death to kill the firstborn male of every Egyptian family. Those to be spared had their doors splashed with the blood from a lamb and would be passed over. But aboard the *Grand Atlantic*, the Angel of Death would be visiting those with a red mark on their door.

At length, David said, "And I have one final request. As you can imagine, the medical staff we have is already overwhelmed with the sick and dying. Besides myself, there's only a nurse, a radiologist, an anesthesiologist, and the ship's doctor who is old and a bit fragile. Add to that a poorly equipped sick bay, and you can see the problem we're facing."

"I guess there are some ways we could arrange for some ventilators and monitoring equipment to be delivered—"

"That won't help!" David cut him off. "All the equipment in the world won't help, because we don't have the staff to set it all up and monitor the patients. From a clinical standpoint, only the nurse, the anesthesiologist, and I can look after the really sick patients. What we need is more medical personnel."

There was a very long pause before Lindberg spoke. "I'm afraid that won't be possible until we know whether the virus is sensitive to the agents we have available. For now, the only personnel who would be allowed to come aboard would have to be wearing Biosafety Level 4 outfits, which require space suits and an external oxygen supply. It simply can't be done."

"Yeah, I guess," David said, making no effort to hide his disappointment.

"Let's hope the virus responds to one of our antiviral agents," Lindberg said tonelessly. "Until we know the results of our studies, you'll have to get by on your own. We'll of course be available 24/7 to help with any new problems."

"Get back to us on those test results ASAP."

"Will do."

The phone line went silent. The light atop the speakerphone stopped flashing and turned from green to red.

Karen looked over to David and asked, "What do you think?"

"I think Lindberg just told us that we're all dead."

FIFTEEN

"Breathe through your mouth," David instructed the nanny. "Take long, deep breaths."

Juanita inhaled deeply, then exhaled slowly. She repeated the cycle twice before her cough kicked in. After swallowing back her sputum, she adjusted her N-95 mask and mumbled, "Sorry, Dr. Ballineau."

"No problem," David said and continued listening to her chest with a stethoscope. He heard some scattered, coarse rhonchi, but only a few wheezes. And again he noticed that her skin color was good. He put his stethoscope in his pocket and smiled at the nanny, who was dressed in a bathrobe and sitting on the edge of her bed. "Your lungs sound good."

"I have the disease, don't I?" Juanita asked, as if she already knew the answer.

"I'm not sure," David told her. "It could be just a routine virus."

"I have the disease," Juanita repeated. "I am certain."

"Oh?" David raised an eyebrow. "Which medical school did you graduate from?"

Juanita smiled weakly, then had another coughing spasm. She paused to catch her breath before saying, "You must not tell the Little One. It will cause her to worry and cry."

"I will tell her it's only a cold," David proposed.

Juanita shook her head. "She will know you are not telling the truth. Like her mother before her, she will see right through you."

David nodded at the veracity of Juanita's words. He had always considered himself a good liar, but Marianne could always sense he was not telling the truth. She said she could read it in his eyes. And apparently so could Carolyn, and so could Kit. "I will say you have a cold, but there's a possibility it's the disease."

"A half-truth," Juanita sighed as she lay back on her pillow. "You will see to it that I am buried in Costa Rica."

"You are not going to die so soon."

"That's for God to say, not you."

"Well, God isn't talking to us," David groused. "He must be on vacation because He sure as hell isn't aboard this ship."

"Sacrilege!" Juanita raised her voice and made the sign of the cross.

David shrugged. "Whatever."

Juanita began to cough again but, with effort, suppressed it. "I wish to be buried with my family in Cartago, which is just southeast of San José. You will remember?"

"I will remember."

Juanita closed her eyes and said, "You should go look after the Little One."

David left the cabin and hurried down the passageway, still wondering if Juanita really had avian influenza. She wasn't nearly as sick as the others, and her lungs sounded relatively good. But, then again, she would be in the early stages of the disease, and all hell could still break loose. And if she had the killer virus, she most likely caught it from her close contact with Will, while chaperoning Kit. But if that were the case, why didn't Kit have the disease? Once more he tried to come up with reasons why Kit was being spared. Was she lucky? Or somehow immune to it? Or was the goddamn virus incubating inside her, waiting to explode? The last thought sent a giant shiver through David. For a moment, he envisioned Kit's face turning purple as the vicious virus destroyed her lungs and deprived her of oxygen. He shook his head and forced the awful image from his mind.

David came to Karen's suite and, after taking a deep breath to compose himself, knocked on the door and entered. Kit and Karen were sitting on the sofa, thumbing through a fashion magazine. Kit's raven hair had been braided into a ponytail, no doubt by Karen. *Women!* David mused to himself. *They know how to push all the shit in life aside. That's why they outlived men.*

"Hi, Dad!" Kit jumped up and dashed over to give him a tight hug.

"Hi, sweetheart!" David hugged her back and gazed at her ponytail, as if giving it careful study. "Your new hairdo looks great!"

"Karen did it for me."

"I figured." David looked over at Karen and winked, then came back to Kit. "So tell me, how are you feeling?"

"I'm fine," Kit replied brightly.

"No fever?"

"No fever."

"No cough?"

"No cough."

"Any scratchy—"

"Dad!" She interrupted, now becoming exasperated. "I feel fine. Really!"

"Just checking."

Kit stared up at her father's face and tried to read it. "You're worried about Juanita, aren't you?"

"It might only be a cold," David said evenly.

"But you think she's got the nasty virus, huh?"

"We'll see."

Kit studied his face even more intently, then tears welled up in her eyes. "Please don't let anything bad happen to her, Dad. Please!"

"She's doing okay so far," David said, trying to comfort her, "and that's a good sign."

"But—but Will was okay too," Kit countered. "At least he was at first."

She's so damn smart, David thought before saying, "But his symptoms were different."

Kit nodded slowly, only half-convinced. "Is Will feeling any better?"

David hesitated, not wanting to be the bearer of bad news. But Kit would learn of Will's death from others soon enough, and it was better she heard it from him. "He didn't make it, sweetheart. He passed away in his sleep."

The tears gushed out. Kit rushed back into his arms and sobbed, "Daddy! Oh, Daddy!"

"He put up a brave fight," David consoled softly, "but it was just too much for him."

"Do—do you think he'll go to heaven, Dad?" Kit cried.

"I'm sure of it," David replied. "And I'll bet God lets him take care of all the little animals up there."

Kit sniffed back her tears and smiled faintly. "Do you really think so?"

"I really think so," David reassured, then slowly ran his hand through her hair. "Now we have to take extra precautions to make sure we don't catch the virus. Okay?"

"Okay," Kit said, wiping her runny nose with the back of her hand. "I'll wear my mask all the time."

"Good," David encouraged. "And remember to take your Tamiflu pills and to stay in here unless you absolutely have to go out."

"Should I check on Juanita?"

"Nah. She'll be sleeping most of the time anyway." David took her hand and led her to the bedroom. "Why don't you lie down now and take a little nap. It'll be good for you."

Kit stepped into the bedroom, then abruptly turned and raced back into David's arms. "I love you, Dad!"

"I love you too, sweetheart." David hugged her and gently guided her toward the bedroom. "You have sweet dreams."

David watched her climb into bed and bring her favorite teddy bear close, and for a moment all the world seemed right.

Quickly he turned and motioned Karen over to the door leading to the passageway. "Can you stay with her for a while?" he whispered.

"Sure," Karen whispered back. "But won't you need me in the sick bay?"

"I'll let you know once I'm down there."

Karen glanced over her shoulder to make certain Kit wasn't within earshot. "What about Juanita? Do you think she's got the avian flu?"

David shrugged. "I can't be sure. But chances are she does."

"If she does, only God knows what it will do to Kit."

David nodded somberly, knowing that Juanita's death would shatter the child. Juanita was Kit's mother-figure, and her death would mean Kit had lost two mothers in her short life, which was two too many. Sighing to himself, he said, "Let's hope for the best."

Karen put her arms around David's neck and brought him close. "If we don't get out of this mess alive, I want you to know that I never stopped loving you."

"I know," David said quietly.

Karen pecked his cheek and said, "Work some of your magic, David. Get us through this nightmare."

David disengaged from her embrace and hurried down the passageway, which was now completely deserted. All the doors were closed and there were no sounds coming from within. It was as silent as a cemetery, he thought just as the ventilation system clicked on and the air began to move. Again David wondered if the ventilation ducts were spreading the deadly virus to every corner of the *Grand Atlantic*. But the system couldn't be shut off because the ship would become unbearably hot, particularly for the elderly and those feverish from the flu. But at this point, did it really matter? The virus didn't need a ventilation system to spread. It was doing very well on its own.

David took the elevator down, all the while trying to think of additional measures to protect Kit. But there weren't any. The only sure way to avoid the virus was to get off the ship. But that was impossible. They were stuck out in the Atlantic Ocean, hundreds and hundreds of miles from the mainland, and the CDC would make sure they remained there.

The elevator jerked to a halt, and David exited on the G level. As he approached the sick bay, he could see the crowd of people stacked up outside the reception area. A few were standing; some were sitting in chairs; most were sprawled out on the floor. There had to be at least a dozen patients waiting to be seen, and all of them seemed to be coughing. Half didn't have their N-95 masks on. *Shit!* David grumbled. Things were going from bad to worse.

He made his way through the mass of humanity, stepping over bodies and trying to avoid their outstretched arms and legs. The reception area was packed as well. People were lying on the floor side by side, squeezed in like sardines. Finally he reached the examining tables. Sol Wyman was on one, Will Harrison on the other. Marilyn was still crying over her dead son's body. Off in a corner, Arthur Maggio was slumped down on a metal stool, his eyes closed, his arms hanging down by his sides. David couldn't tell if he was sick or simply asleep.

Carolyn hurried up to his side. "It's a madhouse down here! It's turned into absolute bedlam."

"So I see," David said, now noticing more sick people sitting on the floor beside the examining tables. "Couldn't you move any of these people back to their rooms?"

"It's the goddamn crew!" Carolyn erupted disgustedly. "They won't help transport the patients back to their cabins. They're afraid to even touch the gurneys and wheelchairs."

"Did you tell them that if they're masked and gloved, they'd be safe?"

"I tried, but they wouldn't listen," Carolyn said wearily. "They see death coming, and they want to stay as far away from it as possible. And there's a definite mean streak running through them as well."

"I'll try to come up with a way to change their minds," David said, remembering a basic tenet in mob control. Find their leader and persuade him. The others will follow. "Is there a member that the others seem to listen to?"

Carolyn nodded. "A tough-looking Asian, with angry eyes and big muscles. I'll bet he spends a lot of time working out."

"I'll talk to him." David's gaze drifted over to Sol Wyman, whose skin color looked good despite his noisy respirations. "How is Sol doing?"

"He seems to be holding his own, but that probably won't last," Carolyn replied, then shook her head sadly. "Every time Sol coughs, poor Marilyn says she wants to die with him."

"The way things are going, she'll soon have her wish." David gestured with his head toward the elderly ship's doctor, who was asleep on a metal stool. "And what about Maggio?"

"I think he's drunk."

David grumbled under his breath. Now the old man would be in the way and totally useless.

The air was suddenly filled with a loud cacophony of coughs and groans and moans. Someone had a throat full of sputum, and it seemed to take forever for him to clear it. Again David noticed that over half the patients either weren't wearing their N-95 masks or had them on improperly.

"Let me see if I can move this crowd out," he said and walked to the space between the reception area and the examining room. Raising his voice so that it would carry into the passageway, David addressed the ever-growing group. "Let me have your attention, please! My name is David Ballineau and, for better or worse, I'm the lead physician down here. Now you must follow my instructions or I won't be able to look after you, and you'll continue to just lie on the floor, which can't be very comfortable."

"We need to be in a hospital," a hoarse voice cried out.

"We don't have a hospital, so we're going to have to make do," David said firmly. "Now I want you to do exactly as I tell you. All of you must return to your cabins immediately. When you leave, give us your name and cabin number, and we'll arrange for someone to come by and examine you. That way, you'll all be seen much quicker and be given medicines to ease your symptoms."

The coughing started once more and seemed even louder than before. Gradually it subsided and some of the sick struggled to their feet and staggered down the passageway. But most of the patients stayed in place, either unwilling or unable to walk back to their cabins.

Carolyn came up alongside David and said in a low voice, "I'll bet they'd leave if we had deckhands to help them into wheelchairs and gurneys."

"Yeah, but we don't."

"So what do we do?"

"Pass out Motrin and Tylenol pills and keep reminding them of the soft mattresses awaiting them in their cabins," David advised. "They'll eventually become tired of lying on a hard floor."

"God!" Carolyn breathed. "They must be absolutely terrified."

"So are we," David said. "It's just that we know how to hide it."

Marilyn Wyman's sobs grew louder. She kept repeating, "No, God! Please, no!" The sick people on the floor around her didn't appear to notice the grief-stricken woman or, if they did, they didn't seem to care. Every person for themselves, David thought. It was always that way when it came to survival. Except for mothers. They would kill for their young, and die for them if necessary.

David sighed deeply and, stepping over people, moved to Marilyn's side. He placed a hand on her shoulder and waited for her to look up. "In a little while, we'll move Will to his cabin, if it's all right with you."

Marilyn nodded, her eyes puffy and bloodshot above the N-95 mask she wore. "I'll want to go with him."

"Of course."

"And will you please bring Sol too?"

"As soon as we get you and Will settled."

"Thank you for being so kind, David," she said and again rested her head on Will's chest. She stroked her boy's arm, as if willing it to come to life.

David walked back over to Carolyn, who was now leaning heavily against the wall. "When we leave with Will's body, give me some Valium pills for Marilyn."

"Five-milligram pills?"

"Yes, but a bunch of them."

Marilyn began sobbing again and murmuring quietly to Will, as if he were still alive.

Carolyn shook her head sorrowfully. "Even if she survives, her life is destroyed."

David nodded. "She'll never get over Will's death, never in a million years."

Carolyn nodded back. "Will was such a sweet, gentle kid. Everybody liked him."

"Particularly Kit."

"Have you told her about him yet?"

"Yeah, a few minutes ago."

"How'd she take it?"

"Badly," David said and looked away. He swallowed hard, his mind going back to Kit's tears. "They were best pals."

Carolyn smiled knowingly. "They were closer than that."

David's eyes narrowed as the revelation sunk in. "Boy-girl stuff, eh?"

"Boy-girl stuff," Carolyn repeated, thinking that men were sometimes so oblivious to emotional bonding. "She'll really hurt for a while, David."

"I know."

"Where is Kit now?"

"I left her with Karen."

Carolyn's face tightened, her dislike for Karen Kellerman obvious. From past experience, Carolyn knew the woman was tough as nails and only softened when she wanted something in return. "I wouldn't have picked her to be with Kit right now, and I think you know why."

David shrugged. "I had no choice. Juanita is sick and may well have the damn flu."

"Oh Christ!" Carolyn moaned and slumped even more heavily against the wall. "Things are really going from awful to worse."

"By the minute," David added and gazed at Carolyn, who appeared weary and drained from handling a sick bay filled with dozens of sick people all by herself. *God! She was holding up so well.* But the fatigue was showing through in her face and posture. "You look beat. Why don't you rest for a while?"

"I'm just getting my second wind," Carolyn said and forced herself to perk up.

"You don't lie very well."

"I know, but I'm getting better at it."

David gave her an affectionate bump with his hip. "I think I could grow to like you."

Carolyn grinned. "You say that to all the girls."

"Just the pretty ones."

The landline phone rang loudly and continued to ring. Other buttons on the phone lit up, indicating even more incoming calls.

"It never stops," Carolyn sighed through her fatigue and picked up the receiver. As she listened to the voice on the other end, her expression changed to dead serious. Almost in a whisper she said, "Yes, I understand."

Slowly she placed the phone down and steadied herself against the desk. The color left her face.

"What?" David asked anxiously.

"Richard Scott has taken over the bridge, and he has a gun pointed at the captain's head."

SIXTEEN

RICHARD SCOTT AND HIS three fellow mutineers were armed with shotguns, and they were holding the weapons like they knew how to use them. Standing at the far wall of the bridge, with their hands atop their heads, were four of the officers aboard the *Grand Atlantic*. Only the new captain, Jonathan Locke, had put up any resistance, and he had an ugly bruise on his forehead to show for it.

"Do you have any idea how many laws you've broken?" David asked pointedly. "You could spend a hundred years in jail."

"Which would be a lot better than dying on this infested ship," Scott retorted. "I'll take my chances ashore in a court of law."

"You're going to have some problems that I don't believe you've considered." David briefly studied the mutineers and decided he could take out one or maybe two, but then the firing would start and some people would end up dead. "Big problems."

"Such as?"

"Such as who will navigate the *Grand Atlantic* and take you exactly to where you want to go?"

"The first officer," Scott answered at once and gestured to the group of officers with his shotgun.

David glanced over and, by the process of elimination, picked out the first officer. He recognized the captain who he had witnessed taking command, and the chief radio officer who had set up the conference call with the CDC, and the security officer who had congratulated him on his fine skeet shooting. That left the new first officer, a chubby man, in his late thirties, with a protuberant abdomen, round face, and wisp of a moustache.

David stared at the first officer and wondered if the man had the know-how and courage to vary the ship's course unnoticed or perhaps sail it in wide circles until all its fuel was used up.

Scott's eyes darted back and forth between the two men, as if suspecting that a silent message was being transmitted. Quickly he interjected, "And the first officer better not play any games. We know where due south is. In addition, Robbie, my colleague with the rose tattoo, has had a fair amount of experience navigating ocean-going yachts. So we'll know if we go off course, and the first officer will be punished for it in a very unpleasant manner."

"But why go through all this?" David argued mildly. "The Navy will never allow you to make landfall in an American port."

"Who said we're going to America?" Scott smirked, then looked over to the first officer. "Due south, and you'd better stay on course."

There was a loud knock on the door. The mutineers abruptly turned and trained their shotguns in the direction of the sound.

"Who is it?" Scott called out.

"Choi," came the response.

"Come in!"

The door opened, and a heavily muscled Asian entered. He was a short, stocky man, with black hair, almond-shaped eyes, and thin lips that seemed pasted together. He gave David a hard stare and waited for him to look away. David stared back and thought this must be the tough who, according to Carolyn, controlled the crew.

"Sir," Choi said, addressing Scott. "All crew with you. They no want to stay on death ship."

"They will leave with us when we reach land," Scott promised. "And you may tell them so."

"Good," Choi said, then asked, "Sir, one problem may be. What if passengers no listen to orders from crew?"

"A little intimidation should take care of that."

Choi smiled thinly.

"Now return to your post and wait for further information," Scott directed. He watched the Asian deckhand leave, then turned to Robbie, who was checking the breech of his 20-gauge Browning shotgun. "Keep an eye on him. I don't trust those sneaky bastards. They'll turn against you as soon as the wind changes."

"They're all that way," Robbie said and closed the breech of his weapon.

Scott signaled Robbie with his hand to follow the Asian, then came back to David. "You will continue looking after the sick people, and as long as you don't interfere with us, we won't interfere with you. If you attempt to contact the outside world, you'll pay a heavy price."

"I'll still have to talk with the Centers for Disease Control in Atlanta," David told him. "They'll be calling the ship for updates. There's no getting around that."

"I know," Scott said, unconcerned. "So we'll monitor your calls in the small, private communications room adjacent to the bridge. Any attempt on your part to alert the CDC will cause us to end the conversation. From that point on, you'll have a shotgun pointed at your head every time you have contact with the outside world. Understood?"

"Understood," David said tonelessly, but he was wondering how Scott knew about the private communications room. Was the chief radio officer a part of the mutiny? Or maybe the security officer who kept the Browning shotguns used for skeet shooting under lock and key? Richard Scott would most likely have tried to persuade someone on the inside to help carry out the mutiny. It would have been the smart move.

"If you have something to say, now is the time to say it," Scott broke into David's thoughts.

"I was thinking about the sick passengers," David lied easily. "In particular, the crew won't assist us in moving patients back to the rooms. I may have to lean on their leader a little."

Scott smiled humorously. "If I were you, I'd be careful around Choi. He can be a very nasty character."

"I'll keep that in mind," David said, unfazed.

Scott gave David a long look before saying, "There's more to you than just being a doctor. You look and act ex-military to me. Maybe you were once an MP. Right?"

Yeah, in a way, David thought. *Special Forces operatives and military police, like cops everywhere, share the common purpose of keeping the slime of the world at bay. I guess that makes me an ex-cop in a generic sense.* David found himself nodding.

"Well, in case you try to overthrow us, I'm going to take some added precautions. We'll post a guard outside your daughter's cabin and keep a close eye on her. She'll be our guarantee that you don't try to upset our plans. Do you get my drift?"

David fought to control his temper, but it still nearly boiled over. For a brief moment, he was tempted to snatch Scott's shotgun from him and quickly pump rounds into the three other mutineers. But it was too risky. Twenty-gauge Brownings didn't require accurate aiming, and even an accidental discharge could blow him to pieces at short range. David took a deep breath and collected himself, then said in a monotone, "If you harm my daughter in any way, you'll be the first to die. And it'll be the worst death you could ever imagine."

Scott shrugged off the threat. "Go about looking after the ill passengers. I'll expect an update every few hours."

David nodded, but Kit was still on his mind. Somehow he'd have to find a way to protect her. "Remember what happens if you hurt my daughter."

Scott shrugged again. "Don't make me come looking for you to get the updates."

As David left the bridge, he glanced out an expansive side window to the pool area below. Dozens of crewmen were strolling about or lounging in chairs, enjoying the bright sun. Some were even splashing in the pool. They were taking the place of the passengers, who were hiding from the virus in their plush cabins. Oh, yeah, David thought darkly, the crew could now enjoy all the pleasures of the *Grand Atlantic*, except for skeet shooting. Only Richard Scott and his band of mutineers would have the shotguns that gave them absolute control. And when the time came for the great escape, the unarmed crew would be let loose and spread ashore like ants, thus providing cover for Scott and his companions. But what was their final destination, and how did they plan to gain entrance to it? David had no answers for those questions.

He hurried down a long passageway, his brain focusing on the weapons Richard Scott had. The shotguns gave Scott an insurmountable advantage and it would be foolhardy to attempt to take him on in a fight. *Without a weapon, I'm at Scott's mercy and there's nothing I can—* David's eyes abruptly narrowed as he remembered the firearms Jonathan Locke had spoken about just after the transfer of command. Was the new captain referring to shotguns or something else?

David picked up the pace, now almost running. He dashed around a corner and came to the section reserved for officers' living quarters. Looking both ways to make certain he wasn't being seen, he quickly knocked on the door to William Rutherford's cabin and entered. The room was stuffy and hot, and had the stale smell of death about it.

Rutherford was dozing and appeared even sicker. He was sweating profusely, and his face was beginning to turn bluish-red, which indicated oxygen deprivation. His strength had ebbed to the point that it required an effort for him to cough.

Opening his eyes, Rutherford slowly turned to David and tried to clear the sputum from his throat. "Has there been some change?"

David nodded gravely. "I'm afraid Richard Scott has taken over the ship. It's a good old-fashioned-type mutiny."

"The imprudent bastard," Rutherford growled. "How did he manage it?"

"He and three of his friends somehow got hold of the shotguns and took over the bridge," David replied.

"And it was easy enough for him to accomplish that." Rutherford paused to cough up some bloody sputum. He wiped the phlegm from his lips before continuing. "All he had to do was say they wanted to enjoy some skeet shooting, and the weapons would have been handed to him without hesitation."

"Or maybe your security officer decided to join them," David suggested.

Rutherford shook his head. "Bob Cooperman has been at sea for over thirty years, half of them with me. He's tried and true."

Well, I suspect one of your officers isn't, David wanted to say, but said nothing because he had no proof.

"Is the crew involved with the mutiny?" Rutherford asked.

"To a man."

"Then Scott has total control of the ship."

"So it would seem."

"There may be a few of the crew who won't voluntarily participate in this cowardly act. They could be of some assistance to you."

"That's unlikely," David told him. "If Choi sees anyone wavering, he'll see to it that they toe the line."

"Be wary of Choi," Rutherford cautioned. "He can be very ill-tempered when provoked, and he's a master of martial arts, which makes him doubly dangerous."

"Have you seen him in action?" David asked.

Rutherford nodded. "A deckhand on the last cruise purposefully tried to provoke a fight with a passenger. Choi stepped in to calm things down, but the deckhand attacked him instead. The deckhand ended up with a fractured jaw and multiple broken ribs."

"Did you actually see Choi do the damage?"

Rutherford nodded again. "From the bridge. He used both his hands and his feet to deliver vicious blows that were lightning-fast."

David guessed that Choi was Korean and knew that country's martial-arts specialty was taekwondo, a tough and brutal form of hand-to-hand combat. In David's estimation, taekwondo was more lethal than karate and more difficult to defend against.

"What about my officers?" Rutherford broke the silence. "Have any of them been harmed?"

"No, they're fine," David answered, again wondering if an officer was involved in the mutiny. Deep down he believed one was, but believing it and proving it were two different things. And he had to know for sure. The last thing he needed at that point was another backstabber. "Can your officers be trusted? I mean, really trusted?"

"I think so," Rutherford said evenly but without strong conviction. "They're all family men, with clean records. But then again, one never knows."

"What about the acting captain?" David asked directly. "Does he have the gumption to stand up to Scott if the need arises?"

"I would say so, as long as his diabetes remains under control," Rutherford replied. "He requires four injections of insulin every day to keep his blood sugar steady."

A brittle diabetic! David groaned. It was another serious medical problem he might have to deal with. "What about the acting first officer? You know, the chubby one with a little mustache."

"He's new to the ship. I can't vouch for him."

Rutherford began to cough violently, bringing up gobs of blood-streaked sputum. With great effort, he cleared his throat, then lay back to gasp and rest. Every breath now seemed a struggle.

David watched the man slowly dying right before his eyes. A good and decent man whom David really liked. But he had to push Rutherford further for more information. It could be critical to his and everybody else's survival. "I've got a few more questions. Do you feel up to it?"

Rutherford nodded weakly.

"We're headed due south on Scott's orders," David said in a rush. "Do you have any idea why and where we're headed?"

Rutherford swallowed heavily, his voice low and hoarse. "My guess is he'll try to make it to some Caribbean island that has no navy or coast guard."

"So he'll sail right in and spread the goddamn virus and start a pandemic."

"Unless someone decides to blow us out of the sea, or somehow disable us."

"Are you referring to our navy?"

"Or the Coast Guard."

"Forget it," David said bluntly. "They'll have no notion as to what's going on. Scott now has complete control of all communications in and out of the *Grand Atlantic*, so there's no way we can inform anybody of the mutiny. I'm afraid we're on our own."

"Bloody Christ!" Rutherford muttered and started coughing again. But the coughs were weak and ineffective and unable to clear the secretions blocking his large bronchi. The captain sucked for air as his complexion turned more cyanotic.

"Just one more thing," David asked quickly. "Locke told me about some firearms the ship has. True or false?"

"True," Rutherford gasped and again tried to clear the thick sputum from his airway. He pointed a trembling finger to a file cabinet beside the desk in his quarters. "The bottom drawer has a combination-lock panel. Punch in two, eight, four to open it. At the back of the drawer is a semiautomatic pistol."

"What make?" David asked hurriedly.

"A Glock, nine-millimeter."

David's face lit up. "How much ammo?"

"A half-dozen clips."

Perfect! David thought, barely able to control his soaring spirits. The semiautomatic Glock could do an incredible amount of damage in only a few seconds. "Do all the officers know about the weapon?"

Rutherford lay back on his pillow, now totally exhausted. He coughed feebly as his eyes closed. "The senior ones do. But they're under strict orders not to touch it unless ordered by me."

David heard a noise in the passageway outside the captain's quarters. It came and went, sounding as if someone was hitting the wall as they walked by. Or maybe someone was opening and closing doors. David crouched down and waited for the sound to disappear. He couldn't believe his good luck. A semiautomatic Glock with 9mm bullets! It was ideal! He could hide the weapon under his short white medical coat until the four mutineers left the bridge and separated. Then he could take them out one by one. He stuffed his stethoscope into the left pocket of his white coat so that it would conceal the bulge made by the pistol beneath it.

Moving quickly to the file cabinet, David punched in the numbers 2, 8, 4 and opened the bottom drawer. He lifted up a stack of papers and stared down into the metal drawer. It was empty! There was no gun or ammunition clips. He rapidly checked the other drawers. No gun! No clips!

David pushed aside his disappointment and glared over to the sleeping sea captain. *Well, Captain Rutherford, now we know for sure that one of your officers was involved in the mutiny.* But which one?

SEVENTEEN

THE ELEVATOR DOOR OPENED on the G level, and David stepped out into a horror show. Outside the sick bay, bodies were stacking up. There were at least a dozen dead and twice the number dying. All the living seemed to be coughing at once, but only a few were wearing their N-95 masks. David shook his head in despair, thinking they were going to need a lot more body bags, and soon.

In his peripheral vision, David saw a pair of burly crewmen emerging from the nearby spa. Their hair was wet and dripping water, like they'd just stepped out of the shower. They gave David a casual look and continued on their way, ignoring the death and suffering around them.

"Hey!" David called out and walked over.

"What do you want?" the shorter of the two crewmen asked.

"I need your help for a while."

"Doing what?"

David pointed to the people on the floor. "Moving these passengers back to their cabins."

"Forget it!" the larger crewman said. "I ain't touching any of those dead people, or any of those live ones either."

"Me neither," the other crewman joined in.

"If you wear gloves and a mask, the virus can't hurt you," David informed them.

"Yeah, right," the larger crewman said sarcastically and motioned to a dead passenger on the floor who had an N-95 mask on. "You mean, like that poor son of a bitch?"

"You won't be actually touching their bodies," David pressed. "Just the wheelchairs and gurneys."

"No way!" the crewmen replied almost simultaneously and walked off.

David glowered after them, furious they wouldn't lend a hand. He wondered if Richard Scott had given them orders not to. After all, the more fear and chaos, the less likely the officers and passengers were to revolt against him. Or were the crew simply frightened of death and the virus that brought it? Either way, David was left with a major problem. The dead and dying on the floor were teeming with the virus and contaminating everything in the sick bay and beyond. And the air would be the most contaminated as patients continued to cough up virus-laden droplets. Again David thought about the N-95 masks being only 75 percent effective at best, with the true effectiveness probably closer to 50 percent. And again he thought they were going to need a lot more body bags.

David entered the reception area and stepped over more sick and dying people. Most were so weak they couldn't call out for help or even reach up to him, like they'd done before. They had given up hope and accepted their impending death. The phones were ringing, all lines lit up. Where the hell were the doctors and nurses? David asked himself, glancing around the chaotic area.

He moved into the examining room and noticed there was now a curtain separating the two tables. To his left, Marilyn was asleep, her head resting on the chest of her dead son. David made a mental note to transfer them out first, then the other dead, then the dying. And by himself, he'd have to put all the dead in body bags. *Shit!* Fighting his fatigue, he pulled back the curtain and saw Carolyn standing beside the examining table, with defibrillation paddles in her hands. The body in front of her was ghostly white.

"David! Thank goodness!" She cried out. "Sol just went into cardiac arrest! He was getting better! I swear to God his breathing was starting to improve, then he crashed!"

David rushed over and looked at the running EKG strip. There was a flat line, with only rare, small blips. "Have you already tried the defibrillator?"

Carolyn nodded hurriedly. "No response at 300 joules."

"Go up to 400!" David directed.

Carolyn quickly reset the defibrillator and placed the paddles on Sol Wyman's chest. "Stand clear!"

The shock caused Sol's body to briefly lift off the examining table, then it settled. Sol remained motionless, his eyes staring up at nothingness.

David peered at the EKG. It showed only a flat line, with no blips at all. "Again!" he shouted.

Another shock went through Sol and lifted his body.

The EKG stayed flat.

"Once more!" David yelled.

The third shock also had no effect. The EKG showed only a flat line.

"Get me a cardiac needle with 1:1000 epinephrine!" David ordered and began CPR, repeatedly compressing Sol's sternum. But to little avail. There was still no evidence for effective circulation. Sol's skin was cold and starting to mottle. The EKG continued to show a straight line.

"Here you go!" Carolyn handed David a syringe with a very long needle attached, and watched him jab the needle through the chest wall and into Sol Wyman's left ventricle. Blood came up into the syringe and David quickly injected a 1:1000 epinephrine.

David gazed down at the EKG and studied the moving flat line. At length, he removed the needle from Sol's chest and discarded it into a nearby trash can. "No good," he pronounced softly.

"Ooooh!" Carolyn moaned and slumped heavily into a metal stool. Her entire body seemed to sag.

David came behind her and began to gently rub her shoulders. "You did everything right and everything you could."

"He was such a sweet man," Carolyn murmured.

"I know."

"And now Marilyn has no one," Carolyn said, "No child, no husband. Nothing. Even if she gets through this outbreak, I doubt that she'll be able to go on."

"She just might turn out to be a lot stronger than you think," David told her.

"Lord! I hope so."

David glanced around at the crowd of sick and dying people, all of whom seemed to be moaning and groaning at the same time. It reminded him of something out of a gothic novel, in which a contagious outbreak decimated the population and quickly overwhelmed the few physicians on hand. But this wasn't the Middle Ages. It was modern-day America, and things like this shouldn't be happening. But they were. And where the hell were the other doctors, who should be helping Carolyn?

"Where is Maggio?" David asked, scanning the sick bay once more.

"He decided to take a break, along with his wife, who's even more useless than he is."

"Terrific," David growled. "And Steiner?"

"With his wife, who has the bird flu for sure."

"Christ!" David grumbled. "That leaves just you and me and Karen."

"And I'm near the breaking point," she said honestly. "In another minute, I'm going to start screaming and yelling and telling everyone to get off their asses and go back to their rooms."

David squeezed her shoulder reassuringly. "You're holding up fine."

"No, I'm not."

A loud chorus of coughs came from the adjoining room. Then someone started to retch, but the sound was drowned out by even harsher coughing. As the noise quieted, a pale, thin pan appeared at the door and appealed, "My wife is about to pass out! Could someone please help me?"

Carolyn sighed wearily. "I'll be right with you."

"Thank you, miss," the man said and hurried away.

With effort, Carolyn pushed herself up and took a deep breath. "I feel like I'm rowing against the tide and close to dropping the oars."

"Can you hold on a little longer?" David implored.

"Not much," she said candidly.

"A little longer," he encouraged. "Now tell me, how many gurneys and wheelchairs do we have?"

"Five wheelchairs, two gurneys."

"So about seven trips to clear out the sick bay."

"But who is going to do the pushing?"

"I'll find somebody," David promised. "In the meantime, I'll send Karen down to lend a hand."

Carolyn made a guttural, disapproving sound. "Any port in a storm, I guess."

"Keep the curtain between Sol and Marilyn closed until I return."

David dashed out and down the passageway, his mind on Carolyn and all the stress she was under. *My God! She's handling a sick bay packed with the sick and dying all by herself. Then she had to deal with a cardiac arrest on top of everything else. And she's doing all this while I wasn't there to direct or assist. It's amazing she lasted as long as she did. Even for an experienced MedEvac nurse like Carolyn, the load is too heavy.*

And she's right about Karen Kellerman not being much help. Anesthesiologists are good at putting patients to sleep and awakening them. Looking after sick people isn't their forte.

Coming to the end of the passageway, David reached for the door to the staircase. As he opened it, there was a loud blast from a shotgun. Instinctively, David dropped to the floor and covered his head while the boom echoed up and down the entire stairwell. In a sudden rush, the flashback came into his mind and caused him to lose his breath. He was back in Somalia, dodging bullets as his Special Forces unit raced across the tarmac to a waiting helicopter. *Jesus!*

Jesus! Got to get back to the 'copter! Got to get out! More incoming! Almost there!

Almost— Then the flashback abruptly ended. Perspiration poured off David's brow and onto the cold floor of the stairwell. He began taking long, deep breaths to gather himself while he waited to see if there would be more shots. Everything stayed still and quiet. Slowly he got to his feet and concentrated his hearing. He heard an angry voice from above.

"The stupid son of a bitch!"

"What the hell was he trying to do?"

"Be a hero, I guess."

"Well, he'll never try it again. That's for damn sure."

David remained motionless as he pondered what to do next. A shotgun had been fired and someone was badly hurt or dead. He had to be careful in case the shooter was trigger-happy or nervous. And in the staircase, he'd be out in the open, with no protection.

"Ahoy, the stairs!" David called out. "This is Dr. Ballineau. May I come up?"

"Come ahead," replied the voice from above.

David cautiously climbed the stairs, keeping his hands in front of him where they could easily be seen. He figured the shotguns would be pointed directly at him. Or would they? For a moment, he wondered if the staircase would be the place to make his move. The two mutineers—assuming there were only two—would be close together. But the space was confined, and that could make things very dicey, particularly when dealing with shotguns.

Up on the next level, Richard Scott and Robbie were waiting for him, their shotguns at the ready. They were standing over a body with the right side of its chest blown off. There were blood and tissue parts splattered against the walls and stairs.

David peered down at the body and saw the face of Arthur Maggio. His eyes were wide open, as if showing surprise at being shot and killed.

"You can't do anything for him," Scott said matter-of-factly.

"Why in the world did you shoot him?" David demanded.

"He lunged at my weapon," Scott replied. "We were coming up the stairs, he was coming down. Suddenly and for no reason, he jumped at us. I barely had time to react."

"Yeah," Robbie confirmed. "He went right for the shotgun. I'll swear to that on a stack of Bibles."

Bullshit, David was thinking. Maggio was a gentle, little man who would never go up against a shotgun. More likely, he stumbled on the stairs and was reaching out to break his fall.

"You look like you don't believe us," Scott said.

David shrugged. "You two were the only witnesses."

"Damn right!" Robbie said, nodding firmly. "The old bastard decided to go out in a blaze of glory."

"Old men don't do blaze-of-glory acts," David countered. "They see the end of their days coming, and they don't do things to hurry it up."

Robbie tensed noticeably and tried to put a mean edge to his voice. "Are you doubting my word?"

David shook his head. "Just Maggio's motive."

"Good," Robbie said and gave David a hard stare. "Because you don't want to call me a liar, do you?"

"No, I don't," David replied, now noticing the changes in Robbie's voice and posture. The mutineer was trying to give the impression he was tough, but David could sense the man's uneasiness. The mutineer was unsettled. He was unaccustomed to blood and guts. "Would you mind pointing your shotgun at something other than me?"

"It bothers you, eh?" Robbie grinned and jabbed the 20-gauge Browning at him.

"A lot."

Robbie's grin grew wider. He kept the shotgun aimed at David.

Richard Scott was examining the body of Arthur Maggio. He used his foot to turn it over, so that Maggio was now on his back. "I'd say his death was accidental and instantaneous. Wouldn't you agree, doctor?"

David nodded, now seeing the full extent of the damage caused by the shotgun blast. The right side of Maggio's chest was blown open, with his ribs and lungs shredded into almost unrecognizable pieces. The liver was completely gone, but the gallbladder and adjacent intestines remained intact. "He never knew what hit him."

"Well," Scott concluded with an uncaring shrug, "he had lived long enough."

"I hope you're not going to leave him here," David said.

"Oh, no," Scott assured. "We'll put all his pieces in a body bag. We have to keep the staircase nice and tidy for our passengers."

Robbie found Scott's last statement humorous and chuckled loudly.

Scott gave him a stern look, and the chuckling stopped. "I want everything cleaned up immediately," he went on. "There's to be no trace of blood or body tissue anywhere. Select two of the most experienced deckhands to do the job."

"How will I know who to pick?" Robbie queried.

"Ask Choi."

David was suddenly aware of how badly he had underestimated Richard Scott. At first, he thought Scott was just a headstrong braggart who was athletically gifted and knew how to handle a shotgun. But Scott was much more than that. The man knew how to plan and carry out a mission, and which men he could use and control. And then there was his reaction to blowing Arthur Maggio to bits with a shotgun at close range. He had none! It was like he'd killed a fly. The man was unfazed by brutal death. David wondered if Scott was a former military officer who had seen combat. Or maybe he was a psychopath. And that would make him even more dangerous.

"What are you going to do with the doc?" Robbie asked. "He could say we gunned down the old man."

"He didn't witness anything," Scott said. "It would be his word against ours."

"I guess," Robbie agreed hesitantly. "But they might believe him—him being a doctor and all."

"Well," Scott said, after giving the matter more thought, "we can always cross that bridge later."

"Yeah, later," Robbie nodded, and when Scott wasn't looking, he ran his finger across his throat and grinned menacingly at David.

We'll never cross that bridge, David thought to himself, *because I plan on killing both of you before you can kill me. And then I'll put you two in body bags, right alongside Arthur Maggio, who you murdered.*

Scott gestured with his weapon to the staircase. "You can go now, Dr. Ballineau."

David started up the stairs, slow and easy, not bothering to look back. He didn't have to. He could sense the shotguns following his every step.

"And you'd be smart not to mention this to anyone," Scott called after him.

"Right," David said, deciding to kill the investment banker first. He'd pick the time and method later.

EIGHTEEN

"I'M DYING!" JUANITA GROANED.

"No, you're not," David told her.

"I feel like I'm dying," Juanita insisted.

"Feeling like it and doing it are two different things," David said. "Now be quiet while I listen to your lungs."

He placed his stethoscope on the nanny's chest and heard scattered crackles and rhonchi, but now there were far more loud wheezes. It was an ominous sign that indicated Juanita's airway was becoming obstructed with blood and mucus. And David knew the worst was yet to come.

"So?" Juanita questioned as she watched him put away his stethoscope.

"So far, so good," he lied.

"Hmm," she moaned, not believing him. Juanita leaned back heavily on her pillow before saying, "I have become a burden."

"No, you haven't."

"I was supposed to look after the Little One and now I can't."

"She's doing fine, and she'll continue to do fine until you get better."

"Please, God! Watch over her," Juanita prayed and crossed herself, then added, "with or without me."

"You're not going anywhere," David said.

"That is in God's hands," Juanita said and gave him a very long look as if trying to read his mind. "You will remember where I am to be buried."

"I will remember."

"And the Little One is not to attend my funeral."

"She'll demand to be there."

"You are her father!" Juanita raised her voice. "You will make that decision."

David shook his head. "She's Marianne's daughter and just as headstrong."

"She will cry."

"Only if you die."

Juanita crossed herself once more and said, "It is in God's hands."

David patted her shoulder reassuringly, but he was thinking that none of the sick aboard the *Grand Atlantic* were going to be buried where they wanted. In all likelihood, the dead would be incinerated, because it wouldn't make sense to put the deadly virus in the ground where it could sit and wait to infect its next host and start a pandemic that would kill millions and millions. For a brief moment, David considered his own mortality. *Whoever thought it would end this way?* he asked himself as he reached for the door handle. *On a luxury liner with a deadly virus, for Chrissakes!*

He opened the door and stepped out into the passageway, and came face to face with Choi. The stocky, muscular Asian was standing outside Kit's cabin, with his arms folded across his chest. He stayed in front of Kit's door, refusing to budge an inch.

"I'd like to see my daughter," David requested.

"No," Choi said curtly.

"What the hell do you mean, *no*?" David growled.

Choi uncrossed his arms and flexed his huge deltoid muscles. "Move on or you get hurt."

Choi never saw the blow coming.

David's fist caught him flush on the forehead, just above the bridge of his nose. Choi sank to the floor, stunned by the vicious punch. He tried to get to his feet as blood streamed out of both nostrils.

David smashed his fist into Choi's forehead again, and the crewman fell to the floor in a heap. Quickly David reached in his pocket for a roll of duct tape and bound Choi's hands together behind his back. He grabbed Choi's collar and dragged him to his feet. A half-smile came to David's face as he said, "We have a little business to attend to."

Choi could barely stand, but David held him up by the back of his shirt and pushed him down the passageway into a waiting elevator. As the elevator ascended, Choi regained his senses and struggled mightily to free his hands.

He twisted and turned, but the tape held. Out of desperation, Choi tried to butt David with his head. David stepped aside and kneed the crewman in the groin, then watched the man bend over in pain.

"Be nice," David said hoarsely.

Choi retched and brought up some bilious vomit, which he spat on the floor. He stared at David hatefully, then again twisted and turned in an effort to free himself from the tape.

David pushed Choi up against the rear wall of the elevator and said coldly, "I've got a surprise for you. I'm going to get you off this ship."

The elevator came to a stop, and the door opened into bright sunlight. David pushed Choi out onto the deck. There were at least two dozen crewmen milling about the pool area or enjoying drinks at the bar. Every one of them stopped and stared at the pair by the elevator, unable to figure out what was happening.

"Take him down!" Choi yelled.

"One more word and I'll snap your goddamn neck," David said in a voice loud enough for everybody to hear.

None of the crew moved.

"Now we're going over to the railing," David went on, watching the crowd and trying to pick out who was the most likely to lead them. His eyes settled on a broad-shouldered deckhand with a jagged scar on his cheek and a sheathed knife hanging from his belt. "If you crewmen are smart, you'll make way."

The crowd of crewmen began to move aside, but the deckhand with the facial scar didn't budge. Instead, he stepped forward, his hand now resting on the handle of his knife. "Let him go, doc, and we won't hurt you."

"Come get him," David said evenly.

The deckhand was a large man, only slightly taller than David but at least forty pounds heavier. His face and posture indicated he'd been in more than a few fights. "Don't do anything stupid, doc," he warned in an Australian accent.

"Right," David said and drove his fist into Choi's ribs. Choi dropped to his knees and tried to catch his breath. "You stay put."

"Bad mistake, doc," the deckhand growled. "Now I've got to hurt you."

He tensed his muscles and sprang forward with remarkable speed. But David anticipated the move and ducked under the deckhand's outstretched arm, then delivered a powerful blow to the Australian's trachea. The man dropped to the deck, clutching his throat and gasping for air. To make sure the deckhand remained down, David kicked him in the base of his spine and watched the man writhe in pain.

The crowd of crewmen froze in place, stunned by the doctor's viciousness. Seconds ticked by before they began murmuring among themselves.

"Jesus Christ! Did you see that?"

"That was mean, man! Really mean!"

"What the hell kind of doctor is that?"

David leaned down and removed the deckhand's knife from its sheath. It was a large knife, with a thick handle and a sharp, ten-inch blade. David held the knife up for all to see. "The next man who comes too close dies."

The crowd remained motionless as they watched David reach for a large coil of rope and tie Choi up in a peculiar fashion. The rope went around Choi's waist and between his thighs, then up the front of his body and over his shoulders before being knotted in the back.

"There," David said and gave the rope an extra tug to make certain the knot was secure. "Now, as I promised, it's off the ship for you."

He lifted Choi up over the railing and slowly lowered him until he was halfway down to the waterline. After tying the rope to the railing, David held the blade of the deckhand's knife against the knot and addressed the gathering of crewmen. "I want seven of you to go to the sick bay and help transport the ill passengers back to their cabins."

Nobody moved.

"Or I start cutting through the rope," David threatened.

Still no one moved.

David began to slowly saw through the rope. From over the side, Choi was yelling, but the wind was blowing and it muted his cries. "I'm about a quarter of the way through," David called out.

"You can't get all of us," challenged a burly crewman, with very thick arms. He stepped forward, unafraid. "And you're backed up into a corner."

David recognized the crewman as one of the two he had seen earlier leaving the spa. "You didn't want to lend a hand before, did you?"

"And I'm not going to lend one now."

"Okay," David said calmly and walked briskly over to the crewman, catching him by surprise. Before the crewman could react, David stomped down on the man's foot and broke all the metatarsal bones. The burly man fell to the deck and, grabbing his foot, howled in pain.

"Now once I've cut Choi's rope and he's in the water, I'll throw this dumb son of a bitch in after him," David continued on. "And then I'll come for all of you, until either you're dead or I am."

"He's bluffing," someone in the crowd said.

"There's one way to find out." David returned to the railing and began sawing at the rope again. "I figure I'm about halfway through, or maybe a little more than that."

"Jesus Christ!" a voice muttered. "He's really going to do it!"

"It'll be murder!" another voice said.

"Who gives a shit?" a third voice joined in. "Unless we reach land soon, we'll all going to be dead anyhow."

The crowd of crewmen went silent, their collective gazes fixed on the doctor holding a knife against the rope. To a man they all wondered if he would cut through the rope and drop Choi into the ocean. And to a man, they all decided he would.

A lanky crewman, in his early thirties, with straight blond hair, moved forward and asked, "Do we have to touch these people?"

"No," David answered. "All you have to do is push wheelchairs and stretchers back to the passengers' rooms."

"O-okay," the crewman said hesitantly.

"And Choi stays where he is until all those people are cleared out of the sick bay," David added.

"Okay," the crewman said again. He walked over to the elevator and a half-dozen others followed him.

From the deck below, Choi was screaming his lungs out in a foreign language. His voice didn't sound nearly as tough as before.

NINETEEN

RICHARD SCOTT GLARED AT David, who still had a knife on the rope that held Choi in suspension over the side of the *Grand Atlantic*. David stared back, his eyes on Scott's shotgun that was pointed at him. The crew was now bunched up behind Scott, all silent and waiting to see which man would give in first.

"Pull Choi up!" Scott demanded.

"Not until every single patient has been moved out of the sick bay," David told him.

"And what if I say that they've all been moved?"

"Then I say prove it." In his peripheral vision, David spotted Robbie high up on the bridge, with his shotgun aimed directly downward. "And order your friend on the bridge to raise his weapon. It's making me nervous, and I might accidentally cut through this rope."

Scott signaled to Robbie, and the shotgun on the bridge disappeared from view. Then he came back to David. "You're making a big mistake."

"Not as big as the one Choi made," David countered.

"Which was?"

"He wouldn't allow me to see my daughter."

"You should have brought that to my attention."

"I did. That's why we're standing out here on the deck."

A hollow smile came to Scott's face, but it vanished quickly. "His mistake can be remedied. Yours can't."

David remained silent and wondered why Scott was dragging things out. The man was either waiting for the right moment to mount a surprise attack or, less likely, for convincing evidence that the sick passengers had all been moved. Which? A surprise attack, David decided.

"The giant mistake you made was dishonoring Choi," Scott went on. "The Asians call it a loss of face. With them, that's very important."

"So?"

"So he'll kill you the first chance he gets." Scott paused for effect and glanced over his shoulder at the deckhands. "And the crew will be glad to help him because of the damage you did to their friends."

The crew joined in, apparently liking the idea of tearing David apart.

"Yeah!" cried out a voice from the rear.

"Damn right!" bellowed another.

"Who needs a doctor now anyway?"

"You do," David answered the third voice. "Because if you get sick, you'll hope to God I'm here to help and maybe ease some of your suffering. And when the experimental drugs come to treat the virus, you'll sure as hell need me to administer them."

The crowd murmured excitedly at the glimmer of hope. A drug! Something that could save them!

"What drugs?" Scott pressed him.

"You'll see," David said vaguely, and knew he'd thrown the crew off balance. And David could see from Scott's expression that the banker knew it, too. The crewmen would be harder to control now.

"You said experimental drugs," Scott argued mildly. "Have they ever been tried in humans?"

David shrugged.

"They probably used the damn things in rats," Scott reckoned. "And who knows what happened to those rats when they received the drug?"

"They seemed to improve," David lied easily.

"I'm still in favor of getting off this ship," Scott said. "I'm not waiting around to catch this killer virus, then be a guinea pig for some drug that might help rats."

"I'm with you," a voice in the crowd yelled out. "I'll take my chances ashore."

"Me too," another chimed in. "I don't want some drug that's never been used in people."

Scott nodded firmly, now certain he had regained control of the crowd. He gave David a stern look and said impatiently, "Get Choi up!"

David stayed motionless.

Scott raised his shotgun and aimed it at David's head. "One last time," he threatened.

David increased the pressure on the blade of his knife. A thick strand of the rope popped and flew up into the air. Choi must have sensed it because he started screaming again.

No one moved or even breathed. It was a Mexican standoff. Somebody was about to die.

Seconds ticked off. The tension in the air was almost suffocating.

David placed more pressure on the knife. Another strand of rope popped.

Suddenly the door to the passageway opened. The lanky, blond crewman who had volunteered to move the sick passengers hopped out onto the deck and announced, "The patients are all back in their cabins!"

The crowd collectively breathed a sigh of relief.

"I need proof," David said at once, his knife still on the rope.

"The nurse knew you would," the crewman said. "She told me to give you the password. It's Beaumont."

David took the knife away from the rope. He hadn't discussed a password with Carolyn, but she knew he'd demand one. *Smart! She was so damn smart! And the word she'd chosen was known to only a very few aboard the ship.*

Beaumont was the name of the private pavilion at University Hospital where Carolyn was head nurse. Finally, David said, "You can have Choi back now."

Scott gestured to the crew with his shotgun, and a dozen men rushed over to the rope and hoisted Choi up. As he was lifted over the railing, the crewmen cheered, as though they were welcoming a hero home.

The tape was cut from Choi's wrists, and he rubbed at them to get the circulation going. As the tangle of rope was removed from his torso, Choi turned to David and gave him a long, mean look. His thin lips seemed to disappear. There was only a slit where his mouth should have been. In a monotone, he uttered something in Korean. It sounded like a death sentence.

David raised the knife he was holding and expertly threw it down to the deck, just in front of Choi. It stuck straight up, deep into the wood. The message David was sending was clear. *Don't fuck with me!*

The message didn't seem to bother Choi. His hateful expression didn't change.

From high on the bridge, Robbie yelled down, "The CDC is on the line."

"Let's go," Scott said and prodded David with his shotgun toward the elevator. The crowd parted to give them room. One of the deck-hands reached out to pat Scott's shoulder in a congratulatory fashion. Scott glowered at the man, who quickly backed away and disappeared into the throng.

"Move faster," he ordered David and pushed him into the elevator.

As the elevator ascended, David concentrated on possible ways to alert the CDC that a mutiny was taking place aboard the *Grand Atlantic*. Maybe he could use a code word that they would hopefully understand. *But then again, they—*

"You're tougher than I thought," Scott broke into David's thoughts.

David shrugged.

"Ex-military, huh?" Scott asked and waited for an answer that didn't come. "MP, right?"

David nodded slowly, as if giving out privileged information.

"Marines, I'd guess."

David nodded again.

"Where were you stationed?"

This was not a casual conversation, but a quiz, David decided. Scott wanted to find out if David had in fact been an MP or something else, like a Green Beret or Navy SEAL. Someone he would really have to fear. Finally, David said, "A lot of places."

"Where was your last assignment?"

"Pendleton," David replied, figuring that an investment banker didn't know much about a Marine base outside San Diego.

"Ah-huh," Scott said, still measuring David.

The elevator came to a stop, and the door opened. They hurried through the bridge and into the small communications room. Robbie was standing off to the side, with his shotgun pointed at the chief radio officer. The light atop the speakerphone was blinking green.

"I've got the CDC on the line," the chief radio officer called over.

As David sat, Scott reached out and put his finger on the phone's hold button. "Remember, any tricks and the call ends."

David again tried to think of a way to stealthily alert the CDC that the ship was now in the hands of mutineers. But nothing worthwhile came to mind. And a clumsy attempt was worse than no attempt at all. That would make future calls to the CDC very limited, and David needed all the help he could get.

He leaned forward and spoke into the phone.

"Ballineau, here."

"Good afternoon, Dr. Ballineau," Lawrence Lindberg said.

"There's nothing good about it."

"Well, it's about to get worse," Lindberg warned. "I'm afraid the virus is totally resistant to Tamiflu and Relenza, as well as all the other antiviral agents. We have a few experimental drugs we are now testing, but they've never been tried on humans."

Scott nodded to himself. It was just as he'd thought. There weren't any experimental drugs to treat them, and there wouldn't be any in the immediate future either. His plan to jump ship and get away from the virus was looking better and better. He jerked his head toward David, now aware that the silence on the other end was lasting too long. "Say something," he whispered to David.

"Never been tried in humans, eh?" David asked hastily.

"Never."

"Well, at the rate we're going, there won't be any humans left to test them on."

"How many sick do you have?"

"Over a hundred and climbing," David reported. "And we already have dozens dead, and only four of them had underlying conditions that weakened their defenses. Two had HIV infections, one with diabetes."

"And the fourth?"

"A young boy who inhaled repeated, huge doses of the virus from the dying bird."

There was a long pause before Lindberg asked, "Are the other flu victims afflicted with the severe form of the disease?"

"So it would appear," David answered. "Dozens more are dying, and dozens more will almost surely follow."

"Bad, bad," Lindberg muttered to himself, then raised his voice. "Did you receive the new supply of N-95 masks and body bags?"

"Affirmative," David replied. "But they were dropped onto the deck by your helicopter, and the heavy crates split the already badly damaged heliport wide open. It's totally useless now."

"Unfortunate."

Was it? David asked himself suspiciously. He wondered if that was done on purpose, in order to make doubly sure no helicopters could land on the *Grand Atlantic*. David shook his head at his paranoia and dismissed the idea, but the useless heliport did make one thing certain. Now, badly needed doctors and nurses could not be airlifted to the ship under any circumstances.

"Ballineau?" Lindberg broke the silence.

"Yeah," David answered, his mind going back to the fact that no antiviral agents were available to combat the virus. "Is some sort of vaccine possible?"

"It would take at least a year to produce, test, and distribute any vaccine," Lindberg said. "With no guarantee for success, of course."

"I figured," David said sourly. "So we just make do and stay on our current course, eh?"

"For now," Lindberg replied. "But there's a storm warning in the Leeward Islands at present. It probably won't reach you, but it's a possibility. How is your weather?"

"Calm," David said, and suddenly saw an opening to warn the CDC that the *Grand Atlantic* was in even greater distress now that a mutiny had taken place. "It's like a day in May."

Scott quickly reached over and punched the hold button on the speakerphone. "Don't try that again," he growled.

"What?" David asked innocently.

"That Mayday bullshit!"

"Christ! You're paranoid!" David snapped, desperately trying to cover his clumsy, foolhardy attempt to warn the CDC. "That's an academic doctor on the other end. He wouldn't know Mayday from a day in June."

"Maybe," Scott said, unconvinced. "Now, finish your call and talk strictly in medical terms." He reached for the phone and switched off the hold button, then aimed his shotgun at David's head. "Strictly medical terms," he repeated quietly.

David leaned to the speakerphone and said, "Sorry about the interruption, but I just got a call from the sick bay, where I'm needed. Is there anything else?"

"One final item," Lindberg told him. "You're going to have to establish a let-die list."

"A what?" David asked, not certain he'd heard Lindberg's instructions correctly.

"A let-die list," Lindberg said again. "You should attend to only those who have a chance to survive."

"There won't be too many of those," David said pessimistically.

"Would the number of survivors increase if we managed to get you some ventilators?"

David hesitated as he considered the offer. "The ventilators would help a lot. But the problem is we don't have the staff to monitor the patients on them. And patients on ventilators need to be constantly monitored or they can develop all sorts of complications."

"Can you do the monitoring?" Lindberg asked.

"Of course, and so can the nurse and anesthesiologist we have on board. But at best, we'll only be able to monitor seven or eight patients, and that's a stretch, particularly if they have to be intubated."

"Then we'll have a Navy ship ferry over eight ventilators, with the appropriate monitors."

"We need more antibiotics as well," David told him. "And a lot more body bags."

"I'll see to it," Lindberg said. "Now let's get back to the let-die list. These are patients who wouldn't survive, even under the best of conditions. This group should include those on chemotherapy, transplant patients, diabetics, the elderly, and anyone with AIDS, cancer, or chronic pulmonary disease. You shouldn't waste any of your resources or manpower on these individuals."

"Are you saying to just move them aside and let them die?"

"That's exactly what' I'm saying."

"Jesus Christ!" David groaned. "It's like being on the train platform at Auschwitz and deciding who should live and who should die."

"Sadly, yes, "Lindberg said. "It does resemble that."

The phone went dead.

TWENTY

DAVID TOOK THE STAIRS down, the let-die list still on his mind. *A goddamn let-die list*, he thought bitterly. It sounded like something Charles Dickens would write. But this wasn't fiction. It was real life, and soon he'd have to devise a triage system to separate the sure-to-die from the hope-to-live. Carolyn could help with that.

David left the stairwell and entered a long passageway. He passed a pair of deckhands who were mopping the interior of an elevator with disinfectant. Both were masked and wearing gloves. They nodded to David and he nodded back. They obviously weren't as hostile as the other crew members and not as stupid either. They were doing their best to avoid the avian flu virus until they could jump ship.

Up ahead he saw a solitary, motionless figure with his hands on his hips, waiting for him. It was Choi. David glanced around and hoped to see one of the armed mutineers who might intercede. But, except for him and Choi, the passageway was deserted.

David slowed and prepared himself, all the while looking for an edge. There wasn't any. And this time he wouldn't have the element of surprise working for him, which was a big disadvantage.

He watched Choi move to the center of the passageway, effectively blocking it off. Then the Asian assumed a fighting stance. His feet were apart, the left in front of the right, his arms hanging loosely but bent at the elbows and ready to spring into action. And now he had a knife in his belt. A big knife.

David slowed even more. He had his eyes locked onto Choi's, but he was still searching for an opening. He moved a few inches to the right. Choi moved with him. Seconds ticked by in the ominous silence. Carefully David wiggled out of his short white coat and wrapped it around his forearm. A hint of a smile crossed Choi's face as he gradually moved his hand up. Now it was at the level of his hip and a lot closer to his knife.

Parry the thrust of his knife, David thought rapidly, then go for the eyes or testicles, whichever was open. He took a measured step forward. Choi's smile grew.

"You're blocking the goddamn passageway!" a voice boomed out from behind Choi.

Choi turned hastily and saw a large man, with reddish-gray hair and a square jaw, staring down at him. He was dressed in a green warmup outfit that had the words FIGHTING IRISH on the front of the jersey.

"You go other way," Choi ordered.

The big man didn't budge. He was two heads taller than Choi and forty pounds heavier, with hands the size of hams. "Don't push," he said hoarsely. "I ain't in the mood for it."

Choi hesitated as his eyes darted back and forth between David and the FIGHTING IRISH. He appeared to be weighing his chances against the two. It didn't take him long to reach a decision. With a scowl, he turned and walked away.

The man watched Choi leave, then came over to David. "They think they own the damn ship."

"In a way, I guess they do," David said.

"Nah," the man disagreed easily. "They're still prisoners, just like we are. This ship is one giant brig."

David nodded, noting the man's use of the word *brig*. He had to be ex-Navy or ex-Marine. Sticking out his hand, David introduced himself. "I'm David Ballineau."

"I know who you are," the man said and shook David's hand with a grip that felt like an iron vise. "I'm Tom Sullivan in cabin 408." He pointed over his shoulder with his thumb. "And I was coming to get you, doc. I think my wife has caught the damn virus. She's coughing her head off."

"Does she have any fever?"

"Some."

"Any shortness of breath?"

"Only after a bad bout of coughing," Sullivan replied. "She's not a strong person, doc, and she has some other medical problems. I suspect that's why the flu is hitting her so hard."

A door down the passageway slammed loudly, then slammed again. They waited for the noise to subside.

"A goddamn bird virus," Sullivan went on disgustedly. "And we took all those shots for the regular flu and swine flu and everything in between, and it hasn't done us a bit of good."

"The avian flu virus is a different type of virus," David told him.

"Yeah, and there's no shot for it." Sullivan coughed and used a hand to cover it. Then he coughed again. "It looks like the virus is getting to me, too."

From the sound of his voice, he didn't seem concerned about having the avian flu. His tone was almost matter-of-fact, David thought. "Are you coughing up blood?"

"Not yet," Sullivan said. "I was told that comes later."

Again Sullivan's voice showed no real concern. "Aren't you worried about it?" David found himself asking.

Sullivan shrugged. "Worry doesn't do anything for you. I learned that during two tours in Vietnam." He paused as a faraway look came and went from his face. "It's always out there, waiting for you."

The *it* Sullivan was referring to was death. David had the same fatalistic outlook as Sullivan, as did most men who had gone into combat over and over again and survived. Death was always out there, waiting for you, waiting for the opportunity to step in and complete its mission. And sooner or later, it eventually did.

"Well," Sullivan continued on. "I'm going up to the dining room to grab a bite, and get a little something for the wife. I want to be there before the crowd arrives."

"I'm surprised a crowd still shows up," David said. "I'd think people wouldn't want to gather in close proximity to one another."

"They only come in during the evening hours, when their appetites get the better of them. But even then, they give each other plenty of space and get the hell out as soon as they can. It's like a mess hall in a brig. There's not a lot of socializing."

David wondered about the mood of the ambulatory passengers and whether they planned to join in the revolt. "Have you had a chance to talk with the other passengers over the past few days?"

"Yeah," Sullivan answered. "I've chatted with some up on deck."

"How do they feel about Scott and his bunch taking over the *Grand Atlantic*?"

"It doesn't particularly bother them. They figure it doesn't change things a whole lot. They're still trapped on a ship with a virus that's going to kill them."

"But deep down they must be hoping that Scott can get them ashore."

"Why, hell yes! That beats staying on this ship forever, doesn't it?"

"I guess," David said, then added as he walked away, "I'll check on your wife in just a bit."

David hurried down the passageway and made a mental note to examine Tom Sullivan's wife after he checked on Kit. He recalled Sullivan saying that his wife had other medical problems, and that could be a death sentence according to the CDC. A *let-die list*, they called it. What a bullshit term! Most of the passengers, if not all of them, were going to die. He didn't need a list to tell him that.

Up ahead he saw Kit's cabin and quickly inspected the rest of the passageway. Choi wasn't around, but David knew he'd be back soon because now it was kill or be killed between the two of them. *I should have cut the rope and let him drown or, better yet, just dragged him into a cabin and thrown him overboard from the balcony*. Nobody would have really cared. Not the self-absorbed Richard Scott, not the passengers, not even the mutinous crew, who would have quickly gotten over it and picked a new leader. *Yeah, in retrospect, I should have killed him*, David thought on, without a hint of emotion. His total lack of feeling didn't bother him because he was aware of what he had become yet again. He was once more the stone-cold killer that he had kept hidden for all those years. But it was never really locked away. It was always there, waiting to surface, compliments of the Special Forces.

He reached Kit's door and, after knocking gently, entered. Karen arose from the sofa and pressed a finger to her lips.

"She's sleeping," Karen whispered.

"Is she feeling okay?" David whispered back.

"She's fine."

They walked out to the balcony overlooking the sea. The water was calm, the air fresh and cool, twilight now setting in. A giant half moon was making its appearance.

Karen rested her head on David's shoulder and said longingly, "We should be up on deck, dressed to the nines, and enjoying chilled martinis."

"The only thing up on deck is a rebellious crew that would happily slit my throat open," David said.

Karen nodded. "Carolyn phoned and told me all about it. Can't anyone control them?"

"Yeah, Richard Scott. But only when he wants to."

"This reminds me of *Mutiny on the Bounty*."

"Except there's no friendly island waiting to welcome us."

Karen paused for a moment before asking, "Is there any way out of this?"

"One," David answered. "But you don't want to hear it. It's not a happy ending."

"So we're all going to die."

"Unless there's some kind of miracle."

"Do you believe in miracles?"

"No."

Karen snuggled her head closer to him, her silky blond hair brushing his cheek. "Why do I keep thinking you're going to come up with a magic answer and save us all?"

"Because you like Hollywood endings."

"I'll tell you something else I like," she breathed softly. "You."

"I'm already taken," David said tonelessly.

Karen shook her head. "Carolyn is not really your type. She doesn't have my spark, and you like sparks, don't you, David Ballineau?"

David shrugged. "Sparks come and go in a hurry."

"They can also start fires," Karen said and pressed up against him. "Real hot fires."

David felt himself stir despite his effort to resist her. *Get away from her!* He commanded his feet, but they stayed in place. There was something about Karen's sensuality that attracted him and always would. But she had betrayed him once, and given the opportunity he believed she'd do it again. He glanced over at her. Even in the bright light, she still had a flawless beauty. But there was a cold, calculating presence to it. Carolyn had once remarked that Karen had the warmth of a blackjack dealer. At length, David said, "What we had together is in the past. You should leave it there."

"No way!" Karen said immediately. "It was too good not to go back to."

David shrugged indifferently, thinking he sure as hell wasn't going back to her. Not when he had someone as warm and wonderful as Carolyn. *The past is the past and I intend to keep it there.*

He pushed himself away and said, "Let's return to the business at hand, beginning with the new flu victims. The really sick are piling up on us, and it's going to get worse."

"I know," Karen said. "Carolyn told me she had moved out most of the people in the sick bay, but it was filling up again with even sicker patients."

"We have to go down there and help her out," David said and glanced back into the cabin. "But I hate to leave Kit alone."

"She's sound asleep and will stay that way for a while," Karen assured. "And she's no longer just a little girl. She'll do fine on her own."

"Yeah, I guess," David said with uncertainty.

He tiptoed quietly into the bedroom and over to Kit's bed. She was sound asleep, hugging her favorite teddy bear, with her raven hair spread out on the white, cotton pillowcase. He stared at her for a long moment, loving her more than anything on the face of the earth. With care, he leaned over and kissed her forehead.

Kit opened her eyes and drowsily said, "Hi, Dad."

"Hi, sweetheart," David said softly. "Karen and I will be gone for a little while. We're going to help Carolyn in the sick bay."

Kit nodded and immediately went back to sleep, still hugging her teddy bear. David kissed her forehead again and tiptoed out of the bedroom. He motioned to Karen to close the sliding glass door to the balcony and, when she had, they left the cabin and gently shut the door behind them.

They didn't hear Kit cough. And they didn't hear her next cough, which was deep and raspy and even louder.

TWENTY-ONE

DAVID KNOCKED ON THE door of cabin 408 and heard a weak voice from within call out, "Come in."

He entered and found a small, slim woman, with dyed black hair, sprawled across a couch in the sitting room. Everything about her was petite except for her chest, which was barrel-shaped.

"Mrs. Sullivan, I'm Dr. Ballineau," he introduced himself. "Your husband asked me to stop by and see you."

"Oh, thank you so much for taking the time," she said and seemed out of breath from the relatively short sentence. "I know you must be very busy."

"I'm managing to keep up," he lied. "Now tell me, how are you feeling?"

"Not so good," she reported and coughed a wet, noisy cough. "I'm afraid my chronic bronchitis is making things a lot worse."

David nodded. Those were the medical conditions Tom Sullivan had mentioned earlier. She had chronic bronchitis and, judging from the shape of her chest, severe emphysema. She would be the first on the let-die list.

"From too many cigarettes," she added.

David nodded again. "I hope you're not still smoking."

"Only when Notre Dame is in a close football game," she said with a smile. "My friends call me Bunny, by the way."

"And you can call me David," he said, liking the woman immediately. "Let me ask you a few questions."

"Sure."

"Do you feel feverish?"

"Only after the chills come and go."

"Are you coughing up blood?"

"A little."

"And your husband told me that your shortness of breath is getting worse."

Bunny Sullivan nodded. "My inhaler isn't helping like before."

David took out his stethoscope and listened to her chest. It was filled with crackles and wheezes. And her skin felt warm. He estimated her fever at 101°. There was no doubt about the diagnosis of avian influenza. "Do you have antibiotics on hand?"

"Cipro," she replied. "And I'm taking it twice a day."

"Stay on it," David told her. "Did you bring a humidifier aboard?"

"Sure did."

"Use it, and have your husband help you clear your lungs."

"He's doing that already."

"Tell him to do it more."

Bunny had a coughing spell that went on and on. It took her a long time to catch her breath. She swallowed back the phlegm in her throat and asked finally, "Are we going to get out of this alive?"

"If we're really, really lucky."

"Do you think we'll be lucky?"

"No," he said honestly.

Bunny fingered the golden crucifix that hung from her neck. "I'll pray for us."

"Can't hurt."

David stopped into the passageway and committed the cabin number to memory. 408. Its door would be painted red. Bunny Sullivan would be left unattended. She would die in cabin 408.

He took the elevator down to the G level, sharing it with a middle-aged couple who were coughing their heads off. Their N-95 masks were bloodstained and clearly overloaded. David could envision the avian flu virus swarming through the soaked masks and pouring into the stale air of the elevator. He kept his head down and a hand over his own mask, giving himself as much protection as possible. The couple kept coughing.

The elevator jerked to a stop. The door opened to a chorus of moans and groans and coughs. The passageway from the sick bay to the beauty spa was again jammed with ill patients. David stepped aside to allow the couple next to him to rush out and join the crowd of the sick and dying. *Yeah*, David thought grimly. *Hurry up and get in line for a doctor who can't do anything for you.*

He moved through the mass of patients, carefully avoiding their outstretched arms and legs. The coughs were coming up at him in sprays. Hurriedly, he put a hand over his mask once more to protect himself from the airborne droplets. But he knew he was hoping against hope. The virus in the droplets would still stick to his clothes, ready to jump into his airway at the first opportunity. As he reached the entrance to the sick bay, he heard Carolyn's voice shouting orders.

"Just separate the sick from the sickest! Don't worry about details!"

"That's not how I practice medicine!" Karen yelled back.

"Well, you're not in charge down here, and I am. So let's do it my way."

"Who anointed you Supreme Ruler?"

"Lord, give me strength!" Carolyn seethed.

David grumbled under his breath. This was the last thing he needed. Two trained professionals fighting over who should have authority in a useless sick bay. And to make matters even worse, there had always been bad blood between the two women, and it wasn't just over him. The women had a mutual dislike for one another right from the get-go.

Taking a deep breath, he stepped into the reception area and waved to the pair. "It looks like we've got a full house again."

"It's a big mess," Carolyn said, exasperated.

"So I see."

"And again they refuse to return to their cabins," Carolyn went on. "It's as if they believe we have magic pills that are going to cure them."

"Let me give it a try." David went back to the entrance of the sick bay and, raising his voice, called out, "Please give me your attention!"

His request was met with moans and groans and even more coughing. Two couples propped up against the far wall of the passageway were arguing between themselves about something. They ignored David, like he wasn't even there. A small dog was barking noisily in the background.

"Listen up!" David bellowed, his voice now hard and loud. "I'm only going to say this once, and if you want to be treated, you'd better listen."

The crowd quieted instantly. The dog barked again, but someone quickly hushed it.

"Here is the way it's going to work," David told them. "All of you are to return to your rooms at once. As you leave, give us your name and cabin number or, better yet, you can phone the information in. Those of you who stay down here will be seen last." He glanced around the crowd and saw he had their full attention, then continued. "If you decide to keep lying on this uncomfortable floor, that's your business. But you won't be seen for hours and hours because the medical staff won't be here. They'll be busy attending to people in their cabins."

"Can—can't you leave one doctor or nurse down here?" a voice pleaded.

"No, I can't," David said firmly. "You return to your room or you don't get seen. It's that simple."

The crowd seemed to hesitate as one, then ever so slowly began to struggle to their feet and move out. Some headed for the staircase; most stood in line at the elevators. The coughing started again.

David walked back into the reception area and noticed a couple still sitting in their chairs. Their expressions appeared to indicate that they expected to be seen since they were already in the waiting room. Both were expensively dressed. She even had on fine jewelry.

David jerked his thumb from them to the door. "No exceptions!"

The couple stood, holding hands, and gave David and Carolyn a displeased look before leaving.

Karen came up alongside David and said, "That was really mean."

"We don't have time for niceties," he snapped.

"A little civility goes a long way," Karen rebuked mildly.

"You want some civility, eh? Well, try this on."

David told them about his phone conversation with the CDC and their instructions to establish a let-die list. He described in detail how they were to select out those who would be left to die. From memory, he went through a list of medical conditions that would ensure a certain death sentence.

The women stared at David, astounded by the concept of a let-die list. It went against everything ingrained in their professional code of conduct. *You just didn't let people die without trying to help and comfort.*

Carolyn slowly shook her head. "It's another way of telling us that the CDC won't be sending any help."

"All they're sending are eight ventilators," David told her.

"And who is going to monitor them?" Carolyn asked at once.

"We are," David replied.

"That's going to be a real stretch," Carolyn said. "We're already overwhelmed as is. If we have to monitor eight ventilators as well, we'll be turning a very difficult problem into an impossible one."

"I know," David said, nodding. "And you haven't mentioned the most difficult of all the problems."

"Which is?"

"Choosing which eight patients get to go on the ventilators," David answered somberly. "They'll be the ones selected out to live."

"Jesus!" Carolyn breathed. "It's like a Nazi triage system."

"We've got no choice," David said simply.

"The part about letting all the elderly die really bothers me," Carolyn thought aloud. "What's the definition of elderly? What's the cut off? Sixty-five? Seventy?"

David shrugged. "If they're old and infirm, they'll be considered elderly."

"And who decides that?"

"All of us," David said. "And remember, there's not a hell of a lot we can do for them anyway."

"But still…" Carolyn let her voice drop off.

"I know," David said consolingly, "but it's the only way we can attend to those who might live."

"I don't like it," Karen interjected. "I don't like playing God."

"Who does?" Carolyn asked.

"You seemed to be enjoying that role a moment ago," Karen said snidely. "Like when you were shouting out orders."

Carolyn glared at her. "Now I understand why you became an anesthesiologist. You don't know how to relate to other human beings while they're awake."

"I'm not going to put up with your—"

"Whoa!" David interceded quickly. "Let's not argue among ourselves. That's not going to help us solve our problems."

The women continued to glower at each other.

"So knock it off!" David directed. "And I mean now!"

Carolyn's expression softened, but Karen's didn't.

"Can't we have a truce while we're in the middle of this nightmare?" David implored. "Is that asking too much?"

There was a long pause before Carolyn offered her hand in friendship. Karen hesitated, then reluctantly shook it.

"All right," David said to them. "Let's concentrate on the major problems we're facing. Namely, how to deal with the sick and how to deal with Richard Scott and his mutineers, because they've increased our peril even more, if that's possible."

"By taking over the ship?" Carolyn queried.

David shook his head. "It's more than that. Have you noticed that very few of the crew are wearing their N-95 masks?"

The women nodded simultaneously.

"That's because I heard one of the deckhands say it was okay with Richard Scott if they didn't wear their masks. So they'll soon get sick and become sicker, and stretch our resources even further. It's like Scott is making sure the outbreak spreads to every part of the *Grand Atlantic*."

Karen asked, "Why would he do that?"

"I have no idea," David replied.

"Won't it eventually spread to Richard Scott and his men?"

"Maybe, maybe not," David said. "For the most part, they've isolated themselves by staying on the bridge and denying entrance to all but the most essential people. Nobody sick gets near them."

"But why spread the virus to all the others?" Carolyn asked thoughtfully. "How would that help Richard Scott?"

"I have no idea," David said again. "All I know for sure is that Scott plans to go ashore somewhere in the Caribbean. And it doesn't matter a damn to him if he starts a pandemic while he's in the process of saving his own skin."

"Wouldn't we all jump ship if we had the opportunity?" Karen asked self-servingly. "I know I would."

Carolyn gave her a look of disgust. "Those of us with an ounce of moral fiber would stay behind and care for all the others."

The women glared at one another again. Their truce was over.

The phone began to ring, all lines lighting up at once.

Carolyn glanced over and said, "That's probably the sick passengers calling in their names and cabin numbers. Who wants to man the phone first?"

"I'll do it," Karen volunteered, then added with sarcasm directed at Carolyn, "assuming the director of the sick bay agrees, of course."

Carolyn flicked her wrist dismissively and watched the anesthesiologist walk away, disliking her even more than before. She turned to David and lowered her voice, "How in the world did you ever put up with that?"

"I didn't," Richard answered. "Remember?"

"But it sure took you a while to come to your senses."

"That's because I'm a forgiving sort."

"Ha!" Carolyn forced a laugh. "I've always had the feeling you're one who holds a grudge for a long time."

"I guess," David said, recalling Karen's dishonesty and duplicity from years back. Her unconscionable behavior still stung, and that was good. It reminded him of what she really was. Self-centered and self-serving. And that would never change. He brought his attention back to Carolyn and her dark eyes that he never tired of looking into. Her signs of fatigue seemed to have vanished. "You look like you've gotten a second wind."

"I'm good at that," Carolyn said matter-of-factly. "But, Lord! It sure took its time coming." She gazed up lovingly at him. "I'm sorry I almost came apart on you. I usually don't go in for pity."

David shook his head. "Pity, hell! You were holding up great."

She shook her head back at him. "I was weak."

"I hope everybody becomes as weak as you were in the middle of that nightmare."

A half-smile came across Carolyn's face. "You're not going to let me fall, are you?"

"It's me who will fall first, not you."

Carolyn's smile grew. "You say the sweetest things, even when you lie."

"Well, here's an absolute truth," David said. "When we get out of this mess, we're going to the nice, white beaches of Waikiki. Just you and me, without Kit or Juanita."

"No way!" Carolyn said promptly. "Either Kit comes with us or I don't go."

David hummed happily to himself. "When are you going to stop being so perfect?"

"When you stop loving me," Carolyn replied.

David brought a finger up to his lips, then reached out and touched Carolyn's nose. "Then you'll be perfect forever."

A female patient appeared at the door of the sick bay. David recognized her immediately. She was the librarian from Ohio who had the oculogyric reaction to Compazine. The poor woman had had nothing but bad luck on the cruise, and now she was holding her left wrist with her right hand.

"I've fallen and hurt my wrist," she said, grimacing with pain. "Can someone please help me?"

"I'll get it," Carolyn said and rushed over to the woman.

"If it's a fracture, see if you can find us some casting material," David called after her.

"Gotcha."

David leaned against the wall as a sudden wave of fatigue swept through him. He hadn't slept soundly since the outbreak began, except for a few hours here and there, and now he was feeling the full effect of it. He needed sleep or he would start making poor decisions and people would suffer because of it. And then there was Choi, who would be difficult to handle fully awake. If David remained sleepless, Choi would take him easily. Again David wished he had killed Choi when he had the chance. That was a big mistake. A mistake that could cost him his life.

Karen came up to his side and said quietly, "David, we have to talk."

"About what?" he asked.

"Carolyn."

"What about her?"

"I'm not accustomed to taking orders from nurses," Karen hissed.

"Well, you'd better get used to it," David said. "She's more experienced at critical care than 99 percent of the doctors I know."

"What makes her such an expert?"

"Her years in the ER, then as a MedEvac nurse before she began working on the Beaumont Pavilion."

Karen nodded begrudgingly, "Yeah, I guess that would do it."

"Damn right, it does!" David emphasized. "Just thank your lucky stars we've got her down here."

Karen took his arm and pressed it against her body. "It's you who we should be thanking our lucky stars over."

Carolyn called out from the examining area, "I think she has a fractured wrist."

"Give Steiner a buzz and tell him we need some x-rays."

"He's on his way down."

David winked at Karen. "See what I mean?"

"And we don't have the materials to cast it," Carolyn added.

"Shit," David grumbled. "What about splints?"

"Nada," Carolyn answered.

"You've got to be kidding!" David groaned in disbelief.

"No splints," Carolyn said again. "And if they do have any splints down here, they've hidden them so well I can't find them."

David disengaged from Karen and sighed heavily. "I'll see if the ship's carpenter can help us."

"She's small," Carolyn reminded him. "The splints shouldn't be longer than a foot or so."

David trudged wearily out of the sick bay and into the passageway. He had his head down, shaking it and struggling to keep his eyes open. He didn't see Choi following him.

TWENTY-TWO

A THOUSAND MILES AWAY in the Oval Office, all eyes were on the recently elected President. John Jefferson Tyler, the first African-American President, was reaching into a large bowl of M&M's. A former two-pack-a-day smoker, Tyler had substituted the small pieces of candy for tobacco, and those closest to him knew they could measure his anxiety by how many M&M's he consumed. He was currently gobbling them down by the handful.

"How many dozens are dead?" Tyler asked, wanting specifics.

"We can't be certain, Mr. President," said Lawrence Lindberg, a heavyset man with a neatly trimmed beard. "We estimate at least three dozen, but it's no doubt many more by now."

Tyler gave the CDC's director of global quarantine a long look. "Why can't they just count and give us a number?"

"It's not that simple, sir. The patients are spread out over the entire ship. Some are in the sick bay, most in their cabins. And there are only a few doctors and nurses to care for all of them. Which means there could be a lot of unnoticed dead."

"Did all the passengers take Tamiflu like they were supposed to?"

"As far as we know, Mr. President."

"And that had no effect?"

"Apparently not."

"And none of the other drugs work either, eh?"

"No, sir."

Tyler reached for another handful of M&M's. "In total, you say there are over a thousand people on board the *Grand Atlantic*. Correct?"

Lindberg nodded. "If you include the crew."

"Will the virus infect all of them?"

"In all likelihood."

"And kill most of them?"

"In all likelihood."

The President rose from his chair and walked over to the window overlooking the Rose Garden. He stared out at the dwindling sunlight for ten full seconds before turning back to the group of national security and scientific advisors. As usual, his Sphinx-like face was totally expressionless. "Can we do anything?"

The scientific advisors shook their heads collectively.

The President directed his next question to Anthony Church, the short, wiry director of the National Institutes of Health. "What about a vaccine, Tony?"

"There is no vaccine available, Mr. President," Church replied.

"How long would it take to produce one?"

"At least a year, if everything went smoothly."

"No good," the President said, more to himself than to the others. He went over to the bowl of M&M's and absently picked up another handful. "So we're left with treating the sick using only supportive measures?"

Church nodded.

"Then we have to get them ashore, don't we?"

His proposal got no response from the group. They looked at him in silence.

"Don't we?" the President repeated.

"That presents a huge problem for us, Mr. President," Church said carefully. "We're talking about hundreds and hundreds of very sick patients who would require strict isolation in intensive care units. Most ICUs are routinely filled to capacity, with very few empty beds. So if you suddenly have hundreds and hundreds of terribly ill individuals that need prompt admission and constant monitoring, they would overwhelm all the ICUs in a dozen of our largest metropolitan areas."

"And, Mr. President," Lindberg added, "those metropolitan areas don't have enough specialists and nurses to care for all those critically ill patients."

The President began walking in a circle around the Oval Office, his shadow silhouetted by the sinking sun. He was a lanky, tall man at 6'4", with the easy stride of an athlete who had lettered in two sports at Harvard. He continued circling because he thought better on the move. Abruptly he stopped and gazed over at Lindberg. "Couldn't we distribute the sick people to hospitals all across the country?"

"That raises another set of problems, Mr. President," Lindberg said. "How do we transport these patients? How do we keep them isolated along the way so they don't spread the avian flu virus? And once they arrive at the various medical centers, there is always the very real possibility that the virus will be passed on to others. Remember, this virus is highly contagious and travels via invisible droplets through the air. One unguarded cough in a crowded room, and you'd end up with dozens of infected people. What I'm saying, Mr. President, is that moving these patients ashore would almost surely start a pandemic."

"Are we talking on the order of the 1918 flu pandemic?'

"Worse," Lindberg said. "With modern-day plane travel to every corner of the world, we could easily see a billion infected and hundreds of million dead."

The numbers were stunning to the President. His jaw tightened noticeably. "So you're saying that taking them off the ship is not an option?"

"Yes, sir. That's precisely what I'm saying," Lindberg told him. "That ship is like a floating reservoir containing untold trillions of this killer virus, and it will remain so for the foreseeable future."

The President let the new information sink in before asking, "Are you telling me they'll have to stay at sea indefinitely?"

"I'm afraid so," Lindberg said. "There is no way we can let that ship dock anywhere without the gravest of consequences."

"Well, they can't just stay out there forever," the President thought aloud. "Their families won't stand for that."

The members of the President's advisory committee shifted around in their seats uncomfortably. All were thinking the same dreadful ending. *The passengers on the* Grand Atlantic *would never reach land. They would never see their families again. They were all destined to die at sea.*

Finally Lindberg spoke, breaking the silence. "Mr. President, the families have not yet been told about the true nature of the outbreak. We decided it was best to initiate a blackout on every aspect of this dilemma, much to the consternation of the cruise line. As you might imagine, they've been bombarded with calls from anxious relatives."

The President waved a hand dismissively. "The passengers know, and they're going to somehow contact their relatives ashore, if they haven't already. You can't stop the news from getting out."

"We *have* stopped it, Mr. President," Lindberg went on. "The executive order you signed empowered us to establish a federal quarantine on the *Grand Atlantic*. To this end, we have EA-18 Growlers continually circling above the ship. These planes can block out virtually all electronic transmissions, including those made on cell phones. The latter is particularly important, since some of the passengers have very influential relatives who will demand the ship be brought into port."

The President asked quickly, "How influential are these families?"

"One of the passengers is Marilyn Wyman, who is the sister of Senator Evans."

The President groaned inwardly. Albert Evans, the Senate Majority Leader, was a close friend and a powerful ally. The President made a mental note to personally call the senator. "How does this blackout help the situation?"

"Sir, if these influential people knew about this pending catastrophe, they'd demand their relatives be brought ashore. Or worse, they'd try to come up with ways to get their relatives to land."

"How? How could they get these people ashore?"

"By helicopters or yachts or by every other possible means they could devise. People do desperate acts in desperate times. And keep in mind, sir, all that's required for a pandemic to start is for a few of these passengers to secretly reach shore. In essence, Mr. President, the blackout reinforces the federal quarantine and makes sure that no one foolishly tries a rescue mission."

The President nodded slowly. "And with a blackout, the position of the ship can't be revealed."

"And its course can't be tracked," Lindberg added.

The President started pacing again, back and forth in front of his desk. "The families have to be told something."

"They have to be told the truth," Lindberg said without inflection. "Namely, that there is an outbreak of a highly contagious bird flu virus aboard the *Grand Atlantic*, and that the ship will remain quarantined and held incommunicado until the outbreak is brought under control with drugs and other—"

"But you just told me that the drugs don't work," the President interrupted.

"We'll tell them we're trying newer, experimental drugs."

"Is there any chance these experimental drugs will work?"

"Almost none," Lindberg said honestly. "But we'll keep trying."

The President rubbed at his forehead, like he was attempting to soothe a headache. "There's going to be a public outcry when the news media gets hold of this story."

"The outcry will be limited and primarily from family members," Lindberg predicted. "The general public may sympathize with the passengers, but deep down they'll want that ship to remain at sea for obvious reasons."

"Particularly when they realize their own survival may be at stake," Church chimed in.

"But that doesn't solve our problem, does it?" the President asked, his tone sharper now.

"No, sir," Lindberg and Church answered simultaneously.

The President knitted his brow, concentrating, all the while pacing the floor of the Oval Office. He mumbled something to himself that sounded like *nightmare.* The others in the room strained to catch his words. Suddenly he stopped and snapped his fingers, as if he had the answer to the problem. "Why not send a bunch of doctors and nurses, and all the equipment they need, out to the ship?"

"We considered that option too," Church told the President. "But we'd require hundreds of doctors and hundreds of nurses to provide around-the-clock critical care. Keep in mind, these highly contagious patients would be in four hundred separate cabins. Then there's the matter of protecting all the doctors and nurses from the virus. They'd all have to wear space suits with external oxygen supplies. And even then, there'd be no guarantee they'd be protected. In all candor, Mr. President, I don't think we could find nearly enough volunteers to go aboard that death ship."

"What about military doctors and nurses?" the President queried. "They could be ordered to go on board."

Church shook his head. "We need ICU doctors and nurses who are specialists in critical care. The military doesn't have enough qualified people to fill the bill."

The President gave Church a prolonged stare. "So we're just going to let those people die?"

"The vast majority will die regardless of what we do," Church said bluntly.

"Couldn't some be saved by sending out medical personnel?" the President pressed.

"A small percentage perhaps," Church replied in a clinical tone. "But we'd be risking the lives of a lot of doctors and nurses to do it. It's not a very good trade-off, Mr. President."

"So we're damned if we send help, and we're damned if we don't?"

"I'm afraid so, sir."

The President started circling the Oval Office again, searching for an answer to the dilemma. He moved past his desk and by the door to the Rose Garden before stopping in his tracks. Abruptly he narrowed his eyes and turned back to the group. "Is there any way to decontaminate the *Grand Atlantic*?"

"Not without destroying the people aboard," Lindberg answered.

The President stepped in closer to the director for global quarantine before saying, "Spell that out for me."

"Well, sir, if you incinerate the ship with all its passengers, the decontamination would be absolute and complete."

"Incinerate!" the President's voice went up an octave. "Like a nuclear explosion? Is that what the hell you're saying?"

"It was never a serious consideration, Mr. President."

"I hope not."

But it was a serious consideration and had been discussed at length. Scientifically it was a viable option. Politically it was not. None of the advisors thought it wise to mention this.

"I need answers," the President commanded. "Workable answers."

"I'm not sure there are any," Lindberg said candidly. "Despite our best efforts, we seem to find ourselves between a rock and a hard place."

"That's a place I don't like to be in," the President said.

"Yes, sir."

The room went silent. All the advisors were concentrating on the insoluble problem, a few pausing to thank God they weren't aboard the *Grand Atlantic*.

The President straightened his tie and buttoned his coat. It was a signal the meeting was over.

The advisors stood.

"Should—should we meet again, sir?" Church asked hesitantly.

The President nodded. "As soon as you come up with a way to save those people and decontaminate the ship."

"But, Mr. President," Church blurted out. "You're asking for the impossible."

"Yes," the President said, "I am. So you gather all the resources you need and do the impossible."

"But, Mr. President—"

The President ended the discussion with a wave and stepped into his small, private study next to the Oval Office. Closing the door behind him, he reached into his desk for a cigarette and lit it.

Screw the M&M's, he thought and, inhaling deeply, concentrated on the terrible dilemma he was facing.

TWENTY-THREE

DAVID LEANED AGAINST THE wall outside the carpenter's shop and tried to catch his breath, all the while watching the door to the staircase. He expected Choi to burst through any moment, knife in hand, ready to kill. Seconds passed. Then more seconds. Then minutes. Still, there was no Choi. *Where the hell is he?* David asked himself as he glanced around the expansive lower level, which contained the carpenter's shop, giant storage spaces, and a huge laundry room that was lined with oversized washing and drying machines. The entire area seemed deserted. It was a good place to kill and an even better place to hide a body. So where was Choi?

David pushed off from the wall but kept a wary eye on the staircase door. He'd been lucky to escape with his life. He had spotted Choi closing in on him in the passageway near the sick bay and had raced for the stairs. Choi came after him and was only a half-flight behind and could have easily thrown a knife into David's back. But he didn't. Why? There were two possible answers. Either Choi wanted to play cat and mouse and terrorize him for a while, or he had orders from Richard Scott not to kill the doctor yet. David favored the second possibility because, at least for now, he was still a valuable commodity.

Ahead David saw the carpenter's shop, its door wide open, the sound of a pounding hammer coming from within. He tried to pick up the pace, but his legs wouldn't let him. The wave of fatigue was coming back and it was more intense than before. Racing down the stairs had used up the last of his energy, and his legs now felt like dead weights. Each step became an effort.

He entered the carpenter's shop and saw Harry Heins nailing two pieces of wood together. David assumed the man was Harry Heins because that was the name on the plaque by the door. And the guy looked like a carpenter, with his short gray hair, stocky build, and tattooed arms as big as telephone poles.

"Have you got a minute, Harry?" David called out.

"Sure, doc," Harry said and stopped hammering. "What can I do for you?"

"I need a man of your talent to make me some splints."

"For what?"

"A broken arm."

"Upper or lower?"

"Wrist."

Harry nodded slowly before asking, "Big or little person?"

"Say five feet, maybe a hundred pounds."

"Like a young teenager?"

"Right."

"A foot long should do it then, eh?"

"Perhaps a few inches more," David approximated.

Harry reached for an unfinished wooden slat and showed it to David. "I could give you this, but it won't work worth a damn."

"How do you know that?" David asked.

"Experience," Harry said easily. "A while back I served on a merchant ship and we had seamen with broken arms all the time. At first, we used just plain old slats like this for splints, but they never really worked. They'd slip and slide even when they were taped in place. And they were damn uncomfortable too."

"So what did you do?"

Harry picked up a thicker slat of wood and fingered its center. "I took a piece like this and scooped out the middle. Kind of made a big groove in which a man could rest his broken arm."

David nodded, aware that he was dealing with a real craftsman who was accustomed to producing quality goods. "Then add some cotton padding and tape the arm in place."

"You've got it, doc."

"How long will it take to make a splint like that?"

Harry gave that some thought. He began moving his lips as if he were counting. "Well, I've got to chisel out the groove and sand it down, then put in some notches for the tape, then maybe add a light coat of quick-drying varnish to smooth everything out. I'll have it done in an hour and a half or so."

"Good," David said, now noticing a cot against the far wall. It had a small pillow and a brown, army-issue, woolen blanket. David fought his fatigue as he stifled a yawn, his eyes fixed on the bed. "Do you mind if I doze on your cot while I wait?"

"Fine with me, but you should know I'll be making some noise while I work."

215

"Just wake me when you're done," David said, then added as a precaution, "and if Choi or anyone else comes looking for me, give me a shout."

"I'll keep an eye out."

David moved to the cot and reminded himself not to get under the blanket. That would cause him to sleep deeper and be drowsier when he awoke. An hour-and-a-half sleep would barely be adequate, but he could manage on it. And he'd have Harry Heins watching his back, just in case Choi suddenly showed up.

"I've got some ear plugs if you want them," Harry offered from across the shop.

"Don't need them."

As David was about to drop onto the cot, his gaze went to the wall off to the side. It had wooden pegs and slots for a wide assortment of tools. Saws. Chisels. Wrenches. Hammers. Screwdrivers. Everything was orderly and clean. Lower down was a first-aid kit, but it was the item next to it that drew David's attention. A hatchet! A small, well-used hatchet!

Quickly he glanced over his shoulder. The carpenter was occupied, measuring out a slat of wood. David inched over to the wall and pretended to be examining the first-aid kit. Then he stepped in front of the hatchet and deftly removed it from its peg. Pausing for a moment, he casually turned and held the hatchet behind his back. Then, in a single motion, he slipped the wooden handle of the hatchet under the belt of his pants and covered it with his short white coat.

"Everything all right, doc?" Harry yelled over.

"Perfect."

And the hatchet was perfect. It was the prefect weapon to counter Choi's knife. It was longer and stronger and could inflict far more damage than a knife. And now it would be he, not Choi, who would pick the place for their final encounter. David already had a plan in mind. He would outwit Choi, then kill him.

With that thought, David lay atop the woolen blanket on the cot. He pressed his head onto the pillow and was instantly asleep.

TWENTY-FOUR

DAVID KNEW SOMETHING WAS wrong the moment he stepped into his cabin. Carolyn's face was drawn and worried, her eyes teary red. She tried to speak, but the words seemed to stick in her throat.

"What's wrong?" David asked.

"Kit," Carolyn uttered.

"What about her?" David demanded.

"I think she's got the bird flu," Carolyn said and fought her tears. "She looks so sick."

David forced himself to breathe. "Does she have fever and chills, like the others?"

"Her temperature is a hundred and two," Carolyn said, nodding slowly. "The chills are coming and going."

David started for the bedroom, but Carolyn grabbed his arm. "I moved her back into the suite with Juanita."

David sprinted out and into the cabin across the passageway. From the sitting room, he could hear the loud, continuous coughing. Juanita's cough was coarse and raspy, Kit's high-pitched, almost a squeal. A little girl's cough. David braced himself and entered the bedroom. His heart sank.

Kit looked deathly ill. Her face was flushed with fever, her forehead covered with beads of perspiration that plastered her raven hair to the underlying skin. She was moaning between her weak, wet coughs. *Oh, no!* David shrieked to himself. *God, no!*

He reached out and gently stroked her arm. It felt hot, hotter than 102°. "Hi, sweetheart," he said, his voice barely above a whisper.

"Hi, Dad," she said and licked at her parched lips.

"How are you feeling?"

"Not so good," Kit licked her lips again and asked, "Can I have some water?"

"Sure." David leaned over to the lamp table for a small plastic bottle of water. He held her head up while she gulped down mouthful after mouthful. "Better?" he asked and waited for her to nod before easing her back to her pillow. Then her cough started again.

"I can't stop coughing, Dad," Kit complained weakly.

"It's that nasty, old virus," David downplayed it, his expression even although his heart was breaking. "It makes you feel really yucky."

"Is it the same virus that Will had?" Kit asked.

"I guess so."

"But I don't have it as bad as Will did, do I?"

"No way!" David lied. "He was really, really sick. And remember, he actually touched that bird with the disease and you didn't."

Kit nodded, apparently satisfied with the explanation. She swallowed back a cough and asked, "You're not going to get sick too, are you, Dad?"

"Not me," David replied promptly. "I've got myself well pro-tected."

"Good." Kit slowly closed her eyes and dozed off. She didn't bother to reach for her favorite teddy bear.

David looked away as his tears welled up. *She's so sick and she can only think of me. Just like her mother Marianne when she was dying with leukemia.* He rubbed at his eyes briefly. Then, gathering himself, he took out his stethoscope and listened to Kit's chest. He heard rhonchi and rales, but no wheezes that would indicate air-way obstruction. But he knew the wheezes would come later, along with the purplish complexion that signified oxygen deprivation.

"I will look after the Little One," Juanita said hoarsely from her bed. "She is my responsibility."

"You're too sick," David told her.

"Do not tell me what I can and can't do," Juanita argued and propped herself up on an elbow. She tried to raise up farther, but her strength gave out and she dropped back down on her pillow. "I will attend to her later, when I have the energy."

"Yes," David agreed sadly. "When you have the energy."

He kissed Kit's forehead and walked back into the sitting room. Carolyn was worriedly pacing the floor, head down, hands clasped in front of her. She spun around and stared at him, as if trying to read his expression.

"Tell me I was wrong," she pleaded. "Please tell me I was wrong."

David shook his head. "You were right. She has the bird flu."

"Oh, Lord!"

"He isn't aboard the *Grand Atlantic*," David muttered.

"What are we going to do?"

"Everything we can."

With effort, David pushed aside his alarm and anxiety. For the moment, he compartmentalized his worries and focused on the enemy he was facing and how to defeat it. Except this wasn't some mutineer or terrorist he could kill—it was an invisible, deadly virus that wanted to take his daughter from him. It was an indestructible foe. *But still, think clinically! Think about what's needed to keep Kit alive!* Quickly he made a mental list of things to be done, then turned to Carolyn.

"Do we have any of those small oxygen tanks left in the sick bay?" he asked hastily.

"A few," Carolyn answered.

"Get as many as you can and bring them back to this cabin," David instructed. "What about those transparent air-flow masks that are used for asthmatics?"

"We have plenty."

"We'll need those too," David went on, "as well as a goodly supply of bronchodilators and antibiotics."

"I should also grab some IV setups and fluids, in case Kit can't take fluids orally."

"Right," David agreed, and reminded himself to check with the CDC on the status of the ventilators that were supposedly en route.

"What if other people see me grabbing all this equipment?"

"Tell them it's for a very sick patient."

Kit started coughing again, and it disrupted David's concentration. The compartmentalization of his alarm and fear evaporated, and those emotions came to the front of his brain again. *If Kit becomes as sick as the others, she'll die*, he thought gloomily. *Her only chance to survive is ashore in an ICU at some medical center. But we can't get ashore unless I strike a deal with Richard Scott. He's in control of everything. He calls the shots. I'd have to beg.*

"I know what you're thinking," Carolyn broke the silence.

"What?"

"Getting Kit ashore."

David stared at her, stunned. "How did you know that?"

"Because I was thinking the same thing."

"And?"

"You won't do it."

"Why not?"

"Because you're you," Carolyn said. "Your type doesn't run from anybody or anything."

"Don't be so sure."

"You won't do it," Carolyn said again, then flicked her wrist at the idea. "Now let's get this show on the road and keep Kit going."

David nodded firmly, convinced beyond a doubt that Carolyn was every bit as strong as he was. She also knew how to compartmentalize problems and worries, which was the real test of one's mental toughness. He gave her a quick hug and said, "I'll stay with Kit while you run down to the sick bay for all the equipment. How many trips do you figure it will take?"

"One," Carolyn told him. "I'll pack everything onto a gurney."

"What about the IV poles?"

"We won't need them. We can attach the bags of fluid to the hooks over the beds."

"What hooks?"

"The ones that hold the paintings."

David shook his head admiringly. "Is there anything else I haven't thought of?"

"Probably," Carolyn said and headed for the door. "I'll let you know when it comes to mind."

David watched the door close, thinking how fortunate he was to have Carolyn at his side. She was an excellent ER nurse, with years of critical-care experience, and that made her worth a dozen doctors who rarely left their offices. For a moment his spirits were buoyed, but then he came back to the stark reality that he had a terribly ill child who was infected with a killer virus. And chances were, all the supportive measures in the world weren't going to save her.

David stepped out onto the balcony and breathed in the fresh ocean air. The sea was becoming choppy again, with whitecaps and whirls coming up from the south. He gazed into the distant twilight and saw no ships, then up at the sky and saw no planes or birds. They were as alone as alone could be. Suddenly the silence was interrupted by Kit's high-pitched coughs. She coughed over and over again, and now seemed to be having trouble catching her breath. David hastily turned to reenter the cabin, but then Kit's coughing subsided and he heard her raspy respirations return to normal. But that lasted only briefly. Then the harsh coughing started again.

David's anger abruptly boiled over, and he made no effort to control it. He glared up at the sky and shook his fist at God. *Don't you do this! Don't you dare do this! Goddamn it! Leave her alone and take me instead! Don't you kill the little girl I love more than anything*

in this world! Don't you take Kit from me, like you took Marianne!
Don't you have any mercy, you no-good son of a bitch? Well, don't you?

God didn't answer.

TWENTY-FIVE

THE FIVE MEN ON the bridge listened intently to the weather report coming from the National Hurricane Center in Miami. Another storm was brewing in the outer reaches of the Caribbean, and it might be headed their way.

The voice from the speaker was female, crystal clear and emotionless.

"The Category 1 hurricane, with winds of eighty miles per hour, will pass over central Cuba in the next forty-eight hours. Its projected course will carry it through the Yucatan Channel and into the Gulf of Mexico, thus avoiding landfall in the southeastern United States. However, a rapidly developing frontal system may cause the hurricane to veer northward and extend its track to the Florida Keys. Further information will be available—"

Richard Scott switched the speaker off and turned to the acting captain, Jonathan Locke. "How close are we to this hurricane?"

"On our current southerly course, we're still in the mid-Atlantic and well east of it," Locke answered.

"And from the sound of the weather report, the hurricane will skirt past the Bahamas. Right?"

"If it continues on its current course, it will. But if it veers toward the eastern seaboard of the United States, the waters around the Bahamas will become very rough and dangerous."

"But it may not veer," Scott argued.

"It's a possibility, Mr. Scott," Locke said evenly. "And at sea, we pay a great deal of attention to the possibilities."

"Yeah, yeah," Scott said dismissively. "But let's talk probabilities. In all likelihood, the Bahamas will be relatively unaffected by this hurricane. Correct?"

Locke shook his head. "The Bahamas are quite close to Cuba. So the islands will definitely be affected, particularly if the storm takes a more northerly track."

"But a Category 1 hurricane is not that powerful. A ship this size can easily withstand eighty-mile-an-hour winds."

"No vessel I know of can easily withstand eighty-mile-an-hour winds," Locke retorted.

"He's right," Robbie Hendricks joined in. He was wearing jeans and a T-shirt with cutoff sleeves, which gave everyone a full view of the red-rose tattoo over his deltoid area. "That wind force can bang a ship around pretty good."

"And keep in mind," Locke said to Scott, "that as the hurricane reaches the warmer waters of the Caribbean, it will increase in strength and become a Category 2 or 3. Trust me when I tell you that you don't want to be anywhere near that."

"A Category 2 or 3 would eat us up alive," Robbie agreed. "It's best to wait until the damn hurricane passes by."

"But we'd have to wait another forty-eight hours," Scott groused.

"Better safe than sorry," Robbie said.

"I guess so." Scott nodded reluctantly, not pleased with the delay, but having little choice. The more time spent at sea, the more chances things could go awry. He reconsidered his entire plan before giving Locke additional orders. "I have two new directives for you. First, you are to continue on our current southerly course. There is to be no variation. If you attempt to do anything other than what you're told, Robbie will detect it on the GPS, and you may find yourself swimming in a very rough ocean. Understood?"

Locke's shoulders slumped submissively. "I understand."

"Second," Scott went on, "you are to slow your speed so that we reach a point parallel to the middle Bahamas in forty-eight hours. At that time we'll know which way the hurricane is headed."

"Assuming it doesn't change speed," Locke stipulated.

"Let's assume that," Scott said. "With that in mind, I have an important question for you. I don't want any ifs, ands, or buts, just a straight answer. Got it?"

Locke nodded.

"Okay," Scott continued, "here is the question. From the place we'll be in forty-eight hours, which should be well east of the Bahamas, how long will it take us to reach the larger Bahamian islands?"

"At full speed?"

"At full speed."

"Ten to twelve hours," Locke estimated.

"You'd better be accurate," Scott warned, then motioned to a third mutineer standing off to the side. "Watch them and make certain no one goes near the communications room."

The third mutineer raised his sloping shotgun up to hip level and pointed it at the captain and chief radio operator. He gestured them away from the speaker.

"Is it really necessary to have that shotgun aimed directly at us?" Locke asked.

"Yes," Scott said simply and headed across the bridge at a quick pace.

Robbie followed him a step behind, appropriate for a second-in-command.

They went through a door and onto the small deck that fronted the bridge. Night had already set in. The sky was pitch-black, with a billion stars twinkling as far as one could see. Below, the main deck was brightly illuminated with floodlights. A dozen crewmen were milling about, enjoying the bar and pool area.

Robbie absently scratched his hemorrhoids and asked, "So we're going to the Bahamas, huh?"

"If all works out with the weather," Scott said elusively.

"Which island?"

"I haven't decided yet," Scott lied. "But as soon as we see a clear opening…" He let his voice trail off.

"Man—oh—man!" Robbie said excitedly. "I never thought I'd be so happy to get my feet on dry land again. And away from this goddamn bird flu."

"Two-and-a-half more days and we'll be ashore."

"I wish we could speed it up."

"Be patient," Scott told him. "Like you said earlier, better to be safe than sorry."

"You bet," Robbie nodded his agreement, then glanced down to the area where the lifeboats were located. "I think I should check the lifeboats to make sure they're okay."

"Good idea," Scott said. "But do it when there's no crew around."

"What difference would that make?"

"If they see you by the lifeboats, they'll get overanxious and be more difficult to control."

"Right," Robbie said. "But I don't think that'll be a problem because a lot of the crew is catching the flu."

"Good."

"Why good?"

"Sick crewmen are less likely to switch sides and revolt against us."

"But I thought you wanted a bunch of them in the lifeboats."

Scott shook his head. "I just want all the boats in the water. I don't care how many of the crew or passengers are in them."

Robbie looked at him quizzically. "I'm not sure I follow you."

"The coast guard will be distracted by the number of lifeboats in the sea. They won't be counting heads in each boat."

"The Bahamas have a coast guard?"

"Probably. So the more lifeboats, the better our chances are to slip ashore."

"But we'll still be seen in a big-ass lifeboat."

Scott smiled thinly. "There are ways around that, too."

On the deck below, they heard a commotion going on. Choi was ordering the crew out of the bar and lounge chairs. Some resisted, but only briefly. Choi kicked the legs out from under one crewman and head-butted another. The crew became silent and moved out without a grumble.

"Choi is tough as nails," Robbie commented.

"And some," Scott said with a nod.

"He really wants to kill the doctor, you know."

"Not yet. Tell him to continue terrorizing Ballineau and keep him off balance."

Robbie shrugged. "The doc has already caused a lot of trouble and he can cause more. Why not kill him and get it over with?"

"Because we need him, if only to talk with the CDC," Scott explained. "If he's not around when they call, they'll become suspicious. They might even attempt to fly in a new doctor."

"But the heliport is all messed up," Robbie reminded.

"They could still lower someone from a hovering helicopter," Scott said. "We'll keep Ballineau alive for now."

Robbie gazed down at Choi, who was now staring up at them. Choi waved. Robbie waved back and said, barely moving his lips, "He's really salivating to kill the doc."

"Promise him he can later." Scott raised his hand in friendship to Choi, not trusting him, not even a little. "Go talk with Choi and emphasize that we need Ballineau alive. And give him this warning. If anything happens to the doctor before I say so, Choi will not be allowed onto a lifeboat. He can stay on this ship and die with the others."

"He ain't going to like it."

"Too bad."

Robbie gave the matter more thought before saying, "You know when Choi slits the doc's throat, we could be considered accessories to murder."

"Really? And who will testify against us?"

Robbie smiled. "No one."

"Exactly. No one," Scott said and headed back to the bridge.

TWENTY-SIX

As Carolyn approached the sick bay, she saw two men running toward her. They were waving their hands frantically and yelling to her, but she couldn't make out their words. *Oh no! Not another emergency! Not now!*

"Are you the nurse?" the larger of the two men asked.

"Yes," Carolyn said. She glanced into the sick bay and noticed it was deserted. "What do you need?"

"Oxygen," the man said hurriedly. "My wife has chronic lung disease and now she has the flu. She's having trouble catching her breath."

Carolyn thought briefly about the CDC's let-die list and decided to ignore it. Her mind raced back to the supply of oxygen tanks in the sick bay. There were only two or three small tanks remaining at last count. And now she'd have to give up one of them. "Do you know how to use the oxygen?"

"No," the man admitted.

"Okay," Carolyn said with a sigh. "I'll help you set it up. What room are you in?"

"Four-oh-eight. My name is Sullivan."

Carolyn rushed into the sick bay, with Tom Sullivan close behind. The other man, small and slender, followed them in. He held a hand over his mouth to cover a raspy cough.

"And I need some antibiotics," he called out.

"For what?" Carolyn queried.

"My cough."

"Antibiotics won't help a viral cough."

"It won't hurt either."

Carolyn didn't argue. If he had avian flu, antibiotics weren't going to matter. He was going to die, with or without them. She entered the examining room, which was now a mess. Trash littered the floor, drawers were open and emptied, and blood-stained masks were strewn everywhere and gave off the stale smell of decay.

She hurried to a nearby closet and opened it. The shelves were bare except for a few boxes of facial tissues. There were no oxygen tanks, large or small. She knelt to check the bottom shelves. They too were empty.

"All the oxygen tanks are gone," Carolyn reported and got to her feet.

"What the hell do you mean *gone*?" Sullivan asked furiously.

"I mean they're gone and probably being used by someone else," Carolyn said.

Sullivan's face turned red with rage. "What kind of goddamn ship is this? They don't even have enough oxygen for the passengers."

Carolyn held her hands out and shrugged in a helpless gesture.

"What about my antibiotics?" the small man inquired.

"Fuck your antibiotics!" Sullivan roared, his eyes still on Carolyn. "I want some oxygen tanks and I want them now!"

"Then you'll have to find them on your own," Carolyn said, unintimidated.

"I'll tear this place apart," Sullivan threatened.

"Be my guest," Carolyn told him. "And if you find any tanks, save one for a very sick little girl."

She watched Sullivan dash into the small laboratory and x-ray room, then heard doors slamming shut and drawers being opened and closed. Something fell to the floor and shattered into pieces. Then another door slammed. A moment later Sullivan returned to the examining room.

"Nothing," he grumbled and stormed out of the sick bay.

The smaller man stayed and asked, "Where are the antibiotics?"

Carolyn pointed to a large drawer under a Formica counter.

The man quickly opened the drawer and studied it briefly before looking back to Carolyn. "It's empty."

"So I figured."

"Well, wh-what should I do?"

"Hope for the best."

The small man nodded slowly, as if accepting an unpleasant fate, and left.

Carolyn gazed around the sick bay, struck by the drastic changes it had undergone. Hours earlier it was packed with the sick and dying, the air filled with moans and groans and coughs. Now it was empty and still, like a morgue at midnight. And it looked as if it had been plundered by a mob. Panic did that to people, Carolyn thought to herself. When their lives were threatened, they would beg, borrow, buy, or steal anything they believed would help them survive. It was human nature. They did it during hurricanes, earthquakes, and other natural disasters. Such as an outbreak of a deadly disease.

She brought her mind back to Kit and the oxygen that might keep her alive. The missing tanks could be anywhere, but most likely they were in passengers' cabins, being used or waiting to be used. There was no way to get them back. Again she glanced about the stripped sick bay. Even the IV fluids and poles were gone. Things were going from bad to worse.

She heard footsteps in the passageway. One person. Slow steps. She wondered if she would have to tell another patient to return to their cabin and hope for the best.

Karen Kellerman appeared in the doorway. She nodded briefly to Carolyn, then trudged over to a chair and plopped down wearily. Her eyes and face were puffy with fatigue, any semblance of make-up long gone.

"Jesus!" she groaned. "What a nightmare! I've been going from cabin to cabin, and all I see is the sick and the dying. And I can't do a damn thing for them."

"Welcome to the club," Carolyn said somberly.

Karen held up her arms and displayed the splashes of red paint on them. "And you can forget about painting the doors red."

"Why?"

"Because we ran out of red paint," Karen replied. "But it really doesn't matter because they're all going to die anyway."

"We might be able to help some if we had any oxygen tanks left to support them."

Karen nodded. "I'm afraid I used the last tank on Maggio's nurse."

"Is she bad off?"

Karen nodded again. "She won't last the day."

"Somehow we've got to find another tank or two for Kit," Carolyn said earnestly. "It may be her only chance to survive."

Karen stiffened in her chair. "Oh, no! Not Kit too!"

"Yeah, and she looks so sick it just breaks your heart," Carolyn said sadly. "But she's a strong little girl, and with the right supportive measures, she might survive."

"David must be devastated," Karen said in a whisper.

"He's barely holding—" Carolyn stopped in mid-sentence as an idea came to mind. For a moment, she debated whether or not to propose it. *Oh hell! Go ahead and say it.* "Since Maggio's nurse is on her deathbed, it wouldn't be so awful to grab her tank of oxygen for Kit, would it?"

"Except that the contents of that small tank are probably depleted by now."

"Shit!"

Karen suddenly snapped her fingers. "Wait a minute! Wait a minute!"

"What?"

"Maggio's nurse mumbled something about oxygen tanks in storage when I told her that she was receiving the last one," Karen said in a rush. "There may be some stored away, but who the hell knows where."

"I think I do." Carolyn reached for the front end of the gurney and rapidly spun it toward the door to the sick bay. "God! Let us be lucky on this!"

"Do you need some help?" Karen volunteered.

"I can handle it. You stay put in case more sick people straggle in."

Carolyn pushed the gurney down the empty passageway and into a waiting elevator. She pressed the button for the level of the carpenter's shop, hoping against hope that she'd find the oxygen tanks in the storage spaces David had vaguely described to her. She wondered if the shelves and cabinets were labeled to show what they contained. Without some kind of direction, she'd be lost.

The elevator came to a stop and Carolyn guided the gurney into a very long, deserted passageway. She looked around the cavernous level and tried to get her bearings. Off to the right was the carpenter's shop, now dark and silent. In front of her was the laundry room, dim and still. Then she came to the huge storage area that was the size of a city block. David said it reminded him of a giant warehouse. She thought it looked more like a Costco store, with wide aisles and oversized shelves packed with supplies, but with far lower ceilings. And like Costco, neither the aisles or shelves showed any labels. She would have to go about the search blind. Goddamn it!

Carolyn decided to start at the north end and work her way south. The first section she searched contained mainly household items. Soap. Detergents. Bathroom tissue. Deodorizers. Then came mops, brooms, and dustpans. The next aisle held sheets, linens, pillows, and comforters. And after that were stacks of pots and trays and other kitchenware. Up and down the aisles Carolyn went, scanning the ten-foot-high shelves for medical supplies. She stopped abruptly and gazed up at shiny, metallic objects, hoping they might be oxygen tanks. They weren't. The objects were bathroom fixtures. Faucets, showerheads, chrome handles, and dust-covered mirrors.

The next section held furniture and drapes and rugs. Then more furniture and more rugs.

On the next to the last aisle, Carolyn found what she was looking for. There were shelves packed with x-ray and laboratory equipment and instruments for minor surgery. The adjacent shelves held dressings and casting materials and boxes of antibiotics. Then her eyes lit up as they focused in on bags of IV fluids and setups, which she grabbed and piled onto the gurney. And next to them was a row of small oxygen tanks! She snatched up a half-dozen tanks and secured them onto the gurney with a wrap-around belt.

Feeling reinvigorated, Carolyn pushed the gurney toward the door. *Maybe this is a good sign*, she thought. *Maybe things are starting to turn around.*

At first she didn't see the man standing in the entrance. But she did when he put out his hand to stop the gurney in its tracks. She jerked her head up and saw Robbie Hendricks staring at her.

"Where do you think you're going?" he asked.

"Back to the sick bay," Carolyn lied.

"Well, you can go," Robbie said. "Just leave all the supplies behind."

"These things are for the sick passengers," she argued. "They are of no value to you."

"We'll let Richard Scott determine that."

"There's a sick child who really needs the oxygen tanks," Carolyn pleaded.

"Needs it bad, eh?"

"Really badly."

Robbie shifted the shotgun in his flexed arm, which caused his deltoid muscle to bulge, and this expanded his red-rose tattoo. "What are you willing to trade for it?"

"What are you talking about?" she asked, missing the point of his question.

"I'm talking about you and me getting it on down here," he explained and patted the gurney. "We could use this instead of a bed."

"You go to hell!" Carolyn spat.

"You seem to forget I've got a shotgun, which can be very persuasive."

"And you seem to forget I've got a boyfriend who would rip you apart," Carolyn snapped, her voice strong despite the fear running through her. They were alone on the huge level. No one was there to help her or even hear her screams. She quickly added, "And he's one tough guy."

"Wooo!" Robbie feigned a giant shiver. "Now I'm really scared."

"You should be, if you had any sense," Carolyn said.

Robbie waved his shotgun in her face. "How do you think he'd measure up against this?"

"That won't help," Carolyn said, not missing a beat. *If he was going to kill or rape me, he would have done it by now. I think!* "Before you could fire that weapon, you'd find yourself over the side, like Choi. Except David won't pull you up."

Robbie stared at her for a long moment. "How do you know about Choi? You weren't there."

"But a lot of others were, and they're still talking about what a mean son of a bitch my boyfriend is."

Robbie pointed his shotgun at her and moved in closer. He suddenly grabbed her left breast and squeezed it hard. "Fuck him!"

Carolyn gritted her teeth against the pain. Her fear returned and sent a chill through her body. *He's going to do it! He's going to push me down onto the gurney and do it!* Desperately, she looked around for a weapon to defend herself. "Y-you hurt me and he'll come after you big time."

Robbie squeezed her breast again, then shoved her away. "After Choi finishes with your boyfriend, there won't be enough of him left to come after anybody."

Carolyn glared at him, hating him and wanting to tell him that soon he would have to face someone from Special Forces who would turn his life into a living hell. But the last thing she needed to do was to provoke him further, so she held her tongue.

"That's enough talk," Robbie said coarsely. "Now you get your smart-alecky ass out of here before I lose my temper."

"I want a tank of oxygen," she insisted. "For the little girl."

"No," Robbie said and aimed his shotgun at her head. "Move it!"

Carolyn seethed at the merciless, tattooed man, hating him even more. She spun around on her heels and hurried down the passageway, with only one wish on her mind. To see that no-good bastard die.

TWENTY-SEVEN

WHEN CAROLYN RETURNED, DAVID was at bedside, taking his sleeping daughter's pulse. Kit looked even worse, with a deeply flushed face and raspy respirations. She seemed to be growing sicker by the minute.

"Her heart is racing at 120 beats per minute," David said softly. "And she's having occasional extra beats."

"Should I get the EKG machine?" Carolyn asked.

David shook his head. "It won't help her or me. If she were to develop an arrhythmia, there are no drugs in the sick bay to treat it."

Carolyn watched David lean over and kiss Kit's forehead. "Still hot?"

"Burning up, despite the Tylenol I gave her an hour ago." He took Carolyn's arm and guided her into the sitting room. Keeping his voice low, he asked, "Were you able to find some oxygen tanks?"

"Yes and no," Carolyn replied.

"What the hell does that mean?"

"It means there weren't any in the sick bay, but I found a row of tanks in the storage space you told me about."

David glanced around. "So where are they?"

"Robbie saw me in the passageway with the tanks and refused to let me have them," Carolyn explained. "He said we needed Richard Scott's approval. But I think he was just being mean and nasty and trying to show who was boss."

"I'll go talk to him," David said at once and started for the door.

Carolyn grabbed his arm. "It won't help. They will make you beg but still refuse to give up the oxygen tanks."

"How can you be so sure?"

"Because they'd like for Kit to stay really sick. That way you'll have to stay with her and be out of their hair."

"You're probably right," David agreed reluctantly. "But I have to somehow get those tanks for Kit."

"I was thinking the same thing, but I don't know how to do it."

"Neither do I," he had to admit.

"But you'll come up with a way, won't you?" Carolyn said and stepped in to hug him. As she pressed up against him, she winced in pain. "Ah!"

"What?" David asked immediately.

"My chest."

"What about your chest?"

Carolyn took a deep breath and rubbed involuntarily at the tender spot. "When Robbie stopped me, he decided he wanted to fool around. I told him to get lost, so he got angry and reached out for me. Before I could move away, he squeezed my breast really hard."

David quickly unbuttoned the top of her blouse and saw a large black and blue bruise across the upper part of her left breast. His eyes suddenly went stone-cold. "That son of a bitch!"

"And some," Carolyn added. "He may also be a sadist. I think he actually enjoyed doing it."

"He won't enjoy what he's about to get in return," David said icily.

"Don't do anything rash, David. They're just waiting for you to make a stupid move, so they can turn Choi loose on you."

"I won't do anything rash."

"Promise?"

"Promise," David said as he remembered the words of a tough Special Forces instructor. *Rash and stupid gets you killed. Smart and controlled gets the other guy killed.* "I won't act out of anger, and that's a double promise."

"Good," Carolyn said. "Now, what about getting an oxygen tank for Kit?"

"Let me think on it," David told her, but a plan was already forming in his mind. It was based on two assumptions. First, Robbie wasn't nearly as bright as he thought he was. And second, like most not very bright people, Robbie was a creature of habit. Those two flaws could get Kit a tank of oxygen and cost Robbie his life. All David needed was a few more details. "Are there any other developments I should know about?"

Carolyn pondered the question at length before saying, "A fair number of the passengers are starting to panic. Some are totally out of control. I didn't think it would happen to so many so soon."

"And it'll get worse," David said, nodding. "When people see death at a distance, it's only interesting. When it gets up close, it scares the hell out of them. They'll do just about anything to survive."

"Including pillaging a sick bay until there's nothing left but trash on the floor."

David nodded again. "Wait until the grand finale. When land is sighted, the passengers will rush for the lifeboats, which will quickly fill up. And more people will pile in until the boats are so overloaded they begin to sink. Then you'll see real panic."

"Do you think Scott will allow that to happen?"

"He wants it to happen. The more people and boats in the water, the greater the distraction."

"So he and his pals can slip ashore more easily."

"Exactly. And if some of the passengers drown, that'll be okay with Scott too."

Carolyn shuddered to herself. "That's cold!"

"And clever."

Kit let out a loud cough, then another, longer and louder yet. Seconds ticked by and the silence returned.

"That was a strong one," Carolyn noted.

"Sometimes she seems to be clearing her lungs, other times not," David said, glancing back to the bedroom. "Unfortunately, the weak ones outnumber the good ones."

"Maybe she'll start having more good coughs," Carolyn hoped.

David shook his head sadly. "It will only become worse and worse. And before long, her airflow will diminish to the point where there's obvious oxygen deprivation."

"Then get those oxygen tanks!" Carolyn demanded.

"Wait," David said patiently.

"For what?"

"A little more time to pass."

"What happens then?"

"Then people's body clocks reset, and their eyelids become heavy."
Carolyn smiled. "And their reflexes slow."

"Among other things."

"How long will—"

There was a loud knock on the door.

"Jesus!" Carolyn moaned. "Who can that be at this hour?"

"Maybe Karen," David said, then called out, "Who is it?"

"Robbie," came the rough reply. "Open the damn door!"

"What do you think he wants?" Carolyn whispered.

"I don't know," David whispered back. "But stay behind me.
Whatever happens, stay behind me."

"Open it!" Robbie barked.

David approached the door carefully. It had a peephole, but he
had learned long ago never to use one. It could mean certain death
if the person on the other side had a gun. All the shooter had to
do was wait for the peephole to darken, then fire a shot through it.
The bullet would go through the eye, into the brain, and out the
back of the skull in a tenth of a second.

David opened the door. Robbie stood square in the center of
the passageway, with his shotgun pointed into the cabin. Choi was
off to the side, his thick, hairless hand on the hilt of his knife.

"What do you want?" David asked.

"You're to come with us," Robbie ordered.

"I can't," David said firmly. "My daughter is very ill and I have
to remain at her bedside."

"This isn't a request," Robbie snapped.

"And this isn't a polite refusal," David retorted. "I stay. You move on."

"We figured you'd play it this way."

"Who's *we*? The two brain cells you have inside your head?"

Robbie poked his shotgun into David's ribs. "It'd be real easy to blow you to hell and back."

"But you won't," David said, unconcerned. "Because you're just following orders. You're not smart enough to give them."

"Not smart enough, eh?" Robbie snarled. "Well, let's try this on for size. I'm going to persuade you to come with us and it's going to be easy. Let me tell you how I'll do it. Rather than have Choi slice you up, I'll have him pick up your daughter and carry her down to the elevator. I'll bet you'll follow us there. And I'll bet you do it really peaceful too."

David's temper began to flare, but he pushed it aside and quickly assessed his situation. He could deflect the muzzle of the shotgun away from his ribs, but Robbie would still pull the trigger. The shot would spray all over the cabin and might hit Carolyn. And then there was Choi and his knife to deal with. That would be far too risky. David sighed and turned back to Carolyn. "You stay with Kit. I'll return as soon as possible."

"Good boy," Robbie said derisively.

"Let me just check on my daughter before we leave," David said in a submissive voice.

"Make it quick," Robbie growled.

David hurried into the bedroom and glanced over his shoulder to make certain no one was watching. *They might frisk me*, he thought hastily. *And then I'd lose the only advantage I have.* He quickly removed the hatchet from the back of his belt and placed it under Kit's pillow. She groaned weakly, but remained asleep. David came back into the sitting room and said to Carolyn, "Keep a close eye on her."

Robbie shoved David into the passageway and kept the shotgun pointed at him.

"Where are we headed?" David asked.

"You'll see," Robbie said and poked the muzzle of his shotgun into David's ribs. "I just hope you make a dumb move and give me a reason to pull the trigger of this fine Browning."

Don't worry, David thought to himself. *I won't make a dumb move. When the time comes, I'll make a smart move you won't see. You won't even feel it. Because dead men can't feel.*

TWENTY-EIGHT

CAROLYN WAS WRONG ON all counts. Robbie hadn't confiscated the oxygen tanks on some sadistic impulse or to show he was boss or to demonstrate how mean and nasty he could be. He was ordered to do it, so the tanks would be available for Richard Scott's flu-stricken girlfriend. David looked down at Deedee Anderson and saw death coming.

"What do you think?" Scott asked.

"It's bad," David said frankly. "Very bad."

Deedee's face was colored a deep blue from lack of oxygen, and her respirations were so weak they resembled squeaks more than breaths. And most of her beauty had disappeared. Her blond hair was a messy tangle, and what little makeup she had on was smudged. She was wearing a scant, silk nightie, but all of her sexuality was long gone.

"Can you do anything for her?" Scott queried.

"Some oxygen might help."

"Then give her some," Scott directed, and pointed to a small tank on the floor near the head of the bed.

David quickly started Deedee on oxygen, using a plastic, transparent mask to deliver it. He adjusted the flow to two liters per minute. Casually glancing around, he searched for other tanks, but saw none. So Scott had only one tank in the cabin, David thought, and Carolyn had used the plural *tanks* when describing her encounter with Robbie. That being the case, where were the other tanks? Probably still down in storage, in a secure place.

"I hear your daughter is sick," Scott said, breaking the silence. His voice was matter-of-fact and showed no concern. "Right?"

"Yes," David said.

"Is she as sick as Deedee?"

"Almost."

Scott nodded slowly to himself. "You've got to be thinking about getting her ashore."

"It crossed my mind," David said honestly.

"You could come with us," Scott offered. "I'd see to it you were in the front of the line to the lifeboats."

Oh yes, David thought, not trusting Scott for a half-second. *We'd board well after you and the other mutineers were already in the water and heading for shore. And we'd be in an overcrowded lifeboat, with chaos all around, and no guarantee of ever reaching land.* Yet still, it was a chance to get Kit ashore. But to what? An isolated island or one with second-rate medical facilities at best.

"Well?" Scott pressed.

"I'll pass," David said. "I'm not going to start a pandemic, which will kill millions upon millions, just to save my own skin."

"What about your daughter's skin?" Scott asked cruelly. "Are you just going to let her die on this ship?"

David looked away and tried not to second-guess himself.

There was a loud knock on the door. Scott and another mutineer named Tommy aimed their shotguns at the entryway.

"Yes?" Scott shouted.

"Choi," a voice shouted back.

"Come in!"

Choi hurried into the room. Ignoring the mutineers, he gave David a *I can't wait to cut your heart out* stare. The glare lasted for a full five seconds before Choi turned to Scott. "Important news! Hurricane pass over Cuba and go to Gulf of Mexico. All clear by thirty-six hours. We now head for port. Yes?"

"Yes," Scott said promptly. "Find Robbie and bring him to me."

"I look," Choi said in broken English. "No see."

"He's guarding the storage area."

Great! David wanted to yell. The not-too-bright creature of habit Robbie was guarding the oxygen tanks, all by himself.

"Tell him to meet me on the bridge," Scott commanded. "You stand guard in Robbie's place."

Shit! David's spirits suddenly sank. Choi would be a lot harder to deal with. And a lot harder to kill.

"I need keep eye on crew," Choi said and raised his right hand. Several knuckles were bruised and bloody. "Make sure they stay in line."

"He'll only be gone for a few hours."

Choi gave some sort of salute and left.

"Tommy," Scott went on, "take the doctor back to his cabin."

"You want him to stay in there?" Tommy asked.

"For now."

David quickly interceded. "I've got a lot of other patients to care for. Dr. Kellerman can't look after all of them. She's already worn to a frazzle."

Scott studied him carefully, as if suspecting that something was amiss.

"There's a big ex-marine in a cabin down the way," David added. "His wife is sick as hell and he demands that she be seen frequently."

"So?" Scott asked, unmoved.

"So I don't think you want to piss him off," David said. "But then, that's your choice."

Scott hesitated before nodding slowly. "Okay. But I want you back here in two hours to check on Deedee."

"In two hours," David repeated, like he was making a mental note.

Tommy escorted David back to his cabin, keeping the correct distance between them. Not up close, as Robbie had done, but rather eight feet or so behind. That gave Tommy plenty of time to squeeze off a round in the event David decided to make a sudden move. And Tommy made no attempt at conversation. He wasn't going to be distracted.

At the entrance to the cabin, Tommy recited Scott's orders. "You show up in Deedee's room in two hours or I come looking for you."

David closed the door, then put his ear to it. He heard footsteps fading into the distance. He waited another minute to make certain the mutineer wasn't creeping back, then dashed into Kit's bedroom.

She appeared even sicker. Her temperature was sky-high, her pulse racing. And her cough seemed weaker.

"Any change?" he asked Carolyn.

She shook her head. "Not really. Except the good coughs are fewer and fewer apart."

"Shit," David grumbled, feeling even more helpless than before.

"David, you've somehow got to get Kit more oxygen."

"I plan to."

"When?"

"In an hour or so. Maybe a little longer."

"What are you waiting for?"

"A changing of the guard."

———

David tiptoed down the staircase, barely making a sound. He kept his ears pricked and listened for any noise that would indicate he wasn't alone. The stairwell remained dead quiet. He checked his watch. 4:40 a.m. An hour and a half had passed since he'd left Deedee's cabin. That was enough time for Robbie to go to the bridge and ascertain that the captain was making the desired course correction, then return to his post on the storage level. David could only hope that Robbie had followed that time schedule. Because if Choi was still standing guard, it would greatly complicate matters. Again he listened for noises and heard none.

He altered the expression on his face to one of urgency and hurried out of the staircase and down a long passageway. The carpenter's shop was dark, the laundry room well lighted but deserted. Ahead, David saw a figure with its back to him. He couldn't tell if it was Robbie or Choi. It was too dim. Abruptly the figure spun around. It was Robbie. His shotgun came up quickly to waist level as he released the safety.

"What are you doing down here?" Robbie asked suspiciously.

"Scott sent me down," David said in a rush. "Deedee needs more oxygen now!"

Robbie didn't budge. "I just took up a tank."

"Well, she needs more," David urged. "She's turning blue."

Robbie still wasn't convinced. "I'm not going to let you carry a tank out of here all by yourself."

"You'd better check with Scott before he gets really mad," David bluffed, and instantly regretted the suggestion. Robbie might use a phone. "Or better yet," he went on hurriedly, "you can follow me and the tank up to Deedee's room. Then you'll be certain she receives the oxygen."

"Yeah, we'll go up to her room together," Robbie said, like it was his idea.

"Where are the oxygen tanks?" David asked.

"Go straight ahead to the door on your right," Robbie ordered. "And don't try anything brave unless you want a load of buckshot up your ass."

David raced down the passageway ahead of Robbie. But now Robbie stayed ten feet back and remained silent. *Maybe he was getting smarter*, David thought. But he still wasn't very sharp. He'd already committed a bunch of mistakes. *If I had a weapon, he would have been dead a dozen times over.*

They came to a large door that led into the dark storage area. Stopping at the entrance, David asked, "Where is the light switch?"

"On the wall to your right," Robbie answered.

"To the right, eh?" David queried, now sensing Robbie just behind him.

"Yeah."

David stepped into the dimness, knowing that it would take approximately five seconds for his eyes to adapt to the dark. He would be virtually sightless during that time. And so would Robbie. "On the right, eh?" he asked again.

Before Robbie could answer, David cocked his elbow and smashed it full force into Robbie's sternum. The sternum or breastbone consists of 1/4-inch of ossified calcium, and is so hard that cardiac surgeons have to use an electric saw to cut through it. Not that this mattered to Robbie. He was sprawled out on the floor, clutching his fractured sternum and grimacing at the terrible pain, totally unaware of what caused it.

David watched him for a moment before deciding how to kill him. He lifted Robbie up, and grabbing his head, powerfully jerked it around counterclockwise. There was a loud snap. David knew from the sound alone that the jerk had been a good one, with enough force to tear through the muscles and vertebrae in Robbie's neck before shredding his spinal cord into a thousand miniscule fibers. Robbie suddenly stiffened in a giant spasm, then went limp. David noiselessly eased the body to the floor and checked for a carotid pulse. None was detectable.

David switched the lights on and waited for his eyes to accommodate to the brightness. Quickly he grabbed Robbie's collar and dragged his body across four aisles to where the rugs were stored. He unrolled a long, fine Persian one and placed Robbie on the far edge. Then he rolled Robbie up inside the rug and hoisted it up onto a large shelf. But one of Robbie's feet was sticking out. David added two more rolls of rug atop the stack. Now Robbie's body was completely hidden.

David sprinted to the next aisle over and found the oxygen tanks and other medical equipment precisely where Carolyn had told him they would be. He stuffed his pockets with IV fluid bags and setups, then grabbed two small tanks of oxygen and dashed for the door.

He nearly stumbled over Robbie's shotgun. David's spirits soared. *Great! Now I can take out those bastards one at a time or as a group.* The mutiny on the *Grand Atlantic* had just ended. Dropping the tanks, he picked up the Browning shotgun and examined it for damage. None was noticeable except for a scratch here and there. Next he checked the chamber to see how many rounds it held. It was empty! The goddamn chamber was empty! It took a few seconds for his surprise to wear off, and another few seconds for him to list the reasons why the weapon was not loaded. Either it was always empty because Richard Scott trusted no one other than himself, or he demanded it be emptied after the fatal shooting of Arthur Maggio. Whatever the reason, David groused to himself, it was bad news. An empty shotgun was a worthless shotgun.

He picked up the small tanks of oxygen and, tucking the shotgun under his arm, ran for the stairs.

TWENTY-NINE

DAVID RUSHED INTO KIT'S cabin and quickly closed the door behind. He tossed the empty shotgun aside before dashing into the bedroom.

Carolyn looked up and smiled broadly. "You got 'em!"

"I got 'em."

"How'd you do it?"

"Later." David checked his watch. It was now 5:10 a.m. Tommy would be coming in a matter of minutes to escort him back to Deedee's cabin. "Here," he said hastily and handed Carolyn the two small oxygen tanks. "Set up one for Kit and hide the other."

"Hide it where?"

"Use your imagination."

David sprinted out to the sliding glass doors leading to the balcony and opened them. After a moment's hesitation, he tossed the useless shotgun overboard. He had considered holding onto the weapon and searching for shells, but that would have been very dangerous. Had the mutineers discovered the shotgun, they would have known it was Robbie's, and David would have been a dead man. Again David wondered how many of the shotguns were loaded. Richard Scott's for sure. The weapons of the other two mutineers—maybe. But who the hell knew? And it wasn't worth the risk to find out. A wrong move could cost him his life.

He spun around and hurried back into the bedroom. Moving quietly to Kit's bedside, he felt his heart breaking once more. Kit looked so sick, with her short, labored respirations and flushed facies. Carolyn already had the oxygen going, and had ensured maximum delivery by placing a plastic mask over the child's nose and mouth. But it didn't seem to be helping much.

"Two small tanks won't last long," Carolyn said in a whisper.

"When she needs more, I'll get more," David whispered back.

"You should have taken all the damn tanks," Carolyn chided mildly.

David shook his head. "They probably won't notice two missing tanks. But if all of them were gone, they'd guess what happened and begin an intensive search for Robbie."

"What happened to Robbie?" Carolyn asked.

"He won't bother you again," David replied vaguely.

"What happened to him?" she asked again.

"I snapped his neck."

"Good," Carolyn said without emotion. "Did you throw the body overboard?"

"I couldn't," David answered. "There was no open balcony down there."

"I hope you hid him well."

"He won't be easy to find," David said and glanced around the bedroom. "Where did you hide the second oxygen tank?"

Carolyn gestured with her head to Juanita. "I rolled it up in a towel and wrapped her rosary beads around it. Then I squeezed it inside her bathrobe."

"Nice," David approved. "They won't bother to look there."

"Don't be so sure," Carolyn warned. "They think you're up to something, and they keep checking on you. About a half-hour ago, one of the mutineers knocked on the door to see if you were still here."

"What did you tell him?" David asked.

"That you were examining your daughter and for him to be quiet."

"And he bought it?"

Carolyn shrugged. "He went away. But I could sense from the sound of his voice that he'd be back soon. And he may come in next time."

"And maybe search around."

"That's what I'm thinking too," Carolyn said, then pointed to Kit's pillow. "And by the way, I found your hatchet under Kit's pillow, so I put it inside the pillow case itself. That makes it a little harder to find."

Kit moaned and coughed, but not with enough strength to bring up sputum. Her face was still flushed and very red, despite the added oxygen she was receiving. She coughed again, the cough even weaker this time.

David reached for this stethoscope and listened to Kit's chest. As before, he heard rhonchi and rales, but now there were wheezes too. A bad sign. Her airways were becoming more obstructed. He quickly examined the mucous membranes in her nose and mouth. They were as dry as sandpaper.

"Let's start an IV," David directed.

Carolyn nodded and reached for an IV setup. "Five percent dextrose in water?"

"For now," David said and leaned over to kiss his daughter's forehead. Her skin was still hot, her fever at least 102°. "And she'll need more Tylenol."

David stepped back, feeling helpless and wishing he could do more. Kit was deteriorating right before his eyes, and there was nothing he could do about it. Once again he considered joining Richard Scott and the others, and taking Kit ashore in one of the first lifeboats. At least that way there was a chance for survival. It was admittedly a slim chance, but nevertheless a chance.

Juanita propped herself up on an elbow and asked in a worried voice, "How is the Little One?"

"Not good," David said candidly.

With effort, Juanita pushed her body to the edge of her bed. She didn't notice the small tank of oxygen roll out from under her robe and clang onto the floor. "I will help her."

David eased her back onto her pillow. "In a little while, you can help us."

Juanita nodded, exhausted by the brief exertion. Slowly her eyes closed. "You will tell me when."

"I will tell you when."

Carolyn started an IV infusion of 5 percent dextrose in water on Kit and taped the needle down securely, then leaned over for the fallen tank of oxygen on the floor. "Not such a good hiding place after all, eh?"

David gazed rapidly around the room. His eyes went from the mattresses to the leatherbound chair to the chest of drawers, then to the closet and lamp tables. *Too much in the open*, he thought. They'd find the tank in a matter of minutes. And they'd take it from the cabin without giving Kit a second thought. His gaze drifted up to the ceiling and to the expensive lighting fixture that had wide blades of glass protruding from it. *Too small! Not strong enough!* Then he saw what he was looking for. He pointed to a large ventilation duct. "We can unscrew the screen and stick the tank in there."

"Perfect!" Carolyn said and reached in her pocket for a coin to use as a screwdriver.

Juanita raised up once more, saying, "I will help the Little One now."

"Later," David told her and waited for the nanny to plop back onto her pillow. But now she kept her eyes open and fixed on Kit.

In a barely audible voice, Carolyn asked, "Where does she get her strength from?"

"From loving Kit as much as I do, I guess," David said and grabbed a chair to position it directly under the large ventilation duct. "Once I get the screen off, you hand—"

There was a powerful rap on the outer door to the suite. A voice yelled, "Ballineau, out!"

"What do you think he wants?" Carolyn asked quietly.

"For me to see Deedee again," David surmised.

Carolyn shook her head. "He sounds really angry. Like maybe they found Robbie's body."

"We'll see," David said and motioned up to the ventilation duct. "You hide the oxygen tank while I'm away."

"Be careful, David."

He darted through the sitting room to the door, thinking that if Tommy was by himself, there was no real trouble. If Choi was with him, it meant double trouble.

David opened the door and saw only Tommy, with his shotgun pointed downward. They obviously hadn't discovered Robbie's body or that two oxygen tanks were missing.

"What?" David asked.

"We're going to the bridge," Tommy answered.

"Why?"

"Because the captain says so."

David squinted an eye quizzically. "Locke wants to see me?"

"No. Richard Scott does."

"He's no damn captain," David said derisively.

"As long as he controls the ship, he is," Tommy growled. "Now move it."

They walked at a fast pace down the passageway and into a waiting elevator. As the elevator ascended, David studied the mutineer in his peripheral vision. Tommy stood off to the side, expressionless, his eyes glued on David. The mutineer carried the shotgun exactly right. He held it waist high, not too tight, ready to fire instantly. Tommy was clearly at ease around shotguns, but that didn't tell David whether it was loaded or not.

David motioned with his head toward the Browning shotgun. "Is that a Citori model?" he asked, already knowing it was.

"Yeah," Tommy said tersely.

"Does it have a chrome-plated chamber?" David asked, again knowing the answer.

"All Citoris have a chrome-plated chamber," Tommy said neutrally.

"How many rounds does it hold?"

"Make a sudden move and you'll find out."

It's probably loaded, David thought to himself. Just the way Tommy held it and talked about it told David that the mutineer had a lot of experience with shotguns. And Tommy didn't learn all that from skeet shooting. He knew how to bear arms.

"Were you in the Army?" David asked casually.

"Airborne."

David nodded to himself. Tommy had checked out the weapon, like any good soldier would. It was loaded for sure.

THIRTY

THEY STEPPED ONTO THE bridge in bright sunlight. It took a few seconds for David's eyes to adapt and see beyond the sunbeams streaking in through the wide glass windows. There were three others on the bridge. Directly in front of him was Richard Scott, who was nibbling on a donut. Off to the side, Jonathan Locke was peering at a radar screen, while another mutineer stood guard over him. David briefly studied the youngest of the mutineers. He was tall and muscular and had red hair, with a buzz cut. He also had a raspy cough that he tried to suppress.

"How is Deedee?" Scott asked.

"I haven't reexamined her," David replied.

"Why not?"

"Because your man hustled me up to the bridge, that's why."

Scott looked over at Tommy. "Well?"

"I figured this was more important than her," Tommy said bluntly.

"You figured right," Scott said, and finished the last of his donut. Licking his fingertips, he turned back to David. "The CDC just called. They want to talk with you."

"About what?" David asked.

"They didn't say, but we're about to find out."

Scott motioned for David and Tommy to follow him and led the way into the small, private communications room. He waited for David to sit, then snapped his fingers at the chief radio officer. "Get the CDC on the line."

David watched the chief radio officer follow orders without the slightest hesitation and wondered if he was the inside man who helped Scott pull off the mutiny and commandeer the *Grand Atlantic*. They needed someone who knew all about ships to take it over and make certain Scott's orders were being followed exactly. It could have been the chief radio officer or Jonathan Locke or any of the other senior officers. David would know for sure when they were about to reach landfall. The one who jumped into the first lifeboat would be the traitor.

"I have the CDC," the chief radio officer called out.

Scott quickly sat across from David and reached over for the hold button on the speakerphone. "Be very careful what you say."

David heard Lawrence Lindberg's voice come over the phone. "Dr. Ballineau?"

"I'm here," David said.

"How are things?"

"Things are awful," David reported. "There are over a hundred dead and twice that number dying. And all of our supplies are exhausted."

"We'll try to get more to you. What do you need?"

"Everything. We need IV fluids and setups, oxygen tanks, antibiotics, bronchodilators, and the ventilators you promised. And most importantly, we need more doctors and nurses. We're way beyond being overwhelmed."

"We may be able to help you with additional personnel."

David leaned in closer to the speakerphone. "How?"

"You have to understand that we're still in the planning stage."

"Cut the bullshit and tell me how," David demanded.

"It's now clear that the newly formed hurricane will head directly into the Gulf of Mexico. It will track well away from the Bahamas. With that in mind, we may be able to transform the *Grand Atlantic* into a floating hospital."

"You *may* be able to?" David asked, losing patience. "What does that mean?"

"I know how difficult it is for you. But you—"

"No! You don't know how difficult it is for me," David cut him off. "We're out of time and we're going to end up with nothing but dead people on this ship. It's not going to be a floating hospital. It's going to be a floating morgue. So stop using words like *may* and *may be*. Tell me exactly what you plan to do and when you plan to do it."

Everyone in the communications room heard the sound of multiple conversations taking place on the other end of the line. Someone raised his voice, but another voice quieted him. There were more loud words in the background before Lawrence Lindberg came back on the line.

"Here are the specifics," he said in a decisive tone. "Your current position is 820 miles northeast of the Bahamas. According to the ship's company, you have just enough fuel to reach Nassau. We will instruct your captain to steam to Nassau, where the *Grand Atlantic* will be refueled offshore. From there, the ship will proceed to an isolated area off the east coast of Mexico where medical supplies and personnel will be waiting."

"Why not some place off the coast of Florida?" David asked. "It's a lot closer."

"For two important reasons," Lindberg told him. "First and foremost, we don't want the *Grand Atlantic* anywhere near heavily populated areas. And second, the weather forecast calls for severe thunderstorms with strong gusts along the Florida coast. That would obviously make things much more difficult. So it'll have to be Mexico."

"Where is this isolated area in Mexico?"

"We're working on that now."

I'll bet, David wanted to say, now certain he was being given the runaround.

"We'll contact you again once we have more definite information."

The phone line went dead.

Richard Scott let out a whoop of joy. He danced over to Tommy and high-fived him. "Perfect! It's perfect! They're going to let us go straight into Nassau and they won't suspect a thing. And when we're close enough to the island, we'll put all the lifeboats in the water and head for land."

Tommy smiled broadly and high-fived Scott back.

"And they'll only have a refueling tanker out there," Scott continued on. "Can you imagine what they'll do when they suddenly see two dozen lifeboats chugging for shore?"

Tommy nodded. "They won't know whether to shit or go blind."

Scott nodded back. "By the time they respond, most of the lifeboats will be near or on the beach." He turned to David and added, "And you can stay on this ship with the goddamn virus, while our government begs Mexico for one of their crummy little islands."

The chief radio officer stepped forward and asked, "Why don't you just wait until we reach the Mexican island, where they can help us?"

"Because there isn't going to be any Mexican island," Scott told him. "There's a hurricane that will move across the Gulf of Mexico, which means we can't go anywhere in the Gulf. And that leaves the east coast of the Yucatan Peninsula, where I've spent many vacations. That's where Mexico has a multibillion-dollar-a-year tourist industry. It's Mexico's version of the French Riviera. They won't allow this ship to come anywhere near the Yucatan and start a pandemic and turn that area back into a jungle. Trust me. They're not that stupid."

Tommy stroked his chin and gave the matter further thought. "So they're just planning to let this ship float around until everybody is dead."

"Except for those of us who reach land in Nassau," Scott said. "This is still a death ship, and it's going to stay that way."

David kept his face expressionless, but he knew Scott was right. There would be no remote island off of Mexico where medical help awaited them. All the reasons Scott gave were valid, but he missed the most important one. If the American government really wanted to help, they would have directed the ship to Guantanamo Bay near the easternmost tip of Cuba. We have a naval base there. We have a harbor there where the *Grand Atlantic* could dock. We have a huge runway there to land giant cargo planes. And Guantanamo is relatively close to Nassau, so we could reach there without refueling. *So,* David thought on sourly, *they are going to let all of us die on this ship. They're going to sacrifice us for the greater good.*

"Well," Scott was saying as he gleefully rubbed his hands together, "we have plans to make, and not a lot of time to draw them up. Let's see now. We're traveling at twenty-eight miles an hour and we're about 800 miles from Nassau. At that speed, we'll reach the island in just over thirty hours."

"Should we alert the crew?" Tommy asked.

"Not yet," Scott said promptly. "We don't—"

The door to the communications room burst open and Choi hurried in. His arms and shirt were covered with dust and grime. "No find Robbie!"

"Did you check his cabin?" Scott asked.

Choi nodded.

"What about the storage area?"

Choi nodded again. "Look everywhere. No find Robbie."

"Sometimes he catches a snooze on the cot in the carpenter's shop," Tommy suggested.

"No there," Choi said.

A worried look came across Scott's face. He knitted his brow and concentrated before asking, "Where was his last duty station?"

"Guard storage area," Choi replied.

"Maybe he's asleep down there," Scott thought aloud.

Choi shook his head. "Too hot to sleep there."

"Check the area again," Scott directed. "Search it carefully, wall to wall."

"Already search."

"Do it again," Scott barked. "Now!"

Choi rushed out of the room, grumbling to himself.

Too hot, David thought miserably. *Too hot in the storage area.* He hadn't considered that when he rolled Robbie's body up in a thick Persian rug. The body would stay hidden, but the smell that would emanate from it wouldn't. In the hot, humid air, Robbie's body would rapidly decompose. David had seen bodies in the jungle do that before, and it happened in a matter of hours.

"I don't like it," Scott was saying. "It's not like Robbie to go missing."

Tommy shrugged. "If anybody messed with him, they'd have to contend with his shotgun."

"Yeah, yeah," Scott muttered under his breath.

David nodded inwardly, now convinced that Scott had unloaded Robbie's shotgun, with or without his knowledge. He knew Robbie couldn't use it to defend himself.

"Without Robbie, we can't be sure the captain isn't fooling around with the ship's course," Tommy said.

"There are ways to make certain he doesn't." Scott reached for a ring of keys, which he held up and jingled. "Very persuasive ways."

Tommy smiled knowingly. "That should keep him real honest."

"Or real sick, if he does something stupid," Scott said, and headed for the door.

THIRTY-ONE

"SHE LOOKS DEAD," TOMMY commented.

"She almost is," David said and pulled the sheet up to Deedee Anderson's chin.

The woman's face was now so blue that it was impossible to tell if she was Caucasian. Air was barely moving in and out of her lungs, causing severe oxygen deprivation and deep cyanosis. And she seemed to be aging by the hour. Her lines and skin folds had become much more noticeable.

"How long you figure she's got?" Tommy asked.

"Not long," David answered as Deedee gasped weakly for air. It was more of a hiccough than a gasp. "Does death bother you?"

Tommy shrugged. "Not particularly."

"Good," David said. "If you're here when she dies, I want you to run up to the bridge and inform Scott."

Tommy shrugged again. "They were never that close, you know."

"Oh?"

"Well, I mean they were sleeping together and all that. But she was more like a toy than anything else."

"Nevertheless, if she dies in your presence, you tell Scott."

"Is that an order?" Tommy asked, with an edge to his voice.

"It's more an act of courtesy," David said. "Do you know what courtesy is?"

"Yeah. But it's not going to matter to him, and it sure as hell ain't going to matter to her." Tommy stared down at the motionless woman and studied her purplish face. "Damn! She really looks gross now."

"Death by suffocation does that to a person," David explained. "It's like her tissues are silently screaming for oxygen."

"Ah-huh," Tommy nodded, as if he understood the pathophysiology of anoxia. "What are you going to do with her body?"

"Put it in a body bag."

"Like the Army uses?"

"Yeah, like the Army uses."

Tommy backed away from the foot of the bed, his shotgun aimed at Deedee, his finger loosely on the trigger. "The kindest thing to do would be to blow her head off and stop her suffering."

"That's called murder," David said.

"I was just saying," Tommy went on. "But I'll tell you this. If I ever catch the bird flu, I'll put this shotgun in my mouth and end it. I'm not going to lay around and suck for air while my face turns blue."

David shook his head. "You'll do what everybody else does. You'll hang on and wait and pray for someone or something to save you."

"Bullshit!" Tommy snapped. "I'm not hanging around and waiting on anything. That's why I'm jumping ship the first chance I get. That's called saving your own ass rather than waiting for someone to save it for you."

"What makes you so certain you'll reach land?" David asked.

"I can't be sure," Tommy said without hesitation. "But I figure it's better to die trying instead of sitting here and waiting for some damn virus to kill me. And if you had any sense, you'd get the hell off the *Grand Atlantic* too."

David nodded. He didn't agree with the plan, but he understood its appeal.

"Okay," Tommy said, his voice all business now. "Have you done everything you're going to do for her?"

"Yes."

"Then move out."

They took the elevator up two levels in silence. Tommy kept his eyes on David, as if expecting him to make some sudden maneuver. His shotgun was aimed directly at David's abdomen. David ignored the stare and shotgun as he again thought about Robbie's body and the stench it would soon give off. They'd surely find it and probably also discover that several tanks of oxygen were missing. Then they'd put two and two together and come looking for him. Somehow he had to take care of Robbie's body. But how? Choi and the others would be searching the storage area, and even if they found nothing, they'd still guard it. It would be doubly dangerous to go back down there. And it might give Choi the one thing he wanted most. The opportunity to kill David.

The elevator jerked to a stop. They stepped into a passageway that was noticeably darker than before. Two of the ceiling lights were out, limiting clear vision to no more than ten feet.

"Put your hands on top of your head," Tommy ordered.

David did as he was told.

"Now walk slowly, like you expected your prisoners to do when you were a military cop."

David took short, measured steps, thinking that Tommy was the exact opposite of Robbie. He had obviously been trained in how to deal with those he had captured. He knew all the right moves.

"If it was up to me, I'd put handcuffs on you and throw you into the brig," Tommy said tonelessly.

"Well, I'm glad it's not up to you," David said.

"You're dangerous," Tommy went on, "but not nearly as dangerous as people think you are. Right, tough guy?"

"If you want to find out, put your shotgun down," David challenged.

Tommy smiled thinly. "Maybe another time."

David walked on, nodding to himself. Tommy was smart, very smart, and he wasn't about to be goaded into a fight he might lose. He already had a winning hand. He would be ashore in under thirty hours. Why take any chances?

They came to Kit's cabin. David stopped and felt the muzzle of the shotgun on his spine.

"Don't wander around," Tommy directed. "Stay put in your room."

"But I have to check on the sick passengers," David argued.

"Make certain that's all you do," Tommy said and backed away in the dimness.

David entered the suite and coughed for the first time. It was a dry, shallow cough, but a cough nonetheless. *Christ! Me too? Is this the start of it?* He collected himself and hastily went through the other symptoms of influenza. Fever, chills, malaise. He had none of those, not yet at least. Pushing his self-concern aside, he hurried into the bedroom. Carolyn was reaching up to adjust the flow of IV fluid into Kit's slender arm. His daughter no longer had the transparent plastic mask over her nose and mouth.

"Why did you stop the oxygen?" David asked quickly.

"Because we're out of it," Carolyn replied. "The first tank was full, but the second one had a big leak and was virtually empty."

"Oh Lord!" David groaned loudly, shaking his head at yet another obstacle. "Was the oxygen helping?"

"I think her color was starting to improve, but her cough is still bad," Carolyn said. "We have to get her more oxygen, David."

"That's going to be almost impossible," he said, and told her about the intensive search currently underway for Robbie's body. He repeated word for word the orders Richard Scott had given to Choi. "They somehow know that Robbie is in the storage area, and they'll scour the entire space inch by inch until they find him."

"Maybe his body won't decay so fast," Carolyn said hopefully.

"Trust me. It will. And the stench will lead them right to Robbie."

Kit coughed up thick sputum that clung to her lips. She coughed again. The phlegm rattled in her throat.

Carolyn used a Kleenex to remove the sputum from Kit's mouth. "Poor thing! She's trying so hard."

"While we just sit and watch."

"We're doing the best we can," Carolyn said softly.

David gazed down at his desperately ill daughter and felt totally powerless. Here he was, a highly trained physician, and he could do nothing to save his own child. *Nothing!* His temper rose up, then spilled over. "Goddamn this flu virus!"

"If He does, He's already a little late."

"I guess." David waited for his anger to pass, then took a wet washcloth and dabbed Kit's feverish brow with a gentle touch. She opened her eyes and smiled weakly before dozing off again. David had to fight to hold back his tears.

Behind him he heard Juanita grunt with effort. When he turned, he saw the nanny sitting up in bed, pointing a finger at him.

"Do not curse God," she told him. "He has a long memory."

David stared at her in amazement. Her color was better and her strength was obviously returning. "How are you feeling?"

"Terrible," Juanita admitted. "But now I must treat the Little One."

"With what?"

"Costa Rican herbal tea," Juanita replied. "The boiling tea leaves help clear the lungs."

David's eyes bore into the nanny as he hoped against hope that the herbal tea contained some potent antiviral agent. "Did you use this tea?"

Juanita shook her head. "It only works in children."

"I see," David said, hiding his disappointment. He leaned over to the nanny and eased her back onto her pillow. "You rest now. It will be your turn to watch over the Little One this evening."

"Good," Juanita said, closing her eyes and drifting off again.

David signaled Carolyn and they tiptoed out into the sitting room. They stared at one another, almost not trusting what they had just witnessed. It wasn't a return from the dead, but it was close.

"Unbelievable!" Carolyn breathed.

David nodded. "There's no question she's better. It looks like she's going to survive."

"Maybe the virus isn't as nasty as we originally thought."

"Oh yes, it is," David said firmly. "Everybody who has caught the avian flu virus has died or is dying. So far, we've got over a hundred dead and twice that number dying. And there have been no exceptions until Juanita."

"But why her?"

David shrugged. "Maybe her immune system was able to mount an antibody response against the virus."

"Or maybe she was plain lucky."

"When it comes to medicine, I don't believe in luck."

They heard Kit coughing. A high-pitched, child's cough. She coughed again and again, trying to clear her lungs.

"I've got to get Kit more oxygen," David said determinedly.

"But how?"

David quickly thought about possible sources of oxygen tanks. There were only two. "First, I'll check Deedee Anderson's room for spare tanks. She's so close to death, all the oxygen in the world won't help her. If I can't find any there, I'll have to go back to the storage area."

"But it's so dangerous."

"I have no choice."

They walked on their tiptoes, arm in arm, back into the bedroom. Kit and Juanita were both asleep. The nanny was snoring softly.

David bent over and kissed Kit's forehead. She didn't stir. He turned to Carolyn and said, "You know, I think her color is a little better. I think the oxygen may really be helping."

"I do too," Carolyn agreed and looked directly into David's eyes. "But while you're searching for more oxygen, please remember that a dead father won't do Kit any good."

"I don't plan on dying."

"But if Choi sees you with the oxygen tanks, he'll stop you and kill you."

David reached into Kit's pillowcase and extracted the hatchet. He tested the sharp edge with his fingertip before saying, "If he tries, it'll be the last thing he does on the face of the earth."

Carolyn shivered at the sudden change in David's expression. Now he had on his war face. Now he was a stone-cold killer.

David tucked the hatchet under the back of his belt and slipped silently out of the room.

THIRTY-TWO

DAVID FOUND DEEDEE ANDERSON dead in her cabin. But some-one had been there before him and played with the body. Her silk nightie was ripped open, exposing her silicone-enhanced breasts, and bright red lipstick had been applied in a careless manner. *Sick!* David thought and wondered who was responsible. Richard Scott? Tommy? Maybe one of the crew? Whoever it was, was sick as hell. He covered her with a sheet and searched around for tanks of oxy-gen. The only one he found was on the floor, empty and discarded.

He dashed out of the cabin and down the deserted passageway, now concentrating on the other way to obtain a tank of oxygen for Kit. First, he would need a diversion of some sort. Something to get the mutineers out of the storage area and him in, unnoticed. But what? *A fire? An alarm bell? A smoke—*

David stopped in his tracks. There were faint footsteps and voic-es behind him. He raced for the first cabin door he saw and entered without knocking. Quietly he closed the door and held his ear to it. There was only silence, then voices approaching. A couple. A man and a woman. It couldn't be Choi or the mutineers or any of the deckhands. A door slammed shut. The voices disappeared.

David relaxed, but only for a moment. Abruptly he brought a hand up to muffle another cough, which was again dry and short. Before he could begin to worry about it, he detected a terrible stench in the air. A body was decomposing somewhere in the cabin. He glanced around the empty sitting room, then over to the sliding-glass balcony doors that were closed and kept the odor in. Holding his breath, he walked into the bedroom and saw two bodies on the bed. A woman and a child were bloated and green and decaying in the hot, humid enclosure. He gagged briefly and looked away. The sickening sight reminded him of rotting bodies he'd seen in the streets of Mogadishu twenty years ago. But unlike Somalia, there were no swarming flies, at least not yet.

David hurried out of the cabin and ran for the staircase. He took the stairs down two at a time, making no effort to conceal the sounds of his footsteps. If he was seen and challenged, he had a ready-made excuse for being there. He was on his way to see a sick passenger. David knew that virtually any cabin he went to would have sick or dead occupants. But the storage area was another matter. If he was caught there, he'd have no excuse. He'd have to kill. And that was bad. More bodies meant more problems.

He came to the storage level and cautiously opened the door. The passageway was still and silent, but well lighted. The stillness made the hairs on the back of David's neck stand up. All of his senses were suddenly heightened. Something was wrong. There should be people, noise, the sounds of an ongoing search. He wondered if they had found Robbie's body and taken it topsides.

David moved along the passageway past the carpenter's shop and laundry room, all the while keeping his ears pricked. He heard nothing but his own soft footsteps. As he approached the entrance to the storage space, he reached back and made sure the hatchet under his belt could be extracted with ease.

The lights were off in the storage area, and there were no sounds coming from within. David took a penlight that he used to examine patients' throats and shone it on the floor. Slowly he moved alongside the aisles, counting them, until he came to the one holding the oxygen tanks. On tiptoes, he walked to the shelf where the tanks were stored. *Shit!* There was only one cylinder remaining. He quickly searched the surrounding shelves for more tanks, but saw only boxes of surgical instruments and bags of IV fluids. Cursing again under his breath, he grabbed the sole cylinder of oxygen and raced to the next aisle over. David didn't need his penlight to locate Robbie's body. The stench of decay told him it was very near.

Not good! Not good! David groused. *A blind man could find the body now. And the smell will linger in the rug, long after the body is removed. Goddamn it to hell!*

Hurriedly he recalled the contents of the adjacent shelves. *Furniture. Mattresses. Linens. Fixtures. Then soaps and detergents and other—*

Oh yeah! Detergents! David turned and sprinted full speed past furniture and mattresses and linens before reaching the shelves that held the huge cartons of soaps and detergents. With his penlight, he found two gallon-sized containers of lemon-scented detergent. He gripped their handles and, with the oxygen tank tucked under his arm, dashed back to the aisle where Robbie's body was. He put down the folded body bag he'd brought along and went to work. It took him less than a minute to pull off the stack of rugs and unroll the one with Robbie in it. The stink was awful. The heat within the rolled-up Persian rug had apparently sped up the decaying process.

David hastily poured the lemon-scented detergent onto Robbie's body and the Persian rug, dowsing both. The stench was muted, but it was still there. Now it was a lemon-scented stench. David spun around to obtain more detergent and perhaps some deodorizers as well. Suddenly the lights came on, bright and blinding. David heard voices. Two or three. He couldn't be sure. But one of the voices belonged to Choi.

In a matter of seconds, David rolled Robbie's body into the thick Persian rug and hoisted it up onto the shelf. After pushing the body well in, he piled two more rolls of rugs atop the Persian to ensure that Robbie was completely hidden. Then he took out his hatchet and, crowding into a nearby stack of rugs, he waited.

The voices grew louder, but were still difficult to understand. David concentrated his hearing to catch every word. There were two people near the entrance and they were having an argument.

"We do like Mr. Scott say," Choi was insisting.

"But we've already searched the place," a second voice complained.

"We do again," Choi ordered. "But this time we throw everything off shelf and onto floor."

"Shit! That will take us all day."

"Not if we find Robbie."

"All right," the second voice said begrudgingly. "But what's so important about finding Robbie?"

"Robbie is Mr. Scott's half-brother, and Mr. Scott want Robbie in boat with us," Choi said. "So we find."

David's brow went up. So Robbie was Scott's half-brother! That would explain how Robbie, who was obviously from the working class, could afford to be on a luxury liner that cost at least $8,000 per passenger. The affluent Richard Scott footed the bill for his brother. And no doubt for Tommy as well, who was probably a personal assistant or bodyguard. David stifled a cough and swallowed it back, then concentrated his hearing as the two crewmen began speaking about the lifeboats and how they would be used, particularly if Robbie was sick.

"The lifeboat might get a little crowded with him in it," the second voice said, then had a harsh coughing spell. "It'll get real crowded if we have to lay him down."

David nodded to himself. The voice belonged to the redheaded mutineer who was coughing on the bridge. Hopefully he'd become sicker, and that would leave only Richard Scott and Tommy to deal with. And of course Choi, who was the most dangerous of the lot.

"Big lifeboat," Choi was saying. "Plenty of room for Robbie, Tommy, Mr. Scott, you, me, Locke, and lady doctor."

Son of a bitch! David seethed. Jonathan Locke was the inside man who helped Richard Scott with the mutiny. A goddamn traitor! And then there was Karen Kellerman, two-faced and self-serving like always. She would be the first to jump off the *Grand Atlantic* along with the mutineers, saving herself at the expense of others. *The good doctor*, he thought disgustedly.

David went back to overhearing the conversation between the mutineers.

"So I take this side," Choi directed. "And you take that side. Start here and go all the way to wall."

Ah-huh, David deduced quickly. They planned to start their search in the center of the storage area and work their way to the sides. That would take time, but it would also prevent him from dashing for the entrance. There was no way he could accurately predict where Choi and the other mutineer would be at any given moment. And if he was spotted, Kit would never receive the oxygen, and he could end up dead, especially if Robbie's body was discovered.

David eased himself out from his hiding place and again concentrated his hearing, listening for sounds that would help him pinpoint the location of the mutineers. He heard the thud of boxes as they hit the floor at least four aisles away. Then came the noise of metallic objects clanging together. Then came a loud, raspy cough. It was the redheaded mutineer and he was moving fast. David quickly gazed around for another hiding place, preferably one that would allow him to attack from the back or front. His eyes went to a large shelf, four feet up, just down the aisle from Robbie's body. It held large cushions for lounge chairs. He climbed up quickly and wedged himself into the shelf, feet first. Then he reached back for his hatchet and pulled two cushions in front of his face, leaving a very narrow space between the two for him to spy through.

With his mind preoccupied, David didn't take into account that he was now encased by thick, heavy cushions, which would cause his core temperature to rise. Degree by degree the heat within the closed-off space intensified. David began sweating profusely in the blackness, drenching his shirt top to bottom. Then the flashbacks came, brought on by the scorching heat. He was back in Somalia, surrounded by Islamic terrorists hellbent on killing the Special Forces unit so they could drag their bodies through the streets of central Mogadishu. David's hands started to shake violently as the terrorists in his mind's eye moved in closer, screaming and yelling, their white turbans swirling in the hot wind. Suddenly his chest wouldn't move, like it was caught in a vise. He gasped for air, his senses telling him he was about to suffocate in the enclosed space. Frantically he punched at one of the large cushions and it fell to the aisle below. Air flowed in. Warm air, but cool enough to evaporate some of his sweat and lower his temperature. As the flashbacks faded, he took long, deep breaths in an attempt to steady himself and ease his tremors. But the shaking continued.

My God! I'm coming apart at the worst possible moment. Kit desperately needs oxygen and I'm the only one who can supply it. And my goddamn brain keeps going back to Somalia. Get over it! he commanded himself. *And concentrate on the two men standing between Kit and the oxygen that could save her life.*

Swallowing back his fear, he turned his attention to the two crewmen who were searching for Robbie. He could only hope they didn't hear the large cushion hit the floor, which had to have made an audible thud. He listened intently and heard the crewmen talking to one another. Their voices were still distant, still calm. *Good!* David told himself, climbing down for the large cushion to conceal himself again. But this time he left enough space for air to get in and circulate.

The crewmen's conversation stopped. Then seconds and more seconds or maybe a minute passed. David couldn't be sure because the blackness all around disoriented him to time. Now he could only hear the sound of his own breathing. More and more seconds went by in the stillness, and David wondered if the mutineers had left. Maybe they had been called away temporarily. That would give him enough— Abruptly the racket made by the searching crewmen commenced again.

The noise of objects crashing to the floor drew closer and closer. David heard dishware and glasses shattering, followed by a string of coughs. Then there was more coughing and the sound of the mutineer hawking up phlegm to clear his throat. Then came more glassware breaking into pieces. *There's no way they'll miss the stench of Robbie's decaying body! No way!* Pushing his legs against the back of the shelf, David readied himself to pounce.

For a moment things went silent. David held his breath and listened intently, now wondering what had—

The silence was abruptly broken by a deafening blast from a shotgun. The loud bang reverberated back and forth across the immense storage area. Again David's mind flashed back to scenes from the firefight in Somalia. Muslim fanatics were all around them, screaming and yelling and closing in on the Special Forces unit. A grenade went off. John E. lost a leg and bled out right before their eyes. *Got to get out! Got to get—*

David blinked rapidly as the flashback ended. Sweat was pouring down his chest, and he had to once more force himself to breathe. *Two goddamn flashbacks in a row!* he thought miserably. *Just like the kind that occurred when I first arrived at Walter Reed. They just kept coming day and night, making it impossible to distinguish between nightmare and reality. And if that happens here, I'm as good as dead. And so is my little girl.* Gradually David's brain calmed, and he regained control of his senses. He pushed his jitters aside and brought his attention back to the mutineers.

Choi was yelling, "Why you shoot?"

"I saw something move up there on the shelf."

"Maybe Robbie, you idiot!"

Then there were heavy footsteps before the conversation started again.

Choi made a brief chuckling sound. "A rat! You shot a big rat!"

"It could have been that doctor," the redheaded mutineer explained. "I remember what he did to you, and I wasn't going to take any chances."

"You no shoot him," Choi growled. "He is mine to kill."

"Whatever. Let's finish up this search and get the hell out of here."

"We both go to my end and go shelf by shelf on both sides of aisle. That way we no miss anything and you not shoot at rats!"

"Suits me."

The footsteps walked away.

David climbed down silently and waited for the sounds of the search to begin again. The footsteps faded. Seconds ticked by, then more seconds. Choi said something, but it was garbled and far away.

The rummaging started.

David secured the tank of oxygen under his arm and tiptoed to the end of the aisle. He peeked around the corner and made sure the way was clear, then dashed over to the next aisle. He did this maneuver twice more and was now only two aisles away from the entrance. He peered out at the door and into the passageway. It was deserted. No guard. No sounds.

The conversation commenced from a distance.

"Less than twenty-four hours and we'll be out of this hellhole," the redheaded mutineer said.

"Stop talk and look for Robbie."

David carefully peered around the edge of the aisle and saw nothing. He waited for the sounds of the search to begin again, then sprinted for the passageway.

THIRTY-THREE

CAROLYN WRINKLED HER NOSE at the strong aroma. "You smell like lemon juice."

"I know," David said. "But it's way better than the stench it's covering."

"Robbie?"

David nodded. "He turned ripe real quick."

"Well, at least they didn't find him."

"But they will, and soon," David told her. "The mutineers were only five or so aisles away when I made a break for it."

"Jesus!" Carolyn breathed. "Will they know you did it?"

"In all likelihood," David replied. "When they see his broken neck, they'll figure only one person could have done that. And that person is me."

"Because you were in Special Forces?"

David shook his head. "They think I was an MP. But when you put that together with what I did to Choi, it doesn't take much imagination to conclude I know how to snap a neck."

"So they'll come after you."

"Full force."

"What are you going to do?"

"Stay on the move and keep in touch with you by room phone," David said and handed her the small tank of oxygen. "It's the only one I could find."

"Let's hope it helps."

They hurried into the bedroom and set up an oxygen delivery system for Kit. The child was sleeping, but her respirations were raspy and rapid. At the foot of the bed was a temperature chart that Carolyn had constructed on a sheet of the ship's stationery. It showed that Kit's temperature had remained at 102° throughout the morning.

David sighed sadly and said, "I'd love to see her temperature come down, if only a little."

"That may be starting to happen," Carolyn informed. "I haven't given her any Tylenol for hours, and she's had no fever spikes."

"But her face is still flushed," David noted, then added, "I guess we should be thankful it hasn't turned that awful blue color."

Kit coughed in her sleep. Sputum rattled in her chest and throat, yet it didn't seem to interfere with her breathing. She coughed once more and tried to clear her lungs, but was only partially successful.

"I think her cough is stronger," Carolyn observed.

"I don't see much improvement," David said.

Juanita turned to him in her bed. "That is because you haven't been listening closely. The Little One has become stronger."

David smiled briefly. "That is your clinical opinion, eh?"

"It is the opinion of someone who is experienced when it comes to the breathing of children," Juanita said firmly.

"Then I'll have to take your word for it," David said, and again realized how fortunate he was to have a nanny like Juanita to help him look after Kit through all the years. He watched the woman try to raise herself off the bed, only to plop back down. "You should continue to rest."

"I will continue to rest," Juanita told him. "And while I continue to rest, I will continue to keep an eye on the Little One."

"Good. We'll be back shortly."

Taking Carolyn's hand, they moved quickly through the sitting room to the cabin door. He paused and listened for sounds outside. There were no voices or footsteps. Cautiously he opened the door and peered out to make certain there were no guards in the vicinity. Then they dashed down the empty passageway and into their cabin. David rapidly began stripping off all of his clothes and handing them to Carolyn.

"Don't let them touch the floor and leave behind a lemon scent," he instructed. "I don't want them to know I was here."

"Right," Carolyn said and tossed his wallet back to him. "What should I do with your clothes?"

"Throw everything into the ocean."

David dashed into the bathroom and turned the shower on full blast. He soaked himself under the steady stream of water, then soaped and re-soaped his body, ridding it of its lemon aroma. But the stench of death and decay was still in his nostrils. And the smell was sure to intensify as the number of dead aboard the *Grand Atlantic* increased. To make matters even worse, they had run out of body bags again. The last bag was the one he'd used on Robbie's—

Christ! David groaned to himself. *I didn't put Robbie's body into the plastic bag.* There wasn't time because the mutineers were approaching. He'd left the damn thing on the floor, directly beneath the shelf that held Robbie's body. They'd find it, and now Richard Scott would be absolutely certain that David had killed his half-brother. David switched the faucet to cold and let the icy water stream onto his face, his mind still on Richard Scott. The investment banker would search high and low for David, wanting him dead before leaving the *Grand Atlantic.* David turned off the shower and reminded himself that Scott wasn't the problem. Choi was. Choi would be the one assigned to kill him.

As he stepped out of the shower, Carolyn handed him a thick white towel. "Take a whiff and tell me what you smell," he requested.

Carolyn stepped in close and inhaled deeply. "No lemon scent."

"Good," David said and began toweling off. "Now listen up because there's a bunch of things you need to know. First, the acting captain, Jonathan Locke, is the inside man. He helped Richard Scott and his men pull off the mutiny. He's a full-blown traitor."

"How did you find out?" Carolyn asked.

"I heard Choi telling another mutineer about Locke. Nice, eh?"

"Bastard!"

"Yeah," David agreed, shaking the water out of his hair. "And you'll never guess who has decided to jump into the first lifeboat, along with the mutineers."

"Karen Kellerman," Carolyn answered at once.

David grinned without humor. "How did you know?"

"She's a me-first kind of woman," Carolyn told him. "She can only think of herself."

"I suppose," David said. "But it still caught me by surprise."

"It shouldn't have," Carolyn said. "You should have been able to predict it from past experience."

"It's just I expected more from a physician."

"Titles don't change the person."

David nodded, thinking about Karen's duplicity in the past and her self-serving behavior now. She hadn't changed a bit, not one iota. He rapidly brought his mind back to the problems aboard the *Grand Atlantic*. "In less than twenty-four hours, we'll reach Nassau, where they've arranged for the ship to be refueled. That's when Richard Scott and the mutineers and the passengers will crowd into the lifeboats and head for shore. Some will be sick, some not so sick, some asymptomatic. But most will be carrying the virus. And that's where and when the pandemic starts."

"Wo-won't the authorities in Nassau try to stop them?" Carolyn stammered.

David shook his head. "They don't know about the avian flu on this ship. All they'll see is two dozen lifeboats in the water and figure the cruise ship is in some kind of distress. Hell! They'll probably send out people to help them get ashore."

"What about the Navy?"

"They won't be anywhere around," David said knowingly. "That would only raise suspicions. And even if they were nearby, what could the Navy do? Blow the lifeboats out of the water?"

"So the mutineers and passengers will get ashore and start a pandemic," Carolyn said dispiritedly.

"Beyond any doubt." David finished drying himself and hurriedly put on a new set of clothes. He carefully eased the hatchet under the rear of his belt and made certain it was secure.

"Maybe one of us should get into the boat with the others and warn the authorities when we reach shore," Carolyn suggested.

"It wouldn't matter," David told her. "By the time we got to the authorities and they verified our story, the mutineers and passengers would disperse to every part of the island. And remember, these people are very well-to-do, with passports, cash, and credit cards galore. They'll buy their way onto boats and planes and helicopters, and be in a half-dozen cities on the mainland before the authorities on Nassau begin to react."

"And there's no way to stop it. Is that what you're saying?"

"That's what I'm saying." David took her hand and moved quickly into the sitting room. He gave her a peck on the lips and said, "I'll call every hour or so to check on Kit."

Carolyn thought for a moment. "Scott may decide to put a guard in Kit's cabin."

"I doubt it," David said. "They know Kit is sick with the bird flu. They won't put anybody in a confined space with the virus."

"Let's hope you're right." Carolyn's gaze went up to the ventilation duct that David had taped over to prevent the air from entering the cabin. "I should remove the tape from the duct in case we need to hide something in there."

"Like what?"

"Like some additional tanks of oxygen, if you're lucky enough to find them."

"Good idea," David said and reached for the door handle. He gave Carolyn a big wink as she mounted a chair beneath the ventilation duct. David's brow suddenly went up. In a matter of seconds, he had formulated a plan that would keep Richard Scott

293

and the mutineers aboard the *Grand Atlantic*. Hastily he asked Carolyn, "Is there a stepladder of some sort down in the sick bay?"

"Not that I recall," she replied.

"But some of those shelves were at least seven or eight feet up. How did you reach them?"

"I used one of the metal stools."

"And how much extra height did it give you?"

"I'd say three feet or so."

"Perfect!"

"For what?"

"For a—"

His answer was interrupted by a loud commotion in the passageway. Voices were yelling, footsteps stomping. It was impossible to tell how many people were out there. At least three, David estimated. Maybe four.

"I want him alive!" Richard Scott shrieked.

David rapidly backed away from the door and took out his hatchet. "It's the mutineers! They've come for me!"

"What should we do?" Carolyn asked breathlessly.

"I want you to walk out into the passageway and go into Kit's cabin," David instructed, thinking quickly. "Leave this door open, as if you're coming back."

"For what reason?"

"Make up one," David said in a low voice. "Now go!"

Squaring her shoulders, Carolyn opened the door and walked out into the passageway.

David slipped behind the open door and, raising his hatchet, readied himself to spring into action.

"Where's Ballineau?" Scott demanded.

"He had to go to the sick bay," Carolyn said evenly. "They have some kind of emergency down there."

"Not in sick bay," Choi interjected. "I already look."

"Well, look again," Carolyn insisted. "He left here just a few minutes ago."

There was a pause while someone coughed loudly.

"How do I know you're telling the truth?" Scott pressed.

"You don't. But why would I lie?" Carolyn asked. "Now please move aside. I want to move Dr. Ballineau's daughter into his cabin, where there is a larger balcony and better cross-ventilation. The child has a fever and it'll be more comfortable for her in there."

Smart, David thought, *so damn smart.* Carolyn explained the open door without being asked about it. That made her reason more believable.

"We are going to find your boyfriend," Scott said menacingly. "And when we do, he'll pay a very high price for killing my brother."

"What are you talking about?" Carolyn asked, raising her voice an octave. "David hasn't killed anyone."

"Tell that to my brother Robbie, who is now cold as ice," Scott said, then gave directions to the other mutineers. "Choi, I want you to check out the sick bay again. Tommy, you get some deckhands and start patrolling and searching the levels, one by one. Mac, you come with me while I think of a way to smoke that son of a bitch out."

"If we find him, do you want him dead?" Tommy asked.

"I want him alive," Scott growled. "I have special plans for him."

And I have a special plan for you, David thought to himself. *One that will ensure that you and your mutineers never leave the Grand*

Atlantic. You'll scream and yell, but you'll stay aboard because you'll have no choice.

He heard the group of four stomp away and waited for the passageway to become dead quiet. Then he peeked around the door and, seeing no one, raced for the staircase.

THIRTY-FOUR

DAVID WAS CURLED UP inside a giant dryer in the laundry room. He considered it to be an excellent hiding place. It was a brightly lighted area, right out in the open for everyone to see, yet chances were nobody would bother to search it. David knew that the clearly obvious would often be the most obscure, particularly when dealing with amateurs. He had learned that a long time ago in places like Mogadishu and Beirut.

With the door to the dryer cracked open, David could hear and see anything approaching. Over the past four hours, he had heard footsteps and voices only twice, both times passing by the laundry room but never entering. David had purposefully chosen a machine at the end of the row, which would give him more time to react to an intruder. He had also taken the precaution of unplugging the dryer he was in, just in case somebody decided to turn it on.

David checked his watch. It was 7 p.m. Darkness was setting in. Fourteen hours until landfall. Time to put the plan in motion. He eased himself out of the dryer and stretched his muscles, all the while listening for sounds. Everything was dead still. Silently he crept over to a phone on the wall and punched in Kit's number.

Carolyn answered on the second ring. "Yes?"

"Is Dr. Balli-not there?" David asked, purposefully mispronouncing his last name. It was a code he and Carolyn had devised in case a mutineer was in the cabin. If one was, the response would be, "He's in the sick bay."

"No one is here," Carolyn whispered. "But they're checking both cabins on a frequent basis. It would be really dangerous for you to come back now."

"I don't plan to," David whispered back. "How is Kit doing?"

"Better," Carolyn reported. "Her fever is down to 101° and she's taking fluids by mouth."

"What about her cough?"

"It's still there, but she's getting a lot of yucky stuff up."

"Oh Lord!" David breathed thankfully. "Don't tell me we're going to get lucky for once."

"Keep your fingers crossed."

"I will," David said, keeping his voice very low. "Now listen carefully, beautiful. There are some things that I'm going to ask you to do that sound crazy. But just do exactly as I say. Okay?"

"Okay."

"In the morning, when the passengers are lining up to get off the ship, I want you to wrap Kit up in a blanket and bring her to the lifeboat area. As soon as you see me, move to the front of the line."

"What!"

"Just do as I say. And when you get there, don't talk or utter a word. Simply stand in place."

"Jesus, David! What's this all about?"

"Saving a lot of lives."

"Should I bring Juanita?"

"No."

David heard faint footsteps and voices over the phone. The voices gradually grew louder. It had to be another cabin check by the mutineers.

"He's in the sick bay," Carolyn said curtly and hung up.

David moved quickly to the door of the laundry room and peeked out into the deserted passageway. He waited another thirty seconds to make certain no one was there, then sprinted down the corridor and to the staircase. Keeping his ears pricked, he went up the stairs on his tiptoes. So now, step one of the plan was in place. Step two would be far more difficult. It would require him to be out in the open again, which was very risky, with half the crew looking for him. But he had no choice.

He came to the level of the sick bay and cautiously cracked the door. The only thing his senses detected was the stench of decay. The smell was so strong that David wondered if there was a cluster of bloated dead people lying about the area. Maybe some of the passengers couldn't make it back to their cabins or maybe some had come down here to die. As he approached the spa, he heard a peculiar noise. It sounded like loud chirping mixed with a background hum. He glanced into the well-lighted spa and winced at the most gruesome sight he'd ever seen. Less than ten feet away, a decaying body was seated upright in a large, leatherbound chair. A pack of giant rats was feasting on the female corpse, while a swarm of flies flew overhead and waited their turn. David felt a surge of nausea and swallowed it back.

"So there you are," a voice behind him said.

David spun around and reached back for his hatchet. But then he lowered his hand. It was Karen Kellerman.

"Everybody is looking for you, David," Karen went on.

"Who is everybody?" David asked innocently.

"Mainly the crew and mutineers," Karen replied. "And they seemed really angry. Did you do something to upset them?"

"They think I killed one of their men," David said tonelessly.

"Did you?"

"Of course not," David said, not trusting her. "But they're convinced I did."

"If I were you, I'd do everything possible to avoid them," she warned.

"That's my plan," David said, then added, "and I'd appreciate you not mentioning that you'd seen me."

"Why in the world would I do that?"

To secure your place in the first lifeboat, David wanted to say, but held his tongue. "I was just referring to loose talk that might get back to the mutineers."

"I'd never do anything to hurt you, David."

"I know," David said, straight-faced, then watched her stifle a yawn. "You look beat."

"Caring for a couple hundred sick patients will do that to you," Karen said wearily and yawned again. "Particularly when you don't have much to offer them. Damn! I've seen so many dead people."

"Like the one next door?"

Karen nodded. "I almost threw up."

"The whole ship is going to be that way soon."

Karen looked away for a moment, then came back to him. "I can't take this anymore, David. I've had enough. That's why I'm getting off this ship with the others."

David was taken aback by her honesty. He had expected her to hide the fact she was deserting. "The sick passengers will still need a doctor."

"No, they won't," Karen said at once. "The ones I've tried to treat all died. And the few who I just left to die, like Mrs. Sullivan, are up and walking around."

David stared at her in disbelief. "Are you referring to the little lady, with dyed-black hair, who has bad emphysema and chronic bronchitis?"

"That's her," Karen told him. "She should have been dead ten times over, but she's currently walking around her cabin with a little fever and cough that's getting better by the hour. And I did nothing for her, other than tell her husband things were hopeless."

David blinked as he rapidly digested and assimilated this new information. Another survivor! That makes two for sure—Juanita and Bunny Sullivan. And if Kit continues to improve, that'll be three. Everybody else was dying horrible deaths, by the hundreds. Yet these three managed to survive. How? Why? What was the common denominator? They were all females, for starters. Maybe females, for some reason, can mount an immune response against the Asian flu virus. *No! That can't be it.* Deedee Anderson and the corpse next door and dozens of other victims he'd seen were all females. Gender wouldn't be the reason they survived. It had to be something else.

"You should get off this ship too," Karen broke into his thoughts. "And take Kit to some big-time medical center where she'll at least have a chance."

301

"Yeah, I guess I should," David said, thinking that Karen could be good or bad, depending on the situation. Touched by her concern for Kit, he reached for her hand and gave it a quick squeeze. "I've got to scoot."

"Me too," Karen said and moved in closer to kiss his cheek. "Catch you at the lifeboats."

"We'll see."

David hurried down the passageway and into the sick bay. He went directly to the high shelves in the laboratory area. There, next to a closed closet, was the stationary metal stool Carolyn had described. It was round, with a corrugated rubber sheet atop it for better traction. But it was only two feet tall rather than three. It would have to do. He picked it up and dashed for the door. But before stepping into the passageway, he carefully peered out to make sure Karen was gone. He still didn't trust her.

————

David's second hiding place was even better than his first, but it was far more dangerous healthwise. He was now in the compartment where Will Harrison had hidden the dying, infected bird. Although the area had been sanitized with disinfectant, David was still concerned that the deadly virus was lingering about, waiting for the opportunity to find a new host. He was careful not to touch anything with his bare hands and even more careful to keep his N-95 mask securely in place.

Shifting his body around, he leaned back wearily against the metal stool he had brought with him. The stool was the second important reason he'd chosen the generator compartment as a hiding place. It was one of the secret locations that was big enough for both him and the stool. But the most important reason for his choice was the possible presence of the virus itself. No one, except for a fool, would search the area where the sick bird had been given shelter.

David gazed around the area, with its bundles of wires and large pipes and screened-off generators. *A good hiding place*, he thought again, but it had one major drawback. It had no back door or exit. He was for all intents and purposes trapped. But so what? It was just a smaller trap aboard a larger trap called the *Grand Atlantic*. That's what the ship was now, a deadly trap. And it was all caused by a sick bird that had lost its way and a thoughtful little boy who tried to help it. And that confluence of seemingly minor events on a cruise ship led to hundreds of deaths and maybe millions more. It was like the perfect storm, except this time it wasn't the weather. It was a God-awful pandemic.

Overhead the ventilation system clicked on. David felt a stream of warm air brush against his face and hair. With a yawn, he leaned back farther against the metal stool, aware of his heavy eyelids and mounting fatigue. *I need a little snooze*, David told himself, *just enough to keep me going.* He checked his wristwatch. Midnight. Eight hours to landfall. Closing his eyes, he set his mind-clock for 3 a.m. and drifted off into a dreamless sleep.

———

David was suddenly awake. The sound of a door shutting echoed throughout the stairwell. Then he heard footsteps on their way down. In a fraction of a second, David was on his feet and searching for a place of concealment. The generators were screened off, so he couldn't get to them, and the space under the pipes was too small to accommodate his body. Off to the side, David saw the ragged blanket that Will had used as a nest for the sick bird. The footsteps came closer and closer, accompanied by a harsh cough. *It's the redheaded mutineer*, David thought hurriedly. He grabbed his hatchet from under his belt and dove for the blanket, then stretched out on the floor and covered himself completely.

The footsteps stopped. For a moment, David hoped the mutineer would turn around and go back on deck. But he didn't. The footsteps started again. David lay perfectly still, even taking very shallow breaths so his chest wouldn't move the blanket. He tightened his grip on the hatchet.

Now the footsteps seemed close enough to touch. Then David felt a hard object poking his kneecap. *Christ! He's probing the blanket with his shotgun! Which is loaded!*

"Well, let's see here," the mutineer said and jerked the ragged blanket back.

He saw a brief flash of metal just before the sharp edge of the hatchet split the frontal bone of his skull into two. Once past bone, the blade easily sliced its way through the cerebral cortex all the way back to the occipital lobe of his brain. The mutineer remained upright for a few seconds, then fell backward, like a dead weight.

David jumped to his feet and, with a tug, extracted the hatchet from the mutineer's skull. Blood poured out onto the floor and began to congeal around the shotgun next to the body. David quickly picked up the weapon and checked its chamber. *It's empty! Shit! But it was loaded before*, David thought back. The mutineer had used it to kill the big rat in the storage area. *And that's probably why it's unloaded now.* Richard Scott had considered the man to be too trigger-happy and removed the shells from his weapon. *Shit!* David cursed again and tossed the weapon aside.

He used the blanket to clean the blood from his hatchet, then glanced at his watch. It was 2:40 a.m. The darkest part of the night. Perfect for what he had to do next. He grabbed the metal stool and started up the stairs.

THIRTY-FIVE

In BRIGHT SUNLIGHT, PASSENGERS began lining up to board the lifeboats. Most were ill, some very ill, a few appeared to be at death's door. *And every one of them is carrying the virus,* David thought from his final hiding place. He was in a storage cabin on the lower deck, with an excellent view of the passengers and the large lifeboats that were suspended over their heads.

Richard Scott was giving orders to the crowd of people, most of whom, like Scott, were wearing life jackets. "There will be room for everyone, but we must allow women and children to board first."

There was a murmur of approval from the throng, although many started to inch forward.

"I'll be in the water, along with some of my men, to see that everything goes smoothly," Scott continued on. "If this is done correctly, we'll be ashore within the hour."

Some in the crowd applauded lightly.

Oh yeah, the Great Savior! David thought cynically. Scott couldn't care less about the passengers. His obvious plan was to surround his lifeboat with a half-dozen of those carrying the women and children. It would be the ideal cover for him and his mutineers. Two-thirds of the way in, they'd split off from others and be the first ashore. All the rest could fend for themselves.

David gazed out the porthole and saw the city of Nassau in the distance. They were at the mouth of the main harbor, no more than a mile from shore. And the ocean was clear, with no ships or vessels between the *Grand Atlantic* and land. From what David had read, the lifeboats were powered by small diesel engines that propelled them along at six knots per hour. At that rate, passengers could expect to reach the beach in ten minutes. But that was only true under ideal conditions. And conditions were about to be far less than ideal.

"Please help me!" a female voice cried out.

David's eyes went to a middle-aged woman who was kneeling over a motionless man. Despite her plea, none of the passengers stepped forward. David couldn't tell if the man lying on the deck was dead or alive.

"Please help me!" the woman implored again. "I think my husband has passed out from the flu. We have to get him ashore."

"Move him over to the side," Scott ordered. "Women and children first. There will be no exceptions."

"Perhaps we should take him back to his cabin," a voice in the crowd suggested.

"Stay put!" Scott said tersely.

David watched the woman drag her limp husband away. The passengers parted to give her room, but no one offered to help. They weren't about to lose their place in line, David told himself. Or maybe they were intimidated by Choi, who was standing beside

Scott and holding a ball-and-chain apparatus. The chain was about three feet long, and at its end was an iron ball the size of an apple. When swung with force, it was a deadly weapon, capable of crushing bone and killing with a single blow.

"All right," Scott called out. "We are about to lower the lifeboats. You will form a single—" He stopped in mid-sentence and abruptly turned as the elevator door opened and passengers in front of it stepped aside.

David had to crook his neck to see what was happening. The crowd moved apart for Jonathan Locke and the mutineer named Tommy. Locke, looking weary and disheveled, was leading the way. It took David an extra second to notice that Tommy had his shotgun planted in Locke's back.

"What?" Scott asked, annoyed.

"The Navy is ready to come in and begin fueling," Tommy replied. "They have instructions they want us to follow."

"Do what I told you before," Scott barked. "Have the captain tell them to wait because we're having trouble with our anchor."

"Locke won't talk to them unless we give him his insulin."

"Put your shotgun to his head."

"I already tried that."

Scott grumbled under his breath, then rushed over and grabbed Locke by the collar. "I don't give a damn about your insulin! You make that radio call now."

"I'm begging you!" Locke pleaded. "I can feel my blood sugar going sky high. If I don't inject myself with insulin now, I'll lapse into a diabetic coma."

"The radio call first," Scott demanded.

"No!" Locke rebelled. "Give me my insulin or you make the call yourself."

Scott's face reddened. He glowered at Locke, trying to intimidate him, but the captain didn't budge. "We can do this the easy way or the hard way."

Locke remained steadfast and returned the stare.

"Then we'll do it the hard way." Scott turned to Choi and gave him a nod.

Choi brought the chain on his weapon up to shoulder level and began to menacingly swing the metal ball back and forth.

The bastard! David seethed. So that was how Scott persuaded Locke to join the mutiny. By blackmailing him and threatening to withhold his insulin if he didn't follow orders. *Christ!* It would only take ten minutes to obtain, prepare, and inject the insulin. But Scott wasn't going to allow it. He was on a tight schedule, and every minute counted.

"You've got five seconds to make up your mind," Scott warned Locke. "If you still refuse, I'll turn Choi loose on you."

Now is as good a time as any, David thought resolutely. He gathered a mouthful of saliva and spat on the floor for luck, just as he'd done in Special Forces. He opened the door of the cabin and walked out onto the deck.

Scott spun around and glared at him with intense hatred. "You killed my brother!"

"He deserved to die," David said matter-of-factly.

"You're going to pay a terrible price for that."

"No, I won't."

"Why not?"

"Because you're more interested in saving your own skin than getting vengeance for the actions of a stupid half-brother."

"We'll see about that," Scott growled and motioned to Choi, who promptly began swinging his iron ball again.

"Save the theatrics," David said without inflection. "And let's get down to business."

"Which is?"

In his peripheral vision, David saw Carolyn move to the front of the line. She was holding a sleeping Kit in her arms. David directed Scott's attention to the two. "I want my daughter to be in the first boat that leaves. I'll accompany her and so will the nurse."

The large crowd murmured their disapproval.

David turned to them and snapped. "Put a lid on it!"

They quieted instantly.

David came back to Scott. "Yes or no?"

Scott hesitated, as if weighing the pros and cons of his decision. "Why should I give you anything? You don't have any cards to play."

"Oh, I have a big one."

"Yeah? Like what?"

"Like what happened to Arthur Maggio in the stairwell," David answered in a low, barely audible voice. "I could conveniently forget that."

Scott shrugged, but he too lowered his voice. "You weren't an actual witness."

"Tell that to a judge and jury," David said in a monotone. "See how well it goes over."

Scott hesitated again, longer this time. "How do I know you'll keep your word?"

"You don't," David said. "Except for the fact that I have this habit of standing by my promises."

"That's not much of a pledge."

"That's all you're going to get."

Scott considered the proposition at length before nodding slowly. "You and your daughter will be in the first boat, but not the nurse."

"Agreed," David said immediately and watched Scott and Choi exchange knowing glances. Choi had been given the go-ahead to kill him. *But when?* David asked himself. *And where?* Probably not here and now because there were too many witnesses. "Let's get this show on the road."

Scott snapped his fingers at a small group of crewmen, who promptly activated the mechanism to lower the suspended lifeboats. Slowly, a large lifeboat descended toward the deck. The passengers stepped back and aside to make room for the orange, fiberglass lifeboat. They applauded as it came down to eye level.

"Son of a bitch!" One of the crewmen hollered. "Someone has scuttled the lifeboat!"

Scott rushed over, with David only a half-step behind. They stared at the damaged lifeboat. There was a broad, foot-long gash in its side. The fiberglass covering was split wide open, the damage irreparable. It didn't take an expert to know the boat would sink within minutes of touching down on the water.

Scott's face lost color. "Check the other boats!" he yelled to nearby crewmen. "Check every one of them!"

The remaining lifeboats were gradually lowered toward the deck. The rate of descent was too slow for some of the crew. A few impatient crewmen climbed up on ladders to perform their inspections.

The passengers kept their eyes glued to the boats, hoping that most were still serviceable. Within a minute, the deckhands began shouting down their reports.

"Scuttled!"

"Scuttled!"

"Scuttled!"

"Scuttled!"

"Same here!"

"And here!"

Scott bellowed, "Are any of the boats intact?"

There was no response.

"What is this?" David screamed. "Some kind of sick joke?"

"It's no joke," Scott shot back, "and whoever did this will die for it."

"Him! He do it!" Choi shrieked and pointed a finger at David. "Him!"

"Piss off!" David hissed, then turned to Scott and Tommy. "Can the damage be repaired?"

"No way," Tommy said. "This isn't wood. It's fiberglass, and we don't have the time or equipment to patch it."

"Are you an expert on boats?" Scott asked sharply.

"No," Tommy replied. "But I know fiberglass."

"Well, let's be sure." Scott signaled to a group of crewmen and yelled to them, "Get the ship's carpenter up here."

"Can't," a crewman yelled back. "He's damn near dead with the flu."

"Christ!" Scott grumbled, then eyed David suspiciously. "How do we know Choi isn't telling the truth? How do we know you didn't somehow scuttle the lifeboats?"

"Yeah, right," David snapped. "I did it so my little girl can die aboard this goddamn ship."

"He do it!" Choi growled and lifted up the ball and chain, then began swinging it like a pendulum. "He die!"

The crowd of passengers quickly backed away, giving Choi and his deadly weapon plenty of room. Then everybody became still and silent.

"You'd better control him," David cautioned.

Scott shrugged. "You'll have to fight your own battle. Besides, Choi owes you something, doesn't he?"

David unbuttoned his white coat and readied himself for what was certain to be a life-and-death struggle. Scott had decided to turn Choi loose and remove the only witness to Arthur Maggio's murder. Choi was now swinging the iron ball in a circle well above his head. His eyes were filled with so much hate, it was almost palpable. David slowly backed up, scanning everything and everybody around him. The crowd of passengers had moved aside and spread out to give everyone a good view of the fight. Scott had his shotgun pointed downward. Tommy had the muzzle of his gun planted on the deck, while he leaned on its wooden stock, like a spectator at a sporting event.

David watched every move Choi made, paying particular attention to the arc of the iron ball. Now it was lower than before, which meant Choi would go for a body blow first, probably to the chest. *That way he can incapacitate me, then move in for the kill. But death by itself won't be enough for Choi*, David thought grimly. *He wants revenge. He wants me to die a slow, painful death. Martial-arts experts like him are very good at inflicting pain and even better at killing.*

Swish! Swish! The moving iron ball drew nearer and caused hot air to stir against David's skin. He had to force himself to hold his ground. Choi began swinging the iron ball in an even wider arc, which left most of his head exposed. And that gave David all the opening he needed. He rubbed his palm against his shirt to dry the perspiration, then he waited.

Choi advanced closer to David as he let out the chain bit by bit. The iron ball swished through the air, going round and round, now less than ten feet away from David's body. *Give him another couple of feet*, David thought and inched his way nearer to Tommy. The iron ball was swishing even louder, now only seven feet away.

"You die!" Choi snarled.

"Try this on for size," David said and reached for his hatchet, and in the same motion threw it at Choi's head. The thick blade sliced off the left side of Choi's face and brain. A giant mist of blood spurted up into the air. A good portion of Choi's brain was now on the deck of the *Grand Atlantic*, its convoluted surface glistening in the sunlight.

Everyone, including the mutineers, gaped at the bloody sight, horrified and transfixed by its gruesomeness. For a brief moment, Tommy averted his eyes. It was all the time David needed. He lunged at Tommy and, before the mutineer could react, grabbed his shotgun and released its safety. Quickly he pointed the shotgun at Scott, whose weapon was still aimed downward. Scott stared back at David, stunned by the sudden turn of events. As the surprise wore off, he moved his finger ever so slowly toward the trigger housing.

"Go for it," David said tonelessly. "Give me a reason."

Scott dropped his hand away from the shotgun's trigger.

"Good," David said. "Now place it down on the deck, with the barrel facing you. Then, very slowly, using your left foot, kick it aside."

Scott did as he was told.

"Now sit on the deck, with your hands on top of your head."

Again Scott did as he was told.

"Good," David repeated, then turned to Tommy and said, "Are you doing all right?"

"So far," Tommy replied.

"Well, 'so far' just ended."

David swung the butt of the shotgun up and slammed it into the side of Tommy's head. The wooden stock broke skin and smashed into bone, producing a thump-like sound. Tommy crumpled down to the deck in a heap, out cold, with blood oozing from the wound above his ear.

"Oooh!" the crowd of passengers hummed simultaneously. Their eyes darted back and forth between the unconscious Tommy and the dead Choi.

A group of crewmen edged toward David and the bodies.

Uncertain of their intent, David hastily reached down for Scott's weapon and tucked it under his left arm. After releasing its safety, he said, "Two shotguns can do a lot of damage."

The crewmen backed off.

David glimpsed over at Carolyn. Kit was drowsy and half-asleep in her arms, but in all likelihood she had seen the mayhem that had just taken place. David could only hope that she'd have no nightmares from the bloody violence. He quickly brought his attention back to Choi. The left side of Choi's skull was holding on to the rest

315

of his head by only a few fibrous strands of tissue. The blood around him was now congealed and was already smelling of decay.

David looked over to a pair of husky crewmen. "Move Choi off the deck."

"I ain't touching him," the younger of the two said.

"If I have to repeat myself, you're going to lose a leg," David said neutrally.

The older crewman pushed his mate forward and said, "Where do you want the body to go?"

"In any cabin that has dead people in it." David waited for them to lift up Choi's body and drag it through the crowd, then called over to Locke. "Do you know where they keep your insulin?"

"In the officer's lounge, under lock and key," Locke called back.

"Can you get to it?"

"No problem."

"Then go!" David shouted. "After you've injected your insulin, call the Navy and prepare to refuel."

Locke hurried over to the still-unconscious Tommy and retrieved a set of keys, then dashed for the elevator. As Locke disappeared into the crowd, Richard Scott saw his chance. He jumped to his feet and ran for the railing at the edge of the deck.

"One more step and you'll be lying next to Choi," David warned.

"You're not going to shoot an unarmed man," Scott said confidently. "Not with all these witnesses."

"You're right," David admitted and lowered his shotgun. "But I don't have to shoot you because, if you leap overboard, you'll already be a dead man. There's no way you can swim through a mile of choppy ocean and strong currents, and safely reach land. Unless you're a fish."

"Or a triathlete," Scott said and vaulted onto the top of the railing. "I've swum a lot farther than this under much worse conditions. So, in the end, I win. I always win!"

Using his heavily muscled legs, Scott sprang out into the air and plunged straight down into the sea, which seemed calmer now. For a few moments Scott stayed submerged, then he popped up through the water, buoyed by his life jacket. He smiled up at the crowd gawking down at him and yelled, "So long, suckers!"

Scott floated effortlessly, basking in the warm sun. He was so busy waving to the crowd above, he didn't see the large rogue wave that was forming behind him. As Scott turned to swim away, the wave caught him full force and drove him back to the *Grand Atlantic*. Instantly Scott knew what was happening, but he didn't have time to scream before the wave crashed down and swept him under the ship's giant hull.

The crowd of passengers leaned over the railing and stared at the sea below, all wondering if Scott had somehow managed to survive. Seconds passed by, then more seconds, without any sighting of Richard Scott.

After a full minute, Carolyn turned to David and asked, "What do you think happened to him?"

"I don't know," David said. "But my guess is he hit his head on the steel hull and, if that's the case, he's a goner."

"Maybe he somehow escaped and is now swimming for shore underwater." Carolyn gazed out at the sea and saw a white object floating in the distance. She handed Kit to David, then turned to a passenger with a pair of binoculars. "May I borrow your binoculars for a moment?"

"Sure," he said and gave them to her.

Carolyn scanned the ocean, looking for the white object she'd seen a moment earlier. She searched back and forth several times before she spotted it again. As she focused in on it, her face suddenly went pale. She passed the binoculars to David and said, "Look at the white thing floating at about two o'clock."

David handed the sleeping Kit back to Carolyn, then surveyed the outer right quadrant of the sea. It took him only a moment to find the white object and focus in on it. It was Richard Scott's tennis shirt. Sticking out on one side was a severed arm. "Looks like he ran into a propeller," David said as more body parts surfaced.

"What an awful way to die," Carolyn said softly.

David shrugged. "It was his choice."

"But he had no way of knowing he'd get swept under and into the propellers."

"Poor planning," David said dryly, feeling no pity for a man who thought only of himself and was willing to hijack a ship and start a pandemic, all in his own self-interest. The world was better off without him in it.

"Well," Carolyn said as an afterthought, "at least we've got the *Grand Atlantic* back."

"But it's still a plague ship," David said darkly. "We're like a colony of lepers stranded at sea, with nowhere to go."

Most of the passengers around them turned and slowly trudged away, hopelessness written all over their faces. A few sank to the deck and stayed there, preferring to die in the sunshine rather than in the darkness of their cabins.

THIRTY-SIX

"How many of the crew can you trust?" David asked.

"No more than half," Locke replied. "And that's a very generous estimate."

"What about the other half?"

"Like the surviving passengers, they're desperate. They'll do anything to get off this ship."

"Even another mutiny?"

"Particularly another mutiny." Locke gestured with his head to the shotguns David was holding. "And I doubt that a pair of shotguns will stop them."

David had kept the loaded shotguns constantly at his side since squashing the rebellion. He knew the crew was still dangerous and just biding their time. Over the past few hours, he'd seen more than a few crewmen performing their duties in a lackadaisical fashion, only doing enough to maintain the *Grand Atlantic* while she stayed on a southerly course. He sensed they wouldn't attempt another mutiny on the open sea. But once they came within sight of land again, they'd go for it, even if it meant using lifeboats turned upside down for floatation. And the disgruntled passengers would happily join in, after coming so close to shore yet not being allowed to disembark. From his vantage point on the bridge, he scanned the vast, blue sea. The water was calm now, with not a single whitecap in sight.

"How far are we away from land?" David asked.

"About a hundred miles," Locke answered.

"I'd keep it that way."

"That's what the Navy advised."

"Did they tell you when we'd eventually make port?"

"They said they were in the process of determining that."

David forced a laugh. "Do you know what *in the process* means in the military?"

"A long time," Locke replied.

"A very long time," David said and left the bridge.

He took the elevator down to the main deck and stepped out into the dazzling sunlight. Crewmen were milling about, most of them disheveled and wearing filthy clothes. Rebellion was in the air, and they wanted everyone to know it. They turned and stared at David, watching his every move, but kept their distance. Still, to be on the safe side, he had his shotguns aimed directly at them.

"When do we make landfall?" a voice hollered.

"Soon," David said vaguely.

"How soon?"

"When they finally get a hospital set up."

"Shit! We'll all be dead by then," a second voice yelled out.

David recognized the man behind the second voice. He was the big, ugly deckhand who had tried to come to Choi's aid earlier. He would be the ringleader of the next mutiny.

"You!" David pointed to the man with the shotgun. "Step over here!"

"You going to make me?" the deckhand challenged.

"I'm asking you," David said politely. "Think of it as a request."

"Say please."

"Please, then."

The crew cheered, as if they had won an important victory.

The deckhand came forward, smiling, and looked down at David. He was at least six inches taller. "What?"

David pressed a shotgun against the deckhand's knee and said quietly, "Try anything and I'll blow your leg off."

The smile left the deckhand's face. "You do that and the other crewmen will—"

"They won't do jack shit," David cut him off, "except watch as you bleed out. Let me describe how it will be. The shotgun blast will rip your leg apart, just above the knee. It'll tear open the femoral artery in your thigh, and blood will spurt out like water from a fountain. It'll take you about two minutes to die, and you'll watch every second of it. How is that for a happy ending?"

The deckhand's eyes bulged. "What the hell kind of doctor are you?"

"The kind you don't want to get on the wrong side of," David told him. "Now I want you to remember, no matter who or what starts a mutiny, you'll be the first to die. I'll make sure of that. So you'd damn well better keep your boys in line."

"I may not be able to control all of them," the deckhand said, keeping his voice down.

"Oh, I think you can," David said and nudged him back with the barrel of his shotgun. "And you can start by having them return to their duty stations."

The deckhand went over to the crowd of crewmen and waited for them to gather around him. He spoke in a muffled tone that David couldn't hear clearly, but a moment later the crew began to disperse. David watched them move out, knowing their change in mood was temporary. As time passed and the deaths mounted, desperation would grow and mutiny would again be foremost in their minds. Well, he thought on, things were calm for now and there were still important medical matters to deal with. Like pest control.

David gazed over to the lounge chairs, where a tall, lanky crewman was straightening cushions. He was the crew member who had fetched the rope that David had used to tie up Choi. *At least the man followed orders*, David thought. *Maybe he could be trusted. Yeah. Maybe. But how much?*

David walked over to the lanky crewman and asked, "What's your name?"

"Chandler, sir."

"Well, Chandler, tell me how good your stomach is when it comes to seeing horrible things."

"Pretty good," Chandler said.

"We'll see." David glanced around the pool and bar area, not finding what he was searching for. "I need some of those canisters that spray disinfectant."

"How many?"

"Two."

Chandler dashed over to the bar and disappeared behind it. A moment later he reappeared, holding two canisters of disinfectant, and rushed back to David. "Now what?"

"Now we go to the sick bay."

They walked rapidly to a waiting elevator and entered. As the elevator descended, Chandler's lips moved silently while he struggled to find the right words. In his early thirties, he had a look of innocence about him, with straight blond hair and freckled cheeks. Sighing to himself, he kicked at an imaginary object on the floor before saying, "You know, I was never really involved in the mutiny. I never wanted any part of that."

"I know," David said.

"Think you might put in a good word for me?"

"If you play it straight."

The elevator came to a stop and the door opened. The smell that rushed in was so putrid that it made them step back and cover their noses.

"What the hell is causing that?" Chandler asked.

"The worst sight you'll ever see," David answered. "Keep your hand over your nose and head for the spa."

They walked slowly down the deserted passageway and heard the loud chirping sound that David was familiar with. Chandler didn't ask about the origin of the sound and David didn't volunteer any information. Just thinking about it was bad enough. At the door to the spa, the stench became overwhelming.

"Brace yourself," David warned. "And get ready to spray."

They entered and stared at the horrific sight.

The swarm of rats had eaten away most of the skin and muscles from the extremities of the corpse, leaving behind only skeletal remains. They had also gnawed every bit of flesh from the face, and were now burrowing into the chest and abdomen to get to the internal organs.

"Spray!" David yelled and switched on the canister of disinfectant.

Chandler gagged and threw up, but only once. He recovered quickly and he too began spraying.

At first, the rats ignored the disinfectant and continuing chewing away. But as the disinfectant soaked deeply into the body, the taste of the human tissue became disagreeable and the rats lost interest. Slowly the rodents began to scatter.

"Keep spraying!" David directed.

They went on dousing the corpse until both canisters were empty. Then they stepped back. All the rats had disappeared, all the flies overhead gone. And the terrible stench was far less noticeable, now replaced by the smell of strong disinfectant.

"Think they'll come back?" Chandler asked, breathing through his mouth.

"Maybe later," David said and gazed around the spa. Seeing a fire extinguisher on the far wall, he darted over to it and came back, then began spraying white foam into the bodily holes made by the burrowing rats. "That should do it."

Chandler nodded. "I can guarantee you the smell won't return after all this spraying."

"I didn't do it for the smell," David told him, then explained how rats and insects might act as vectors that could transmit the deadly virus to humans and animals. "So they could spread the disease to others on this ship and even to those on shore. Remember, rats are good swimmers and even better survivors."

"Too bad we didn't get down here sooner," Chandler commented.

"Better late than never," David said and discarded the empty fire extinguisher. "Now, there are a few other things we have to do to slow down the spread of the virus. So listen up."

"I'm all ears," Chandler said attentively.

"Tell me, what color paint is the most plentiful in the storeroom?"

"White. Just about everything we pain on this ship is white."

"Good," David went on. "I want you to gather up some deckhands who you trust and all the white paint and brushes you can find. Then go level by level, looking in each cabin. When all the occupants in a given cabin are dead, lock the door and paint a big white cross on it. You'll notice that some doors already have a red splash on them. Ignore the red paint. Got it?"

"Got it!"

"Then go!"

He watched Chandler sprint for the elevator, thinking that the young crewman could be trusted. Maybe not absolutely 100 percent, but close enough, and that could be very important later on. He gave the corpse a final glance and left the spa, closing the door behind him.

As he turned away, he heard a cacophony of sounds coming from the sick bay. Furniture was being moved, boxes overturned, metal objects hitting the floor. Someone was searching, he decided. They were probably scavenging for oxygen tanks or maybe antibiotic tablets or perhaps narcotics, if the person was an addict.

David released the safety on his shotgun and silently moved to the sick bay. At the door, he peered in cautiously before advancing through the reception area. All the noise was emanating from the examining room. He glimpsed in and saw Marilyn Wyman on her knees, rummaging through boxes and cartons.

"Hey, Marilyn," he called over.

"Hello, David," she said, now looking under the examining table.

"Did you lose something?"

"Not me," she replied. "It's something of Will's. I noticed that one of his shoes was missing and I thought it might be in here. It's so important that I—" She paused to choke back her tears before continuing. "It's very important to me. I want to hold on to everything he owned, particularly his clothes and books. And I couldn't stand the thought of Will having only one shoe on. I simply couldn't. I had to find the missing shoe. You—you probably don't understand all this."

"I understand," David said softly and thought back to Marianne. When his wife passed away, he wouldn't let anyone clean out her closet or chest of drawers or remove any of her personal items. To do so would have meant she was really dead, and he couldn't accept that. Not for a very long time. At length, David asked, "May I help you look?"

"Thanks, but there's no need," Marilyn replied and held up a small brown shoe. "I found it."

"Good," David said. "Now I'm going to ask you to accept my apology. I know I promised to stop by and chat with you, but I never got around to it, and I'm sorry for that."

"Oh, I realize you've been very busy."

"But I'm not busy now, so let's talk."

"I don't have much to say," she said quietly as her eyes again welled up with tears. "All I keep thinking about is that I have no reason to live. Everything I loved and cherished is gone. My son, my husband…." Her voice trailed off while she dabbed her eyes with Kleenex. "I wish I would have died with them. But it wasn't to be. They caught the terrible flu and it killed them. All I got was a hacking cough and a little fever that lasted a few days. And so I'm here and they're not."

David blinked. My God! Another female survivor! That makes four! And Marilyn should have been the least likely to survive. She'd had close intimate contact for hours on end with Will and Sol, who were both heavily infected. She must have inhaled a massive dose of the virus, yet she was barely affected. Why?

"There are moments when I just want to jump overboard and end it," Marilyn went on, after blowing her nose. "There's a sad irony to all this. As you may have guessed, Sol was a millionaire many times over. So now I can have everything I want in the world. Everything except the people I love the most. All that money and nothing to live for."

"Live for Will," David said gently.

"He's dead, David."

David shook his head. "Will is alive in your heart and mind, and he'll be there forever."

Marilyn nodded and smiled faintly at the memory of her son. "Every time I see his goldfish or hold his books, he comes back to me."

"As he should," David said, suddenly thinking of a way to boost Marilyn's spirits. "Say! I've got an idea that Will would really like. Why not use Sol's money to establish a veterinary center to look after sick and stray animals? You could name it after Will."

"He'd love that," Marilyn said, perking up.

"You bet."

"And there's a university not far from our house that has a very fine veterinary school," Marilyn continued on. "They could advise me on how to establish such a center."

"It's a perfect place to start," David said and reached out to help her up. "Come on. I'll walk you back to your suite."

They rode the elevator up two levels, then strolled to Marilyn's cabin in silence. But at the door, she turned and spoke. "I should tell you that I opened Will's body bag so I could still see and touch him. I probably should close it, eh?"

"That would be best," David said.

Marilyn nodded as the awful sadness returned to her face. "In a little while, if that's all right."

"That'll be fine."

David decided to take the stairs up to his cabin. He wanted time alone to think about Marilyn and the others who had survived the deadly avian influenza. All were female, all sick with the illness to varying degrees. And the sickest should have been those exposed to the heaviest dose of the virus, like Kit. But Marilyn Wyman had also received a large amount of the virus and for a much longer duration. So survival wasn't dose dependent. Nor did age seem to matter. Kit was twelve, Juanita sixty-five. Thus, the only common feature the survivors shared was gender. They were all female. But there was no known infectious disease that tended to kill men and spare women.

The elevator door opened and David came face to face with Edith Teller, the librarian from Ohio who had suffered an oculogyric reaction to Compazine. She appeared much more attractive now, with her perfectly applied makeup.

"How are you, Mrs. Teller?" David inquired.

"Fine, doctor," she reported sprightly.

"No more facial contortions, eh?"

"None at all. My only problem is this nagging cough that won't go away."

"Oh?" David's brow went up. "Did you have any fever or chills?"

She nodded. "I had that a few days ago, but it's gone now. This cough just hangs in though. Is there anything I can do for it?"

David was about to say *It's only a virus*, but wisely decided not to. "It'll pass," he advised. "Just drink plenty of fluids."

"Should I continue taking my cough drops?"

"If they're helping."

David walked on, shaking his head in wonderment. *Another survivor! Another female!* Hundreds of passengers were dead, hundreds more dying, yet five females survived and returned to health. Something must have protected them. But what? Was it something they did or didn't do? Was it something in their blood? He concentrated his mind and searched for an answer, but drew a total blank. David decided to present the problem to the CDC on their next teleconference call. Maybe they could figure it out.

David entered Kit's cabin and found Carolyn asleep on the sofa in the sitting room. He walked over quietly and kissed her forehead, then watched her eyes open.

"Hi, beautiful," he said lovingly.

"Hi, handsome," she said and sat up. She brought up a hand to stifle a yawn, then stretched her arms out wide. A moment later she was patting her hair into place. "I must look like hell."

"You look great to me."

"You say that to all the girls."

"Nah! Only to the pretty ones."

Carolyn smiled. "You should see your daughter now. She's talking a mile a minute between spoonfuls of soup that Juanita is feeding her."

David hummed happily. "That's music to my ears."

"But she's worried about you."

"Why?"

"She's worried you'll get the flu from all the sick people you're looking after."

Kit was just like her mother, David thought yet again. That natural caring and sweetness must be in her genes. "Did you reassure her?"

"About a thousand times," Carolyn said as she studied David's face. The lines seemed deeper, the circles under his eyes darker. "You look like you could use some sleep."

"I guess."

Carolyn's smile returned. "That great performance you gave up on deck must have tired you out."

"Did you like it?"

"It was outstanding!" Carolyn enthused. "You had me completely fooled until those damaged lifeboats came down. That's when I put two and two together. You used the hatchet to scuttle the boats, but you know you weren't tall enough to reach them, even on your tiptoes. That's why you needed a stepladder or metal stool. Right?"

"Right."

The smile left Carolyn's face when she asked, "Did you know you would use the hatchet to take off Choi's head?"

"Pretty much so," David said without a hint of emotion.

Carolyn hesitated before asking the next question. She thought she already knew the answer, but she still had to ask. "Would you have really shot the crew with those shotguns had they rushed you?"

"Oh yeah," David said at once. "When the choice is between my life and theirs, I'll choose mine every time."

"But you could have killed a dozen men."

David shrugged. "When your survival is at stake, numbers don't matter. You kill as many as you have to."

"And you could still sleep after doing that?"

David nodded. "Except for the nightmares and flashbacks. But on the positive side, I'd still be alive."

Carolyn stared out into space for a long moment before coming back to him. "You've got to be the most unusual person I've ever encountered."

"Why so?"

"Because you're a chameleon. You can go from sweetness to savagery in a split second." Carolyn paused to snap her fingers. "It happens that fast, in the blink of an eye. Do—do you actually feel the change coming on?"

"Sometimes," David said, but that was a lie. He never sensed the change. He simply went on automatic pilot. "Yeah, sometimes I do."

"Jesus! It's as if you're a mixture of contrasting personalities," she went on. "Do you have any idea how many people you are?"

"A lot."

"That's not a very good answer."

"All right then, five."

"Where did you get the number five from?"

"A Somerset Maugham novel," David told her. "In it, one character asked another the question you just posed. The answer was five. Then the questioner asked how one individual could possibly be five different people. The response was 'You tell me the situation, and I'll tell you who I am.'"

From the bedroom, Kit coughed, wet and loud, then coughed again before clearing her throat.

David helped Carolyn to her feet and grinned wryly. "I just turned into a father, and in ten seconds I'll be a doctor."

"I should write a book about you," Carolyn said. "The only problem is no one would believe it."

They walked into the bedroom and saw Kit sitting up in bed, coughing between spoonfuls of soup that were being fed to her by Juanita. Her color was much improved, her raven hair carefully combed and held in place by a yellow ribbon. Juanita was nicely dressed in a pink blouse and skirt. She looked like her old self.

"Hey, sweetheart!" David called out.

"Hi, Dad!" Kit called back and gulped down more soup.

"How are you feeling?"

"Better," she said and coughed loudly. "Except for this cough."

"It'll pass."

"When?"

"In a couple of days."

"Darn virus!" she said and shook her head to more soup. "How could I catch the stupid thing? I got all those shots for the regular flu and swine flu."

"This is a different virus," David explained. "Those shots didn't give you any immunity against it."

"I'm living proof of that," Kit said sourly. "And so is Juanita. She also got both shots and ended up sick with the virus too."

David's brow shot up. *And both of you survived,* he thought immediately. *And Carolyn and I and probably Karen, like most healthcare providers, took both shots and never became ill, despite being exposed to God-only-knows how many people infected with the avian flu virus. Jesus! Could that be the answer? Could the combination of vaccines against the regular influenza and swine flu viruses give the individual enough immunity to protect against the avian flu virus? Did the three similar viruses share enough common antigens so there'd be cross-reactivity between them?*

Kit saw the strange expression on her father's face and asked, "Dad, are you all right?"

"I'm fine," David said hurriedly and continued his thought process. *Is that really the answer? If so, why did Kit and Juanita come down with such a severe form of the disease? Why?* David blinked as the answer came to him. Because Kit was exposed to a massive dose of the virus when she was with Will. The huge virus load overwhelmed her immune system. And Juanita was a senior citizen who, like most with advancing age, had less resistance and a weaker immune response to all invading microorganisms.

"Dad," Kit broke into his thoughts, "did I say something wrong?"

"You said everything right," he replied and kissed her forehead.

David's mind was now concentrating on Kit's survival, despite the enormous load of virus she'd been exposed to. Somehow she survived, but poor Will, who also received a huge dose of virus, didn't. *Maybe Will was exposed to even more of the virus than Kit. Yeah. That would explain—*

David's eyes suddenly lit up. Maybe, in Will's case, it wasn't a matter of viral dose, but rather a matter of immunity. Quickly he came back to Kit. "Sweetheart, do you know if Will had gotten the same shots as you had?"

"I don't know," Kit said through a cough. "But Will told me, after you got that gumball out of his throat, that he was glad nobody had given him a shot because he was allergic to eggs or something like that."

Eggs! David thought at once. *The flu vaccines are produced in incubating chicken eggs! The manufacturing process is egg-based! People allergic to eggs can't receive the vaccine. Will never received the flu shots. He had no immunity to the avian flu virus.* "Was anybody else in Will's family allergic to eggs?"

"I think so," Kit replied and reached for her diary. She flipped through pages until she came to the one she was looking for. "Yes, here it is. His stepdad, Sol, was also allergic, but his mom wasn't."

"I'll be damned," David muttered as all the pieces of the puzzle began to fall into place. "It's so straightforward it's unbelievable."

Kit misinterpreted his remark and proffered her diary to him. "Here, Dad. You can see for yourself."

"No, no," David said hastily. "Your observations are perfect and right on."

"Good," Kit said and closed the diary. "Accuracy is important, you know."

"I know," David leaned over and kissed his daughter's cheek, loving her with every ounce of his body and soul and then some. "How did you get to be so smart?"

"I got it from my dad, I think." A smile came across Kit's face, but it was interrupted by a coughing spell.

Juanita moved in rapidly, with a steaming bowl and spoon. "You must eat more soup to dampen your cough."

"We'll be back," David said, taking Carolyn's arm and guiding her out to the sitting room. While he waited for Kit's cough to abate, he rethought his scientific reasoning. All the facts fit, but the numbers bothered him. He was basing his conclusion on a small sampling of people, and that was always dangerous. Finally he said, "I may know how to stop the pandemic."

"How?" Carolyn asked promptly.

"This is how." David went over all the facts in detail, explaining why some had survived and others hadn't. He paid particular attention to the vaccines against the regular influenza and swine flu viruses, and how the combination could protect against the avian flu. "It's the only logical explanation, but I can't be sure until we do a survey of everybody aboard the ship. If the surviving passengers received both flu shots, we'll have the answer."

"Jesus!" Carolyn breathed. "Let's hope you're right."

"If I'm not, then God help us," David said grimly. "Because this virus will eventually get to land, and when it does, a pandemic is an absolute certainty."

THIRTY-SEVEN

CHANDLER HEARD THE WHISPERS coming from halfway down the passageway. The words weren't meant for his ears, but the people uttering them didn't know that Chandler had supernormal hearing. Sounds that others could barely detect were crystal clear to him. It was an unusual trait that he had possessed for as long as he could remember, and it had always served him well, but never more so than now. The voices thirty feet away were talking mutiny! Not a fly-by-the-seat-of-your-pants–type mutiny, but one that was planned by experienced crewmen. They wouldn't make the same mistakes that the civilian mutineers had. Chandler pricked his ears, not wanting to miss a word, while he painted a white cross on the door in front of him.

"With a knife at the little girl's throat, that doctor won't dare use his shotgun," a burly, tattooed crewman was saying.

"Right," the other crewman agreed. "That'll hold him until we can run this bloody ship aground off Cozumel."

"Have you been to Cozumel before?"

"Aye. It's a nice little island with fancy hotels and lots of tourists."

"Any police?"

"A few fat Mexicans who can be easily bought off."

"Perfect."

Son of a bitch! Chandler groaned to himself. They were going to wreck the ship and swim ashore, along with the infected rats, just like the doc predicted. And that would spread the disease everywhere. Chandler wanted no part of that, and he wanted no part of a mutiny either. He was a sailor who loved the sea as much as life itself, and he knew that those involved in the mutiny would never sail again under any flag. Screw that!

He stared down the passageway, a brush in one hand, an empty can of paint in the other. The crewmen stopped talking and eyed him suspiciously. The one with the tattooed arms stepped out and blocked Chandler's way.

"Where are you headed?" he asked hoarsely.

Chandler pointed at the empty can. "I need more paint."

The crewman examined the can and moved aside. "Don't take all day."

Chandler continued down the passageway at a slow, even pace. But when he reached the stairwell, he tossed the can and brush away and dashed up the stairs, running as fast as he could.

———

David was having trouble with his survey. There were too many dead, and he had no way of determining whether they had received the various flu vaccines. *So far, 203 dead and eighty alive*, he thought. And of that eighty, fifty were very sick, twenty moderately ill, and ten with few or no symptoms. He concentrated on the ten who had mild or no disease. Eight of them had received both the regular and swine flu vaccines. So, he calculated, 80 percent of those immunized appeared to be protected by the combination of vaccines. That was an impressive result except for the fact that the number of people studied was far too small to draw any conclusions. Only ten passengers with mild or no disease had been surveyed, and that wasn't nearly enough. If, for example, the 203 dead had also gotten both vaccines, the total protection rate would have been less than 5 percent, which would be a poor outcome by any measure. *Shit!* David growled and hoped that the CDC could help him make sense of the numbers.

He moved on to the next cabin and, after knocking, opened the door. The smell alone told him there was only death within. Peeking into the bedroom, he saw two fully dressed, decaying bodies on the bed, still holding hands. Now there were 205 dead. In the following cabin, he found an elderly man sitting on the sofa across from his dead wife. The couple's names were Roy and Mary Mitchell.

"Is there anything I can do for you?" David asked.

The old man shook his head.

"I'm sorry to bother you with questions," David went on, "but I need to know if either you or your wife had gotten the regular flu and swine flu shots."

"I had both," the man replied in a monotone. "But she took only the regular flu shot. She was frightened of the swine flu vaccine because it was so new and all."

David nodded and walked out, thinking one more passenger protected, one not. He jotted down his observations on the Mitchells.

He heard footsteps coming down the passageway and turned to see Chandler running toward him at full speed. He wasn't carrying cans of paint or brushes, and he was waving rather than crying out. David immediately sensed something was terribly wrong.

"What's up?" David asked at once.

"Trouble!" Chandler said between gasps. "Big trouble!"

"Like what?"

"Like mutiny!" Chandler hurriedly repeated the conversation he had overheard in the passageway, remembering most of it word for word. "And they're going to run the ship aground at Cozumel. They've got this thing planned down to the last detail, and that includes throwing you into the brig with the mutineer named Tommy."

"Are they armed?" David asked.

"No, and they're not worried about your shotguns either," Chandler replied, taking another deep breath. "They're taking your daughter hostage to prevent you from interfering."

David's eyes narrowed sharply. "Have they already got her?"

Chandler nodded. "It sounded that way."

David's face reddened as his temper rose to the point of boiling over. *My little girl! A sick little girl! And those bastards using her as a hostage!* With effort, he suppressed his anger and calmed himself. Then he concentrated on the typical behavior of hostage-takers. Their first order of business was to secure the perimeters. "Did they mention anything about posting guards?"

Chandler shook his head. "Only that Joe Barrick would be holding a knife to your daughter's throat."

"Who is Joe Barrick?"

"The big, ugly guy with a scar on his face."

David stared out into space for a moment and thought about the two basic tenets of hostage rescue—deception and execution, which were euphemisms for distract and kill. He turned quickly to Chandler. "It's about to get really messy, so if you want to split, I'll understand."

Chandler shrugged. "I got nowhere in particular to go."

"Follow me."

They dashed down the passageway and up the stairs, taking them two at a time. David led the way, with shotguns at the ready, not for firing but for threatening. A loud blast would remove the element of surprise, which was essential for a hostage rescue. David tried to keep his brain focused, but a picture of Joe Barrick holding a knife to Kit's throat stayed in his mind's eye. *God! She must be so frightened! She must be wondering where her dad is. Well, he's on his way!* Then David sent a silent message to Joe Barrick. *Want to play hardball, eh? Good! I'll show you what real hardball is.*

They came to the level of Kit's cabin and cracked the door that led out to the passageway. Halfway down the corridor, standing outside Kit's cabin, was a short, stocky guard. He was unarmed but vigilant, constantly looking from one side to the other.

"Do you recognize the guard?" David asked in a whisper.

"His name is Poston," Chandler whispered back.

"How tough is he?"

"Plenty. He won't back down and he doesn't scare easily."

"We'll see," David said, his face now stone-cold. He pointed to the paint can and brush that Chandler had discarded earlier. "Pick those up, one in each hand, then walk down the passageway swinging your arms widely. I'll be at your side and just behind you. He won't see my face."

"But he might see your shotguns."

"I'm not taking the shotguns." David removed his white coat and wrapped the shotguns in it, then knelt down to hide the bundle beneath the stairs. Straightening up, he reached for his hatchet and held it close to his thigh. "All right, go! Walk normally, not too fast, not too slow."

The moment the door opened, the guard turned to them, his senses heightened. He kept his eyes on Chandler and watched the paint can and brush swing back and forth in the crewman's arms. As the pair came closer, he called out, "Where the hell are you going?"

"To paint crosses on the doors of the dead passengers," Chandler answered, now less than twenty feet away from the guard. He didn't slow the pace. "It's a real shitty job, but I was ordered to do it."

"By who?" the guard challenged.

"The man."

"What man?"

"Me!" David said and slammed the flat side of his hatchet into the guard's testicles. The guard went down, with a low-pitched, guttural groan, and groped his groin. In an instant, David was on top of the man, pinning him to the floor. Then he waited for the guard's pain to ease before showing him the sharp edge of the hatchet. "One wrong move and I'll do a Choi-job on you. I'll spit your head wide open."

Poston's eyes bulged.

"You stay real quiet and I might let you live," David said before looking over to Chandler. "Go into the next cabin and rip the drawstring from the drapes and bring it back." He watched Chandler hurry away, then came back to the guard. "I'm going to ask you a few questions. You answer by nodding or shaking your head. Got it?"

Poston nodded hastily, his eyes still on the hatchet.

"Is Barrick the only mutineer in the cabin with my daughter?"

Poston nodded.

"Are they in the bedroom?"

Poston shook his head.

"The sitting room?"

Poston nodded.

"With the nanny?"

Poston nodded again.

Chandler rushed back in, holding a long piece of sturdy drawstring. "Do you want me to tie him up?"

"No," David said. "I want you to pull down his pants."

"What?"

"Pull down his pants and undershorts," David directed. "Then tie the drawstring securely around his balls."

Poston's face went pale. His eyes seemed to be coming out of his head, but he didn't resist being undressed.

"Good," David approved as the guard's testicles were roped off. "Now let's stand him up."

With the weak-kneed guard on his feet, David gave Chandler another directive. "Pull on the string, but not too hard."

Chandler performed the task and watched as Poston's scrotum was lifted away from his body.

"Hold it right there," David said, then leaned close to Poston's ear. "You make one wrong move or say one wrong word, and my hatchet will separate you from your private parts. And you'll have the pleasure of watching your balls roll all the way down the passageway."

Chandler gulped. "Do you think there's a password?"

342

"You never know," David said and pushed Poston in front of the door's peephole. "Knock on the door and tell Barrick you've got to use the head. And remember, if my daughter gets even a scratch, you lose your balls."

Poston rapped on the door.

A moment later a gruff voice answered, "What?"

"I—I got to use the head," Poston said.

"Use the one in the cabin across the passageway," Barrick barked.

"Say okay," David whispered immediately.

"Okay," Poston said loudly.

David, staying away from the peephole, jerked Poston down the passageway and into the next cabin. He shoved the guard onto the floor and asked Chandler, "Do you know how to hogtie?"

Chandler grinned. "I grew up on a farm in Ohio."

"Then hogtie him and gag him," David said. "And if he starts to squirm or make noise, kick him in the balls again."

"What are you going to do?"

"Wait," David said and dashed out of the cabin.

He positioned himself at the side of the door to Kit's cabin and listened for sounds from within. He heard only silence. David wished he had a revolver because then he could end everything quickly. Barrick would eventually look through the peephole and the peephole would suddenly darken. One shot into the peephole would go straight through Barrick's eye and into his brain, and the hostage situation would be ended. But David didn't have a revolver, and he couldn't use a shotgun because the blast would be too wide and might hit Kit or Juanita. So he'd have to do it the hard way. A minute passed by, then another minute. David bent down and put his ear to the door again. He heard a rustling sound.

Something was moving. Quickly he went back to the side of the door and raised his hatchet.

"Poston!" Barrick hollered. "Where the hell are you?"

Ten seconds ticked by before Barrick growled loudly, "God-damn it!"

More seconds passed by.

"Leave the child alone!" Juanita pleaded. "You are frightening her."

"Shut up, granny, or I'll slice an ear off."

The door handle turned and the door opened.

Barrick stepped out, holding Kit in front of him. He had his knife pressed against her throat. He didn't see the dull edge of the hatchet swinging toward him, but he felt it smash into the front of his skull. The knife dropped from his hand and he went down face first onto the floor. He tried to struggle to his feet, but David kicked him viciously in the chest, breaking ribs. Barrick howled in pain and rolled from side to side. David kicked him again for good measure, this time in the head.

"Daddy! Daddy!" Kit cried out and ran into his arms. "I'm so scared!"

"I know, I know," David said soothingly and hugged her close. "But it's all over now."

"I want to go home, Dad," Kit said in a little girl's voice.

"We're going to do that soon," he promised and gently rubbed her back, calming her. "Real soon. But now I want you to go with Juanita. Okay?"

"Okay."

He glanced over at Juanita, who was glaring at Barrick. "Are you all right?"

"I am fine," she said strongly and spat on Barrick. "Pig!"

"Take Kit and hurry to the elevator," David told her. "Hold the door open for me. I'll be right behind you."

Juanita grabbed Kit and dashed down the passageway.

Chandler stuck his head into the cabin. "Do you want me to tie him up too?"

"No," David replied. "I want you to check every level until you find my girlfriend, Carolyn. Then both of you scoot up to the bridge. Got it?"

"Got it!"

"Go!"

David walked over to Barrick's outstretched body. The mutineer was breathing in short gasps, with his arms extended out to the side. He was mumbling words that sounded like, "No more."

"A little more," David said tonelessly. Then he stepped on Barrick's right hand and ground his heel into the bones, snapping and crushing all the metacarpals. Barrick screamed in agony and jerked his fractured hand away, but his other hand remained exposed. David crushed its metacarpal bones as well, all the while ignoring the deckhand's shrieks.

"Let's see if you can hold a knife to a child's throat with those hands," David said and ran for the elevator.

THIRTY-EIGHT

THE BRIDGE WAS UNCOMFORTABLY hot, and with the sun blazing
in through the windows, it was growing even hotter. David gazed
around the glass enclosure, thinking they had traded one hostage
situation for another. The seven occupants on the bridge were
trapped and had no way out. Juanita was sitting on the floor, with
Kit asleep in her arms. Jonathan Locke was at the helm, while nearby Chandler was peering at a radar screen. Everyone was stationary, except for the chief radio officer, who was wandering around
with little to do since he was now cut off from the communications room. David watched him pace aimlessly and thought the
man was like a fish out of water, helpless and doomed. *But then
again, so are the rest of us. We are just as helpless and just as doomed.*
David sighed deeply and turned his attention to Carolyn. She was
crunching the numbers of their incomplete survey and trying to
make sense of them.

"Any luck?" David asked her.

Carolyn shook her head. "There are too many blanks that need to be filled in. And I can guarantee you the crew won't allow us to roam the ship and gather more information from the passengers."

"There's a lot of things the crew won't be allowing us to do, and that includes letting us continue to set the course for the *Grand Atlantic*."

"Do you think they'll storm the bridge?" Chandler asked over his shoulder.

"They don't have to," David answered. "The temperature in here will keep rising because they've shut off the air conditioning. Soon we'll become dehydrated, and without any water we'll grow increasingly weak and unable to put up any resistance. So they can just wait us out."

"How long do you think that'll take?" Chandler asked, with concern.

"A day," David estimated. "Two, if we're lucky."

"And then there's my diabetes," Locke added. "I require insulin injections every six hours, and I can't get to my supply now."

"And we can't call for help," the chief radio officer joined in, "because we can't reach the communications room."

"Which puts us at a double disadvantage," Locke said discouragingly. "Now we don't have access to the weather forecasts. We could be sailing into another hurricane."

"That shouldn't be a problem," the chief radio officer told him. "The last weather report from six hours ago called for calm seas except for a thunderstorm brewing along the eastern coast of Florida. We're presently well clear of that."

"Well then, score one point for our side," Chandler said.

"Not really," David countered. "In rough seas, the mutineers would have trouble grounding the ship and swimming ashore. Calm seas make it easier for them."

"Shit," Chandler muttered, then immediately looked over at Juanita and apologized. "Sorry, ma'am."

Juanita nodded briefly, accepting the apology.

David's eyes drifted back to the expansive bridge, with its rows of consoles and computers and electronic displays. All were useless now, as were his two loaded shotguns. Oh, he could kill the first wave of mutineers, but the remaining ones were mean and desperate enough to kill him in return. And they might decide to kill the others as well and feed them to the sharks, figuring it was in their best interest not to leave any witnesses behind. David concentrated his mind and tried to come up with a doable solution to their problem. He couldn't give in to the mutineers, because they would eventually start a worldwide pandemic. He couldn't do that. He just couldn't. *Maybe if—*

There was a loud bang on one of the large metal doors to the bridge. Then another bang, louder yet.

"What's that?" Chandler asked, spinning around. "Are they trying to break in?"

"I don't think so," Locke replied. "That door is made of reinforced steel. They could smash it with a sledgehammer and barely cause a dent."

For a moment, everything was quiet. Then a voice hollered from behind the door. "Listen up in there! The CDC wants to talk with the doc."

"It could be a trap," Chandler warned immediately.

David nodded. The mutineers knew he was the group's leader, and if he was captured, the others would quickly surrender. But, on the other hand, David needed to talk with the CDC. It could be their only way out. He hurried to the door and yelled, "What do they want?"

"They didn't say," came the answer.

"Then ask them," David said, buying himself time. "I want specifics."

There was only silence outside the door now.

David rushed back to the others and asked the chief radio officer, "Do they know how to use the ship-to-shore radio?"

"For sure," the radio officer said. "Some of the crewmen who work with me are experts in communications."

"It could still be a trap," Chandler advised. "After what you did to Choi, they'd happily tear you apart."

Carolyn asked anxiously, "Is there any way to determine if it's a trap?"

"First, let's see if the CDC really wants to talk with me," David said. "And about what. It could be vitally important."

"Important enough to risk your life?" Carolyn asked.

David nodded. "About five hours ago, before we started our survey, I contacted the CDC and told them my preliminary findings. I wanted them to find out which of the passengers had taken the various flu vaccines and which hadn't."

"How in the world could they do that?" Carolyn pondered. "They'd have to track down hundreds of family members and hope the family members knew who their relative's doctors were, and then hope the doctor kept accurate records of the flu shots their nurses probably gave. It's an impossible task that would take forever to do."

"I know," David said dispiritedly, realizing the odds were stacked against him. "But I had to try."

"It's a very long shot," Carolyn said candidly.

"But that's better than no shot at all."

There was another loud rap in the large metal door, followed by a booming voice. "They need to talk with you about the vaccine. They say it's really important for you to give them more information."

David took a deep breath and squared his shoulders. "I've got to go."

"Don't!" Carolyn implored. "Once you've spoken with the CDC, they'll never let you come back onto the bridge. They'll have you as a hostage, and we'll be goners."

"Maybe not," David said. "Particularly if I give them a good reason to allow me to return."

"Like what?"

"Like this," David said and turned to Locke, then gestured to the rows of electronic equipment on the bridge. "Can you disrupt all the navigational systems that are essential to guide the *Grand Atlantic*?"

Locke thought for a moment. "Yes, I guess I could, but I won't."

"What if your life depended on it?" David pressed.

"Tell me what you've got in mind."

"I'm going to threaten the mutineers," David told him. "And I'll do it by saying the following: If I'm not back on the bridge within twenty minutes, you will proceed to destroy all the essential navigational instruments. Then the *Grand Atlantic* can float around in circles until it runs out of fuel or the next big hurricane comes along."

"That will scare the bejesus out of them," Locke agreed, nodding firmly. "Without guidance, they couldn't run the ship aground anywhere near shore."

"Exactly," David said. "Now I want you to name all the important navigational instruments for me, so I can sound like an authority on the subject."

Locke slowly reeled off a short list of the critical instruments, giving David ample time to memorize each. "Even the dumbest seaman will recognize those."

"Good," David said and headed for the door. He handed Chandler the shotguns. "If they try to burst in, aim for the leader's head and blow it off."

"Gotcha!"

"Be careful, David!" Carolyn cried out after him.

David quickly opened the large metal door and moved back. He was now face to face with Poston, the deckhand whose genitals he had threatened to cut off. David hastily glanced around the entrance. There were two crewmen behind Poston, none to the sides.

David stepped out and saw a malevolent glint in Poston's eyes. "I see something in your eyes I don't like."

"Yeah?" Poston challenged. "Tell me what you see."

"A plan to take me hostage once I've spoken with the CDC."

Poston smiled thinly. "That crossed my mind."

"Well, you'd better uncross it," David said brusquely. "Because if I'm not back on that bridge in twenty minutes, the captain is going to use my hatchet to disrupt the entire navigational system of the

Grand Atlantic. I'm talking about the fiber-optic gyrocompass, the self-tuning autopilot, and all the radar screens and electronic displays. Then you and your mates can paddle this goddamn ship to shore."

The smile left Poston's face.

They walked down a short passageway and entered the communications room. Two more crewmen, with hard looks on their faces, and a junior radio officer were waiting for them. The crewmen blocked David's way, and only moved aside when Poston ordered them to do so with a gesture of his head. So Poston was now the leader of the mutiny, David thought, and probably the most dangerous. David hurriedly envisioned the fastest way to kill Poston if trouble broke out. A chop to the larynx, he decided. Then he could deal with the other two crewmen.

"You shouldn't have done what you did to Barrick," Poston said, and the other crewmen in the room nodded their agreement. "That's a fact."

"What I should have done was rip his head off and thrown it overboard," David said gruffly.

"Barrick is going to kill you the first chance he gets."

"Yeah? How is he going to do that? Paw me to death?"

Poston gave David a long stare. "Your time will come."

"So will yours," David said evenly. "Now let's stop wasting time and get down to business."

The junior radio officer called out, "I've got Dr. Lindberg from the CDC on the line!"

David sat at the small conference table and, clearing his throat, spoke into the speakerphone. "David Ballineau here. What information do you need from me?"

"The health status of 220 passengers," Lindberg answered. "That's how many we know for sure did or didn't take the vaccines."

David's brow went up. He brought his chair in closer and hunched over the speakerphone. "You were able to track down the vaccine history of 220 people in under six hours? Is that what you're saying?"

"That's what I'm saying."

"How in the world did you do it?"

"We had some help from the ship's company," Lindberg explained. "They gave us the passenger manifest on the *Grand Atlantic*, which of course contained the people's names and who to call in case of an emergency. Luckily for us, they also required the passengers to list their doctor's name and phone number. I guess they did this because so many of the passengers were elderly. In any event, it was the big break we needed. So we immediately put twenty of our investigators at the CDC on twenty different phone lines and began the calls. There were more than a few doctors we either couldn't reach or didn't have the information we wanted. But we finally collected 220 verifiable vaccination histories, and we figured that was enough."

"Damn right it was!" David said excitedly.

"Now here's how we'll determine the effectiveness of vaccines," Lindberg went on. "We'll read from our list, one by one, calling out each passenger's name. You will check your list and tell us the health status of that particular passenger. Then we'll tell you whether or not they received the two vaccines. Is that clear?"

"Perfectly. I'm going to put you on hold." David quickly pressed the hold button and looked over to the junior radio officer. "Connect me to the bridge. I need to speak with Carolyn."

Poston stepped in closer to the conference table and asked harshly. "What the hell is this all about?"

"Saving a lot of lives, if we're lucky," David said.

"With a vaccine?"

"With a vaccine."

The junior radio officer snapped his fingers. "She's on line two."

David pushed a button on the speakerphone and said, "Carolyn, I want you to come in here and bring all the patient survey data with you. All of it, yours and mine."

"Are—are you sure?" Carolyn asked hesitantly. "Are you positive, Dr. Balli-not?"

David smiled to himself. Carolyn was using the code word, his mispronounced last name, to determine if the mutineers were forcing him to make the call. "Everything is fine and may get even better. Now get a move on."

"I'm on my way."

David leaned back and thought hurriedly about Lindberg's plan to find out if the vaccines were effective. It had one big flaw. Lindberg's list of passengers, which he would call out first, was probably in no particular order. David's list went by cabin number. It could take hours and hours to match up names since there were sure to be some passengers on Lindberg's list that David and Carolyn hadn't seen in their survey. They would have to go down a long list of passengers, over and over again, looking for matching names. But David saw a way around that.

The door opened and Carolyn rushed in, carrying a stack of sheets from their survey. She quickly drew up a chair and sat beside David.

"What's going on?" she asked.

"Maybe the end of this nightmare," David told her, then gave her the details of his conversation with Lindberg at the CDC. He saved the best for last. "So we have the vaccine histories on 220 passengers."

"What a stroke of luck!" Carolyn breathed.

"Only if it works out for us," David said and reached for the hold button on the speakerphone. "Lindberg?"

"Here."

"We're going to do things a little differently," David proposed, "because your way will take too long. Your list may be in no particular order, while ours is by cabin number. So we could be here all day matching up names. I suggest we give you the passenger's name and health status first, then you inform us if he or she received the vaccines."

"Good," Lindberg agreed immediately. "Give me a second to get the names up on my computer screen."

Carolyn bowed her head and mouthed a silent prayer as David arranged the survey sheets by cabin number.

"Go!" Lindberg said.

David began without looking at the survey sheets. "Will Harrison—dead."

Seconds later, Lindberg reported, "No vaccine."

"Sol Wyman—dead."

After a long pause, Lindberg said, "No vaccine."

"Marilyn Wyman—mild disease."

Another long pause. "Received both seasonal and swine flu vaccines."

David and Carolyn nodded and smiled to each other.

David went back to his survey list. The next two names were the HIV-positive passengers he'd seen at the very beginning of the outbreak. "Thomas Berns—dead."

There was static on the line as seconds passed by. "He received both flu vaccines."

"Ralph Oliveri—dead."

Another delay before Lindberg reported, "Received both vaccines."

David gazed down at the next two names on his list. They were the dead, decaying old couple he'd see in bed, still holding hands. "George Davenport—dead."

More static and prolonged pause. "Both vaccines."

"Rose Davenport—dead."

"Both vaccines."

David's spirits began to sink. Four passengers in a row had received both vaccines and all had died. At first glance, the vaccines were looking less and less effective. "William Rutherford—dead."

A long pause. "Received only the seasonal flu shot."

"Deedee Anderson—dead."

"No vaccines."

"Albert Murray—dead."

Thirty seconds passed before Lindberg reported, "Both vaccines."

David frowned. The numbers were again looking less and less promising. "Richard Scott."

Lindberg asked, "What's his health status?"

"He jumped overboard," David said.

"Suicide?"

"Desperation."

"Should we list him as death by drowning?"

David nodded to himself. That sounded better than death from a sharp propeller blade. "That'll do."

"He received both vaccines."

"Arthur Maggi—" There was a loud burst of static that went on and on. David tried to speak above it, but with little success. Finally the line cleared. "This is taking far too long. At this rate, we'll be here all day," David groused.

"Let's simplify things," Lindberg proposed.

To speed up the process, it was decided that David would call out the passenger's name and health status, but not wait for the CDC to respond with the passenger's vaccination history. That correlation would be done after all the passengers' names and health status were gathered. It took almost an hour for the exchange of information to be completed, then David leaned back and waited for the personnel at the CDC to double-check the numbers and complete the statistical analysis.

David kept staring at the speakerphone as he thought about all the people who had died such a horrible death aboard the *Grand Atlantic*. Their faces began to flash in front of his mind's eye. Will Harrison, Sol Wyman, William Rutherford, Deedee Anderson, and so many others. All had died because a thoughtful little boy had tried to help a bird. Despite his best intentions, Will had set loose a vicious virus that turned a billion-dollar luxury liner into a Third World country, with people fighting for survival any way they could. And that included himself and the savage acts he had committed. But he had no regrets for what he'd done, and he'd do it again without hesitation, particularly when Kit's life was at stake.

"This waiting is awful," Carolyn whispered nervously.

"It would be a lot more awful if my theory doesn't hold up," David whispered back as he envisioned the catastrophe that would occur if the combination of the vaccines didn't work. Hundreds and hundreds of passengers would soon die, and they would be followed in death by hundreds of millions more once the virus reached land. And there was no question the virus would reach land. One way or another the mutineers would make it to shore and set off a monstrous pandemic, unlike anything the world had ever seen. It was doomsday, waiting to happen.

"Here are the results," Lindberg's voice came over the speaker-phone.

David and Carolyn quickly leaned forward and held their breath. In the background they heard the sound of papers being shuffled, followed by a loud continuous burst of static. It seemed to take forever before Lindberg spoke again.

"Two hundred names were matched," Lindberg went on finally. "Of those, 102 received both vaccines, seventy-nine received only the seasonal flu vaccine, and nineteen got no vaccination. From a statistician's standpoint, the numbers are ideal. Half got both vaccines, half either no vaccine or a single vaccine. The results are striking. Ninety percent of the passengers who received both vaccines survived and have no disease or moderate disease at the worst. In the group who got no or only one vaccine, 80 percent died with severe disease. Thus, the combination of vaccines worked beyond any doubt, and we can now make arrangements for the *Grand Atlantic* posthaste."

"Hallelujah!" Carolyn cried out.

David breathed a long sigh of relief. "We're home safe now."

"Well done, Dr. Ballineau," Lindberg congratulated before signing off. "Well done indeed."

Poston nervously looked at the other deckhands, then came back to David. "What does all this mean in plain English?"

"Did you get both flu shots?" David asked.

"Yeah. So what?"

"That means you won't get the disease."

Poston didn't look relieved. "What happens now?"

"In all likelihood, they'll arrange for us to be transferred to a fully equipped hospital ship that will be manned by doctors and nurses who have been immunized with both vaccines," David said, guessing that's the plan the CDC would come up with. No one would be allowed ashore until it was certain they weren't carrying the avian flu virus. "Then we'll be checked and eventually released."

Poston swallowed hard. "I meant what happens to us? You know, the crew?"

"Are you referring to the deckhands who took part in the mutiny?" David asked bluntly.

"Yeah."

"Nothing I suspect," David said. "The ship's owners aren't going to want a trial that would publicize there was a mutiny aboard the *Grand Atlantic*. That's the last thing they would want."

Poston and the other deckhands smiled broadly.

"But I can guarantee that you'll never sail again on any ship," David went on. "The owners of the *Grand Atlantic* will see to that."

The smiles left their faces.

David came over to Carolyn and helped her up. "Let's go get Kit and Juanita."

As they strolled back to the bridge, Carolyn rested her head on David's shoulder. "So it's really over."

"I guess," David said and placed his arm around her waist. "But we were lucky, very lucky."

"Lucky!" Carolyn looked at him oddly. "Lucky, after what we've been through?"

David nodded. "We were lucky that the combination of vaccines worked against the virus. We found that out by pure luck and happenstance."

Carolyn slowly nodded back. "And we're lucky to have a potent vaccine if the virus decides to return."

"Don't be so sure of that."

"But we know the combination of vaccines works," Carolyn argued mildly.

"Against the virus as it is today," David said. "But what happens when it mutates and changes the antigens on its outer coat? What happens when the vaccine then produces antibodies that don't react with these new antigens?"

"Then the vaccine no longer protects against the virus," Carolyn said and shuddered to herself. "It would be useless."

"Exactly," David told her. "And keep in mind that viruses tend to mutate in order to adapt to their environment. That's how they survive."

"Jesus!" Carolyn groaned. "Are you saying that another outbreak is going to occur?"

"I'm saying it's possible."

"You're mincing words."

"Probable, then."

"You're still mincing words."

David smiled humorlessly and gave her a quick hug. "That's what I told the CDC when they wouldn't give me a straight answer to the question you just asked."

"They beat around the bush, eh?"

"For a while."

"What did they finally say?" Carolyn pressed.

"That it's sure to happen again," David said as he reached for the door to the bridge. "It's only a matter of where and when."

EPILOGUE

THE FLOCK CONTINUED ALONG the Atlantic Flyway, unaware that yet another member had become ill. The sick bird struggled to keep up as the avian influenza virus multiplied within its tissues and destroyed its muscles and lungs.

The bird had no defense against the virus because the microscopic organism was again undergoing a mutation that changed its surface antigens. The new antigens allowed the deadly invader to completely avoid detection by antibodies in the bird's blood.

Thus the virus multiplied without resistance, weakening the bird to the point it was losing altitude in the face of the approaching thunderstorm. Desperately it searched for a landing area where it could feed and rest. Ahead it sensed land, but the oncoming wind grew stronger and the bird dropped even farther, with nothing except rough seas below. Instinctively it pushed on, knowing that a lush feeding ground was not far off. The bird beat its wings furiously as it lost more and more altitude. The storm came closer and the weather suddenly worsened. Dark sheets of rain now pounded against the bird, making it impossible for it to see the coast of Florida and the huge housing developments being built on its shores.

Then there was lightning and thunder, followed by more lightning that caused the sky to momentarily light up. In the distance, the bird saw a broad stretch of land that jutted out into the sea. With all of its remaining energy, the bird veered off from the flock and made a last-ditch dive for survival. Now the wind was at its back, propelling it forward and downward. So close to land. So close. If only it could reach the feeding grounds. If only it could reach...

THE END

© Dennis Trantham

ABOUT THE AUTHOR

Leonard Goldberg is the internationally best-selling author of the Joanna Blalock series of medical thrillers. His novels, acclaimed by critics as well as fellow authors, have been translated into a dozen languages and have sold more than a million copies worldwide. Leonard Goldberg is himself a consulting physician affiliated with the UCLA Medical Center, where he holds an appointment as Clinical Professor of Medicine. A highly sought-after expert witness in medical malpractice trials, he is board certified in internal medicine, hematology, and rheumatology, and has published over a hundred scientific studies in peer-reviewed journals.

Leonard Goldberg's writing career began with a clinical interest in blood disorders. While involved in a research project at UCLA, he encountered a most unusual blood type. The patient's red blood cells were O-Rh null, indicating they were totally deficient in A, B, and Rh factors and could be administered to virtually anyone without fear of a transfusion reaction. In essence, the patient was the proverbial "universal" blood donor. This finding spurred the idea for a story in which an individual was born without a tissue type, making that person's organs transplantable into anyone without worry of rejection. His first novel, *Transplant*, revolved around a young woman who is discovered to be a universal organ donor and is hounded by a wealthy, powerful man in desperate need of a new kidney. The book quickly went through multiple printings and was optioned by a major Hollywood studio.

On the strength of the critical and popular reception of *Transplant*, Leonard Goldberg was off to the races as an author of medical thrillers. He began writing a series of new books, with a continuing main character named Joanna Blalock. The Joanna Blalock series features a forensic pathologist at a prestigious university medical center who has a Holmesian knack for solving murders. These books include *Deadly Medicine*, *A Deadly Practice*, *Deadly Care*, *Deadly Harvest*, *Deadly Exposure*, *Lethal Measures*, *Fatal Care*, *Brainwaves*, and *Fever Cell*.

Leonard Goldberg's novels have been selections of the Book of the Month Club, French and Czech book clubs, and the Mystery Guild. They have been featured as *People* magazine's "Page-Turner of the Week," as well as at the International Book Fair in Budapest. The series has been optioned on several occasions for development as a motion picture or television project.

His best-selling novels have also been praised by fellow writers, as:
- "Loaded with suspense and believable characters." (T. Jefferson Parker)
- "Medical suspense at its best." (Michael Palmer)

Dr. Goldberg is a native of Charleston, South Carolina (with the accent to prove it), and a part-time California resident. He currently divides his time between Los Angeles and an island off the coast of South Carolina.

Please visit his website, www.leonardgoldberg.com.

WWW.MIDNIGHTINKBOOKS.COM

From the gritty streets of New York City to sacred tombs in the Middle East, it's always midnight somewhere. Join us online at any hour for fresh new voices in mystery fiction.

At midnightinkbooks.com you'll also find our author blog, new and upcoming books, events, book club questions, excerpts, mystery resources, and more.

MIDNIGHT INK ORDERING INFORMATION

Order Online:

• Visit our website www.midnightinkbooks.com, select your books, and order them on our secure server.

Order by Phone:

• Call toll-free within the U.S. and Canada at
  1-888-NITE-INK (1-888-648-3465)
• We accept VISA, MasterCard, and American Express

Order by Mail:

Send the full price of your order (MN residents add 6.875% sales tax) in U.S. funds, plus postage & handling to:

> Midnight Ink
> 2143 Wooddale Drive
> Woodbury, MN 55125-2989

Postage & Handling:

Standard (U.S. & Canada). If your order is:
> $25.00 and under, add $4.00
> $25.01 and over, FREE STANDARD SHIPPING

AK, HI, PR: $16.00 for one book plus $2.00 for each additional book.

International Orders (airmail only):
> $16.00 for one book plus $3.00 for each additional book

Orders are processed within 12 business days. Please allow for normal shipping time.
Postage and handling rates subject to change.

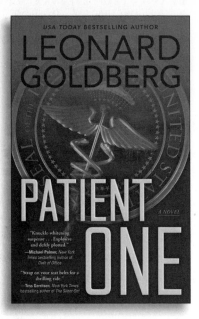